The Other Side of Paradise

by

Chris Lea

A Paradise Novel

Text copyright © 2019 Chris Lea
All Rights Reserved

Published by Regency Rainbow Publishing
Cover by Maria Spada Design at www.mariaspada.com

Introduction

In this my second compendium I've decided to flip over to the other side; toss the coin or turn the tables – and combine a small selection of my gay stories for your pleasure – stories that will tickle your tonsils, flutter your fundamentals and amuse your anus as they regale you with some fun-filled days and nights. In a number of my stories there's a certain amount of heterosexual stuff included because in each instance, it's there to lead you astray, to twist your mind and then throw you energetically into the gay side of life.

This compendium isn't so clearly age-graded as my first. There I progressed from a callow teenager to a mature man whereas here, although I begin as a student, I progress through to middle age in jerks and starts. You'll also notice that my form of employment changes and that's simply because this compendium doesn't chart one character but several and while using my own name in most stories, I've had to change names in the final story otherwise the story doesn't make sense.

It also suits me to have several forms of employment because I've always been one to keep as many strings to my bow as possible and in doing so, a number of various ways of obtaining an income have been interwoven throughout my life. Sometimes one career takes ascendance; another time that fades and is replaced by one of my other 'trades' – I try to be as versatile in work as I am in my sexuality!

Please do also bear something else in mind – I am far from a wholly committed gay man – I float happily between the sexes almost at will and the result is that my stories are as seen from my perspective, using my descriptive language and generally avoiding overly gay idioms and expressions

College Blues

I left school in Surrey, England in July 1975, when I was a month short of my 18th birthday... a child by all intents, because I had no idea what I wanted to become. I seemed to have done well enough in my exams and my career had been 'planned' for me by the school careers master and my dad, but no-one seemed to have considered me! Because the last thing I really wanted to do was to follow my dad into accountancy or to do as my careers advisor suggested and try to become a lawyer – heaven forbid, all those dusty tomes and lines of numbers; not to mention all those years and years of study!

And so I passed my 18th birthday while on extended summer holiday, with no more school or a job to look forward to and I wasn't in the least bit worried! Why wasn't I worried? Because I'd just found myself a real live girlfriend – not just someone from school to take to the cinema or to the café... no, this was real love, and she was gorgeous! Very quickly we passed from both being virgins to practiced lovers and our romantic future was looking rosy as it always is with your first love.

However, I'm not going to let that get in the way of my story – because romance was nipped in the bud as my mum soon saw better things for me than becoming a full-time Romeo and packed me off to a college well away from home for a two year Business Studies course.

So, in the September following my 18th birthday, my parents set me up with some 'digs' – a small bed-sit near the college, which was some 80 miles from home and with a bit of financial help from them and then a small inheritance from a great-uncle, I was sitting pretty! All I had to do was to attend lectures and try to behave...

I think that my mother was more canny than I believed though, because no sooner had I settled in, than they moved and ended up some 150 miles further away and I was left to make my own way in life. The truth was actually that my father almost simultaneously received a promotion and had to go to Head Office to work, but with the timing it didn't seem that way to me.

In reality, my parents were only on the other end of a phone line if I wanted a chat or a bit of loving, or even cash, but I certainly felt alone and I also realised that, without my own transport, I couldn't easily get to see the love-of-my-life – and my crusty old landlady certainly wasn't going to let her come and stay with me! So now what to do?

I soon realised that if I was to pacify that damn thing that kept rearing its head in my trousers, I'd have to find other outlets for my sexual needs, and I became a real expert at wanking. I could make myself cum in a matter of a few minutes or I could edge myself along for perhaps an hour or more before I just had to let it out. Usually I'd lay on my back on my bed to wank, allowing my spunk to spurt onto my abdomen and chest and I'd long ago found out about the taste, which I now rather enjoyed. Sometimes I'd lie on my side and then I could catch my cum in my hand and lick it all up, but I tended to vary my activities, so I always had an old towel handy.

Since I started wanking, I'd always wanted to be able to suck my own cock, but I was short of a few inches of flexibility – or a few inches of cock! Instead I'd managed to arrange myself, upside-down with my back up against a wall and then succeeded in jerking cum from my cock but it had splattered all over my face and pillow so it wasn't a huge success. It was also a bit of a worry to be in that position because at home, mum or dad might have walked in and once I was in 'digs' I was always concerned that my landlady, who had a key to every room, might come in and find me in that unexpected position... so I seldom tried that position and I'd yet to properly obtain sperm direct from the source despite my desires.

But wanking, while good to release the pressure, isn't the same as having sex with someone else – it's a "solitary vice," to quote the old 18th Century view – a lonely way of having sex and I needed more than that. I sorely missed my girlfriend.

My walk to and from college took me either through or past a local recreation ground, past the tennis courts, the children's playground, the putting green and the bowls clubhouse. There were a number of bench seats around and it soon became my habit to take my lunch there, where I was able to feed the birds and watch whatever games were being played. There was also a block of public toilets close by and I was fortunate that they existed because it was there that I found something better than plain masturbation.

I think I ducked into the toilet entrance that particular afternoon mainly because it started raining heavily and then I realised that I might as well have a pee while I was there, so I moved from the doorway into the men's toilet proper. There was a wall of porcelain urinals – perhaps six or even eight of them if I remember and at the far end a well-built man, perhaps in his forties stood, looking down at the urinal in front of him. I moved to one further down the line away from him, shuffled close to the wall and pulled my zip down. I fished out my penis, pulling back my foreskin as I did so and since my bladder wasn't under any great pressure, I waited for the wee to start.

For a while nothing happened and as I waited I glanced down the row of urinals and realised that the man was looking in my direction. My glance also told me that he was holding his remarkably large penis in his left hand so that my view was unobstructed and as I looked, my eyes now captivated by the sight of his cock, I saw him run his hand up and down it, slowly and smoothly. He was smiling too as he stroked himself.

3

I had to look away because suddenly my own penis was starting to swell... and since I was holding it in my right hand, its enlargement from a limp object to around seven inches of tumescent flesh must have been at least partially visible to the man. I simply couldn't stop it from growing and stiffening.

I also couldn't help but take another sideways glance and now discovered that the man had half turned away from the urinal and was now facing towards me. More than that, he was holding a penis which was now massively erect!

'Oh my god,' I thought, 'I can't believe this is happening! This is so sick! What do I do – what the fuck do I do?'

My somewhat panic-stricken mind wanted me to run away but my stiff cock had other ideas, as did the man. Before I could come to my senses, he shuffled towards me until he was standing at the next urinal. He looked down at my erection and then back at his own, which he was gently stropping while I just stood there, perhaps too scared to move. My cock too was now a rigid length in my hand, and I was trembling with, well, not fear but anticipation, I think.

"Nice one you've got there," the man said quietly, still rubbing his own organ, "Do you think I could hold it?"

'Oh God' I thought again, 'Do I let him?'

I was panicking really – never in my life had I let anyone anywhere, or for any reason, touch or hold my cock apart from me. I'd never even wanted to let a doctor touch me – nor even my mum... not since I was a baby and I felt myself shaking my head in denial.

"Not to worry. Feel mine then," the man suggested, reaching out for my hand.

And like a zombie, I let him pull my hand across the small space between us and rest it on his penis.

"Get hold of it then," he said as his hand closed my fingers over his shaft, "Beauty, ain't it? I got about seven inches, how about you?"

"Errrr, dunno," I said, flustered, speaking for the first time.

"Looks good mate – not far off, I reckon," he said, "Let me feel it and I'll tell you."

Releasing my own grip from my penis I let him grasp me and his firm fingers made my cock jump with what must have been delight, because it stiffened further with the touch. The man ran his hand over my cock, smoothing his rough palm over and around my knob and spreading the little dribble of lubrication that had oozed from the tip.

"Feels good mate," he said, "Reckon you might be a bit longer than me, you lucky bugger! Come on, give mine a rub, will yer."

I could hardly stop my hand from moving, partially because he was now moving his hips so that his cock was pushed through my fist and partially because I now really wanted to feel that cock, so similar and yet so different to my own. Somehow his flesh felt hotter than mine, but the loose skin felt just like mine as I moved it up and down his shaft.

"Ohhh, do it harder," said the man, now moving his hand on my cock more quickly, "Grab hold tighter and do it a bit faster."

For a little while we just rubbed each other, not talking, but both breathing quite heavily.

"It's getting good, mate; have a play with my knob," he asked, because I'd been concentrating on the enjoyment of feeling his hot smooth shaft, "Rub my knob for me – underneath, you know."

I moved my hand towards the end of his penis and admired the bulbous plum-coloured end to his cock that now throbbed in my hand then found that I actually wanted to explore him, to feel his stiffness and slipperiness. My fingers stroked over his knob and then, as I looked at it, so a long stream of lubricating syrup dribbled from his penis and stretched to the ground.

"Oooooh," said the man, now breathing faster, "Look what you made me do! I always make a lot of that stuff when I get excited. Catch some of it, would yer mate?"

Ten minutes ago I wouldn't have dared to get my hand anywhere near such a thing, but now I not only wanted to feel all of his cock but I actually wanted to feel his slippery precum as well.

I slid my hand up and over onto his knob, loving the stiff flesh of the ridge of his knob, before moving my hand to cup and gently squeeze his slippery, shiny knob end. It seemed to pulse in my hand as his penis jerked hard, then the warmth of his knob seemed to increase.

'Oh fuck,' I thought, 'I can feel him oozing into my hand! I'm actually holding someone else's cock and it's making my hand wet!'

Sure enough, he'd oozed another load of precum but this time into my hand. It ran between my fingers and I found myself swirling them around until they were liberally coated with it.

"Ahhh, that felt good," moaned the man softly, "Keep doing that mate."

I just had to squeeze his knob a bit more and another slow spurt of precum ran into my hand as I did. I smoothed the viscous fluid all over his knob – it felt so slippery and sexy as I turned my hand over and around his penis. I wanted to just keep on doing that for ever, but the man brought me back to earth.

"Don't forget the rest of my cock now mate, spread that stuff all over me," he said, then "Ooooh – fuck – here comes some more!"

I was committed now – I was really into this despite the newness and the way it made me feel scared – but I now really wanted to keep playing with him. I was hooked!

Quickly I slipped my hand back to his knob and was in position as another pool of precum drooled from his cock. I caught it all and brought it back to his shaft, where I spread it over him and started to rub him again.

In the meanwhile, his hand wasn't idle as he played with my cock too. He'd managed to get both my balls out of my fly as well and he kept touching them and rolling them in his hand, before returning to my cock to continue masturbating me.

I too was leaking precum, but not as copiously as he was and his hand on my cock felt absolutely out of this world! I hardly knew what sensation to feel – there was panic, shock, delight and above all a feeling of great excitement. My legs had turned to jelly because my cock was being wanked and not by me... and I was going to cum before too long if this kept up!

The man must have realised from my breathing or possibly because of my hip thrusting my cock through his busy fist, that I was getting close.

"Gonna cum soon?" he asked, and I nodded my head.

"Good, good!" he said, "I ain't far off either, keep rubbing me and I'll try to cum with you!"

Together we wanked, panting hard together, surrounded by the gentle slapping noise of lubricated flesh as our hands worked on each other's cocks.

"Fuck it – I'm cumming!" he said, beating me to it, "Feel it cumming up – ooooh – faster, bit faster!"

"Come on then, do it!" I said, suddenly wildly excited, "I want to see you cum!"

"Out the way then!" he grunted as his hips jerked, thrusting his cock powerfully through my fist, "Ooooh yeahhhh, that's it – I'm cumming! Here it is! Uuuuugh! Uuuuugh!"

As he grunted and as I continued to rub his penis, I felt it swell slightly and his hips jerked powerfully as his first jet of ejaculate erupted from his penis.

Still rubbing him, I watched in awe as he punched the air with his cock and blasted one, two, three, four, five long streamers of white-streaked spunk at the urinal wall.

"Uuuuh! Uuuuuh! Ohhhhh!" he groaned as the last spasms of his orgasm jerked the final dribbles and blobs of cum from his cock over my fist and onto the ground.

Everything slowed down and he pulled his penis from my hand to wring out the last of his cum, which he flicked from the tip onto the wall with his finger.

"Fuck me, that was good," he said as he put his cock away and zipped up, "You've got a lovely hand – but hey, what about you? You haven't cum yet, have you?"

I still felt almost speechless, so I shook my head as I looked at the sperm that now clung to my hand. Not knowing what else to do with it, I wiped it off on the wall.

"Bit of a waste doing that," he commented, "Could have made use of that."

The idea of using his cum to lubricate my cock felt shockingly wrong for a moment, until the man spoke again.

"Still nice and stiff, aren't you," he said, now starting to rub his hand up and down my shaft, "You've not cum have you, I can feel you've still got it."

"No, I haven't cum," I agreed, "I was nearly there but then you came off and we sort of forgot about mine."

"Soon remedy that mate," said the man, "Turn 'round this way a bit more so I can get at you better."

I moved to stand facing him as his hand, well, both hands occasionally, began to work me up again. It wouldn't take long for me to cum now – I was still so excited at seeing his cock erupt.

And then he shocked me again.

"Mind if I suck you?" he said and as he spoke, he dropped to his knees before me.

Gobsmacked, I just couldn't do or say anything – and anyway, his hand was still working on my cock and it was feeling so damn good that I wanted to let him do whatever he liked.

Taking my silence for approval, he opened his mouth and let my knob and then several inches of my shaft slide smoothly into his mouth as I watched. Oh god – it felt simply out of this world – it was a thrill I'd never had before – a sensation like nothing else. It was simply superbly erotic and numbingly sexy as his lips started to move around my knob... although my knees were still trembling like anything. The fact that it was a man sucking my cock didn't matter – the sensation was too good for me to care about such niceties... and he was rapidly bringing me to the boil.

The man began sliding his mouth up and down my cock, sliding my penis deeply into his mouth and then out again, until it was just his lips sucking at the tip of my cock. Then he'd repeat his actions and all the while my orgasm was building and building.

"Gonna cum soon, gonna cum," I said, galvanised at last, "Let me out – let me cum!"

"In my mouth mate, do it in my mouth," he said, to my shock and perhaps horror!

It seemed a disgusting idea and yet at the same time I felt myself thinking back to his orgasm and wishing I'd had the guts to taste his cum, but suddenly I had no objection or option left as my climax arrived.

Visions of my attempts to make myself cum in my own mouth suddenly popped into my brain too.

"Waaah – I'm cumming!" I cried as I froze briefly before I erupted, "Ohhhhh! Oooooh god! Uuuuuugh!"

My own jets of spunk were now filling his mouth; overflowing down his chin and dribbling back to drool around his hand and beneath the shaft of my jerking, thrusting, cumming penis.

"Ooooh fuckin' hell!" I cried again, "Oh yeahhhh! Oh god – Oh god!"

I felt the mouth release its grasp on my cock and then the coolness of fresh air on my wet, slippery, sticky penis. Breathing deeply through his nose, the man stood up and ran his finger up his chin, collecting the blob of whitish sperm which he looked at briefly, before popping it into his mouth. He opened his mouth to show me what I'd done – I'd filled his mouth with my spunk; his entire mouth was coated and puddled with strands and smears of my cum. Briefly I stared before he closed his mouth and I saw his throat work as he swallowed my offering.

"Yeah – that was tasty, mate," he said, "Nice gob-full that was. You cum a lot too, don't you matey, all nice and hot. Not too salty like some of 'em."

I stood there dumbfounded, wondering what to do next before he spoke again.

"Oh sod, I left your cock all sticky! Can't have that!" he said as he bent down – and before I knew it, he was sucking me again.

"Ooooh shit, no, not again!" I gasped, "I don't want to do it again!"

Well, I did really, but it wasn't to be – he was merely sucking my cock clean – although as he stood up, my newly-sprung erection stood out before me.

"Oh, look at that! Fucking eager, aren't you!" he said, giving my cock a quick tug, "Love to suck you off again, but I can't stay much longer. But thanks mate, I enjoyed that."

"So did I," I managed to reply, "Thank you."

"See you again?" he asked, "Same place."

"Dunno," I wavered as I tucked my penis back into my trousers, "Might do."

"Ok – cheerio then mate," he said and a moment later he'd gone, leaving me there, totally shattered from the new experience and yet totally satisfied – for now!

I never had that pee – and I never even found out his name! At least the rain had stopped.

I walked back to my digs in something of a daze... this was the first time I'd ever, EVER, had any kind of sex outside a bedroom – let alone with a MAN!

The sheer wonder of it struck me once I was home and could retire to lie on my bed, contemplating things. Because what was going through my mind was the fact that, once I'd got past the original butterflies, I'd really enjoyed what we'd done together. I began to think back – to the feeling of holding another man's penis, feeling it stiffen, feeling it pumping its cream out. The slipperiness of his precum and the erotic smell of his spunk lingered in my mind.

I need hardly add that I was erect again by now and as I lay there on my back, I slid my trousers and pants down and started to wank. I re-ran the action in my mind, seemingly unable to put it into a seamless timescale. Somehow the best bits kept jumping up and leaping from the mental video and every time he spurted his cum in my mind, another pulse of pleasure shook my body – until suddenly, well before I was expected, I felt my orgasm engulf me.

My cock leapt into action – three quick but energetic pulses of cum shot up my body – the first splashing down across my face and hair; the second and third spurts landing on my chest while several lesser squirts fell on my abdomen and dribbled into my pubes. I don't think I'd ever cum that hard before and certainly never as far as my face.

No stranger though to the taste of my own cum, I quickly gathered what I could from my face and licked it up, imagining that it belonged to that man. I did my best to clean off the cum from my hair with a tissue, but I didn't know if I'd got it all – I'd check once I'd cleaned it all off my body too.

"Damn – that was quick!" I muttered, licking my lips, "Fastest cum ever I reckon and I've never cum so hard either."

I felt far from satisfied that night though and I just mooched around my digs doing useless chores and feeling quite fidgety. I tried to read and study – but I couldn't settle. I tried to cook something – and burnt it, so I gave up, eventually deciding that I might get a takeaway later. I didn't even want a drink although I had some beer in the fridge – I just wanted more of what I'd had. I couldn't believe just how desperate I'd become to experience a man's cock again. But I wasn't about to go wandering off to the park after dark, not least because it would probably be closed, so I just had to be patient tonight.

Eventually somehow, I must have drifted off to sleep, but I awoke with a hard-on that returned even after I'd had a pee. I jerked myself off again which at least took the pressure off, long enough that I could get ready for college and finally, feeling far from organised I managed to get out on time.

From choice I walked to college through the park again the next morning but although I passed right by the toilets, I had no desire to go in to see if anyone was around – much as our tryst had been exciting it was also way too scary to contemplate a repeat! I somehow doubted that anyone would be in there at that time of the day anyway. Instead I meandered on to our lecture room where I joined the other students. For a while I felt as if I was somehow marked now and I felt almost alone among my friends and colleagues, but gradually my mind returned to normal and before too long I became just another young man aspiring to learn more of the Big Business world.

When the lunch break arrived, I was in two minds. Should I go to the park as I usually did or eat here at college? More often than not I'd buy some sandwiches from the local corner shop then enjoy my lunch and drink in the park but today, just as I decided to go to the shop, I noticed rain splattering on the windows and quickly changed my mind. The refectory it was then, despite their uninspiring selection of food.

I joined the queue and got myself a portion of something labelled cottage pie, which at least smelled nice and meaty and found a place at a table with several other students. Almost as soon as I arrived, two of the three at the table finished their meal and left, leaving just myself and another young man to eat in peace. For a while we didn't even look at the other; but when I did take a very quick glance, I saw that he was looking at me too. I smiled somewhat self-consciously at him and he smiled back.

"Hiya. Crap food, isn't it?" I managed to ask, waving my fork over my meal and when he smiled back, I followed that with, "What course are you doing?"

"Economics," he said gloomily, "What about you?"

"Business Studies," I said, "Dry, boring and hard work."

The other guy laughed happily, his cheerful response inspiring me to introduce myself.

"I'm Chris, by the way. Who are you then?" I asked.

"Peter," he answered, extending his hand and we shook – the touch of another man sending sharp shock waves right down to my penis.

"I don't often come in here," I said, glancing around at the uninspiring room, "I prefer a sandwich in the park but it's raining isn't it. Sometimes they're playing bowls and I can watch them for a while."

"I'm a bit new here actually. Had troubles with my enrolment paperwork and only just made it," said Peter, "I've got a little flat down the road, but I don't know my way around yet. Mind if I join you occasionally? I'm not impressed by this canteen either."

"They call it a refectory," I said laughing quietly, "Same thing really – and no, I don't mind you joining me. Be nice to have a bit of company sometimes."

We moved until we were opposite each other, then chattered vaguely until the break was finished.

A few days later, I bumped into Peter as lunchtime came around and this time, with the sun shining today we nipped off to the corner shop, bought a roll and a drink each and headed to the park. Soon we were stuffing our faces, side by side on a bench, peacefully alone apart from the occasional passer-by, it turning out to be one of those lunchtimes when no-one was using the sports facilities.

We made some idle chatter, during which I found that he was all of two weeks older than I was, rather to my annoyance, as his 18th had been back in late July, while mine was in August.

Leaning back after I'd eaten, I burped gently and looked at Peter with a shy grin.

He was a couple of inches taller than me but somewhat slimmer – not that I was exactly fat either. I weigh in at around 150 pounds so I reckon he might have been ten pounds lighter, considering his extra height, which took him to perhaps 6'2". His face was longish rather than round and his mop of somewhat unruly light brown hair was everywhere. We both had blue eyes and much the same coloured hair and somehow I felt at ease in his company. Oddly enough, we were even both wearing much the same – blue jeans, trainers, a t-shirt with a garish pop logo on and a light leather jacket.

Peter looked at me as he finished and leaned back too, managing a sociable burp as well.

"Agreed," he said convivially, "Hey, that roll tasted a lot better than the stuff at the college."

We sat and contemplated the empty playing fields before us before Peter asked the question that changed our worlds.

"So, where's your girlfriend then – have you got one?" he asked simply.

"Well, I had a girlfriend, but she lives too far away from here, so I'm on my own for now," I told him, "Where's yours then?"

"Never got around to having one," he answered with a shrug, "Can't be bothered!"

"What?" I said in astonishment, "So what do you do for sex?"

I didn't mean it to come out like that, but I think I was so astonished by his claim that I just said the first thing that came into my mind, but fortunately Peter didn't seem to mind.

"I'm just good at wanking!" he said, laughing, "I guess you're in the same boat now then?"

"Yeah," I replied, somewhat abashed, "Well yes – I guess I am actually."

Now that I'd admitted to the charge the ice had been broken and suddenly I somehow didn't mind being very personal and I found myself opening up to him.

"I'm always doing it," I said, miming wanking with my hand, "Morning, noon and night! Can't really leave the bloody thing alone!"

Peter was laughing now and put his hand on my shoulder to gently push at me.

"Takes over, doesn't it?" he said, his hand squeezing my shoulder, "Your cock, I mean. Always randy – never satisfied."

"Bloody right," I said with feeling, "But at least it's enjoyable when you wank. So how often do you do it?"

"When I get up and again before I head out if there's time; I went to the college toilets yesterday for a wank, and then I do it every evening, sometimes more than once," he said, "Mind you, the college toilets are so busy that you've got to be dead quiet... "

There was a lull in the conversation before he spoke again.

"Hey, speaking of toilets, do you know if these ones are clean – I bet they're quiet today," he asked jerking his thumb in their direction, "Why don't we nip in there and rub one out? Got time, haven't we?"

"Should we?" I asked, somewhat worried that the man might be there again and would recognise me.

'What if he's there? What do I do?' I thought to myself in a sudden panic... because here was me, planning to go in there with another man.

"Well, I need to, Chris, look at this!" said Peter.

He looked up to check that no-one was around then spread his legs wide apart and down the leg of his jeans his penis raised a long and straight ridge with a small damp spot at the end – he was hard and in need of some release.

"See! All we had to do was to talk about sex and 'bang', up he comes!" he said as he rubbed his hand up and down his jeans over his penis, "Aren't you getting hard then?"

At the sight of his erection I'd almost instantly become rock-hard, but I wasn't as forward as he was. Nevertheless I nodded quickly.

"Yes, I am actually," I said somewhat coyly.

"Show me then!" Peter said, still smoothing his hand over his cock.

I pulled back my jacket which was hiding the long tent that my penis was making up towards my belt and Peter slapped the bench seat between us.

"See, you can't keep the little bastard down either! Come on then," he said, laughing and standing up, "Let's do it!"

As he stood, now facing me, his erection seemed to almost reach out to me. I wanted to put my hand on that ridge and feel its heat and hardness, but I was completely shy and actually shook my head to say no.

"Oh come on, I can't leave it like this!" said Peter impatiently, "It'll feel so much better afterwards – you know it will!"

Still in two minds, I rose with him and we walked to the toilets; me furtively looking around as we entered – but they were empty. A big sigh of relief left me and suddenly I felt better.

"Let's go in a cubicle in case someone else comes in," said Peter, pulling me down the room and soon we were shut into our little world, just the two of us.

The cubicles, like the building itself were built of brick and had big solid doors – it felt very private inside.

Peter shrugged off his jacket and hooked it on a nail on the door and I put mine on top of his. And by the time I'd turned around; Peter had his zip down and was starting to pull his penis out.

"You done it with anyone else?" he asked quietly.

"Once," I replied, feeling somewhat ashamed and yet also superior.

"Was it good?" he asked as his erect penis appeared at his fly.

I nodded hard and fast – in time with my heart it seemed, as his hand extracted his cock and held it out, already hard and glistening in the feeble light. There was already a small tear of precum at the tip.

He waved his hand at me by way of encouragement.

"Come on then, let's see yours," he said softly, and I knew that this was the moment of discovery.

Was I going to like doing this or had my experience with the man been a one-off? Inwardly, I felt certain that I already knew the answer.

Slowly, almost but not entirely reluctantly, my hand moved to my fly and I pulled my zip down. Peter was watching ardently, his hand smoothly and gently moving up and down his shaft as I reached into my pants and with a bit of adjustment to my clothing, I was able to bring forth my pride and joy which I stretched out before removing my hand. My cock wasn't entirely stiff, but he was making a good impression on Peter.

"Wow!" he said quietly, "That looks really hot, Chris. He's not hard yet, is he; does he get any bigger?"

"A bit," I said, gripping my shaft and rubbing my hand up and down for a while, "Ohhh, that's better, he's woken up!"

And he had – now he was throbbingly hard. My foreskin had now rolled back to expose my shiny purplish knob and like Peter, a bead of precum had oozed from the tip. With my fingers, I spread it over my knob, making it all glossy and slippery.

Together, facing each other, we wanked for a little while, both carefully examining the other person's penis until Peter spoke again.

"I've never done this before," he said, "It's good – I like it."

"So do I," I said and greatly daring yet emboldened by my experience, I asked, "Could I touch you, Peter?"

"Do you want to? Really?" he asked, his eyebrows lifting in a show of surprise and delight.

I nodded enthusiastically. We shuffled a little closer and I stretched out my hand. Carefully and gently I grasped his shaft and for now I just held it and squeezed it, savouring the feel of a live penis in my hand again. His cock was a bit thicker than mine and what was sticking out of his jeans was just as long as the part of me that was exposed, so he too was probably around seven inches long. He'd still got his foreskin, like me, which slid back as I started to move my hand slightly up and down his length.

"Oooooooh" groaned Peter, shuddering all over, "Oooooh fuck – that feels so different."

"Nice is it?" I asked, feeling the thrill of his warm, quivering stiffness, "Feels amazing to me."

"Oh it's good alright," breathed Peter, "So much better than using my own hand! Ooooh yes! That's definitely feels good! Yeah, rub it for me, please Chris."

Changing my grip, I now held my palm beneath his cock with my fingers and thumb wrapped up the sides of his cock – it was too fat for my fingers to reach all around. His penis felt just as hot as the man's had, but this time the penis was quite a bit younger, more rigid and smoother too... not that I really cared about those finer points at this moment! All I knew was that I was holding another man's cock in my hand and I was loving it!

With my new grip, I was able to move my hand further and with more feeling. I made sure that his foreskin was being pulled back over his knob each time so that some of his lubrication would be spread around. I wanted to feel that moisture on my hand; I wanted to be able to smell the incredible scent of hot man-flesh afterwards on my hand and most importantly, I wanted to see that spunk shooting out again. Inside me there was also another desire bubbling up – actually and truly, I really wanted to be able to taste him!

'Oh my God, where did that thought come from?' I questioned myself, *'Just 'cos that bloke sucked me now I want to do it! What is it – contagious?'*

Peter's hand had been holding his balls as I stroked him but now he moved it and, pushing my hand off my cock, he replaced it with his. He started moving his hand up and down his cock faster than I'd been doing it.

He smiled at me, a big silly grin!

"You're being too gentle. But hey – this is hot. I guess it's all right to touch yours?" he asked, having grasped me without waiting for my permission.

19

His long slim fingers seemed to curl right round my cock, sending shivers of delight all up and down me and thrills of pleasure up and down my cock. It jumped hard as he touched it and seemed to stiffen even more. For a little while longer we sociably manipulated each other's penis, both just enjoying the unaccustomed feelings we were getting and giving, but my desire to taste him kept resurfacing.

"Can I do something?" I finally plucked up enough courage to ask, "I want to get down and look at your cock properly."

Ok, I chickened out of asking the real question, but I was getting there!

As he nodded, I dropped to my knees before him and changed my grip on his cock again and now my fingers were wrapped round his shaft from above, with my thumb below. I looked straight ahead at this fascinating piece of male meat and inspected the way the flesh of his knob was drawn together underneath, leading to the vestiges of his frenulum, which, like mine, was almost non-existent. I observed the seam beneath his cock that continued all the way to his balls... and then I realised that his knob was no more than two or three inches from my mouth.

I was shivering with anticipation and excitement – was I about to suck my first cock?

"Can I suck it? Would you mind?" I asked, politely because I was scared; my voice quivering as I spoke.

"Mmmmmm," Peter murmured in reply and I turned my mouth towards his penis.

Slowly and carefully I stuck my tongue out and gently let the tip slide over his knob. The sensations that were engulfing me were causing butterflies in my stomach and shivers in my spine – but I just knew I had to do it then a sudden thought filled my mind.

'If that man could do it then why can't I?'

Steeling my resolve, I slid the end of his penis into my mouth.

'Done it!' I thought, elated by my daring, *'Wow!'*

A long drawn-out happy-sounding sigh rose from Peter as his cock sank into my mouth. It felt warm and firm yet so smooth and sexy that I knew immediately that I was doing the right thing.

Gently I applied some pressure to the tissue of his knob and discovered that wonderful spongy, firm and yet giving, smooth texture of a penis that made me want to feel more of him. Slowly I let his cock sink deeper into my mouth, sliding and smoothing over my tongue and eventually reaching the back of my mouth. I backed off briefly and returned to his knob, which now felt so good to me.

I could taste a vague trace of urine; not a nasty taste; and then suddenly there was a new flavour that was slightly salty but almost non-existent.

Peter groaned at that moment and I guessed he'd just let loose with some precum.

Urgently now I sucked harder on his knob – I wanted more – I was becoming consumed with the need to feel and savour his cock. My tongue worked him over, sliding around his knob, probing into the little slit at the end and around the ridge separating his knob from his shaft. I was sucking hard too, wanting more of that slippery precum and sort-of hoping for his greater offering.

I too was groaning quietly to myself – this was a form of heaven that I'd seemingly been wanting ever since I learned to wank! Unable to suck my own cock, this was the next best thing in the world!

Now I was sliding my fist up and down his shaft as well as sucking and licking him and the inevitable was about to happen. I felt Peter tensing up and shudders seemed to shake his body. His cock kept jerking into my mouth as uncontrollable spasms drove Peter towards his orgasm.

"Careful!" he said, breathing heavily, "You'll make me cum soon, Chris, if you keep that up. Let me take him out."

I stopped sucking for a moment. Did I want his cum in my mouth? Part of me definitely was saying 'yes' while other parts were rebelling against the idea and I knew I soon had to make a decision...

I went for it!

"Let me finish you off Peter, cum in my mouth," I said, releasing his penis from my lips but still wanking him, "I want to suck you off!"

"Oh god – really?" said Peter, his voice quivering, "Oh yes please – make me cum!"

No more words were needed for a while as I continued to swirl my tongue in his increasing flow of precum. The taste and feeling were wonderful precursors to the main event – his spunk – his cum – filling my mouth. So often had I licked up my own pools of cum from my hand or belly and now I was about to taste cum direct from the fountain at last.

I worked harder on him and Peter began groaning quietly and breathing faster now as his orgasm began to overwhelm him.

"Oh fuck, that's it!" he said, pushing his penis deeper into my mouth, "Watch out! It's cumming, it's cumming! Oh god – here it is!"

And as I clamped my lips round his shaft, a warm gush of wetness suddenly coated my tongue and the back of my mouth and a new scent filled my nose. I felt another splash of cum and another and another filling my mouth. Unaccustomed to such a happening I didn't expect there to be so much and before I could swallow any, a last jet filled my mouth to overflowing. I felt it squirting out past my lips and I quickly held up my spare hand – the other one was holding his pulsing penis – to ensure that the overflow wasn't wasted.

And finally Peter heaved a last big sigh and his body relaxed, together with his cock, which started to soften in my mouth. I let it go and his cock, still with some off-white spunk clinging to it slid from my mouth.

Not accustomed to knowing how to handle all the cum that still filled my mouth, I quickly realised that there only one decent way to deal with it – to swallow it and then I suddenly understood that I really, really wanted to swallow it anyway. I drew a breath in through my nose and leaned my head back... and let it slide down my throat.

It was nectar! Ambrosia! Food of the Gods! It was delicious! It felt so alien and yet so good! I ran my tongue round my mouth to clean up the residue, which I swallowed too, along with the little tear of cum that had escaped onto my hand.

As I came back to Earth, I noticed Peter's cock still hanging there, lightly covered in his slime. I reached out for it and without a care in the world now, I sucked it back into my mouth to clean it up. I felt a last little dribble of sperm leave his slit before I let him loose, giving the tip of his cock a parting kiss.

Peter leaned back against the wall of the cubicle with a vacant but happy look on his face and eventually he looked down at me, still on my knees.

"Did you really do that?" he said, "That was awesome – incredible – fuckin' brilliant!"

"Was good, wasn't it?" I agreed as I stood up, "My first time and it was like something I've always ever wanted to do."

"Honest – your first time?" asked Peter, now tucking his cock back into his jeans, "God – you were fantastic!"

Then, as we both came back to reality, I suddenly realised that my cock was still standing up and very nearly hard and hadn't been fulfilled yet. I touched it and it immediately sprang back to life.

"Oh Chris – you haven't cum, have you," said Peter, reaching out his hand to hold my cock, "Oh sod it! We've got to be back in five minutes – there isn't time to get you off now. Oh fuck!"

"I'll manage," I said with a rueful grin, "I'll just have to concentrate on something else until I get home."

"Come back to my place after college," suggested Peter, "I'm on my own this week – the other flat's empty and it'll be peaceful. I'll get you off then if you can wait, I promise."

"Yeah, ok Peter, sounds good," I said, tucking my erection away as best I could, "Meet you at the gates later then."

Together we left the still deserted toilets and headed back to college and for some reason I put my arm over his shoulder as we walked – it seemed the right thing to do.

"Don't know what to say about all that," I said, slowly shaking my head in wonderment, "I never thought that would happen to me."

"Me neither," said Peter, "I didn't expect anything – I just wanted us to be friends."

"More than friends, eh, mate!" I said, smiling broadly and pulling him tight against me, "Am I pleased I met you!"

It was almost four in the afternoon before Peter appeared at the gates where I'd been waiting impatiently for some while.

"Sorry," he said cheerfully and bumping shoulders with me, "Had to call in at the office and I got held up. Never mind – it's only a five-minute walk."

Well, it was nearer ten minutes before we reached his place and it seemed to be even longer and then Peter was pulling me into a gateway and up to the door.

"My own front door key," he said smiling happily, "I can come and go when I like. Go on – up you go."

The flat below had its front door on the other side of the house and we climbed the stairs to his landing and his flat.

"It's been converted and sort-of opened up," he said, "Strange layout, but it works ok. Go on in..."

The flat was really just the upper floor of the house, so everything pretty well opened off the lounge-diner, but it looked fresh, airy and clean. As I glanced around, I spotted his bed – a double, of all things!

"You lucky sod!" I called out, "Double bed – what a luxury!"

"My parents had to get a bed for me and this one was in our spare room, so they brought it over for me. Most excellent to spread out on."

"And to do other things!" I said, laughing.

"Hah – what other things?" replied Peter, "There's only been me... but then I've only been here a week."

"That was last week," I retorted, "This week there's me as well. And you promised!"

"Oh yes, I did, didn't I," said Peter, winking at me, "Well you can darned well wait while I get us a drink – what do you want, lager, tea, coffee or water?"

"Wow, a choice! I'll have a can if that's ok," I said, dropping my jacket over the back of a chair and a moment later there was a chilled can in my hand.

Peter came and stood near me as we both imbibed some deliciously cold lager. He looked at me and smiled happily.

"Better?" he asked.

"Much," I replied as I continued to absorb my surroundings, "Should I take my shoes off in here, by the way?"

"Well, I'm going to, so you might as well too," Peter replied and by now we were both feeling much less tense.

25

College was already a distant memory. He stripped off his socks then took off his t-shirt too, revealing a nicely smooth and lightly muscled body.

"I'm sweaty," he said by explanation, "Get your off too. Oh fuck it, I might as well strip down!"

I looked at him in some surprise as he dropped his jeans, to stand there in just his boxer shorts.

"You stripping off?" I asked, perhaps taken aback by the pace of the situation.

"Why not? Warm enough, isn't it? Get yours off too. Then we can get on the bed!" Peter said as he adjusted his visibly somewhat inflated penis inside his shorts before striding into his 'bedroom' recess on his long smooth-looking legs.

He bounced on the bed and then crashed, flat out onto it.

"Damn – bring my can with you," he said from his prone position.

With nothing more to delay me, I gathered our cans and moved to the side of the bed where I put them down on the bedside locker. Quickly now I unzipped my jeans and stepped out of them, stripping off my t-shirt too then removing my shoes and socks.

Peter patted the bed.

"Come and lie here – come and join me on my untested bed!" he said, chuckling and soon I was there with him, two young men lying side by side on the bed, clad only in our underpants.

"Hey, this is better already," said Paul, rolling over towards me, "This bed's too big to be alone in. Nice to have you here!"

His hand reached out and he laid it gently on my chest where he began to move it around, feeling, smoothing, massaging down to the top of my abdomen, up across my ribs and around my nipples. Gently he tweaked each one in turn before continuing his caresses.

"You're like me, aren't you?" he said, now feeling higher up my chest, "Smooth skin and not hairy and no fat either. I do like these muscles of yours – your pecs, aren't they?"

"Yeah," I said, somewhat losing myself in the moment, "Yeah – I've been trying to build up a bit of muscle, I'm too skinny really."

"Hmmmh!" said Peter, moving his hand down my body, "The muscle I saw didn't need building up!"

And he didn't! He was already up and waiting! No-one, not even my erstwhile girlfriend had touched my body like that, and my cock had responded rapidly and enthusiastically. I looked down my body and saw the tent that my cock was making, and Peter saw it too.

"Liked that, did you Chris?" he asked, his hand now reaching down my abdomen to my waistband, "Do you want me to continue?"

"Mmmmmm yeahhh," I agreed happily, "Mmmmmm, don't stop!"

Peter wriggled closer to me across the bed until our bodies were almost touching. His face was perhaps a foot from mine, but more importantly to me, his hand now began pushing down beyond the waistband of my shorts until he was gently stroking across my pubes.

My penis was so stiff that the head was raised well above his hand, but Peter was obviously teasing me – just making me wait.

I was already twitching and shivering with anticipated excitement and Peter had a big smile on his face as we both now watched his hand's movement.

"Would you like me to touch you?" asked Peter, his hand moving ever nearer to my penis.

"Please, please," I gasped, "Oh yes, oh god, yesssss!"

The back of Peter's hand had just grazed past my erection before moving away…

"Let's get your underpants off first," Peter said, and I quickly lifted my hips to allow him to help me to slide them down and off my hips, so that I could soon wriggle my legs free as well.

My penis was now standing naked and proud, pointing up the bed towards me; my foreskin had slid back and my knob now almost glowed with readiness.

"That's better," said Peter; his hand poised to tease me, "Looks good, doesn't he? Are you ready for this?"

"Ooooh! Yes, yes, please Peter – I'm more than ready!" I groaned, somehow stopping myself from taking hold of my own cock, "Come on, please hold me. Rub me, please!"

Peter didn't respond but his hand did instead. Returning to my abdomen, he let his hand wander around, teasing me more, before sliding down, down, down to the base of my straining cock.

Then his warm fingers wrapped themselves round my length, making my cock jerk uncontrollable and making me shudder and breathe in quickly.

"Ooooooooh yessssss!" I moaned, "Ohhhh! Oh Peter, more, more, please! Fuck sake – come on!"

Peter's hand began moving up and down my shaft, occasionally brushing up against my knob, faster and faster. I started to jerk and twitch all over as he brought me towards my orgasm, but it wasn't to be a quickie – not now we had time to enjoy the act at our leisure. His hand slowed and now moved to my knob to gather some of my precum that had begun leaking out. He smoothed it over my penis from end to end, gradually soaking my whole length in my slippery secretions but now just running his fist steadily up and down my cock.

"Mind if I take my pants off too?" asked Paul out of the blue and before I could object, not that I had any intention of doing so, Paul was naked there beside me.

His own penis was as stiff as mine and as he lay on his side, his erection, now released from its enclosure, pressed against my hip.

'Oh fuck,' I thought, *'Two more firsts – the first time I've ever been in bed with a man and the first time another cock has ever touched me – well, properly, that is!'*

I looked at Paul and asked what was really a silly question...

"Would you mind if I held your cock?" I asked still somewhat timidly yet expectantly.

Paul nodded furiously, his eyes sparkling with excitement.

"Yessssss of course!" he hissed softly as my hand wrapped round his penis, "Ooooooh yeahhhhh!"

It was a bit awkward for us to reach and play with both cocks and for a while we struggled – Peter had to roll his hips back to let me get at him properly and he then had to stretch to reach me.

"Turn around," said Peter, "You know – head to tail. You move."

Understanding quickly, I reversed my position on the bed while Peter moved down the bed somewhat and then we both rolled partially together. And now his cock was within easy reach of my hand – or of my mouth for that matter, I realised.

I took hold of his cock pretty well just as he grasped mine and we both started wanking each other, quietly and steadily bringing each other the stimulation needed to reach a climax, but then Peter's hand stopped moving and I wondered what he was up to. I didn't need to wait for long as I felt his hand pull on my cock and then without warning, it was absorbed into a wonderfully warm welcoming cavern, a cavern with a slippery sliding tongue that worked its way round and over my penis; a cavern with succulent lips that squeezed and caressed my shaft.

"Ahhh Peter!" I gasped, "Oh yesss, that's brilliant!"

I gasped again as he began sucking me before realising that here before me was his cock just waiting to be sucked as well.

29

I leaned forward a little bit and, holding his penis in the right direction, I just opened my mouth and sucked him right in!

Peter let out a gasp of surprise and delight, before returning his mouth to my cock and then, apart from occasional approving hums, the only sound was that of our gently slurping lips sucking happily on hardened lengths of penile flesh and of us two breathing somewhat noisily through our noses... but nothing that good lasts for ever.

Actually, it was never going to last for very much longer, but it was going to get a whole lot better as we both neared our climaxes.

"Do you want me to carry on?" I asked, knowing what was to come and Peter stopped his sucking for a moment.

"Oh god – yeah! You were brilliant last time," he groaned, lifting his mouth from my penis for a moment before returning to his devotion.

I let his cock slide into my mouth and concentrated on the big finale.

By now I knew for certain that I was starting to get close and I guessed that Peter felt the same way. He now had his hand over my hip and was holding me with his hand over my buttocks, his fingers actually reaching into the cleft by my arsehole as he pulled my cock into his mouth.

My own free hand was over his hip as well but I was feeling his balls from behind, pulling them down from his cock and rolling them in my hand, a bit like that man had done to me and whatever I was doing, Peter seemed to like it.

Suddenly Peter tensed up and gasped.

"Gonna cum Chris!" he said through gritted teeth, "Gonna fuckin' cum any moment!"

"Yeah Peter – let me have it – all of it," I said, totally determined that I was going to take his full load this time.

I sank his cock back into my mouth and sucked hard, while wanking his shaft as well and it was too much for Peter.

"Aaaaaah! Oh yeahhhhh! Uuuuugh! Uuuuugh!" he cried thrusting his penis hard into my mouth, "Oh god, cumming, cumming!"

Somehow I managed to stop it from pushing down my throat but despite that his knob was wedged right at the back of my mouth as the first several squirts left his cock. I managed to hold him back until I only had the knob and an inch or so in my mouth – which was just as well, because his sperm just seemed to keep on flowing.

I swallowed a mouthful and another – deliciously warm and bittersweet and slippery and then as his flow eased off my mouth just retained the last small globules of spunk. Gently I pulled my mouth free so I could breathe better then glanced at his cock. It was glistening with saliva and cum and kept jerking – the remnants of his climax producing another small bubble of cum which I licked up eagerly.

I also needed air because I was just about to cum – the excitement of Peter's orgasm had tipped me over the top and I was on a rapid slide to my own eruption.

"Peter – Pete, alright to cum?" I asked, pumping my cock in and out of his mouth – and then, unable to wait for a reply, my body froze momentarily, and my orgasm let rip.

I really felt my first pulse of hot spunk travel up my penis and I certainly felt it exit the little slit – which must have been stretched to the limit! My next three pulses also felt as if I was peeing – they weren't just little jets; they were full power blasts!

"Ooooh – yea... yea... yeahhhhhh!" I cried as I began cumming, "Oooooh fuuuuuck – yeahhhhh!"

Peter coughed gently as my eruption took him by surprise, but in moments I could feel his mouth sucking at my cock to extract as much of my cum as he could.

I was filling his mouth – the excitement of the day had kept me loaded and tonight, at last, I could release the tension.

And as I filled his mouth, I realised that his hand was right on my bum and that his fingertips seemed to be probing just inside the tightness of my arsehole! For a second I wanted to rebel – to scream in horror or something – and then I relaxed as my mind quickly pointed out just how intimate we'd been... so to explore my arsehole wasn't really going much further.

Now that we'd both cum and with mutual pats on the back, we disengaged and turned to face one another again – and without a word, we pulled ourselves close together... and we kissed!

Now I don't actually know which was more of a shock – having my arsehole played with or having my lips kissed by a man, but I do know that I was trembling as our lips met. We came together almost spontaneously; our lips meeting and locking even before we could think – then we pulled apart fast. Peter looked at me with smiling eyes, although I think that mine must have been wide open with shock, and then he pulled us together again and this time we came together willingly and with feeling.

It was weird to kiss someone again – and a man, of all things! I'd kissed my parents and my aunt and obviously my briefly acquired girlfriend, and with her we'd got pretty heated – but this was simply scalding hot! I was shaking from head to toe and I think Peter was too. To add to the intensity, there was the taste of our cum, sliding between our mouths as our tongues twisted and turned and interwove. As we lay there kissing, our arms held and pulled each other close and we managed to get our legs interlocked, so that our cocks were rubbing against the other's body.

And you know what happens when you rub a cock? Yep – they were both hard again almost immediately!

After an unconscious length of time, we parted our lips and moved our upper bodies a little way apart, both breathing heavily. Our lower halves remained woven together, our cock rubbing gently on our abdomens.

"That was intense," I said in wonderment, "I'm not complaining though – I liked that. Really different from kissing a girl, isn't it?"

"Why?" asked Peter, licking his lips, "Same action, same position and no reason why your lips or mine are any different."

"It's not that – it's what else happens! What gets me is that as I kiss you I can feel my cock hardening and pressing against you... and then I can feel your cock doing the same... that's what's different," I said, "So it makes our kissing even more like a sex act."

"Better do it some more then!" laughed Peter, throwing himself on top of me.

I grabbed him as he fell on me and held him tightly against me. We kissed again, quickly and excitedly, because now our two stiff cocks were rubbing together and the site of our feelings began moving from our lips to our groins.

I rolled him off me and managed to reverse the situation until it was me who was pressing down from above. We were sort of wrestling for position, but at the same time we were both revelling in the exciting feeling of having our two bodies so close together – so intimately entwined.

Eventually I lifted my body up on extended arms and feet and looked down between us and there, where our bodies met, our two stiff penises crossed, each having left a small wet patch on the abdomen of the other person. A few viscous threads wove a sticky net between us. I jiggled around, making our cocks slide together when suddenly we both jerked forward at the same moment, which pushed my cock to slip past Peter's and slide down over his balls.

"Ooops, sorry!" I breathed although I didn't feel at all sorry – it felt really good.

"Mmmmm, no worries, that's nice!" said Peter, lifting his hips up at me and causing my cock to slide further down past his balls, "Yeahhh, that feels good!"

With my penis out of the way I was able to drop my body completely down on Peter's and I could now feel his hard erection squeezed against my belly. In turn, my cock was pressing and rubbing along his perineum, between his balls and his arse and, remembering how strange yet how nice it had felt when he used his fingers on me, I thought I'd return the compliment by giving his arsehole a touch or two, but this time, with my cock.

I adjusted my position and also reached down to hold and to better direct my cock as I pushed it against his body. Peter was writhing beneath me, loving it all and now tipped his hips up to facilitate my access to his rear end and it was at that moment that I felt the pucker of his arsehole, the firm, crinkled, pulled-together flesh against my knob. It flexed as I touched it, seeming to stretch open against my cock. I pushed against his hole a bit harder, feeling the puckered flesh give way a little more as I did so.

I looked up at Peter – his eyes were closed and his mouth was smiling.

"Is that nice," I asked, "Do you want me to keep doing that?"

"Ooooh yesssss – that's lovely Chris, I like that," he groaned, "I've always liked my arsehole played with."

"You like to play with your arse?" I repeated, not having considered such an idea before, "Is that why you touched my hole?"

"Yeahhhh," moaned Peter dreamily as I continued to rub my knob around and against his hole, "It feels great – sort of secret, you know. And if I put my finger inside me I can make myself cum more quickly – I've put other things in there too every so often and it's brilliant. One day I think I want to have you inside me."

"What? You want me to put my finger in you, like you just did to me?" I asked, somewhat shocked and certainly not thinking of us doing anything more than wanking and sucking.

"No Chris, not your finger – your cock!" said Peter to my amazement, "I want your cock inside me. I think I want you to fuck me."

While the internet is now full of fucking of all kinds, back in the 1970s in England there was no such fountain of smut, porn and learning.

Magazines, such as there were, were usually in black and white, with 'naughty bits' airbrushed out and they weren't readily available to anyone under twenty-one if I remember and they certainly weren't on display in shops. Purloined copies of usually American or German magazines did circulate – but usually at a price. Sex had yet to be liberated and we were definitely just having to find our own way!

And so we explored as if blindfolded, feeling our way into our sex and working mainly from information reluctantly and often incorrectly passed down by one's elders. If you were in the right group, there was bound to be a loudmouth who'd be happy to tell all and sundry about what he'd done and how he'd done it... but I knew no-one like that.

So Peter and I had only my limited experience, and a modicum of 'birds and bees' knowledge – the rest we had to discover for ourselves and therefore, at that time, things like homosexual sex and anal fucking were really unknown to me.

Peter's proposal had shocked me deeply therefore and I hardly knew what to do next. Sex, as in wanking and sucking with another man was shocking enough but doing something as unnatural as playing with someone's arsehole was taking things too far!

A month or two ago I'd been a virgin; a week or so ago I'd been a one-girl guy – then I'd had sex with a strange man and now, here I was, lying naked in bed with another man! Things were happening too fast... but we were in a compromising position and truthfully, it was great!

My cock was pressing lightly on his hole, Peter was responding, and I wasn't complaining... but I wasn't ready. I moved back so that I was lying on top of Peter.

"Pete," I said, talking into his face, "I'm new to all this and I don't know how far I want to go. I'm amazed that I'm here with you and it hasn't sunk in yet. You see, I'm not a homo, I loved my girlfriend... errrrrm Brenda... but now I'm here having sex with you. What's happened?"

"See," said Peter laughing gently, "You've almost forgotten your girlfriend's name already! And as for having sex with me – you're obviously bisexual – you like men as well as girls... so make the most of it!"

"How?" I asked, lost for ideas, because apart from some vigorous fucking in a few basic hetero positions and lots of wanking, my knowledge was almost zero.

Peter, on the other hand, was a bit more worldly than me, it seemed.

"Look Chris, I've got some mags, they're really hot, as in 'wow!' and you can have a look at them, if you like," Peter explained, "They're homosexual mags and they show everything and I mean everything!"

"You what!" I exclaimed, "Really – can I see them, please!"

"Yeah, 'course you can, mate," he said, waving his hand, "They're in the locker by the bed."

I reached over and opened the drawer and there they were and even just the first one blew my mind as I opened it!

Lurid photographs of hunky men, often in leather, but always with huge oiled erect cocks!

Page after page of sex – oozing from the pages – starting with kissing and fondling; progressing through the magazine to sucking and mutual sucking... and then to anal sex!

I flicked the pages over slowly, my mouth agape at the sight of all this eroticism – all this unknown world of men having sex with men.

Finally, on the last few pages were the cum shots – buckets of cum pouring from hugely erect cocks into waiting mouths and stretched arseholes... I was speechless.

But although my head was spinning, my lower brain was wide awake and raring to go! The organ it controlled, namely my penis was throbbingly hard, dribbling and quivering with excitement!

Paul had been laying on his side as I scanned through the magazine – the first of a pile – gently caressing his erection as I took in the almost alien scenes.

I looked over to him in wonderment.

"Does this really happen?" I asked, incredulously, my eyes having trouble leaving the page.

"Of course it does, all though not all men are as big as they are. They're porn models – we're normal humans," he said, smiling at me, "Not that what you and I have are anything to be ashamed of! Now come here and forget them."

Rather reluctantly I pushed the magazines away and then, less reluctantly, Peter and I enfolded our arms and pulled our bodies together. For a while we just held on, revelling in the feeling of another person's hot flesh, but soon our two erections began to demand attention.

"Let's do a 69 again," said Peter, moving and reversing his position on the bed, "Think you could cum again?"

"Bloody right!" I said as I settled myself with his penis just in front of my face, "No problem!"

"Hang on," said Peter and before I knew it he'd climbed on top of me and now straddled my face. His erection now pointed down at me and I automatically jerked as I felt his lips touch my own cock.

"Oooh, fuuuu..." I cried, sucking my breath in quickly as his mouth sucked my erect penis into it, "Oh my god – Oh that's gooood."

I could hardly avoid his penis, not that I wanted to and so I grasped it; pulled it towards my mouth and by raising my head just a little bit, I was able to let him slide down between my soft lips and into my mouth. It was lovely – his penis was smooth and yet so hard; his knob was firm and yet so soft; his taste was bland and yet so savoury – I loved it!

As we mutually gave oral pleasure to each other, the only sounds were the occasional slurps as we changed the grasp of our lips and our breathing – which was gradually becoming faster but well before we'd reached our peaks, Peter lifted his head.

"Touch me there again," he said, and I realised what he meant.

I lifted my hands and ran them over his wide-spread buttocks as he straddled my head. Gently feeling the muscular structure of his arse, I worked my way closer to his anal core. Peter seemed to be holding his breath as I did so – and suddenly I touched his arsehole with my fingers!

Instantly I recoiled but fortunately it was merely an inbuilt reaction that I soon repressed. I touched him again, running my fingers around his crinkled skin and causing Peter to cry out happily.

"Oh Chris – yessss – do that! Do that! Please!" he pleaded, panting now around my cock, "Oh yeah – pleeeeease play with me!"

"Ok," I said, "Hang on."

I pushed my finger at his hole and got some response, but something was missing – there was no way I could even try to slide my finger inside, it was too dry. I brought my finger back down to my mouth and wetted it with spit and then tried again, but still it wouldn't penetrate him.

"Peter," I said, "We need something to make things slippery."

"Try Vaseline, there's a pot of it in the drawer," he said, "Won't need much."

I reached out rather blindly as I lay on my back and fumbled around until I located the corner of the drawer and was able to inch it open. There were a number of items in the drawer that my fingers encountered before I found a little jar which I brought back to inspect – and I was right! Deftly under the circumstances, I opened the pot and gathered a little smear of the jelly on my middle finger before discarding the pot and lid on the bed. I brought my Vaseline-laden finger back to his anus, trying to avoid spreading the stuff where it wasn't needed and finally I was able to smear it onto his little hole. I pushed at the centre of the star and my fingertip just slid inside – easy as you like!

There was a brief 'ooooh' from Peter as I poked inside and then quickly withdrew... I still wasn't entirely at ease with this.

I continued to just run my finger around his puckered flesh, feeling the ripples and indentations as I did so and occasionally sliding my finger in towards his hole – and each time I probed it seemed a little easier to do. And every time I did that, there was a small intake of breath from Peter, who otherwise was remaining silent, mainly because he was still sucking on my cock. I'd almost forgotten his penis despite it hanging not more than a few inches from my mouth... somehow I was somewhat preoccupied with my new task.

I pushed my ring finger at his hole a bit harder and felt the top of it and perhaps down to the second joint slide inside him, causing Peter to gasp again. Slowly I moved it in and out, feeling Peter's anus gripping and squeezing my finger as I did so.

"Ooooh Chris – I like that," said Peter, removing my penis from his mouth, "Try using two fingers and see if you can feel my prostate gland."

"Your what?" I replied, hardly aware of what was inside a human body.

"My prostate – you know, it's a gland that makes your spunk white," he said, and in retrospect he was partially right at any rate, not that I knew anything about it at the time.

"Put your fingers in and curl them down and you'll find it – I'll soon tell you if you do," Peter said, "Go on, give it a try."

His body heat had now melted the Vaseline and it had become really slippery around his hole – so much so that when I pushed my two fingers into him, they slid in with no trouble at all although entry was probably helped by Peter pushing out with his arse – I could feel his flesh stretching – his hole expanding...

And suddenly I had two fingers buried most of the way to the knuckle inside my best friend – inside another man's arse, for heaven's sake!

"Oh fuck Chris – oh yeah – right in me – that's lovely!" groaned Peter around my cock, "Ahhh, you've found it – rub my prostate please, try."

I began to explore the spongy mass that I'd found, my actions making Peter groan anew as I stroked it with my fingertips.

"Ahhh, that's it!" he gasped, "Ohh Chris, that's amazing!"

"Are you really enjoying that?" I asked, still uncertain yet pleased that I was making him happy.

"Oh Chris, yes, yesss – now suck me, suck me!" cried Peter and as I drew his cock into my mouth I tasted that incredibly erotic yet so bland taste of precum again – quite definite now whereas before it had been just a lingering hint of flavour.

"Ooooh! Ooooh" Peter moaned as I explored his insides, "Oooh, I like it!"

Peter's cock was now as hard and as extended as I'd ever come across it and he was leaking his slippery fluid into my mouth constantly – and I was sucking it up as fast as he could deliver.

I was getting into this now – my initial reservations dissolving. I was giving Peter pleasure and he was doing as much for me and it was too good to quibble about or worry over. The many unknown factors that seemed to have filled my life over the past few weeks were being blown away and while my mind was still reeling I understood that I'd also decided inside that I'd take whatever came my way – and enjoy it!

Slurping happily at Peter's cock, I was settling in for a longish period of oral sex – the pair of us pleasurably sucking on each other's cocks, edging each other along when Peter interrupted my reverie.

"Can we change positions please?" he asked.

Acceding, I slid my fingers from his anus and slapping him gently on the bum, I slid upwards until I was almost sitting up. Peter, releasing his mouth from my cock as we moved, crabbed down and around then came and sat on my thighs facing me, almost squashing my erection.

"Will you try, please?" said Peter, holding his hands on either side of my face to concentrate my thoughts, "For me. Please?"

"Try what," I asked, wondering where this was going, without thinking about what we'd been doing.

"Try putting your cock inside me?" he asked, simply, as he reached down and took hold of my erection.

"Ummm... errrrr... dunno!" I flustered as Peter's hands excited my penis and pushed it downwards towards his arse.

"Come on – you don't have to do anything really – let me do the work," said Peter.

"Why?" I asked, considering in my mind that oral and – once-upon-a-time, vaginal sex – were quite enough.

"Because I like it. Because I enjoy having things up inside me. Because I want to see what it feels like to have your cock up inside me!" said Peter.

I didn't know what else to say, so I just remained silent and as I did so Peter lifted his body above mine.

"Come on, slide down the bed a bit," said Peter, and I did.

"That's better," he replied, "Stay there for a minute."

Peter quickly climbed off the bed and located the pot of Vaseline. Then he bent over and applied a blob to his arse, then climbed onto the bed once again and stepped astride me, lowering himself towards me. He reached down and took hold of my penis, then aimed his arse at my upheld erection.

"Ok, here I come," he breathed, and I shuddered as I felt the closeness of his body to my cock.

I watched as Peter lowered himself closer and closer to my penis until he'd pressed it upright against his arse... and although I couldn't see the action as he settled down, I could guess what was happening. Soon I felt his body against my cock... I could feel pressure on the end of it, pressure that seemed to spread around my knob, pressure which slowly eased – right at the moment that Peter let out a deep sigh. Then suddenly his body was pressing down on mine... and I realised that he'd embedded my cock deep inside his anus.

"Aaaaaaaahhhh!" cried Peter – not so much a cry of pain but one of ecstatic pleasure as my penis invaded a place where little had been before, "Oh fuck!"

Peter was now sitting firmly on my lap and my solid erection was right up his arse!

"Fuuuuck, Peter – what're you doing?" I asked, rather stupidly.

This was all a lifetime away from my previous existence – a culture shock in every sense of the word. Actually I wasn't just shocked; I was almost frightened at the speed at which my sex life had done a complete about turn. And then Peter brought me back from my musings as his buttocks slammed down onto my groin, causing me to grunt and also take notice!

"Not what I'm doing; it's what you're doing! You're fucking me!" he replied, lifting his body up and then dropping it back onto my cock, "I'll do the work if you prefer, but if you want to join in..."

Could I not join in? It felt incredible – the tight warmth of his anus was sliding over my penis and stirring my arousal so much that I simply couldn't help but join in!

My body reacted to the pressure on my cock by pushing back, which sent a shockwave through Peter; who squeezed me; which made me thrust again; which made him squeeze again... and suddenly we were fucking one another hard! In time with one another now my hips pushed upwards as he bounced his body downwards onto my penis; my cock driving deeper into his guts as he thumped his body onto mine; my cock throbbing as his arse pulsed around it and things were getting hot.

Our orgasms just couldn't be that far away as the scent of our hot fucking climbed from our bodies in waves... a scent that was new to me but one that I knew I'd soon come to love.

Peter's cock was bobbing up and down on my abdomen in front of me, so I took hold of it and began to wank him, making Peter lift up and sink down even faster. My hand was sliding in the copious quantities of precum that he was now leaking, and it was quite hard to keep good tight grip on his erection but I succeeded – I wanted to see Peter cum while he sat on my cock.

Peter's tight arsehole was still sliding up and down my penis, giving me feelings that I'd never had before but which were quickly bring me to the boil.

"Peter, I'm getting close," I said quietly, my voice quivering, "What do you want me to do?"

"Cum in me – cum in me!" he replied urgently, "Don't stop – I'm almost there too!"

"Can't stop Peter – here it cums!" I cried, because his arse was now squeezing me tightly and bringing me off, "Just cummmmming!"

"Wha – yeahhhhhh!" cried Peter, as he too reached his pinnacle.

"Uuuuuh god! I'm cumming!" I yelled as I felt my first eruption of cum squirt directly and deeply up into his bowel, "Fuckin' cummming up you!"

And I was – jet after jet of my hot cum was blasting up into his arse, deep into his bowels – just as jet after jet of Peter's cum began blasting right at my face. We were both cumming together, gloriously!

Peter slumped sideways and rested himself on one arm, breathing heavily. He was still impaled on my cock which was giving no indication that it was going to go limp yet; Peter's tight arsehole was keeping the blood from flowing back.

"Shiiiiiit!" he exclaimed, punching the air with his other arm and almost falling off me in the process, "We've done it!"

"Done what exactly?" I asked, feeling his arsehole spasmodically squeezing my cock.

"Made my dreams come true!" said Peter somewhat dramatically, "I told you I like to play with my arse – I told you I like to feel things inside me. I've always felt that way and now that I've had a cock cumming inside me I'm sooooo happy!"

"So have we made love or just fucked?" I asked.

I felt Peter squeeze my cock harder with his arsehole.

"I think that was making love. Anyway, I'm sure I love you already!" he replied, "You're the best thing that's ever happened to me."

He went silent and cocked his head slightly in a quizzical look.

"And you?" he asked, "How do you feel about me then?"

'How did I feel?' I mused. A month ago I was a one-girl guy and now I've just had a wonderful time with a man. Was there any going back? I thought not...

I reached up my arms to Peter.

"Come here then, my lover and I'll show you how I feel," I said, "And then, when I've shown you, perhaps we can do it all over again."

44

"Wow!" said Peter, feeling my cock stiffening again, "And maybe next time I can fuck you instead!"

I smiled.

A Tale of Two Opposites

College was fun, to be honest. The course I was on held few mysteries and while it was no breeze, at least I completed it and came out with a good quality pass despite my energetic sexual activities. At least I kept mine private – well, we had to in those days and seemingly no-one was any the wiser. Peter and I really were lovers for a while though but once college was over we parted company, not least because Peter's parents moved across the world to America while I stayed put. It was about then that computers were slowly coming into their own and, eager to learn about something new I delved deeply into the business, soon finding myself to be quite expert in the field. Oh, I was no whizz-kid, but I knew what I was doing and found that there was a distinct market for someone with my know-how – which led to this next encounter.

Thump!! Ouch!!

"UUUUGHHH!"

"AAGGHH FUCK!"

Damn and fuck and ouch – I didn't mean to run into him. Damn, I didn't mean to run into anyone, but I just did – literally.

I'd just panicked as I realised that I'd left a brand-new high-performance hard drive on the back seat of my car. I'd just bought it along with a small fortune's-worth of other computer bits and pieces… and while I'd carried indoors several large boxes full of bits, I'd left the hard drive behind, still in its box.

The law of the street said that if I left it there for much more than five minutes then some thieving git would come along, smash one of my windows and nick it – so I was hot-footing it out to the car, when it happened.

There was this heavy, somewhat oblique impact; some guttural grunts, an impression of flying and falling, a fair amount of pain and some groans and then I was lying there in the gutter alongside a somewhat rotund and rough-looking guy who I'd suddenly and violently met.

"For crying out loud!" I exclaimed, shaken to the core and wringing my hand to get rid of the pain, "What the fuck were...? Why don't you watch where you're bloody well going!"

"No – what the fuck were YOU doing?" the other guy exclaimed angrily as he sat up, "I was just walking past your fuckin' gate and you fuckin' well came rushing out..."

Suddenly I realised that I was indeed almost entirely in the wrong... I'd just galloped out of my gateway without even looking, never thinking about there being anyone right in my way. I've got one of those older houses with a high wall and heavy brick pillars at the front, so I couldn't see anything, but I should have looked first, shouldn't I?

"Ah – oh fuck – oh shit! Ummm, look, sorry mate – I'm really, really sorry," I exclaimed, contritely now, "Yeah – you're right – guess it was my fault. I'm so sorry – you ok?"

"Just about," the other guy said as he sat up, "No thanks to you."

"I am – I'm really sorry," I said, now feeling very contrite, "I wasn't thinking... I wasn't looking either and I was in a real hurry."

We both stood up – actually I helped him up and we began brushing the dust and dirt off our clothes. I looked at him as I did so and oh typical – there was a trickle of blood running down the side of his face.

"Shit – you're hurt," I said pointing at his head.

"Whereabouts?" he asked, his hand feeling for the blood – which he soon found.

"Oh bugger – you got a tissue or something?" he asked as he dabbed at it ineffectually with his hand and made the trickle into a smear.

"Yeah, yeah – come in the house and I'll fix you up. Oh – I am so sorry," I said, now feeling like a complete idiot for crashing into him.

I linked my arm into his to help him up the path – he seemed to be a little unsteady on his feet – and eventually got him into the utility room where I sat him down. In a few moments I'd found some soft lint and some plasters and a little later I was bathing his wound – a small nick on his temple.

"You'll live," I said, hoping to relax him and it seemed to work.

"Yeah – I'm ok. Have you got a plaster I can put on it?" he asked, wincing as he touched the wound.

"Yeah sure," I quickly answered and no sooner said than done and he was repaired.

"That better?" I asked and he nodded.

"Could I have a drink of something?" he asked, "And if you've got a couple of painkillers, they might come in handy too. Banged my head a bit – it's spinning..."

The utility room cupboard was filled with such useful things and I got him a glass of water to wash the pills down and soon they were gone.

"Hey, um – stay there for a moment would you – I must get something from the car," I said, having suddenly remembered my hard drive once more and inside a minute I'd fetched it and now felt very much more relaxed.

"You alright now?" I asked, "Feeling any better?"

"I'll do – bit sore in places but I'll be ok. Better let those pills go down though before I get on my way," he said, "But thanks for your help anyway."

"Least I could do since I caused it," I said but he held up his hand to stop me talking.

"Just bad luck us both trying to be in the same place at the same time," he said with a small smile, "Never mind – worse things have happened…"

"Absolutely," I said and then I realised that I didn't even know who I was talking to.

"Oh sorry – I ought to introduce myself – I'm Chris, Chris Lord," I said, and the other guy held out his hand which I grasped and shook. It was warm and his grip was very firm.

"I'm Paul, Paul Clark – Nobby, they call me," he said with a smile, "Us Clarks all get called that."

I laughed, knowing that I too was lumbered with a silly nickname.

"Ha – they call me Streak – guess you just found out one of the reasons why!" I said laughing, "I'm always running around but I'm also tall and thin as you see, so that's another reason."

"You're not really thin," said Nobby, eyeing me up and down, "Tall yes, but not thin."

"Oh all right," I said, "Slim perhaps – 32 inch waist but I'm not skinny."

I gave Nobby a good once-over to assess him mentally and perhaps physically, soon realising that he was probably six inches shorter than me, if not more and definitely somewhat more rotund, possibly somewhat fat-looking or equally possibly quite muscular – it was hard to tell. He was a cheerful looking guy; short dark hair; blue eyes like me and generally reasonable enough in appearance, if a bit on the rough side perhaps thanks to a day or two of stubble. He was wearing a rather over-sized t-shirt, and baggy jogging trousers – the kind with an elasticated waist.

"So what do you do then?" I asked having assessed his body shape, "I reckon you look as if you're either a lorry driver or stuck in an office."

"Office! Far from it! Seldom see an office, never been in a lorry," exclaimed Nobby, "I'm into sport – I coach hockey players; men that is – well, goal-minders in particular and in my spare time I wrestle."

"Bloody hell," I said, "And there was me thinking you were a bit...oh damn – sorry, I mean more suited for a sedentary life."

"Oh – you mean fat?" he said, "Nah – not a bit of it – it's all muscle, mate."

With that he stood up and quickly stripped off his t-shirt to reveal his upper body.

My jaw dropped as he displayed his remarkably well developed muscles; his bulging pecs; his massive biceps and his ripped abdomen...not to mention his profusion of hairs and tattoos. He was solid – all man!

Don't get me wrong – I'm not a homo – I don't really like blokes at all but his upper body was a bit like something you'd see in a weight-lifting magazine and something of a complete surprise too.

"Wow!" I exclaimed, "Bloody hell – I got you wrong then!"

"You're not the first," he said remaining stripped down as he sat once more, "So, what do you do then – you look as if sport is definitely your scene."

"Hah, you're wrong too!" I exclaimed, "Right shape – wrong mind. And as it happens, I'm the one who spends his time behind a desk. Can't stand sports actually."

"Ahh come on – you must do something sporty – you're just built for it!" Nobby said, "Show me your chest."

Never having been shy of my body, I too quickly removed my t-shirt and I saw Nobby's eyes open wide.

"Hey – you look like a model or a swimmer," he said, "All smooth and clean. Do you shave? Where's all your hair?"

"Never had much – parentage I guess," I explained, "Not that I miss being hairy."

"What about your bollocks – surely they're hairy?" said Nobby, rather to my surprise, "Mine are simply covered!"

I shook my head.

"Just a small clump in the usual place but no hairs elsewhere," I said, smoothing my hands over my chest, "Not even under my arms."

"Is that right?" he said, "Hey – look, I'll show you! This is how hairy I am."

Suddenly he stood up and with his thumbs he pushed down the waistband of his joggers – not actually revealing his hairy balls but at least revealing that his broad and dense forest of hairs continued below his belt and out of sight. The root and perhaps a couple of inches of his cock appeared briefly until he pulled his trousers back up again.

He chuckled heartily.

"Haha, haha!" he chortled, "That was stupid of me! I was going to show you how hairy my balls are without thinking that they're right down there! I'd be showing everything, wouldn't I! Must still be a bit woozy!"

I laughed with him at the absurdity of the situation and we banged knuckles together to show our camaraderie – although we were hardly life-long friends...

"Ah well – so, what are you into? Is it modelling or swimming?" asked Nobby, but I shook my head.

"No, sorry, I don't mind a quick dip but I'm into computers I'm afraid," I said, "Completely geekish I guess!"

"Oh – now that is interesting," said Nobby, his eyes brightening up, "Do you know much about them then?"

"I build custom made PCs for my customers and sort out their problems," I said airing my specialist knowledge, "All kinds of weird and wonderful set-ups and stuff... good business."

"Huh! All I know about computers is that they keep going wrong!" he said ruefully, "Wouldn't have a go at fixing mine would you? The hockey club got it for me. I was trying to do something a while ago and it kept shutting down on me. I've hardly used it since then and I miss it when I do the team lists."

Now I'm not usually into doing computer work just as a kindness but I felt somehow that I owed this guy something so I decided that I could probably spare him a couple of hours for free, so I nodded.

"I'll give it a go if you like," I said, "What is it – a laptop or a PC?"

"Just a PC that I run at home," said Nobby, "Keeps locking up or doing strange things... I dunno."

"Ok – bring it round – this evening any good?" I said and this time Nobby nodded.

"Yeah, great," he said, "I'm free – about sevenish?"

"Done!" I agreed and we both stood up to close the conversation and our meeting.

As we did so Nobby suddenly staggered forward a couple of steps and I just about managed to catch him in my arms. I held him firmly and closely as he shook his head, his eyes looking decidedly wobbly.

"Whhoooo!" he said, "Came over all dizzy – sorry."

"No problem – you'd better stay a bit longer. Come on, sit down again," I said.

Still clutching him fairly tightly I walked him backwards towards the chair he'd just vacated and as I did so I realised that something was prodding into my thigh – something hard but flexible... it could only be his cock! It was my turn to shake my head...

I managed to sit him down and there it was, quite a sizeable tent in his joggers, which I did my best to ignore. Nobby was still a bit dazed I think and seemed to be unaware of his predicament but from my position it was unmistakable, even to the extent of a small damp spot that stained his joggers a darker colour.

'Why the hell is he hard?' I wondered, not having thought of anything sexual at all until now, *'Oh fuck – he's starting to make me hard too!'*

About then Nobby seemed to pull himself together and his arms, once limply by his sides now quickly swung across his lap, more or less successfully hiding his erection.

"Sorry mate," he said, blinking his eyes, "Feeling better now. Didn't realise I was so shaken up."

"Bit like after you've given blood," I said, "You're ok until you go to walk outside! Hey – that's an idea – a cup of tea with plenty of sugar's supposed to be good – could I make you a cuppa – perhaps you'd prefer that to water?"

"Won't say no – but any chance you could make it coffee not tea?" he replied, "Never liked tea much."

"Yeah – no problem – come on through to the kitchen – you'll be able to see my set-up too," I said and Nobby stood up again, still not too steadily.

My eyes automatically fell down to where his penis had been tenting his trousers but apart from a generous bulge there was no indication of an erection – at least he was under control, even if my own cock was still at least half-hard. But at just six inches long, my cock didn't cause much of a tent... and then I shuddered involuntarily as I suddenly realised how long Nobby's cock must be to cause that sized tent! My eyes were very reluctant to leave his groin – I was incredibly curious now!

But why was I interested? Was I gay and didn't know it? Nah – it was just plain curiosity I guessed!

We walked down the hall and through to the kitchen, passing my spare downstairs room that was now my office-cum-workshop – piled and littered with computer bits and pieces, boxes and other junk.

"Work in progress," I said as we stopped and peered inside, "Not to mention a load of clutter!"

"Wow," said Nobby, "How on earth do you know where everything is? I'd get lost just looking."

I laughed, because that indeed was one of my problems.

"Yeah – I can never find the bits I want – they're always somewhere else," I said, "Spend half my time going out and buying new parts and then finding that I've already got them at home somewhere."

"You need organising," said Nobby, "Some racking over there; a decent worktop; get some of those storage units to sit on the top for all the little bits; a few more power points won't come amiss by the look of it; a few other things – easy!"

"Oh yeah, just the thing," I said, "I'm terrible at organising that sort of thing though!"

"I could do it!" he said, sounding entirely sincere, "Right up my street. I'm great at getting things into order and I love doing a bit of DIY work. Let me see what needs doing tonight; I'll see if I can come up with some ideas. Might cost you a few quid for materials but it'd be worth it, I think."

"Ok," I said, feeling quite relieved at the idea of getting the place more shipshape, "Yeah, good plan – we can have a look at that while I'm fixing your machine."

We moved on to the kitchen which opens off the lounge and I sat Nobby on one of the breakfast stools while I stirred up some tea and coffee – then we went and sat in the lounge.

"Come on then, tell me a bit about yourself," I said by way of something to talk about.

"Ok – where do I start... ummmm... I'm 30 this year," said Nobby, "I'm five foot six; I'm about 240 pounds and I've got a flat just around the corner from here. I only rent it but it's what I call home anyway. And I work at the gym and down at the sports club; the gym for my wrestling and the sports club for the hockey. Yeah – and I told you I train goal minders and I do but I actually also manage our local hockey team. And I'm single – well, divorced and er, what else?"

"Nah – nothing – better tell you about me then," I replied, and he nodded with interest.

"Right – well I'm 29 next month. I'm six three and about 170 pounds... and this is my house – all paid for," I said proudly, "Nice little inheritance from my grandfather helped pay for it, thank heavens. And that's meant that I didn't have to get a proper nine to five job so I've had a chance to build up my own business. I'm something of a specialist computer person – I've always been good with IT stuff. So now I'm well set. That's my Range Rover out there – bought it new last year – and I'm single too."

Nobby looked ruefully at me.

"Range Rover," he said, cheerfully scornful but a bit enviously, I thought, "I can hardly even afford to park my bike around here! Still, I don't often need a car. I borrow the van from the sports club when I want to shift some gear around."

"I need my transport," I said, "Some of my clients are out of town and I try to provide a complete service for them, home installation and back-up included."

"Good for you! So you're tall, slim, handsome and rich!" said Nobby cheerfully and I shrugged my shoulders.

"If you say so!" I agreed.

"I do – and you're the complete opposite to me!" said Nobby, "Not that it matters really. Chalk and cheese – but opposites attract, they say."

I didn't want to admit that he wasn't beautiful, but he was a bit rugged to look at... and yet quite appealing somehow.

"We must be well opposite then, from the way we met!" I said, laughing and Nobby joined in.

"Magnetic personalities more like!" he said, "The way we came together!"

We high-fived together, then sat back.

"Hey – N for Nobby and S for Streak. North and South, like magnets – no wonder we collided!" he added and we both fell about laughing.

The conversation degenerated into an amiable chatter about life around the neighbourhood, the weather, the TV (which as it turned out, neither of us watched much); the local 'talent' such as it was and many other inconsequential subjects before we both put down our mugs and stood up once again. Immediately my eyes fell to his groin and although there was definitely something quite large in there, there were no signs of an erection or other unexpected protrusions. I found myself feeling a bit let down somehow! Soon Nobby was on his way, waving back to me and reminding me of our seven o'clock date and then there was peace again.

I busied myself finding places to dump my latest purchases, getting myself a drink and some food and dealing with my emails – and soon seven o'clock was upon me. Minutes later the doorbell rang and Nobby was back, still dressed in jogging bottoms and a t-shirt and lugging his PC under his arm.

I let him in and, taking the computer from him, I took it into my workshop and connected it up.

"Ok – let's have a drink while we're waiting," I said, "Wine, scotch, vodka, lager, coffee, water?"

He laughed and said he'd enjoy a scotch – but since I then discovered that my ice tray was empty, he accepted vodka and coke instead and I joined him... while filling my depleted ice rack.

With the computer now fired up and loaded I sat down to see what I could find. And I was far from impressed. Viruses – loads of them, to mention but a few of his problems! And everything was so out-of-date too. Well – what else was I expecting!

"Don't think much of your protection!" I said laughing as I installed a good program and started it running.

"Don't know much about that kind of thing," said Nobby innocently, "I've just ignored things like that I guess..."

I watched the progress of the clean-up, but I soon realised that probably only a complete re-installation would deal with his problems – everything was wrong. I explained the problems to Nobby who looked somewhat crestfallen.

"Is that going to cost me?" he asked but I was able to shake my head.

"Nah – it's mainly down to time and loading newer stuff," I replied, "Anyway, I owe you, don't I so I'll clean it all up and add a bit more RAM for you too."

Nobby put a burly arm over my shoulder and patted me to express his thanks... his patting was more like a rough blow than a love tap, that was for certain, but it was meant well!

A little while later I'd backed-up all his Documents folders and set the machine to do a full re-installation.

"Ok," I said, "Let's leave the computer to run while we have a break – come on through to the lounge."

Together with fresh drinks we headed to the lounge where we settled comfortably among the plants inside the sunroom and there we chattered about hockey and wrestling – about which I knew nothing – and about computers – about which he knew nothing... but somehow we both enjoyed our chatter.

Eventually I guessed the programs should have completed so we returned to the 'office'.

Damn – things weren't quite complete but almost... seconds were counting down...

Nobby was sitting at my left elbow as we watched the screen and we idly chattered from time to time, each having another drink as we waited – and eventually things began to end their run and normal service was up and running. There was still work to do but at least I could see that his computer was now clean and safe.

I moved to an old PC that I kept, fired it up and loaded the contents of his documents folders into it. It was a mess and definitely needed sorting out so I explained what was needed and what I intended to do and Nobby nodded enthusiastically.

"Yeah, that's brilliant!" he said happily, "I don't know much about all that – I'm a bit iffy about it really. I know where to find the bits I want and that's about it."

"We'll tidy it all up while we're here," I said as I settled to work, "Won't take too long."

Nobby was silent as he watched me work – and indeed, his Documents folder looked as if a bomb had hit it – there were all kinds of unnamed 'new' folders everywhere, not to mention loads of random bits and pieces just dumped there.

"Blimey," I said, "Thought you were good at organising things?"

"Yeah, but..." replied Nobby, looking a bit shamefaced, "Inside the computer is another world – I get lost in there."

"Ok then, let's get things straightened up for you. Makes things a lot easier if you give folders names for a start," I said, as if I was lecturing to a student.

I carried on, "And keep things in groups too. I'll have a go at getting some basic plan up and running for you. Let's set up and rename some folders for starters... have you got any names you want to use?"

"I'd like a place to put the wrestling club photos and stuff and the same for the hockey club, but apart from that..." Nobby said, obviously not feeling very confident.

"That's a start," I said as I made and named some folders for him and soon I was able to pile some assorted documents into their proper places.

"Ok – let's do some proper organising now," I said and so saying I clicked on a folder that had merely a string of numbers as its name and opened it.

Assorted images of hockey players appeared; some pictures of what had to be some local female talent; one or two from a beach somewhere and some more hockey photos – he'd obviously downloaded his camera memory and just left it.

Nobby looked somewhat ashamed.

"Total mess – I agree," he said as I started to create some more new folders and began renaming them.

Soon the contents of several unnamed folders had been moved and sorted and some of the loose documents had been sorted and filed away and it wasn't long before I had a fairly logical collection of folders covering various specific topics.

There were still plenty more unnamed folders though and I clicked on another one and some twenty or so thumbnail photos came into view. They appeared to show a pole of some kind but I wasn't immediately sure.

"What's this lot – anything special?" I asked and without thinking or waiting for a reply I clicked on one at random and actually jumped back as the picture filled the screen.

"Oh wowww!" I said, as my hand jerked away from the mouse, "Look at that!"

There before me was a massive, solid, erect penis that looked obscenely over-long. It filled the screen from bottom almost to the top – an enormously long cock that rose from a hairy nest, it's foreskin already peeled back; the knob gleaming with moisture. Considering the length, the cock should probably have been as thick as a beer can but although it looked to be no thicker than mine it was the length that was amazing.

"Oh shit!" exclaimed Nobby, "Fuck – I'd forgotten they were in there!"

There were some twenty or so photos – all more or less the same and even in thumbnail view I could now recognise that they showed the same fully erect penis, some views with a hand around it and the latter third with what looked like cum erupting from it.

Unable to stop I clicked through the photos with the first half dozen or so all being much the same, then the next few showed a hand around the penis with glistening streams of precum streaking it's length. The final five or six were the most captivating, showing the cock erupting thick spouts of cum, gushes that had disappeared from view at first and were then depicted having fallen back on and around the cock to cover it and the hand that held it with thick coatings of creamy white spunk.

"Wowww!" I said again, my eyes locked onto the incredible instrument, "Sorry, sorry – I should have asked..."

Nobby shook his head.

"No – not your fault. Until you opened the folder I'd completely forgotten about those pictures," he said, "You weren't to know..."

I felt my own cock jerk hard with excitement as I viewed the erotic image.

Although it was shocking it excited me – not because of the homosexual content but because it was just erotic – hot and amazing and very erotic.

And suddenly my cock jerked even harder... because at that moment I just realised that this was very obviously the penis of the man sitting right next to me; the man who'd had an erection right in front of me; the man who's cock had pushed against my thigh not that many hours ago!

"That's you, isn't it?" I said in amazement looking at Nobby, and he smiled, somewhat self-consciously and nodded.

"Yeah – I set up the camera one evening – I was bored!" he said sheepishly.

"Lonely too!" I said light-heartedly and he nodded.

"Guess I was," he said quietly, "Don't know that many people who I can really call friends..."

I looked back to the photos and clicked on several of the other ones and they all showed his penis in excellent detail.

"At least they're good photos," I said, although as I looked at the penis, somehow the length just didn't seem real...

I tried to estimate how long it was; his muscular-looking thigh was perhaps eight... nine inches across; his hand which was wrapped around his shaft in several photos would be perhaps five inches across... so that scaled up to make the penis the best part of... a foot long!

I felt my mouth fall open.

No – never! Joking!

"Did you Photoshop these pictures?" I asked suspiciously but Nobby looked blankly at me.

"Do what?" he said, "Photo what – oh no – no way. Yeah, I've heard of that – who hasn't I suppose – but I wouldn't have the first idea how to use it though."

"It's a tool for manipulating images – for doing things like stretching things – making things longer for example," I explained but Nobby shook his head again.

"Definitely wouldn't know how to do that," he said, "That's just how they come out."

"Fucking hell," I exclaimed, looking at the displayed image again, "Then your penis must be eleven, twelve inches long – is that right?"

Nobby nodded once more.

"Yeah you're right – but I can't help it!" he said quietly.

I examined the penis in the photo more carefully, noting the texture of the skin, the scribbled lines of the veins beneath, the high gloss of his knob, the profusion of curly hairs from which it stood, the generosity of the stream of glistening precum and the sheer quantity of thick white cum. I shook my head in disbelief and looked at Nobby – who appeared to look quite flustered.

"What's up – not feeling so good?" I asked, worried that he was perhaps feeling unwell from his earlier knock, but he shook his head.

"This is what's up," he said and as he lifted his hands from his lap, there once more was a towering tent that his penis had erected.

Without thinking I moved my hand and hovered it an inch or two above the tent to gauge the height and even within the confines of his joggers his cock was lifting the material some five inches, I reckoned, but Nobby misunderstood my actions.

"Yeah – you can have a feel if you like," he said, and his hand descended on mine and pushed it down and onto the crown of the raised penis.

"Ooooh, bloody hell," I exclaimed, shocked but excited as my fingers automatically curled to enclose the shaft of his penis.

It felt massive, hard and hot even through the material and I could feel what must have been his foreskin as it slid around under my touch.

I was captivated now – utterly curious and somehow eager to find out more.

This wasn't homosexual in my eyes – not yet – this was just raw sex – something I never seemed to get enough of!

"Put your hand round a bit lower," said Nobby, pushing my fingers down his shaft, "Nice?"

"Yeah and you feel so hard," I said, "Just like it looks in the photos."

"Do you want to see him in the flesh then?" said Nobby, his breath coming quickly and for some reason I nodded.

Nobby stood up and slid his joggers down to his ankles – revealing that he wasn't wearing anything underneath and quickly sat down again and there beside me was the mirror image of the screen photo!

"Bloody hell!" I exclaimed, because in real life and at close-quarters his penis seemed even longer!

And that was even though it was part-buried in his curly forest and a bit recessed under his wrestler's belly.

"What's it look like if you stand up?" I asked for some reason and Nobby pushed himself into an upright position again.

And now his cock was on view in all its jutting glory – the full length of his shaft and bulbous knob stood out proudly, somewhat above horizontal and looking entirely majestic. I felt proud to be in its presence! I watched as it jerked upwards several times and leaked a bubble of precum.

"Wow!" I exclaimed, my hand rising to my chest, "That is some cock!"

"Come on then, touch it again, feel it properly," suggested Nobby and this time I had no hesitation in reaching out for it realising as I did so that I too was hard as a rock down there.

I let my fingers wander up and down his shaft before venturing out and onto his knob where I could feel the slick stickiness of the exposed flesh. I slid my fingers that were now encircling his penis down the length until I met his wiry pubes; then I slid them back up again, now gathering his foreskin as I moved towards the crown.

"It's massive!" I exclaimed, "It's incredible!"

Nobby's breath was slow and deep and he was letting small groans escape from time to time. I looked at his face, but his eyes were closed in ecstasy. I moved my grasping fingers up and down his lengthy shaft, slowly and gently masturbating him, but the pleasure was mine as I explored that massive weapon.

Eventually I'd got my fill of the feel of his cock, so I took my hand away and Nobby opened his eyes and looked at me.

"Why did you stop?" he asked plaintively, "I was enjoying that!"

"I'm not tossing you off, if that's what you think!" I said, one hand rubbing over my own erection, "I was just amazed..."

"You didn't have to stop," said Nobby, his erection still straining and stiff, "I don't mind if you carry on. No-one else has ever done that to me, not since my wife and I separated."

"Why did you split up then?" I asked, somewhat nosily.

"My missus couldn't take all of me," he said, "We use to row over sex until she just said she was leaving... And anyway..."

Somehow his sadly unfinished story gave me an incentive to touch him once more – I just couldn't help myself. Perhaps I felt sorry for him; perhaps I was just using his story as an excuse to hold his cock again; perhaps I really wanted to do it.

Nobby breathed in hard as my hand wrapped around his shaft once more and he shuffled a little closer to me.

"Do you want to suck it?" he asked, the tip of his tongue licking his lips, "I can suck it myself. I can get my knob in my mouth quite easily – about three or four inches actually if I strain, but that's enough."

"You can? You lucky bastard!" I exclaimed, rather giving the game away, "Wish I could do that with mine!"

"Well, come on then, open up!" said Nobby, the end of his penis held just a few inches from my face, but I was reluctant to take that step.

Holding his cock was one thing – sucking it was really getting into homo stuff; not the kind of thing I'd ever been a part of.

"Dunno," I said as I reached up and took hold of his penis again, "Not sure..."

But despite my reservations, my fist was now running up and down Nobby's cock once more and I could feel his hips pushing forward with each stroke and his cock was stiff and pulsating under my fingers.

His penis was beginning to leak now and although I'd missed the first dribble, which had splattered onto the floor, I'd managed to catch the subsequent trickles of precum and had spread them over his knob and down the shaft. Most of his cock now glistened with moisture, as did much of my hand and there was an incredibly erotic scent of raw hot male sex in the air now. I found out how exciting it was when I suddenly realised that my free hand was now holding and gently stroking my own erection. I didn't stop though – the whole event was way out of my control.

For some while I just continued to rub his penis while caressing my own and I was getting well into it when Nobby spoke again.

"You're getting me a bit close," he said softly, "I'll cum if you carry on..."

I slowed my hand although I didn't entirely stop my rubbing as I pondered my next move.

As I said, I'm not a homo but right here and now this was just plain sex in the raw – a bit like a craving that had to be fulfilled. I really wanted to make him cum, but I was full of concern.

"If I let you cum, will he go down then?" I asked, sort-of hoping that once he'd cum then life would return to normal.

And then I realised that if his erection went down then that would be the end of it – no way – this was too much fun! I was trapped – loving and yet hating this man-to-man experience!

"Hmmm – not sure. Sometimes I have to cum twice or even more before he's satisfied," said Nobby, his eyes closed as I stroked him, "But don't stop now though, please."

My mind was now made up; somehow I just wanted to continue; to watch him cum; to see the expressions on his face as he blew his load. Somehow the sensation of rubbing that extremely long penis was overcoming any feelings of revulsion or horror at doing such a wicked act. Slowly I continued to rub his throbbing cock while thinking of a suitable response, almost willing him to cum.

Nobby sucked in his breath hard and groaned.

"Oooooh god – I'm getting really close now," he said between gritted teeth, "Pleeeeease don't stop!"

I don't think I could have stopped if I tried; I was that absorbed in my task.

"You going to cum for me then?" I said, inciting him to let it go, "You're going to squirt your sperm from your lovely big hard cock, aren't you?"

"Fuck – yes, yes – any minute," he replied, "Nearly there."

Nobby was standing facing me, side-on to the computer screen and I suddenly had a thought.

I grabbed the mouse and clicked on one of the thumbnails and up on the screen appeared one of the later photos – a picture of his cock caught just as it erupted!

"Aaaaahhhh! Oh god, yes!" cried Nobby as he saw the photo, "Don't stop now... its coming – its coming! Oh yessss – here it comes!"

And with that Nobby grunted; his cock stiffened even more and a long streamer of white sperm blasted from the tip and past my shoulder. It must have flown six feet and I heard it splattering down somewhere behind me. A second eruption followed it but this time I'd pulled his cock downwards somehow and this thick pulse of cum splashed against my chest and oozed down my t-shirt.

Another one followed – this time I made sure that it hit me too – this time I actually wanted his cum to land on me and I wasn't disappointed. His third jet was as powerful as the second and a fourth followed a few moments later. A fifth eruption managed to be stronger and splattered just under my chin.

I was so excited that not only did I actively want his spunk on me but I was practically urging his cock to produce more and more.

"Yeah – yeah – come on – squirt for me!" I exclaimed excitedly tugging away at his cock, "Let me have your cum!"

"Yeah; fuck, still cumming!" Nobby said, breathing heavily, "Oh god – uuuuugh!"

Another lesser spray of sperm landed on my thigh and yet another one sprayed my lap but that was the last, apart from small dribbles that adhered to and coated my fist as I finished stropping his erection.

Finally I stopped my actions and returned to reality. I looked down at myself and realised that I was now simply covered in his hot strongly-scented spunk – thick white spunk that was slowly slithering down and soaking into my t-shirt, to join the volleys that had rained over my lap.

I released my grip on his penis and without thinking, I brought my hand to my mouth where I stuck out my tongue and began lapping up the big blobs of sticky white cum; savouring the slightly salty flavour and the thickness of his spunk.

"Oh my god!" I suddenly exclaimed, "That's your cum I'm licking up!"

I looked up at him, aghast at my actions.

"I swallow my own cum," I explained, "I wasn't thinking..."

"Was it any different?" asked Nobby, "Probably tasted a bit different but apart from that..."

I shook my head, realising that not only had it not been all that different to licking up my own cum but that I'd completely enjoyed it – I'd been lost in my own fantasy and it didn't matter that the cum wasn't mine.

But now, before I could do anything more, Nobby sank to his knees before me and leaned towards me, his hands coming to rest on my hips.

"What're you doing?" I asked without thinking.

"I want some of my cum too," he replied, "I'm going to lick it off your shirt."

Moments later there was the sensation of his tongue pushing against my chest as he gathered a big blob of cum and swallowed it. This was just so erotic I couldn't have stopped him if I tried; his hard tongue slid over my nipples and up under my chin and shortly afterwards I felt the pressure of his tongue on my trousers. I sucked in a huge breath as his tongue swabbed over my throbbing erection and Nobby looked up, a small dribble of cum hanging from his lower lip.

"Did you like that," he asked, "When I licked over your cock?"

"Fuck yeah," I replied as I tried to stand up, "I'm so horny I'm going to have to go and have a wank."

"No, no – don't go," said Nobby, holding me in my chair, "I'll do it for you!"

I was about to object when Nobby pulled down my zip and before I could do anything, his hand was searching around inside my trousers.

"Hey!" I complained, sucking in a big breath as his hand made contact, "Who said you could?"

"I think your penis gave me permission," said Nobby, his hand now wrapped around my underpants-clad erection, "He certainly needs some help!"

Nobby's attention to my penis was making it throb with anticipation and illicit excitement and when I happened to glance at the photo on the screen I felt my cock jerk wildly once more.

"Stand up," said Nobby and I just did so – I was putty in his hands...

Even as I began to stand up, Nobby began to undo my trousers and with a small push they fell to the ground, quickly followed by my underpants.

"That's better," he said, "Oh yes – I know just what you need!"

I could hardly look as I felt Nobby's breath on my abdomen – in fact I actually had my eyes shut for a while, but they flew open as I felt the smoothness of what had to be his tongue sliding over my knob. Somehow I remained standing while I sucked in a long breath then I sighed ecstatically as I felt his lips engulf my knob.

"Oh fuck – what are you doing – that's so nice," I said quietly.

"What do you think I'm doing? I'm sucking you off of course," said Nobby, raising his head from my cock, "I'm going to make you cum in my mouth."

"Oh what!" I exclaimed.

I'd only ever had a few blowjobs and they'd all been performed by women, so this was a 'first' in a big way! But more than that, his lips and tongue were doing such an incredibly good job – so much so that I wasn't going to last long!

Actually I wasn't going to last at all – I was so excited that it was coming up already!

"Ahh – watch out – you're making me cum!" I cried feeling my body begin to tremble, "Careful – I'm cummmmming!"

"Mmmmmm!" moaned Nobby as he sucked harder and immediately a sharp spasm ran through me as I started to erupt!

"Oh fuck, oh yeah!" I cried as I felt my sperm pulsing and rushing into his mouth, "Fucking cumming!"

"Mmmmmm!" repeated Nobby as his constant sucking and squeezing of my cock caused it to erupt time and again until I was drained.

"Oh God – that was excellent!" I said with feeling, "Where did you – how did you...?"

Nobby released my penis and looked up at me. His lips were all wet and shiny – just like my cock!

"I'm sure I'm what they call gay or maybe bisexual," he said, one hand still holding my penis, "Just love sucking a good cock – not that I get to suck that many!"

"What! Gay!" I replied, now somewhat horrified as reality sunk in, "You're gay?"

"Yeah – always have been, I think. I married because I wanted to but it may have just been for show, I reckon," he said with a big smile, "Why – does it show?"

"Hardly," I admitted, not actually knowing how a gay person should look.

"And what about you? Are you gay or hetero or bi?" asked Nobby and I had to stop everything as I concentrated on thinking.

"Dunno," I replied somewhat lamely, "I think I'm just finding out..."

Nobby stood up beside me and wiped his mouth on the back of his hand.

"That was tasty," he said with relish, "And you came off so quickly!"

"Always do," I said, "Always cum quickly but that was amazing – you made me cum really quickly."

We both looked downwards and simultaneously chuckled as we realised that we were both erect again – Nobby's cock protruding almost twice as far as mine though; his penis complete with a small blob of white cum at the tip.

I reached down and grasped it, rubbing the spunk around his knob; now wanting this exercise in sex to continue, despite its hundred percent gay content and Nobby grasped mine too.

"Need some more?" he asked, "I know I do!"

I nodded and wondered if I dared to invite Nobby up to my bedroom, when he raised the subject for me.

"Could we lie down – on your bed perhaps?" he asked and once again I nodded.

"Yes please – let's," I said, even though only a few moments ago I'd been dithering over the idea; not to mention being somewhat horrified to find that he was gay, "Come on."

Giving his lengthy penis a last quick rub, I turned and led the way upstairs and into my bedroom where I stood beside the bed. Nobby's gaze took in my king-sized bed; the fitted wardrobes with their full-length mirrors and the en suite shower and a smile lit his craggy face.

"Nice set-up," he said, "Love the mirrors!"

"What are we going to do?" I asked stupidly, knowing full well that we were going to play with each other's cocks, but Nobby understood and took over.

"Don't know exactly, but let's get undressed first," he said as he pushed his joggers down and stripped off his t-shirt and moments later, I'd done the same and we stood side by side by the bed, both of us naked.

71

"The original odd couple!" I said, laughing and we were.

Short and stocky with an eleven or twelve inch penis and tall and slim with a six inch one. At least mine was a fair bit thicker that his – my cock tried to make up for being short by being really thick.

"Come on," said Nobby as he let himself down onto the king-size bed, "Ooooh – that feels lovely!"

"I like a comfy night's sleep," I said as I carefully lay down beside him; ensuring that our bodies didn't touch but Nobby had other ideas.

"Come on, come here," he said, and one powerful arm reached over me and literally dragged me towards him!

"Ooooh god," I groaned as I felt our chests meet; his wiry hairs scraping against my smooth skin – but somehow I wasn't so much as complaining as groaning with desire and excitement.

And naturally I also felt his erection push against my abdomen and as Nobby moved us closer together I felt his length slide upwards over my stomach. I just had to put my hand down to feel it once more...

"It's so long," I said, running my hand up and down his length, "It's incredible!"

Already his cock was slippery, presumably with precum or possibly with leftover spunk from his earlier orgasm and my hand slid easily over him.

For a little while that was all we did; our bodies firmly against each other as I explored but finally Nobby stopped me.

"Would you like to fuck me?" he asked, making my eyes and mouth fly open.

"Fuck – you?" I asked incredulously, "What – me?"

"There's no-one else here!" said Nobby, "I haven't been fucked in too long – could you... do you think you could?"

Whatever I thought didn't matter because my cock was as hard and enthusiastic as he'd ever been. Even just the thought was making him throb and jerk happily and Nobby clearly understood.

"Have you got any lube – you know – KY or something?" he asked, "Bet you have!"

"In the drawer," I said, pointing my thumb behind me to the bedside cabinet.

Nobby rolled up and over me, his heavy body squashing me into the mattress; his hard cock thrusting firmly against my stomach. Soon he rolled back, a small tube of KY in his hand.

"Great!" he said, "Really helps with wanking, doesn't it – not to mention fucking! Hold still – I'll do it for you."

"Do what?" I asked without thinking.

"Lubricate my arse and I'll put some on your cock too," he said, once again startling me with his forthright words and I looked blankly at him.

"I'll need some lube in there for your nice fat cock," he said, "And you'll have to be careful at first."

"But – but – I never said I'd..." I blustered, but Nobby killed my objections.

His hand slid between us and grasping my cock he spread some of the KY over my penis, making me gasp from the erotic sensation. Then, in a moment or two his hand left my cock and was between his legs, sliding underneath his balls to his arsehole.

"You'll have to come up on top," he said as he rolled onto his back and then, using his powerful arms he pulled me up on top of him.

My extra body length automatically meant that my knees now fell between his legs and I found myself supporting my weight with my knees and at once felt my penis nudging between his buttocks – slithering around in the slippery lube.

"That's it – just there, yeah, there," said Nobby as he spread his legs wider and lifted his pelvis up, "Feel with your fingers."

Hardly considering what I was doing I reached down; my hand sliding over his crinkly hairy balls and past my penis as I did so. I followed my cock until I reached his arse, until I felt the tight lips of his arsehole.

"Push your finger in," Nobby said, "Get me ready for you,"

No way – I was reluctant to go that far... until he came to the rescue.

His hand snaked down under his buttock and locating my fingers, he pushed my index finger against his lubricated, firm, puckered flesh. Moments later we both moaned as my finger entered his arsehole, sliding smoothly in the gel. He pushed me further in until at least half my finger was inside him, then left me to it and to be honest, it wasn't as nasty as I'd expected. It was warm and felt moist in there; everything was soft, slippery and pliable except the ring of sphincter muscles that kept firmly squeezing my finger.

Then I remembered a prostate examination I'd had once. The doctor hadn't done or used anything special (except gloves and some gel, inevitably) and I suffered no pain, even when he located my prostate and pronounced it to be normal. Emboldened by my medical experience I pushed my finger further inside until my knuckles were against his hairy arse. It was tough going now, straining one finger without the other fingers getting in the way and Nobby seemed to realise.

"Put another one in," said Nobby, "You're doing fine so far – and you're being so gentle!"

"Am I?" I asked, not having thought of doing otherwise, "You're ok then?

Nobby sucked in a breath sharply just at that moment.

"Oh sorry – second finger!" I explained, "That's tight!"

"Guess I'm out of practice," grunted Nobby, "But keep going."

74

I angled my fingers inside him until I could feel the spongy mass of his prostate, which I rubbed for a little while.

Nobby groaned as I did so, and I saw and felt his cock jerk each time I stimulated his prostate. Soon a little trickle of precum; and another and another slithered from his cock, pooling on his abdomen below me. It was almost as if I was making him cum, from the inside...

While I'd been exploring his anal extremities, Nobby hadn't been idle, although I'd not really taken much notice until now. His spare hand had been on top of me, holding my body close to his; his fingers spread out over one of my buttocks and I'd quite got used to the feeling – shocking as it may have been for a non-gay person like me.

But I was suddenly alerted to his hands' presence as I felt his finger slip down my cleft and come to rest on my own arsehole. But again, instead of me finding it nasty, I felt my arse moving against his finger; actually pushing outwards as if to greet his exploring digit.

"That's it – do that," Nobby said quietly, "Don't worry – I'm just feeling you..."

Now his finger was actually at my arsehole, pushing gently inwards; stretching the skin sideways – testing my pliability, it seemed.

"Stop it, no don't..." I said, unconvincingly but utterly frightened by this new experience, "Stop it – oh it's nice, but stop it!"

"Ok," he said, "Let's try another approach then."

And with that his hand moved away – leaving my arsehole feeling suddenly unwanted and lonely – not to mention exposed! But a few moments later his hand was back, exploring blindly once more until he located my hole again and this time his finger was cool and very slippery. My hole squeezed shut as my body quivered with the sensation, causing Nobby to stop.

"Let it go – relax, I've put some KY on my finger," he said, "I'm not going to hurt you."

His finger pushed against my hole a little harder and I found myself complying with his request – now knowing full well that his finger would soon be embedded inside me just as my fingers were inside his arse. But now I wanted him to explore; to take me; to return the feelings; to finger-fuck me too!

I just couldn't say much – all I could do was to groan occasionally and allow my raw and inexperienced body to comply with his bidding but finally I found my voice.

"Don't – please be careful," I groaned, "It's going to hurt... I know it will."

"No it isn't," said Nobby gently, "Just relax everything; push out a bit and it'll be good!"

I shut my eyes as if that would cancel out all the 'gay' things that were happening and felt my body go almost limp and moments later there was a stretching feeling; an uncomfy one for a while – and then a feeling of fullness – and I realised that his finger was now inside me.

"Oh fuck! Oh fuck me!" I cried, kind of in horror; a large part of me still completely rejecting this sexual happening.

"If you want me to!" said Nobby with a chuckle, "Did you mean that?"

"Wahhhh – NO!" I cried in panic as I realised what I'd said, "No way!"

"All in good time then," said Nobby chuckling affably, his finger now sliding smoothly in and out of my arsehole, "Come on then, how about you fucking me now?"

He withdrew his finger and suddenly I felt unwanted again – I almost needed him back in there but my attention was now elsewhere.

Having exceeded my own health and safety guidelines, so to speak, I suddenly felt quite relaxed now that I was no longer invaded and as my senses returned to something like normal, I realised that my cock had lost none of its hardness and was nudging up against my fingers which were still embedded in Nobby's anus.

It seemed second nature to remove my fingers and replace them with my cock and as I fumbled around, Nobby fell silent – until suddenly I found that everything was in place. The tip of my lubricated penis became seated in the already opened indent of his arsehole and I felt his flesh pushing, well, almost pulling at me; willing me to enter.

"That's it – you're there. Come on then – push it in me," said Nobby, "You know you want to."

And taking a deep breath, I did just that; my thick, stiff, slippery erection sliding suddenly into Nobby's body.

"Yessss!" hissed Nobby, "Oooooh! Aaagghh! Oh, oh yes – you feel so good now you're in. You're stretching me wide open – ohhh, that feels lovely!"

"Ooooh," I answered as our union was consummated.

"Brilliant!" groaned Nobby as I sank deeper, "You feel good."

"Yesssss," I groaned, "I'm inside you – oh fuck, how did I get here!"

"You wanted me," said Nobby, his eyes finding mine, "You didn't know it but I'm what you needed."

"How do you know that?" I asked, pushing my cock inside him once more and feeling his flesh stretching as I penetrated him; feeling the welcoming grasp of his anal cavity.

"You just never said 'no' – well, not convincingly," he said, pulling me into him, "It was obvious you wanted to try something, but you were just scared. Don't blame you really but just look at you – here you are, fucking a man and fucking away happily!"

And I was! I thrust hard into him, pushing my penis as far into his anus as I could, until our stomachs mashed together, squashing his oozing, slippery, lengthy penis between us. I pulled almost all the way out and thrust again, realising now that this was good; this was plain simple fucking regardless of the sex of the participants; this was what my cock needed!

"You planned this, didn't you?" I said, accusing Nobby but he shook his head.

"No way!" he said, "It all just happened...you were helping me with my computer and all of a sudden we're in bed and fucking! Why – you complaining?"

"No – not now," I said, "But I wonder how I'll feel afterwards?"

"Drained and happy I hope!" said Nobby, "Now come on – fuck me properly and make us both happy!"

So saying, he wrapped his legs around my buttocks, pulling my thrusting penis harder and harder into his hole and causing us both to grunt as our bodies came together. But it was good rutting – an animalistic fucking that was about to relieve a load of 'dirty water' from my somewhat stagnant sperm reservoirs.

Each time I plunged into his body I could feel my foreskin being pulled back by the tight ring of muscles around his hole; a feeling that was creating sensations that were building rapidly into an orgasm. I ploughed on quicker now; my excited penis shaking and quivering with pent-up need; a need to fulfil my 'duty' and a need to empty sperm from my body into his.

As my mind allowed those thoughts to spin through my consciousness, I very slowly came to realise that I was having gay sex! There was a sudden explosion of homophobic shock inside me – and then, as if realising that the pleasure far outweighed the stigma, a weight lifted from my shoulders.

I was indeed fucking a man – and I was loving it!

"Play with me, Chris," said Nobby and as I thrust down from above him I looked at his cock, jutting up, long and stiff; its foreskin stretched back to reveal his glowing shiny knob and somehow it just seemed right to give him a helping hand.

Supporting myself on one arm I reached down and grasped his shaft, my fingers sliding up and over his knob. I felt my fingers getting wet as his penis dribbled precum onto my palm and I caressed his cock with the slippery fluid.

"Oooooo yesssss," groaned Nobby, "That's nice – oooo, so good, keep doing that! And keep fucking me too!"

And it seemed almost natural to masturbate him as I fucked him, my body and my hand now moving together and if Nobby was enjoying it, I certainly was as well. It was now that those pre-orgasmic feelings were starting to surface... little shudders and shakes – involuntary ones – were happening and I could feel sweat beginning to form over my shoulders and chest.

I was breathing faster too, as was Nobby and his eyes were now half closed as his body concentrated on his own orgasm. I moved faster too, no longer in cadence with my hand; my movements becoming somewhat irregular and jerky as more and more uncontrollable responses took over my body.

"You getting close?" asked Nobby and I nodded my head, finding myself unable to speak.

"Good – good – me too – cum inside," said Nobby quietly, "Cum inside me."

My eyes sprang open with a kind of delighted shock. I'd been starting to wonder if I should pull out and I knew that I'd feel unfulfilled if I had to spray my seed on his stomach. It would be a case of coitus interruptus; an incomplete job, even if my seed would never make him pregnant. And there was a certain satisfaction in unloading my sperm inside my partner; a degree of contentment that nothing else could achieve.

"You sure?" I asked and it was Nobby's turn to nod.

"I want to feel you cum – I want to feel it all happen inside me," he said and as he spoke I felt his arsehole squeezing my cock ever more tightly.

"Ok, yeah," I said, "Won't be long now."

"I'll be with you," Nobby replied, his hand closing around my fist on his penis, "Do it a bit faster – hold me tighter."

I didn't reply because I was now absorbed in my up-and-coming orgasm – it was getting really close. And silently, punctuated only by the slap of the meeting of our hot sweaty flesh and our laboured breaths, we neared our climaxes.

"Yeah – yeah – yeah!" I grunted as my last few thrusts came faster and faster – until I froze up; my body rigid for a second or two – before the dam gates opened and my orgasm overwhelmed me.

"Uuuuuuh!" I cried, shuddering violently and feeling the first pulse of sperm travelling up my penis, "Ooooooh yeah!"

"Yesssss – felt that!" ejaculated Nobby, "Aaaaagh – making me cum too!"

With that his cock jerked in my grip. I felt it swell and thrust through my fist as his own orgasm let loose – his first jet of sperm spraying well up his body, almost to his chin. Quickly I wanked his pulsating cock causing several more sprays to erupt and all the while my own penis was jerking out volley after volley of cum deep inside Nobby's arse.

"Oh damn – that was good!" groaned Nobby, "Oh yeahhhhh!"

"Needed that," I replied, panting hard and I saw Nobby's eyes open wide.

I don't think that either of us expected me to say that!

I looked down at my hand and it was liberally covered in Nobby's oozing white cum and when I lowered my sight further, I saw that my cock had a ring of frothy cum surrounding it. I let my eyes wander back up his body, now taking in the extensive sprays of wetness covering Nobby's body and somehow I just had to be part of that. Relaxing my arms, I lowered my body down onto his, feeling the still-warm cum slide and spread between us – it felt deliciously nasty but erotic!

I was still panting somewhat when I suddenly realised that our faces were now mere inches apart and I smiled broadly at him and at that moment Nobby's hand reached behind my head and pulled me closer. For a moment I wondered what was happening, until our lips met – his wet and welcoming; mine drier and still uncertain. I felt Nobby's tongue attempt to insinuate itself between my lips and I was partially horrified and partially aroused by the action.

'Oh, go for it!' my mind told me and seconds later my own tongue met his. Moments thereafter, our lips parted; our bodily fluids mingled, and our tongues began their own love-making and moments later I felt my cock stiffen once more and Nobby's too began jerking between us; our oral action creating wicked waves elsewhere in our bodies. We both moaned simultaneously, deep soft moans of contentment and yet of unfulfilled lust – we hadn't finished our sexual pleasures yet. I guess we were lip-locked and tongue-duelling for the best part of five minutes before we parted; probably to allow us both to draw in deep lungfuls of air – we'd been so involved in our lust that breathing had almost been forgotten!

It was as we surfaced that we both realised that my still stiff cock had slipped from Nobby's hole, although its tip still rested against his flesh.

"Ooops, sorry," I said but Nobby wasn't complaining.

"No, it's ok – let's have a break," he suggested and soon we'd rearranged ourselves side by side on the bed.

I fetched a towel and once Nobby's hole and my cock had been cleaned up we just lay there relaxing, a hand on each other's erect penis; our hands just slowly and languidly sliding up and down each shaft.

81

"I think I want to cum again," said Nobby and I hummed my agreement – I too needed more but I wasn't about to cum by being wanked – I wanted some more of that incredible anal action.

But Nobby beat me to it...

"How about we try a 69?" he suggested, "You'd better be on top – I don't think you'd like me pushing my cock down your throat!"

"69?" I questioned, "That'll mean you want me to suck you."

"Well, yeah," said Nobby, "Come on – you've tried everything else! Give it a go!"

And while we'd been speaking, Nobby had started to get us organised; his strong arms almost lifting me once more until my body was reversed above his, my face now looking straight at his ramrod-stiff penis.

Yet again large parts of me were eager to try this new experience while many other parts were rebelling against the awfulness of this act... was there anything more sordid than taking a man's penis into my mouth? It just didn't seem possible that I could do it...

Then Nobby spoke up, presumably realising that I was in a dilemma.

"You worried?" he asked, and I hummed an acknowledgement.

"Ok – ok – look at it this way... when I told you I could suck my own cock, you said you wished you could do the same – yeah?" he said, and I agreed.

"And when I came off over your t-shirt you were there, swallowing my sperm, weren't you?" he continued and once again I agreed.

"So if you can't suck your own cock, why not try mine? And while you're at it, why not try my sperm direct from the tap, so to speak?" said Nobby, completing the circle.

I couldn't answer – I just didn't know what to say, because he was right – and anyway, Nobby had just allowed my cock to slide into his mouth!

"Oooooh guess I could," I groaned and Nobby took my cry as acceptance of his argument.

"Good – good – well, just grab hold and open wide!" he said as he began to suck away at my penis.

"Oooh fuck," I groaned, "That's nice, don't stop..."

"See – it's nice!" said Nobby, briefly removing my cock from his mouth to speak, "Come on then, get busy!"

And now that he was demonstrating just how pleasurable cock sucking was, it seemed churlish to refuse to suck his penis, however much some parts of me still objected. After all, I had indeed yearned to suck my own penis, so therefore why not his?

I shut my eyes as I placed my hand round his shaft – his very long, very hard, very slippery shaft... and I pulled it more upright. And even with my eyes shut I knew it was only inches from my mouth as I could smell the hot aroma of male tumescence – but instead of being revolted, I was now becoming highly aroused. I just had to try him out!

Opening my eyes a fraction I saw his cock; the helmet exposed and glistening in a coating of precum and actually it looked remarkably inviting. I opened wide and slowly lowered my mouth towards his knob, suddenly feeling an inadvertent contact between his hot flesh and my damp lips.

I moved away briefly and Nobby sucked in a quick hissing breath; then I felt his penis thrust once more up at my mouth – I felt it jerk into my mouth before he got his body under control again.

"Ooooh I felt that," he said, "Your lips... do it again."

"In a minute, in a minute," I said, trying to buy time because I still wasn't at all sure that I wanted to do this.

But to support his words, Nobby's lips were now caressing my penis, his tongue swirling around near the crown and attempting penetration into the little hole from whence my essence would soon be pouring. His actions were driving me crazy with lust; crazy with sexual excitement and I could hardly refuse to reciprocate. Quickly and before I could find cause to object, I allowed my head to drop down; my mouth still wide open to accept Nobby's slender pole. It was only when I found myself rebelling against my gag reflex that I realised that I must now have some four or five inches or more of his cock inside my mouth – but instead of feeling disgust as I might have done some few hours ago, I was now welcoming the invasion. I tightened my lips around his shaft, feeling it slide smoothly in and out of my mouth and I allowed my tongue to wrap itself around his flesh.

"Oooooh – that's nice," said Nobby, "You alright with that?"

"Mmmmm," I murmured, "Like it!"

"Don't overdo it," he said, "You're doing so well..."

There wasn't a whole lot I could say with a mouthful of cock but now I'd started, I had every intention of continuing, although before long Nobby spoke again.

"I won't be cumming for a while," he said, "Not from sucking anyway. Do you want to try something else?"

I raised my head and looked back down my body at him.

"Like what?" I asked.

"Like, how about trying my cock somewhere else?" he replied.

There was only one place...

The thought made me lift my body from his and I was simply gobsmacked! Was I really ready to try taking his penis inside me?

"Ummmm..." I pondered, but while I was doing so, I felt Nobby's finger at my anal opening once again, making me draw in my breath quickly.

But the KY that he'd deposited earlier saved me from pain as his finger easily slid deep into my arsehole once more.

"Ohhhh yessss!" I groaned, this time rather enjoying the sensation, "Do it again! Push in deeper."

"I'm in up to my knuckle," chuckled Nobby, "I'll have to use something else..."

"Yeah – anything!" I cried, erotic delight building in my penis, "Touch me inside; it's making me so hot!"

"Ok – ok – hang on – we need to move a bit," said Nobby, his finger still sliding in and out of my hole and such was my involvement in my own pleasures that I hardly seemed aware that Nobby had moved round behind me and parted my legs as I now lay on my side.

The angle of his finger had changed now and he was rubbing against my prostate, making me moan and groan with pleasure.

"Oh God – that's nice – so nice," I groaned, "More, more!"

"Hang on then," said Nobby and I felt his finger slide from my hole, to my extreme disappointment.

"Oh no! Put it back, please!" I cried and at that moment I felt him re-enter my hole and I gasped out loud.

"Oooooooohhh – that's it," I moaned, "Lovely! Ooooooh fuck – oooh fuck me!"

"Yeah – I am!" said Nobby quietly behind me, "I'm fucking you!"

"Ahhhhh!" I cried in abject horror as I realised exactly what he meant, "No – no – don't!"

But instead of withdrawing from me, Nobby pushed his penis deeper inside my body, sending waves of sexual excitement through my entire being – and instead of recoiling from his penetration I was thrusting my body back at his.

"Ooooooooo!" I cried out, "Ooooooh yessss – fill me – fuck me, please!"

"Oh yes – this is fantastic!" groaned Nobby as his lengthy spear thrust into my innards time and time again, "You're so nice and tight – you feel good, so good!"

"And you're so long!" I exclaimed as I felt his cock penetrate way up inside me, "Please don't stop now!"

"I'll only stop when I cum," said Nobby, causing me to jerk with concern.

"No – not inside me!" I cried, "That's gay!"

Nobby burst out laughing raucously and moments later I did too, having suddenly realised the incongruity of my statement!

"Oh fucking hell – what did I say?" I asked, "Stupid! Stupid!"

"So can I cum inside you?" asked Nobby, still sliding his penis in and out of my hole, "Won't be all that long now."

"Oh yes – fill me! Don't you dare take him out! I want to feel you," I said, suddenly at peace with myself.

Suddenly I'd realised that I'd been loving all this gay sex – this was what I'd been missing – this good wholesome gay sex. Neither Nobby nor I might appear to be gay but so what – our bodies were just made for each other today.

Behind me Nobby was now holding my hip as he powered himself into my hole. My cock was leaking steadily as his penis worked hard inside me; his breath now hot on the back of my neck; his hairy chest wet with sweat against my back. I too was sweating – no longer with fear but with sexual delight as we both neared our climax... I was going to cum without even touching myself! And Nobby was going to cum soon as well; the vigour and jerkiness of his thrusts attested to the nearness of his orgasm and soon he spoke up.

"Getting very close now," he said, still thrusting hard but slower, "Oooooh yes – just holding it... coming up... feel it!"

"Let it go!" I cried as my own penis jerked hard, "I'm cumming!"

Quickly I cupped my hand over the end of my cock and began catching as much of my sperm as I could as it leapt from my cock. I could hear it splashing into my hand just as Nobby grunted hard and went rigid.

"Yeaaaaahhhhh! Oh my god – cumming, cumming!" he groaned and I felt hot flushes of spunk spraying inside my body, filling my anus with his hot emissions, time after time.

"Ooooh that's good!" we echoed, "That's so good!"

Slowly Nobby's actions slowed and ceased until all I could feel was his penis still occasionally jerking gently inside me. I brought my sperm-filled hand to my face and licked at my cum – before offering it to Nobby. Quickly he finished my offering before slowly sliding his penis from my body – it seemed to take ages to extract all of his length...

"Ohhh, that was amazing, it was so good," said Nobby, his breath warming the back of my neck, "Was it ok with you?"

"Brilliant!" I enthused, "That was simply brilliant!"

"I tried to be careful too," said Nobby, "Perhaps I'll try and go a bit deeper next time."

"Next time?" I asked, not having even considered such a thought and I felt Nobby nodding strongly.

"Of course!" he said, "You don't want this to be a one-off, do you?"

"No, I guess not," I admitted, "I wonder how much of you I can take?"

Nobby chuckled and patted my thigh.

"Bet you can take all of me!" he laughed, "And I bet you enjoy it too!"

We lay back and cleaned ourselves off, side by side as we considered our situation.

What had started, just those few hours ago with an accidental and violent meeting had culminated in a shocking and violent rutting – life had turned full circle! We looked at each other, now knowing full well that this was the start of something that was to shake both his world and mine.

We'd both exposed our lives to other people, well, to one another at any rate and in doing so we'd both come to really discover what we'd been missing. Nobby had been hiding his sexuality in his physical contact sports while I – well, I suppose I'd been hiding my sexual orientation in my work and now... we'd both more or less 'come out'!

I chuckled to myself at this moment and Nobby looked at me questioningly.

"I was just thinking," I said as I wrapped my hand round Nobby's shaft, "Complete opposites who find themselves completely as one! Strange world!"

Nobby mulled over my comment.

"And completely by accident too," he added, giving my cock a friendly rub, "Makes me glad it happened!"

Much as I'd like to bring this story to a 'lived happily every after' ending, it didn't happen that way. Nobby needed the physical roughness of the hockey and wrestling life while I preferred my peace and privacy and so after our initial introduction things cooled down gradually.

There was a short period during which I set up some computer programs to help him with his activities and he almost rebuilt my office and during that time we had some wonderful sex on a number of occasions but thereafter we tended to go our separate ways. That's not to say that we never met again – sure we did – but never again quite so violently and we definitely had plenty more amazing sex together from time to time but we eventually drifted apart.

Whether or not he ever passed my way thereafter I'll never know but I do know that, despite the incredible sex that followed our meeting, I took a lot more care as I approached my gate!

Misguided Love

My meeting with Nobby did have its other beneficial points because he was able to help me get the best out of exercising, showing me what equipment to use and how to use it – while I was able to teach him some rudiments of using his computer too. I used to spend far too long at my desk, and I needed to firm up my body... and Nobby showed me how and then, with his guidance I joined a gym locally and soon became a regular there, building up some amazing muscles. Soon I was there pretty well every day and actually became one of the star keep-fit men – a firm favourite of the manager, Don.

It was during the process of building my body that I realised that a desk-bound job wasn't entirely good for me and so it was that, using a mixture of computer aided design, my fast talking, my love of gardens and my newly acquired physical strength I settled down to become a landscape gardener. I could combine all my abilities into one job – and still have time to deal with some of my regular computer customers in the evenings and everything worked well. Soon I had a big selection of great customers and plenty of lucrative work – and still found time for the ladies too.

And it was when I was at the gym the other day when I spotted her; a picture of health and loveliness standing inside the glass walled offices, watching us few men working out. The low sun was illuminating her features perfectly, casting her golden hair into a wonderfully glowing cascade that seemed to dance on her shoulders with every slight movement of her delectable body.

Even from where I was I could see that her lips were full and looked enticingly moist, no doubt the result of almost professionally applied make-up and looking as alluring as ripe cherries while her cheeks looked as soft as peaches and twice as kissable. Her long eyelashes curved perfectly upwards from her dark eyes, providing a perfect backdrop to her mascara that faded to soft purple.

As I absorbed her features I took in her magnificently curvy body; her generous bust that seemed larger than life above her trim waist; hips that were generous but not broad and her legs, bare from below her shorts to her ankles, which were the best looking pair of pins I'd seen on a woman in real life.

Oh yes, there were those perfect airbrushed models in magazines, but this was a real live woman and she was at the peak of her glowing vitality.

I simply had to get to know her better...

Easing my weights into their stands I stood up and relaxed, my body glistening with sweat and oil, my muscular chest and biceps heaving and throbbing as my heart and lungs pumped fresh air and blood to my extremities. I grabbed a towel and after a quick and perfunctory swipe over my upper body I was about to go and introduce myself when suddenly I noticed that Don, our manager and trainer had arrived too and was motioning her to sit down across from his desk. I had to move fast...

I almost sprinted across the gym then skidded to a halt near the offices and having raised my hand to say "Hi" and receiving a similar response from the trainer, I opened the door and entered the room, my eyes now entirely betraying my interest.

"Yes Chris, what can I do for you?" asked Don, already an insignificance in my view.

"Ah, hmmm, yes, errrrr, I was errrrm, I was going to ask you if I could change my routine a bit," I said, desperately seeking a way to prolong my viewing but my trainer saw through me.

He laughed, making me feel very self-conscious all of a sudden; he knew that my words were merely subterfuge for my visit.

"No problem Chris, come and see me later when you're through," he said, "But that's not what you're here for is it?"

"Errrrr, ummmm, what d'you mean?" I blundered about with my words.

"You just wanted to have a closer look at Miss Young, didn't you?" said Don, smiling broadly, "Well now you've seen her!"

"Beautiful!" I blurted out before I could even think, "Just bloody beautiful!"

Don laughed at the woman.

"See – he's smitten already!" he said to the woman, "You'll fit in perfectly here!"

He turned back to me.

"Miss Young will be our new office manager," said Don, "So you might just as well get to know her, you'll be seeing a lot more of her when she starts work in a few weeks' time."

God – didn't I just want to see a lot more of her – as soon as possible!

But now was not really the time for that; instead I extended my hand politely and Miss Young raised her perfectly manicured hand to mine and we shook hands gently.

"Pleased to meet you, errrr Chris, is it?" she said, her voice like sparkling champagne to my ears, yet as soft and gentle as a feather and I found myself shivering with such intense desire that I had to release her hand quickly.

I stuttered out some welcoming words but I'm certain that I sounded more like a schoolboy than a grown adult.

"Thanks Chris. I'm Karen," she continued, "You might as well call me by my first name – I guess you come here a lot, so I'll be seeing you quite often."

Her eyes swept up and down my muscular body, from my feet, up my powerful thighs, across my toned and hard abdomen and up over my 50" chest to my short spiky blond hair. She smiled broadly as she surveyed me.

"At least the view will be worth looking at!" she said as she turned to Don, "Handsome bloke isn't he?"

"He's worked hard to get all that," he said approvingly, also sweeping his eyes over me as I stood there, "Stays clean, scrubs up well!"

I felt I was blushing now, but I'd achieved my target; I'd met and spoken to that vision of desirability; now all I needed to do was to chat her up and make her mine!

But feeling that my arousal was now rapidly moving southwards I decided it was time to get out of there before things became too evident, so with a quick goodbye I left them to their discussions and headed off to the showers. I still had some ten minutes left on the exercisers, but I needed to get away from that delectable sight and at least I was cheered to some small extent as I remembered that Don was gay, so he'd be no threat to my interest.

As I'd finished my session early the showers were empty and I stripped off my shorts and vest and turned on the shower at the far end, the best of the four nozzles. Soon I was luxuriating in the sensation of cascades of warm water washing over me, somehow relaxing my muscles as it did so... although one muscle refused to relax. Because as I let my mind wander as I unwound, so that magnificent piece of womanhood stood there before me in my dreams, slowly divesting herself of her clothes – and suddenly I realised that I was quickly getting a hard-on!

93

"Oh fuck!" I groaned, feeling unstoppable forces at work, "Fuckin' marvellous I don't think!"

And at that fateful moment I saw another person appear, already stripped down for a shower – it was another devotee to the gym, Gary, who'd been exercising not far from me. We'd become members on the same day a few years ago and we'd had a sociable link ever since, even though we'd never made anything of it. Buddies at the gym – merely acquaintances out of it though... although we'd have made a good matching pair had anyone wished to pair us up.

I kind of half turned to hide my rising erection as Gary waved a hand to me and turned on the shower next to me, but he'd already seen my arousal.

"Mmmmmm," he said languidly and sexily, "Who's that for?"

I felt certain he was kidding with his imitation gay style and I found myself chuckling and feeling a lot less self-conscious now.

"Sorry mate. Couldn't help it; bloody thing's got a mind of its own!" I said defending my erection, "Happens – just happens when I see someone as good looking as that bit of stuff in there with Don."

"Know what you mean," replied Gary, his own penis far from flaccid now.

I turned back, my cock now above horizontal and raised considerably from its normal hanging position... but now, having explained things I wasn't so concerned about my arousal.

"She was a bit hot, wasn't she?" I said, knowing full well that Gary would also have seen Karen and Gary nodded.

"Bloody right she was," he said, smiling broadly, "And I noticed you were in there damn quick, weren't you? She certainly has an amazing body, hasn't she?"

I laughed as he spoke before I replied.

"Do you blame me?" I said, feeling more blood rushing to my penis, "Best thing on two legs I've seen in ages; gotta get me some of that!"

My cock was almost erect now and the thought of a potential pussy hunt drove him upwards until he was pointing at the ceiling but since we seemed to have got over the fact that I was erect, I was no longer shy about it. Instead I flexed my seven or so inches, making him jerk up and down.

"She's going to get all of this!" I said, proudly showing off my penis, "Bet I can get it up there inside a month – maybe even a week!"

"Yeah? You reckon?" said Gary, "Is she yours already then?"

"Well, not yet, but I bet I can make her mine," I said, strutting around vainly, "I could see by the way she looked me over that she was interested – she'll be a walk-over!"

But Gary had a kind of mischievous look on his face... and through all the soap suds I noticed that his penis was now rising fast, even as I tried not to watch it.

"Don't bank on it," he said, "Don't know what you might be up against – assuming she's free anyway."

And now, as Gary's penis rose, so he revealed it to me by washing away the bubbles and his cock now stood there, jerking just like mine, but probably a good inch or so longer!

Fuck me – of course he was interested in her too, that was now very apparent.

"You bastard!" I said gently, "I thought you were happily settled with what's-her-name, errrm, Dawn."

Gary shook his head somewhat slowly, a sad moue coming to his lips.

"Nah, we fell out, didn't we, couple of weeks ago," he said, "All about having kids it was. She wanted loads – I don't really want any, at least not yet."

For a few moments he was silent as he considered what he was missing.

"She was a bloody good fuck though," he said brightening somewhat, his cock jerking again, "That's all I've got on the brain these days now I'm not getting any!"

He rubbed his hand up and down his cock a few times, his actions entirely unrestrained, his long shaft dripping with water from the shower. I wasn't entirely sure if I wanted to see his hand at work on his penis but somehow I couldn't tear my eyes away either, nor would my own erection go down.

"Damn, I feel fuckin' horny now," he said with a rueful chuckle, "Shame you can't help me out; never mind, I'll errrr... I think I'd better go and get rid of it."

So saying, he turned off his shower, quickly dried himself and with the towel wrapped around his middle he trotted off towards the toilets, leaving me to deal with my own erection.

But the actions of rinsing off and drying myself took my mind off my cock for a while and I was able to complete my shower and dress without further complications.

Soon I was heading back out into the world, my bag over my shoulder, my body feeling energised and refreshed and ready to return to my work.

I'm fortunate in that I work for myself – hence I can find the time to come to the gym quite regularly. I'm a landscape gardener; "Landscape Artist to the Stars" I call myself nowadays – yeah it's corny, but it gets me the business. I'm pretty good at my work and after I landed a decent contract a couple of years ago with a couple of (relatively minor) pop stars to look after their gardens, I 'upped' my business name and now even my truck is bespoke, all complete with some nifty artwork. Life is good – lots of fresh air and exercise and the money keeps rolling in too! And I even have spare time for the gym and to go pussy hunting!

My life moved on for a few more weeks; a busy time for me, getting my client's gardens tidied up for the autumn and winter; even permitting myself some time to go over my own garden – I guess I needed to keep up my own appearances too. Then I needed some paving slabs for a job one day so I headed off to the merchants, my big 4x4 truck handling the damp roads with ease and soon I was parking up near their loading area while I checked over the selection of slabs.

And I was intent on my work when suddenly I heard a voice that I thought I knew – a female voice no longer dripping with warmth but raised in anger.

"Stop being so bloody bossy!" the voice yelled, "We're supposed to share things – and I'm not your bloody slave either!"

"Aaah, shut up and stop fucking moaning," a male voice returned, "Bloody woman – you're being a fuckin' nuisance."

"How dare you call me a nuisance!" came the woman's voice, even louder, "You fuckin' twat! You bloody waste of space!"

I looked cautiously around a huge pile of concrete blocks and there indeed was Karen having a major face-off with some guy who looked almost old enough to be her father. Perhaps he was, but I doubted it from their words.

"I've just about had enough of you!" the man yelled.

"And I've more than had enough of you too!" screamed the woman, who despite pretty well losing her rag, looked entirely delectable.

Her straightened hair was up in a long pony-tail; she wore a lovely plum-coloured fuzzy form-fitting roll-neck jumper which smoothed down from her bouncing boobs to her graceful waist and to her hips while her skin-tight jeans and long leather boots finished the desirable vision perfectly. And even through her anger, her face was beautiful – anger sometimes makes a person's features so much more alive... and she was well and truly alive!

"Time you found someone else to sponge off isn't it?" she said, strutting angrily around the yard, "Just fuckin' go will you – go on, fuck off!"

"Why the fuck should I?" the man replied causing Karen to instantly cease her strutting.

"Because you're fuckin' useless, that's why," she yelled, bending from the hips, "I work hard to keep you and what do you do – sweet fuck all!"

The guy was deflated now.

"I try..." he said, mumbling somewhat, "Can't help it..."

"Well, fucking DO something or get out of my life," she almost screamed.

I knew how she felt – I'd been through much the same some years before when my partner had become demanding, lazy, obsessive and controlling – and expensive to keep – and how good it had felt when I eventually blew my top and kicked her out.

I wanted to go and shelter Karen from this dumb idiot but I didn't want to show too much interest right now and it wasn't really my place to do or say anything, so instead I merely watched as they continued to growl at each other for a while before getting into a rather tatty car and driving off, their visit to the merchant seemingly wasted. Quickly I jumped into my truck and followed them; fortunately they seemed more intent on arguing than on rushing and so I was able to keep them in my sights until they turned into the driveway of a rather nice house in one of the outer suburbs – a mere three doors away from one of my clients.

I noted the address, now planning some form of approach I could make... then drove back to the merchants' yard where I completed my purchases.

Back at home I began my campaign of seduction...

I checked that I had a good supply of visiting cards – mine all glossy and bedecked with flowers, stars and my credentials. I even checked the house all over, removing untidiness and signs of overt masculinity, fetching out long forgotten ornaments and pictures with which to 'soften' my home. I checked the freezer and the range of options in there and then resumed my life, just awaiting my moment. I'd give him a decent chance to 'get out of her life', as I hoped he now would before I made my play for her.

A day or two later and I found time to drop off a visiting card at her house, just as an innocent introduction... but I had plans for this lady! One day, or perhaps one evening would be more appropriate, I'd follow up on my card drop with a personal visit. Then I'd have a chance to invite her to come out for a meal, then perhaps back to my place... and then into my bed. I could but hope and plan but I also had work to do and so, for a week or so I allowed the idea to float around.

I continued with my daily life and my regular visits to the gym, seeing Gary there occasionally until one day I was at the gym again, on this occasion working on my arms and upper body muscles. I spent much of my time lying on my back, pushing weights upwards so I had no idea who else was in the gym, not that I really cared that much. Then finally I finished my workout and sweating and breathing heavily I headed for the showers once more. I could hear the water falling so I knew that someone was already there and I undressed – not that I was wearing much – and headed into the shower area.

The showers were divided into three sections; the entry, then an area for dressing, drying and undressing and finally the showers themselves. A screen wall initially hid the shower area, but as I entered, a sight that I'd never come across in there before met my eyes. There, kneeling on the floor was Gary, his mouth around the erect penis of some other guy, his head moving steadily back and forward; the pair absorbed in their ecstasy!

99

Silently I edged back behind the screen and stood there, captivated by the erotic scene, entranced by the action – and entirely aroused. My cock was hard in seconds, as hard as Gary's appeared to be; as hard as the cock in his mouth definitely was.

But it wasn't hard for much longer.

"Here it cums!" the man said, his hips starting to pump and twitch raggedly, "Get ready!"

"Uuummphhh!" grunted Gary, "Ummmm – ooooh yeahhhh!"

His cheeks bulged as his mouth filled with spunk, then his throat worked as he swallowed a mouthful, then his cheeks bulged again before he swallowed once more.

"Damn – that was a big load!" he said as he allowed the penis to slip from his lips, "More than last time. You been saving that?"

The other guy chuckled and shook his head as he stripped the last of his cum from his cock.

"No – you just bring out the best in me!" he said, "You always make me cum hard."

"You're always hard!" chuckled Gary as he stood up, "When can we do that again?"

"I'll be here on Thursday," the other man said as they turned on the showers and began covering themselves in soapy suds, "Same sort of time, ok?"

I pulled my shorts back on, backed down the corridor and then reversed once more, now slapping my feet on the concrete floor and humming loudly, to find the two men now both innocently showering at adjacent nozzles.

"Hi fellas, oh hello Gary," I said innocently as I stood in the doorway to the shower area and dropped my shorts, "Good workout?"

"Hi Chris. Yeah, just the job!" said Gary brightly, "All I need now is a good massage."

'Oh yeah,' I thought, *'I know which bit you want massaging!'*

Instead I chuckled, chucked my shorts onto one of the benches, stepped into the shower area and turned on my own shower head, turning slowly under the spray to wet myself all over.

"Cheers buddy – see yer!" came a voice and the other man departed, his shower finished.

I turned to Gary.

"How's your search for crumpet coming on?" I asked sociably, "Found anyone yet?"

"Not a damn thing. Bloody boring lot around here!" he exclaimed from beneath the cascading water, "The pubs are full of dykes; the clubs are full of kids and the streets are full of old grannies! And I'm still full of spunk!"

We laughed together but because the subject of sex had come up, because memories of what I'd just seen had resurfaced and because I too was not a little short on pussy-time, my cock immediately began to respond, obviously wanting to join in somehow.

"Bloody thing!" I said to myself as I felt engorgement stiffening my length, "Why the hell won't you leave me alone!"

I got busy with the soap but still my cock rose, my moistened foreskin sliding back off my knob and sending a thrill through me as my exposed nerve-filled flesh was exposed to the water. Unbidden I drew a heavy sigh of pleasure, causing Gary to look around and notice my erection. He smiled broadly.

"Look at you!" he said brightly, "Guess who else is full of spunk. I can see what you need!"

I didn't answer, fearing that I'd say the wrong thing and Gary continued, now coming to stand under my shower with me.

"Chris," he murmured carefully, "What would you say if I helped you? Wouldn't it be nice for you?"

I didn't reply but my cock did – he jerked up and down as if to nod his approval and Gary smiled.

"Looks as if someone would like some help anyway, so could I ummmm... rub him for you perhaps?" asked Gary carefully.

I shuddered, not knowing how to respond but Gary took my silence to imply approval and now I shuddered again as I felt his hand grasp my cock!

"Ahhhh, what the fuck?" I said, shocked and yet aroused, "No don't, you're not supposed to!"

"What do you mean, not supposed to?" asked Gary, his hand now sliding up and down my length, "I'm just helping a friend, aren't I?"

His hand was moving faster now and I was simply unable to or unwilling to move away – instead I just let him carry on, his firm fist feeling wonderful on my rampant and fully loaded instrument.

"Oooooooh fuck," I moaned, "Bloody hell – that feels good!"

I sucked in a deep breath as his hands stimulated me, my hips jerking back and forward, thrusting my cock through his fist as he brought me steadily towards my orgasm. Seconds turned into delightful minutes and still he worked away and still I couldn't stop him. No way could I end this now – this was too good to stop; too many sensations were now awash in my system and there was only one way that this could end.

"Ooooh fuck, you're gonna make me cum! Don't stop now!" I moaned, my body now shaking all over, "Oh God, I'm gonna cum!"

"Let it go!" said Gary quietly, "Come on – let it all go!"

I was panting now as I neared my climax – any moment now I'd be spraying my seed everywhere; any moment...

"Aaaahhhh – yeahhhhh!" I cried as Gary's hand stropped my cock vigorously, "Uuuuhhhh! Ooooh! Oooohh yeahhhhh!"

A long streamer of white sperm jetted from my upheld penis, splashing some four or five feet away against the wall. Another generous eruption followed, quickly followed by two more as Gary continued to wank me, until I held his hand to stop him.

"Let go, too sensitive..." I moaned, "Oooh fuck... what was that?"

I saw Gary lift his hand and lick at it before he spoke.

"That.." he said, "Was a most excellent orgasm! That really looked as if you enjoyed that."

"Bloody right I did, you were good," I replied, not quite certain if I should have said that, "Thanks Gary – feel better now, cheers!"

"Any time!" said Gary, "Ummmm, you don't fancy doing the same for me do you?"

And quite honestly, I hadn't noticed amid all my excitement that Gary's cock was as stiff as mine had been and the tip now bumped into my hip as Gary urged me to take part.

"Uuuummmm, not sure..." I said hesitantly, "I've never done that before."

"Same as doing it to yourself!" said Gary, "Come on, I'll help you."

And with that he grabbed my hand and pulled it towards him, planting it quickly on his penis, my responses too shocked to get away. His fingers curled around mine, causing my fingers to grip his hot stiff cock and making him gasp loudly.

"Oooooh, yesssss, oooooh Chris, yesssss," he hissed, "That's what I need, yesssss, rub him for me, please, please do it!"

His hand pushed and pulled mine up and down his lengthy shaft until suddenly I realised that I was doing it unaided – I was tossing him off... and actually I was quite enjoying it!

It was really rather exciting and very different to rubbing my own cock – his seemed a bit more slender and the extra length was noticeable and he felt warmer too somehow. His cock felt just as firm as mine, but it was the sensation of holding another penis in my hand that struck me hardest. And yet I wasn't horrified – instead I was getting to rather like it – I was getting into the action and now my fingers were actively seeking out the most delicate and excitable points on his penis, doing my best to stimulate him and please him. I could hardly believe what I was doing – yet I couldn't stop!

"Ooooh yesssss," moaned Gary, "You're wonderful Chris, your touch – it's brilliant, this is so good..."

"You're enjoying it?" I found myself asking, my tongue wetting my lips, "Am I doing it right?"

"You're doing it perfectly," moaned Gary, "I'm getting there – please don't stop Chris."

"You gonna cum, are you?" I asked, my eyes now fixed on his penis, my hand now sliding up and down his shaft with enthusiasm, "You gonna cum for me?"

"Yeah, yeah," groaned Gary, "Not long now... just a bit more!"

My hand moved faster and gripped his penis a little harder and now I could feel his upcoming orgasm; his cock was thickening and stiffening, freely oozing precum and his hips were thrusting at my fist.

"Just there... ooooh fuck – yeahhhhh! Nearly, nearly..." he groaned dramatically.

Faster and faster I rubbed him until suddenly he put his hand on mine and held me still.

"Ahhhhh – here it cums!" he cried, "Aaaaaahhhh – yeahhhhh!"

His hand held mine on his penis as pulse after pulse after pulse of cum rose and erupted, splattering over the floor, sticky white deposits now painting the tiles before the cascading water washed them clean once more. Dribbles of cum poured over my fingers before his orgasm ended and he pulled away from me. Quickly I allowed the water to clean my hands; I was happy enough with my own cum on my hands, but not someone else's somehow.

And then we stood there looking at each other.

"No more," I said, "Dunno what happened there, but no more."

"Yeah, I'm sorry Chris, I don't know what came over me either," said Gary, "I think it was just because I was all horny – I just needed some sex."

"Just as well I was there then, wasn't it?" I replied, "Anyway, thanks, guess I enjoyed it."

"Mmmmm, so did I!" replied Gary brightly, "Any time you need help, just ask."

But I needed to escape now that the urgency had gone and quickly I finished my shower and headed back to the changing room. It didn't take me long to towel dry and climb into my shorts and t-shirt and I was out of there before Gary even reappeared from the shower, thank heavens.

I headed out and down to the car park and I was in the process of climbing into my wagon when a car I recognised drove in and pulled up, so I paused and watched.

Eagerly I waited as the passenger door opened and Karen climbed out, quickly slamming the door shut again. Anger was still there on her face, even from some thirty yards away, the look barely leaving her countenance as the car pulled away.

Then, unable to resist, I beeped my horn and climbed out of my wagon, strolling across the car park to where Karen was still standing, legs apart, hands on her hips.

"Bastard!" she said as I got closer – then she smiled at me.

"Hi there, oh its Chris isn't it," she said, "Sorry – that's my partner – I'm getting SO pissed off with him..."

"Problem?" I asked innocently and Karen's face said it all.

She sighed heavily but her eyes belied her feelings and thoughts as they swept me all over.

"I'm going to be starting work today, but I've got a few minutes spare," she said, "I suppose I'd better tell you..."

With that she began to walk towards my truck, her eyes obviously admiring the artwork and wording.

"Hmmm, 'Artist to the Stars' are you?" she said, "I wonder if I could use an artist?"

We both climbed into the spacious interior and sat on the bench seat, her long bare legs captivating me, her firm, thrusting bust thrilling me.

Then she spotted the clip of visiting cards I keep in the truck and she smiled.

"Hey, didn't I see one of these at my place?" she said, picking the cards up, "I thought at the time I might ring them up whoever they were – and it's you – I didn't realise."

"Top quality work!" I said, chuckling proudly, "Best landscape gardener around – all my customers are well satisfied."

"Hmmmmm, I bet they are!" said Karen, her eyes sweeping over me again, "Wouldn't be at all surprised if I can find a use for you!"

I let her words hang in the air – the next move would have to be up to her...

She sighed heavily before she looked me in the eye.

"Said I'd tell you about my partner," she said, her teeth gritted, "He's such a bloody waste of space. He lost his job about a year ago – he was fine then but now he just won't get up and find another one – all he's doing is living off me, using my place as a kind of dosshouse. He goes off to stay with his mum quite a lot, thank heavens – sometimes wish he'd go and live with her instead."

I tutted in sympathy but let her carry on.

"He's never been all that much use anyway – don't know what I saw in him in the first place," she said, "Guess I took pity on him or something. Just as well he doesn't actually live with me all the time."

She looked ruefully at me.

"But now he's got nothing better to do he seems to think he's in charge of me – not that he ever was in the first place," she continued, "He's become so bloody controlling – such a pain in the bloody arse!"

"Are you married?" I asked but Karen shook her head sharply.

"No way – what – marry that!" she spluttered in horror, "You're joking!"

"Why don't you get rid of him then?" I asked and Karen looked at me.

"Don't think I haven't tried to get him to go away," she said, "He's just too fucking lazy to even do that for me and I guess I'm stupid or something because I keep taking pity on him."

"Do you need some help?" I asked, "A bit of pressure perhaps...?"

"Could you...?" she replied, hope suddenly springing into her eyes, "Honestly?"

I realised that I'd have to be careful what I did to him so it seemed really sensible to call in some reinforcement and without further consideration I suggested that Gary would help too. I explained my vague plan to Karen, knowing she'd be happy.

"We'd need to work it out, but I reckon we could help – be glad to try anyway," I said and Karen reached out and put her hand on my arm, now smiling at last.

"Please see if you can," she said, "I'll help too if I can."

It was just a matter of a few quiet meetings at the gym with Gary and Karen and myself and we had a plan. Ok, it was basic and simply came down to Gary and I more or less physically removing him – well, coercing him into moving by our very presence, hopefully without the matter coming to any violence. Neither of us was concerned using some of our physique but we both felt it would be far better and less complicated if we could get him out peaceably.

A week or so later and the deed was done! Her now ex-partner had been sent packing and Karen had her house to herself once more – her ex having been told exactly where to go.

It had all worked out relatively easily – once Gary and I had appeared, our two solid frames with Karen between us towering over his meagre body, he was suddenly all in favour of moving his gear out! Part of his reluctance to move was to do with finding somewhere to put all his possessions and as I now found out, Gary owned a warehousing company and he quickly found a spare corner for his few bulky belongings to be dumped into until he could collect them.

And then I managed to find her a half-way decent car, a convertible and fairly sporty thing that I got from a client who owed me money and her life began blossoming at last... and my interest in her climbed once more.

Of course, Karen wanted to be able to thank us both and so she invited us both over one evening for "a few drinkies" as she put it. It would have felt much nicer if she'd been able to thank me alone, but these were early days and I knew that my chances would come. I'd laid some pretty solid groundwork and was entirely confident of my prospects! But it was great – two mates from the gym, both arriving within minutes – two guys who'd combined their efforts to make her life that much better. I was doing so well – it was just a pity that Gary had to be there too...

Karen was looking incredible! Gone was her unhappiness and instead she looked radiantly beautiful and beamed with love and warmth. We were each welcomed with a massive hug and a warm kiss; Karen's ample bust squashing firmly against my chest, her soft, generous lips attaching themselves to mine like warm limpets and both Gary and I were left feeling almost visibly lifted as Karen made us welcome.

Soon we'd had a lovely meal and were settled in her lounge with brandies, each of us revelling in her warmth and friendliness. There was plenty of light chatter until Karen locked her eyes onto me.

"I've been thinking," she said, "I've always wanted one of those rose arbours – you know, a nice little place in the garden with a swinging seat in, all surrounded by sweet scented roses. What do you reckon Chris?"

"You've got the space," I said as I looked down the garden from the patio doors, "Down there on the left, past those trees, I'd suggest perhaps?"

"Ideal place," agreed Karen, "I think that's where I would have wanted it. Ok – could you do me a quote, fairly soon."

"No problems," I said, knowing that I'd do it for almost nothing for this woman, "I'll need a few days..."

"That'd be sweet of you," Karen said, smiling at me and I felt all warm inside and I even smiled at Gary, my smile being somewhat smug of course.

The conversation resumed until another subject surfaced – her parents.

"Mum's got a huge load of stuff she wants me to store for her," she said, the subject of relatives having come around somehow, "Dad was something of a collector before he died. Now Mum wants to move nearer and to downsize so she won't have enough room left. All the stuff's for me eventually and there are some lovely antiques there so I don't want to give them away but I don't know where I can keep it all."

It seemed that her dad had passed away a few years ago and now her mum was living alone, some seventy miles away from us, surrounded by all his possessions. Karen wanted her to be nearer and had found a lovely little bungalow for her, except for the one problem of her possessions.

"You don't want to sell them then?" I asked but Karen shook her head.

"No, dad collected them all and I want to have them with me," she said, "Perhaps one day I will sell them because it's my inheritance I suppose and there's some nice stuff too, but there's too much for me to find room for here."

I was about to say that I'd look around for her when Gary piped up.

"I'll look after it all for you," he said, deflating me in an instant, "How much do you reckon there is?"

"Ohhh, I reckon there's about a large room packed full," Karen replied and Gary smiled.

"That's easy then – I've got some shipping containers in my warehouse," he said, "I'll put one aside for you; nice and dry and safe. I can get one of my vans to pick your stuff up on an empty return run. We'll arrange something."

"Oh you darling!" breathed Karen happily, "Oh, that'll be so helpful; Mum will be delighted – thank you so much Gary."

With that she launched into telling us that she'd now be able to help her mother sell her house and hoped that the bungalow would still be on sale and that would be perfect... and so on, while I listened somewhat half-heartedly. I felt deflated somehow – Gary had trumped me and I had no answer...

Nevertheless, the evening went well enough overall, Karen having enough charm for the both of us and by the time we departed Gary and I were still friends, linking arms to show our united pleasure. It had been a good evening really; certainly one that had changed Karen from being just someone we knew into a real friend... a friend I still intended to take to bed as soon as possible!

My work kept me very busy for a while but between jobs I managed to find time to nip over to Karen's place and measure up the site for her arbour – and then to spend an evening or two designing a suitable structure. Fair enough – it would cost me a bit but I could use some of my stock of posts, other timber and paving slabs – my labour and some cement were the only real 'expenses' which could be easily offset somewhere else. Yep – I could do it for a nominal sum for Karen – the least I could do. An erection in her garden was merely the first erection I aimed to produce at her place!

In the meantime, I'd learned a bit more about Gary. He'd built up a removal and storage business and now shipped stuff worldwide as well as having several storage depots scattered around the country. I guess I'd never really noticed his businesses or his connection with them because it was none of my concern – until now. But now, as a love rival of some kind, it was necessary to know how to circumvent his interest in my girl – or at least that's how I was beginning to see Karen.

She was now the woman of my dreams – even of my wet dreams! How often had I woken up to find spunk everywhere; my mind's eye full of visions of her ripe body spreadeagled on my bed... How often had I spent quiet evenings at home just allowing my mind to rerun those moments when Karen had been close to me; touching me; holding my arm; kissing me.

I had a bad case of lust for her – until this one particular day...

Having a few hours to spare one afternoon I decided I'd pop over to drop in on Karen on the pretence that I wanted to check the levels in her garden where I'd now agreed to build her arbour. My target was just to spend a moment or two checking levels and the rest of the afternoon checking her. Well preened and brushed up; a bunch of flowers at the ready; my wagon now all clean and shiny too, I drove across town and into her driveway and stopped dead.

There outside her house was a large van – with a removal company's name on it.

"Fuckin' hell!" I exclaimed, banging the steering wheel in frustration, "What the fuck's that doing here? Bloody typical that she's got something happening just when I call."

Quietly I climbed out, gently closed the door and walked to the side gate. Yes, I had intended to do lots of socialising but that would have to wait – but since I was here and since my visit was wasted as I was no longer alone, I reckoned I'd better get on with business. I guess I didn't need to see her to check the measurements...

Still quietly I walked around the house and onto the patio, to mentally survey the scene; to check to see if the ground needed to be lowered or raised for best effect and I was just standing there when I heard it.

A woman's cry; a cry of excited bliss; almost a scream; certainly a scream of delight; suddenly followed by the bellow of an obviously masculine climax. I froze as I located the source – it came from an upstairs window and was now followed by several more such cries, each one a bit quieter until finally there was just a single long drawn out release of air – a sigh of contentment.

'Someone's fucking her!' I thought to myself, 'Some bastard's just fucked her!"

Then the penny dropped.

'That's fucking Gary, isn't it?' I found myself thinking, realising the truth.

I was quivering with suppressed anger, desire and frustration as I turned on my heels and almost ran out of the garden to my truck. Of course it was one of his vans, wasn't it, I realised. Quickly I jumped into mine and reversed out of her drive, all my instincts telling me to gun the

engine and leave burning rubber behind. Instead I crept away quietly –
then headed home, with actual tears on my cheeks.

Indoors I was panting with anger as I tore the ring off a can of lager
and gulped down half the chilly contents before I grabbed a second one
and went and sat down to cool off. I shook my head as I calmed down
and considered the situation. Well, Karen wasn't "mine", much as I
desired her – she was very much a free agent and who she chose to fuck
was up to her – but why with my mate Gary? But why not? He too was
very much like me – his own boss – affluent enough – good looking and
healthy – young and energetic too, but I did have something on him,
didn't I? I'd caught him in the shower, hadn't I? Now how could I use
that against him?

Back at the gym things were quite normal though. I could hardly
raise a scene there and anyway, this was between Karen and me and not
to be aired in public, so I greeted Karen in her office and Gary too with
my usual bonhomie as we sweated away together the next time we met.
Don was all animated now as Karen had started work but now it seemed
that he hadn't thought to provide her with enough privacy, so the offices
were being renovated and new walls were being fitted. He too was full
of talk about Karen – he seemed almost as smitten with her as we were!
As we went through our paces and exercises I managed to mention to
Gary that I'd got the details for her arbour all sorted but once again he
deflated me by telling me that he'd arranged to pick up Karen's mother's
stuff later that week and that he'd be storing it for her free of charge.

'*Damn you*,' I thought as I pumped an extra twenty pounds of
weights up and down, '*I'll get you...*'

Some two weeks passed and with the weather forecast offering a
long spell of some unseasonably warm and dry weather coming up I
phoned Karen and arranged to spend a few days erecting her arbour.
Naturally she was delighted, and the date was set – and bright and early

I arrived with my trailer piled with materials. It was Friday and I'd be able to complete the job before Monday returned.

Karen greeted me warmly, then left me to it as I shifted everything into the garden and got to work and by the time I'd done my first day's work the site had changed remarkably. Now the skeleton of the arbour was rising, and it already seemed to be enhancing that corner of her garden, I was pleased to note.

Karen came out onto the patio as we surveyed my efforts, her arm linked into mine, her hand resting on my forearm.

"That's going to look absolutely lovely," she said, her head now pressed against my shoulder, "It'll be so restful down there; it's going to be wonderful."

"Ah, it's nothing," I said, "I'm just pleased to do something for you."

"Hmmm, I wonder what I can do for you?" said Karen, her warm eyes locking onto mine, "Anything you fancy?"

I almost growled – was she really making that kind of offer? Gently but firmly I pulled her until we were facing each other, close together. It was time to make the first real move...

"I fancy you Karen," I said simply, pulling her tightly to me, "You're just so gorgeous, so lovely. I've wanted you since the day I first saw you. "

I let her go so she could breathe and so I could let my eyes run over her.

"You're just so – so..." I lost my words.

"So fuckable, isn't that what you mean?" said Karen, her face split by a huge smile.

"Oh fuck – yeah, yeahhhh Karen, yes!" I cried, "I want to love you; to fuck you; to be part of you – let me, please, please!"

"Not out here!" replied Karen softly, her eyes sparkling, "Come indoors Chris, come on."

She led the way in through the patio doors, where we stopped as I took my shoes and socks off before she looked me over.

"I think you could do with a shower first, don't you?" she said, a look of lust now on her face, "Would you like me to join you?"

"Oh god, yes!" I exclaimed, hardly able to keep myself under control, "Honestly?"

She grabbed my hand and pulled me.

"Come on then, up here," she said as she led the way to the stairs and I followed, my eyes full of her pert cheeks as they rose and swayed as she climbed the stairs ahead of me, my penis already rising fast. Moments later and we were in her bathroom, a large shower cubicle prominently occupying one end of the room.

"There's room for us both," she said as she turned and faced me, "Come on, off with them!"

Karen's hands reached for my t-shirt and lifted it off my head before she stood back and looked me over.

"Look at those lovely muscles!" she enthused, her hands now sliding over my pecs, "Wow – you look so powerful, so manly!"

I flexed them before undoing my belt and jeans and Karen's eyes followed my hands, her tongue licking her lips, I noticed.

Moving smoothly, I slid my jeans down and off until I was standing there in just my boxers which were already pushed out of shape by my eager penis.

"Shall I take them off?" I asked, mischievously, "Or do you want to do it?"

"You do it!" she said, "I want to watch!"

Like a slow-motion stripper I tucked my thumbs inside the waistband and inch by inch I pushed my boxers down, my rigid cock now caught in the material and showing as a lengthy outline with a damp spot at the tip.

"Ooohhh, look at him!" moaned Karen, "Come on – uncover him for me!"

I pushed my boxers further down and now, with my penis still trapped, the elastic waist was stretched well clear of my body as my pubes came into view. Karen was almost praying; her hands clenched together; her mouth open with her tongue on her upper lip, her eyes fixed on my groin – so I suddenly pushed my boxers to my knees.

With an audible slap my cock sprang out and upwards, slapping against my abdomen before standing proudly, pointing at the ceiling. My foreskin was, as I looked down, just peeling back from my knob, my glistening, purple shiny knob that was so very eager to get to know Karen's hole. He jerked violently as the thought passed my mind.

"God, he's beautiful," moaned Karen, "He's gonna feel so good!"

I'd already realised, or at least hoped that we'd end up making love but her words now completed the story – now it was certain that we'd fuck! Shaking her head quickly she pushed me towards the shower before lifting her own t-shirt up and over her head. Her magnificent breasts now stood there before me; clearly firm and full enough to stand unaided but contained within a lacy bra that merely enhanced their allure. And then, reaching behind her she unclipped her bra and let it fall into her hands while I stood there, mouth agape, cock erect, captivated.

I just couldn't find words to praise her enough, to express my excitement and pleasure at seeing her fantastic breasts bare and revealed to me. Her nipples were still flattened somewhat, but they were small and brown and captivating; I knew that soon I'd be sucking and chewing them...

Karen continued to undress, stepping out of her shoes and now undoing the clasp on her skirt, which fell to the ground. She stepped out of it and now stood there clad in just sweet little knickers that delicately hid her charms. She turned and bent down to pick up her skirt and her lovely posterior was now revealed to me, her cheeks pert and rounded, her thighs separated by a small gap through which the lips of her pussy could just about be made out.

My cock jerked anew at the sight until she turned towards me and moved closer.

"Take them off for me," she said, her hands sliding down to caress my cock, "Take them off."

I knelt before her as I reached up and took hold of the sides of her knickers and I looked up. There above me her generous breasts stood out, her nipples now aroused and erect, her cleavage framing her mouth as she smiled down at me. Holding my breath I began to slide her knickers down her thighs, pulling them gently over her arse before I moved them far enough for the material covering her pussy to fall away.

Karen moved her legs slightly apart to facilitate the easier removal of the last vestiges of coquettish cover and her knickers suddenly fell to her ankles. I breathed again, now with my eyes locked onto her pussy; a slippery-shiny slit; a very protuberant clit and a small landing strip of pubes above it all.

I leaned forward and planted a kiss on her clit, bringing out a low moan from Karen.

"Ooooh don't!" she moaned, "Later Chris, later."

Her hands pulled me upwards and we stood there, my cock almost brushing her navel, her nipples rubbing gently on my chest as she swayed gently to and fro.

"Come on Chris, let's get in there," she said, "Let's get wet!"

I'm not going to tell you all that happened in that shower – I'll let you imagine the action as we soaked and soaped and scrubbed and rinsed – before we emerged and wrapped ourselves in towels.

What I will tell you is that we got to know one another a lot better and now we were ready for the main bout... so much so that Karen couldn't wait. She pulled me across the landing into her bedroom where she flung herself onto her bed.

"Take me Chris – I need you," she said, "I'm all ready for you!"

Quickly I finished drying; climbed onto the bed and poised myself above Karen's writhing body. My cock was so hard I could have driven him through concrete; instead I was about to drive him through some warm, wet soft flesh as Karen pulled me down, her hands bringing my mouth to hers, her lips already wet and parted. We kissed deeply, her tongue urgently exploring my teeth and mouth before my tongue was able to intercept hers and intertwine erotically. She parted her legs further and I felt my penis rub against her crinkled pubes and then between her slippery lips.

"Get him in me Chris," she moaned, "I'm all ready – I'm soaked!"

I reached a hand down to her pussy and slid it experimentally down her slit – she was indeed dripping wet and so very slippery. I teased her clit, which was now even larger than before, then brought my hand up to our mouths to lick my fingers clean of her juices. They tasted so delicious that I just had to have more so I quickly changed positions, sliding down the bed until my face hovered over her pussy.

Karen knew what was coming but when my lips found her clit she still responded as if I'd given her an enormous electric shock! With a scream of pleasure, not pain, she leapt vertically, her clit squashing hard between my lips, her wet slit engulfing my chin before she sank once more to the bed, now panting heavily.

"Oooooh Chris," she cried, "Oh fuck – I didn't expect that! Your tongue; your lips – oh god – they're wonderful!"

I lifted my head and looked at her over the small and dainty forest of her pubes.

"You're sweet," I said, "You taste so sweet, you're gorgeous!"

"Mmmmmm," moaned Karen, her hips writhing as I took her clit back into my mouth, "And you're so good at that!"

She had a lovely clit; well and truly big enough to take into my mouth – no monster, but larger than many I'd discovered. I could feel its entire design; its little shaft; the tiny head covered by its mobile hood. I could feel the different textures in my tongue as I stimulated her clit, Karen's body responding with every swipe and suck.

Karen was also moaning and groaning as I played with her body, exalted cries and sudden gasps coming loudly until my penis reminded me that he needed part of the action too!

"You're getting really wet Karen, do you want me to carry on?" I asked after a while, but Karen grasped my ears and pulled me upwards.

"No Chris – get him in me now – I need your cock inside me!" she said eagerly, "Leave that bit – I'm wet enough!"

I slid back up her body while Karen hummed contentedly, her body moving to prepare itself for mine as my hand pushed my cock down and into position.

Silently I rubbed him up and down her slippery slit, allowing the tip to enter her little hole only once I was content that he was lubricated enough.

I looked into her eyes.

"You ready?" I asked unnecessarily and Karen nodded, her eyes slowly shutting.

Carefully I lowered my body and my penis began to penetrate her pussy, my knob stretching her flesh until suddenly he was lodged inside her. Karen let out a long breath and a low moan as I applied more pressure and as my cock slid further and further inside her. She felt hot and smooth and I could feel the muscles inside her pussy grasping me, caressing me and milking me as I began to move in and out of her hole.

She certainly had a warm and welcoming hole, one that was obviously as delighted to be filled with a hard penis as I was delighted to do the filling and with our bodies now rubbing together, her wonderfully exciting breasts, her firm abdomen and her sleek skin pushing and sliding against my flexing muscles, the whole deed became an activity that brought massive pleasure to us both.

Gradually we picked up the action, both of us moving up and down; our bodies now beginning to slam together; my penis now driving all the way up her vagina; my balls banging against her thighs; her breasts squashed between us as we fucked and fucked. Our breaths were coming more quickly now as we built up the tempo – this was no gentle bit of loving – this was becoming a genuine rut; we were fucking each other hard; both in need of release and satisfaction; both of us fulfilling our desires.

Then finally the tempo built and with almost violent thrusts our exertions drew to a climax; a shuddering of breaths and bodies; a jerking of uncontrollable muscles and a wave of hot sweat that coated us both.

"I'm gonna cum," I gasped, "Can I cum inside you?"

"Yes, yes, oh Chris yesss," moaned Karen, "I'm safe – let it go Chris – I want to feel you cum!"

I was really pounding at her now, bringing myself inside just a few seconds to a massive peak and hopefully taking her there too. Karen's hips were responding; our hotness driving waves of sexual odours from our bodies until we both reached the top simultaneously.

"Cummmmmmm!" I yelled, "Oh Karen – yeahhhhhh! Yeahhhhh! Yeahhhhh!"

"Aaaaaahhhhhhh Chris, yesssss!" cried Karen, her body shaking violently, "Oh fuck – can't stop – can't stop – ohhhhh, yesssss!"

Finally we both collapsed, immediately falling side by side on the bed, my penis dislodging from her so-slippery hole although I was just too knackered to notice or care.

And I was about to say something when a raucous cry rose from the garden area.

"Wha-hey! Nice one, both of you!" came the cheerful call – it was Gary's voice.

What the fuck was he doing here, right now, interrupting our love-making?

In a matter of a few seconds both Karen and I were at the window, the window flung open wide.

"Fuck off!" I yelled, feeling none too polite, "Just bugger off – she's mine!"

"Calm down Chris," said Karen, her hand on my back, "We'd just about finished, hadn't we?"

"Hmmmmm, guess so," I rumbled, thinking that it would have been nice to do it all over again, "Yeah, guess so."

"What on earth are you doing here?" called Karen as she leaned out the window, her bare breasts perched on the sill like a pair of cute pink robins.

"I thought I'd just pop in to say hi," said Gary brightly, "Didn't know you'd have company, so I'll leave you in peace. There's a little something on the mat for you Karen."

"You could have stayed and waited," offered Karen, but Gary shook his head.

"Nah – I'll be off – see you another day, bye," he said and he was gone – and a few moments later we heard his truck roar away too.

But the mood had been broken and now Karen had covered up, some tissue between her legs; her thick dressing gown on as she escorted me downstairs.

"Not the same now, is it," she said, and I shook my head sadly, not really knowing what to say or even what to do.

Then Karen sealed the matter as she looked at the clock.

"Hey look – it's gone seven... didn't realise," she said, "Look, you'll have to be gone anyway – I always chat to my Mum on Friday evenings. I'm going to have a quick shower; can I'll let you find your own way out, will that be ok?"

"Guess so," I replied, "Thanks for that anyway – enjoyed it!"

"Bye," came the somewhat vacant reply from Karen, already climbing the stairs again, "See you!"

'*So much for that*,' I thought as I walked through the door, Karen already having retreated out of sight upstairs, '*Bloody Gary.*'

I nearly kicked out at the little package that Gary had left on the step – instead I picked it up and placed it indoors for safety – I wasn't that nasty...

I was back the next day to complete my work on the arbour, but my mood wasn't the same now – I felt deflated again somehow, especially when she sprayed some perfume on herself and invited me to smell it.

"Gary bought it for me," she said, "It's gorgeous, isn't it; it's one of my favourites!"

I now wished that I had kicked the package but at least Karen was nice to me as we went out and checked again to see if I'd left any tools around; I had to do something... I'd put a lot of love and effort into it and although there were no roses at this time of year, it would look just right come spring and summer.

But though Karen was indeed nice to me, softly rubbing herself all over me as she kissed me, she deflated me further by telling me that she couldn't let me stay that night. She told me she had some girlfriends coming around for a social evening – no men included, so I almost crept away and headed home where I spent a quiet and boring night.

I felt flat and almost lifeless over the next few days. I mooched around and almost sullenly worked off my miseries. Tuesday and Wednesday seemed to slip by... then on Thursday things began to look up a bit once more. I was considerably buoyed up by a phone call from a company who'd accepted my quote to look after their office gardens, the gardens being part of an old, well established and quite famous estate. My knowledge got me the job, I reckoned, and I was quite proud of myself once again – the contact was worth a few notes and a fair bit of kudos too. That evening I felt better and made myself a light dinner; a good steak and lots of salad which went down well with a drop of wine.

Then it was Thursday evening already and I suddenly realised that I hadn't been to the gym for a while; I'd better get there soon, I decided. With a quiet evening ahead there was no time like the present, so I grabbed my things and headed out – the gym being open late on Thursdays.

Don was there as usual with his warm welcome, but the place was reasonably quiet otherwise.

"Only a few of you in," said Don lightly, "The world's getting lazy!"

"Been busy," I said, "Too many other things to do."

"Never mind the excuses," said Don, "Go and get on with it. Don't want to see you get out of shape, of all people!"

I changed into my work-out gear and settled to my routine; not even thinking about whom else might be there. Instead I got busy – peddling, pushing and lifting to a schedule that Don had planned for me. A sweaty hour passed before I even took a decent break at which point I found that I needed a pee so I trotted off towards the toilets.

It was as I passed the changing rooms that I heard sounds that I recognised as being sexual; a slapping sound of flesh on flesh accompanied by grunts and heavy breathing. Someone was up to no good! Carefully I edged forward to see who was doing what with whom – and immediately saw that once again it was Gary, who, bent at the

123

waist, was holding onto a grasp rail... with another guy very busily shafting his arse.

Not only was I speechless but I was struck rigid – I just didn't know what to say or what to do... apart from watch, open-mouthed, as their actions became even more energetic. Anyway, the sight was amazingly erotic and exciting somehow. Gary's shorts were around his ankles and as I was viewing them from partially behind, all I could see was part of his cock as it swayed from side to side and the other guy's balls swinging low below his hairy, clenching, pumping arse.

"Yeah, yeah, come on, harder, harder!" moaned Gary causing the other guy to grunt as he applied more effort.

"Oooohhhfff ooooohhhffff, oh fuck; you gonna let me cum in you?" the other man said and I heard Gary's reply.

"Yeah, yeah – don't take him out, for heaven's sake, don't!" he cried, "Shoot it all up me, please!"

"It's cumming up, I can feel it," he replied through grunted breaths, "I won't be long."

I could see Gary's hand as he held and rubbed his own penis now while I listened and watched as the pair of them approached their crescendo, the slapping noises now louder and faster.

"Here it cums!" groaned the guy, "I'm cumming – any moment now – it's cumming, cumming!"

"Let it go! Fill me!" exclaimed Gary urgently, "Let me have it – I want it all!"

"Uuuuuhhhh – uuuuuhhh!" grunted the man, his hips thrusting and tightening hard, "Ooooooohh yeahhhhh, yeahhhhh!"

"Yeahhh, lovely!" moaned Gary, "I can feel you shooting, ooooh yessss!"

My penis was as hard as a rock as I watched, completely absorbed in the lurid action and now seriously throbbing as Gary's hand brought his own climax – his white cum jetting out at his feet. Somehow I now wished I'd been closer and able to see the details – and perhaps even to touch Gary's cock as he shot off, or Gary's clenching arse or even the other guy's penis as it drove into Gary's hole.

I shook my head as I wondered at my reactions to the scene I'd just watched, then accepted that it was simply that any sex turned me on these days.

Thank heavens that the toilets were separate from the changing rooms – I could just bypass them and dodge any repercussions. Quickly I scarpered, not willing to be seen as they finished and very eager to get rid of my erection.

But as I dashed into the toilet block, I saw that the bucket and mop of the cleaner was at the door, along with a "Wet Floor" notice board; I could use the toilet but a quick jerk-off would definitely be noticed. Damn! I went to a cubicle where I sat down and just waited for my erection to subside, finally having a pee once my cock would point at the water and not the ceiling, before returning to the gym and the running machine.

"Back to the grindstone," I muttered to myself, "And don't get thinking about what you've just seen!"

I was not a little scared of getting another erection if I let my mind wander, so I concentrated on my jogging, steadily eating up the miles until a voice broke my concentration.

"Hi Chris," said Gary right beside me, "How're you doing?"

"Oh fine – yeah, oh hi Gary," I replied, taking a moment or two to get back to reality, "Yeah, fine mate – and you?"

"Couldn't be better," he replied, "Just coming back for a second round."

"Pardon – a second round?" I queried but Gary put me right.

"I've been lifting, then I had a break and a shower and now I'm back to do some running," he said, "How long have you got left."

"About half an hour or so," I replied, which caused Gary to smile broadly.

"Ah – should be finished about the same time as you then," he said, "I'll expect I'll meet you in the showers after that."

Instantly I felt my cock jerk and almost as quickly I told him to behave before I had the mind to reply.

"Guess so – I'm just off to do some pec work; I'll do some bench pressing I think," I said, aiming at getting as far away from Gary as I could, "Done my time running."

"Ok – see you later then," he replied as I walked off.

Soon I was on my back lifting what felt like enormously heavy weights; even though somehow my mind just wasn't focussed today, but I needed to keep up my exercise regime. I'd been at it for a while before I realised that someone was watching – inevitably it was Gary.

"You need a hand spotting," he offered, "You're pushing a fair load there. Don't want to see you drop that lot on yourself!"

He came and stood at my head, his hands at the ready as I lifted the weights but as he moved so I nearly dropped the weighs immediately. I was now looking almost straight up the leg of his shorts and I was being provided with a view of his balls and a considerable length of his penis, which seemed to be threatening to fall out of his shorts entirely!

"Gary," I said as I hefted my weights back into their stands, "You're showing everything!"

He looked down and pulled up the leg of his shorts and there indeed was his penis and balls, which now flopped right down just inches above me!

"Oh fuck, the bloody elastic's gone," he said as he stuffed his penis back under cover and held it there with one hand, "Thought it felt a bit slack, damn!"

"Better go and take these off; that's them finished; glad I've got some spare shorts," he said, then changed his theme, "You due for a shower yet?"

I looked at the clock and saw that I had less than five minutes left, so I might as well pack in.

"Yeah ok," I said, thinking more of my lack of concentration and less of his display, "Might as well call it a day."

Together we sauntered down the room and into the changing room; a really peaceful haven after the music and the rattle of metallic weights and machinery out in the exercise arena and Gary slipped out of his shorts in seconds, chucking them in the bin.

I too stripped off and then, gathering our shower bits and pieces, we headed to the showers, passing as we did so what seemed to be the last two guys to leave the place. We were on the late side; the club would be closing before long, hence the lack of other people.

With the water now running to our liking, Gary and I soaped up and idly chattered as we refreshed ourselves, until he set things off.

"I'm off to see Karen tonight," he said, "Promised I'd take her out for dinner; I wonder if she'll be in a good mood?"

"Hmmmmph!" I grunted, wondering if he'd get further than I had on my last visit, "That reminds me; what the fuck were you doing yelling up at us the other day?"

"Haha, haha!" laughed Gary loudly, "I just popped in to see if she'd be interested in a bit of fun, but you got there first, didn't you. And you were shouting loud enough to hear down the road, so I just had to join in! Anyway, she's open to all comers, isn't she – she's not your property yet, is she?"

I had to admit that he was right and so I let the matter drop, although I felt a tremor of excitement shake my groin at the mention of Karen and realised that my cock had awoken from his slumbers. Quickly I rubbed more soap onto my chest and shoulders to divert my attention, but it was an action that didn't help, as it happened.

Gary couldn't see my rising erection, but he saw me stretching over my shoulders and now he moved under my shower, turned it off and reached out for the soap.

"Here, let me," he said as he grabbed the squeezy bottle and moments later his hands began rubbing over my shoulders and back, sending calming yet stimulating waves of foam and pleasure to all parts.

"Ahhh, that's nice," I answered, "Cheers Gary, good of you."

"Always welcome," he said, his voice now almost teasing, "Anything else I can do for you?"

As he spoke his soapy slippery hands were moving over and then down my back and began to reach around my hips until they were moving on my abdomen, his fingers gently caressing and massaging my muscles... muscles that seemed to be directly attached to my cock. Behind me I could feel the firmness of his penis pushing against my buttocks and in seconds my cock began to rise; an unstoppable force responding to erotic stimulation that left me gasping with pleasure.

Before I could respond intelligently, Gary's hands came together over my penis, which immediately stiffened entirely, now quivering under his touch.

"Shiiiiit," I moaned, unable to remove his hands though, "Quit that, I'm not into that!"

"Bet you are really," said Gary quietly from just behind my ear as he gently pulled me from under the shower, "Wouldn't you like me to help you? Wouldn't you like me to make you feel good? You liked it the other week, didn't you?"

128

Whatever I felt mattered little – my cock spoke for me by remaining very stiff and dribbling slippery precum down over his fingers, it's eagerness for attention overriding my reluctance and with Gary's hand moving slowly up and down my slippery soapy length, he was sending me dizzy with excitement and erotic feelings.

"No, now cut it out," I repeated, my voice almost a whisper, "I told you, I'm not like that."

But somehow I wasn't moving away – somehow the feelings of his touch and the pressure behind me were so exciting that I was frozen – not with fear but with anticipation. Part of me wanted to pull away but somehow I just couldn't; somehow Gary's actions were rooting me to the spot... even as I felt his penis starting to press firmly against my arse.

"You feel as if you could do with unloading," he said, his voice wheedling, "You're all tense – you need to relax. I can help; come on, let me."

For some reason I found myself humming my assent, wondering immediately why I was letting him manipulate me so easily. Gary obviously took my hum as approval and now moved until he was in front of me with both his hands working on my erection. I was completely rigid, yet I was like putty in his hands...

"Is that good?" asked Gary as his fingers teased the ridge of my knob, "Feeling any better yet?"

I hummed again, then I don't know what impelled me to say it but I just blurted it out.

"I saw you earlier on when you were with that guy," I said, "You were enjoying yourself, weren't you?"

"Oh fuck – you didn't, did you?" replied Gary, his hands still at work on my cock, "Shit, that's blown it, I guess!"

"You're gay, right?" I said but Gary shook his head.

129

"Nah – not gay – I'm bisexual; I love 'em all!" he said, "I can give it or take it! And yes, I was enjoying it, since you ask."

He looked into my face, his hands still gently caressing my cock.

"Why, do you want to try me then?" he asked, his tongue licking his lips, "I'd love to suck you off... or perhaps you'd like me to try your arse for size?"

"You're joking!" I exclaimed, "You're not sucking or fucking me, thank you!"

"Well at least do something for me," pleaded Gary, his fingers teasing my penis, "Let me feel you inside me – please."

I felt a thrill rush through my penis and balls; a tremor that expressed excitement and desire and I then I felt myself nodding, quite without really meaning to. Gary saw my nods and smiled before bending down and quickly kissing my cock.

"Come down to the toilets then," he said, pulling me by my newly-kissed and tingling cock, "Don't want to risk it here."

"You did earlier," I countered as he pushed us both under the water again.

"Yeah, well, we thought the place was good as empty," he said as we washed off the soapy bubbles, "But at this time of night Don might come down to check that we've all left. The toilets will be safer."

Like a lamb on a rope I followed Gary from the showers to the changing room, where we paused to dry off then, with towels wrapped around our bodies we headed towards the toilets. I noticed that Gary took something from his bag before we moved on, while I also noted that Gary's own cock was at least partially erect and actually looked as if it would soon be as stiff as mine was.

Before I could think further, we reached the toilets and Gary pushed us into a cubicle before he locked the door behind us. We stood facing each other, our two erections almost meeting between us and in a moment of massive excitement Gary leaned forward and kissed me on my lips!

I felt myself shudder all over; partially because I was shocked; partially because of the physical intimacy and partially because I'd never done such a thing before with a man.

I felt my breathing get quicker as Gary's tongue found mine and sparred with it, before retreating back into his own mouth. His lips sucked at mine before we disengaged, leaving me shaking and excited like never before, my mind in complete turmoil, my cock throbbing.

"You want to do it? Please say yes," pleaded Gary, his hand now back on my cock and once again I nodded almost unintentionally.

"Oh brilliant – hang on," he said as he began to squeeze some gel from a little tube, "Let me get myself ready."

So saying, he reached between his legs and squirmed around a bit before rising again to wipe his fingers on some toilet paper. He turned around and leaned forward, his smooth slippery arse now presented to me, merely inches from my cock.

"Ok – I'm ready, put him in!" he said, "Take it easy please – you're pretty big."

It was obvious what had to be done and in the heat of the moment I just couldn't back off – I simply had to fuck him. Perhaps it felt in some way that I was getting some form of power over him; some way of getting my own back for his philandering with Karen but all such thoughts disappeared as my penis touched his flesh. There was a sudden flash behind my eyes as if of lightning; a shockwave that tore through my body; that seemed to echo to all extremities and then to return to my cock, which trembled and shook with excitement and horror.

So far, the limit of my bisexual activity had been to have a mutual wank with Gary, but that was that. Then we'd just kissed a moment ago; another bisexual gesture; but that was my limit... but now I was about to insert my penis inside another man – not just into his mouth but into his anus!

I was shaking as if I was a naughty schoolboy and yet my penis was so damn stiff. Not only that, it was drooling precum copiously; hardly a sign that my cock was scared...

I took a deep breath and leaned forward, the tip of my penis now resting within the crack of Gary's arse, the warmth of his body already evident. With my hand I pushed my lubricated penis downwards to lodge at his equally lubricated arsehole, then I applied a little pressure, bringing forth a low moan from Gary.

"Ooooooh, feels lovely Chris; push gently; let me get used to him," said Gary softly, "He's quite big, isn't he?"

I couldn't say anything; my whole mind was absorbed in the simple act of pushing my cock into a hole; a hole that was so alien that I'd only ever remember seeing my own once, when I'd had a spot on my arse and I'd used a mirror. It wasn't exactly a place that I spent much time even considering and yet here I now was, pushing my penis right into one such hole. I felt some muscles around my cock inside Gary give way and Gary moaned anew while my cock began to slide into his body.

"Yeahhhhh," he moaned, "I think you're in now – that's better."

And it was – the mental comfort level had risen and instead of the alien feeling of puncturing an arsehole, I was now sliding my cock in and out of a warm slippery sleeve; a much more anonymous place that actually felt really nice to be in.

"Well, say something then?" asked Gary after I'd been silent for a while and I dragged my mind back, "Is it nice – are you enjoying yourself?"

"Oh sorry Gary, I was just letting myself wander," I said, "Now I'm inside you it almost feels like a warm pussy – it actually feels pretty good!"

"Mmmmmm," grunted Gary, "Only 'pretty' good – have to do something about that!"

As he spoke his arsehole began to squeeze at my cock; internal muscles rippling up and down my length; Gary's hips rotating to change the angle of insertion; his hands now behind himself pulling my hips towards him to drive my cock ever deeper.

"Yeahhhhh," I groaned, the feelings now re-energising my cock, "That feels better now; feels nice – really good now."

For a while I just worked away, pumping my cock into Gary's arsehole time after time; the only sounds being the slap of flesh; our breathing, which was becoming faster and faster and the occasional murmurs of encouragement from Gary. My legs were starting to tremble but that was a minor problem – well and truly overruled by my cock which was now threatening to explode.

"Ooh fuck," I grunted, "Yeah, yeah, getting there, I'm getting there!"

"Make sure you cum inside me," said Gary suddenly, concentrating my mind on my cock and answering a query that I'd been about to ask.

"You sure?" I asked anyway and Gary nodded strongly.

"Mmmmm, definitely Chris – you make sure you're inside me when you cum!" he said, "I want to feel that big cock of yours empty itself – gonna feel really good!"

I got back to work, driving my penis in and out faster and harder until Gary began moaning again.

"Cor fuck Chris, you're getting right up me, aren't you?" he said, "Fuckin' deep!"

Certainly I was buried to the roots as I pushed in to him, my entire penis within his body. I'd long since found his prostate and rubbed my penis against it but now I wanted complete insertion, for all the world as if I was trying to empty my spunk deep into a woman's womb. Still I powered on until I passed that moment when nerves reach their apex; when nothing you can do will stop the escalation of events.

"I'm gonna cum Gary," I said, feeling things building nicely in my groin, "Won't be long!"

"Good, good Chris – let it cum!" said Gary, his anus squeezing me even tighter, "Fill me up, please!"

A last rapid burst of powerful thrusts and that was it – I was definitely cumming, like it or not!

"Ahhhhh, ahhhhh, yeahhhhh!" I cried, "Uuuuuhhh yeahhhhh!"

I felt the first volley squeeze from my little hole and spray out into his bowels before pooling back around my cock. A second volley did the same as I pulled Gary's body as close to mine as I could; the pleasure of release overpowering any unusual thoughts of whom I was fucking or what I was doing.

"Ahhh, I can feel you!" gasped Gary, his anus squeezing me firmly.

"Yeahhhhh! Oooooh yeahhhhh!" I groaned as my final burst of spunk emptied itself from my body and entered his, before I found myself leaning against his back, my breathing deep and quick as I recovered.

"Wow – that was excellent Chris," said Gary, as he looked back over his shoulder, "Not bad for a first time!"

Yeah, it was, wasn't it? My first gay fuck; my first real trip into that 'other' world; my first proper experience of same sex interaction – and I'd really enjoyed it! Gary moved and allowed my penis to slide slowly from his anus while he covered his hole with some toilet tissue. He turned and looked at me.

"Wasn't that bad, was it?" he asked, and I found myself smiling at him.

"No, it was great," I said, "Got a load of my chest, so to speak – feel better now."

He wrapped his arm around me and pulled me in for another kiss – one that I didn't recoil from, an action that now felt quite enjoyable.

"I'm glad – I liked it too. Come on, let's get a quick shower before Don locks up," said Gary and wrapping our towels around us we trotted off down the corridor to the showers, which were still illuminated and therefore would still be working.

Soon we were soaping away the evidence of our tryst, our light chatter in line with our buoyant mood and before long we were pulling on our clothes and gathering our things and heading out of the gym with a last wave goodbye to Don.

Once out in the car park the thought came back to me. Gary was apparently having a dinner date with Karen tonight so while I may have enjoyed his body he was now going to enjoy hers. Somehow I felt left out – but I wasn't sure now who I wanted... but it didn't seem fair that Gary should be getting his kicks at both ends, so to speak.

My 'good night' to Gary was quite muted, a low-key adieu that was quite unlike our exuberant fucking. A sense of irritation had quickly fallen over me; a mood that clung to me as I reclined alone on my bed that night.

But despite my gloomy mood my cock still needed emptying again; the memories of our fuck were still strong in my sub-consciousness. I found myself taking my cock in hand urgently that night, my penis quickly rising to my caresses.

I turned on my laptop and instead of my usual pornographic fare I brought up some hot gay porn clips that thrilled me for the first time. Steadily I rubbed my penis as I watched the unfamiliar scenes unfold and I was almost taken aback when my cock erupted exceptionally quickly and with some considerable force.

Shaken somehow, I lay back, my urgent need now sated, but underneath there was a deeper need; a need to enjoy more of that incredible arse fucking; more of that exciting male to male action. I even found myself wondering how it would feel to be on the receiving end...

Languidly I lay there as I headed towards sleep. It would be nice to have a good regular bed partner, I decided; perhaps it was time to settle down once more. Simply a good regular fuck would be excellent, to be honest, although a nice bit of loving wouldn't come amiss as well.

And with those thoughts sleep overcame me and the next thing I knew it was daylight once again and time for work.

I looked at my agenda for the week as I breakfasted and noted that I'd be working at the home of one of my pop star customers just a few doors away from Karen's place once again and I immediately wondered if I'd find time to drop in. The very thought buoyed me for the morning and time flew by and suddenly it was lunchtime – time to grab a few minutes and to see if Karen was around.

I left my truck where it was and light-heartedly I walked down the road and turned into her driveway, mindlessly looking at her plants as I strolled along, only to be suddenly struck by the sight of a brightly shiny sports car in her drive. It wasn't hers unless she'd managed to upgrade hers and that was soon confirmed as her front door opened and Karen and a man emerged, Karen more or less draped over him, looking utterly dishevelled and wearing very little indeed!

I froze and quickly did my best to blend into the foliage of a large bush as I watched her fawning over him, kissing and feeling him and seemingly imploring him not to leave, but with a final lingering kiss he climbed into his car and drove off – her horseshoe-shaped drive meaning that he didn't have to pass me on the way out.

"See you tonight sweetheart!" she called out as the guy in the car waved back at her.

I waited until Karen had disappeared before slinking off, my tail now decidedly between my legs, then I retired back to my wagon to while away my lonely lunch break.

I spent the afternoon working hard and musing about Karen as I did so. Was she playing the field; were we merely pawns in her world, toys to be used and discarded? Were we nothing more to her than a good fuck and some company, to be offered nothing more concrete? It certainly looked like it unless I'd got things wrong.

The day flew past and I vented my anger on my work then returned home tired and exhausted, to crash out almost as soon as I'd showered and eaten.

The following day was another busy one – and profitable, I might add and eventually I returned home, found myself something to eat; changed into something more comfortable and a bit less dirty and pondered on what to do next.

As usual the gym called on my conscience; I'd missed several sessions and I really needed more exercise to keep in good shape, so changing into running shorts and a singlet and grabbing my kitbag I headed out, arriving at the gym some fifteen minutes later. Instantly I recognised Gary's car in the car park and a thrill of excitement shook me, a thrill that gathered and focussed in my groin, causing my cock to lurch. I shook my head as I realised what I was thinking about.

"You can cut that out!" I said to myself, "What the fuck are you thinking of?"

Yeah, I'd been thinking of Gary's cock – or maybe his arse! My subconscious had instantly made the connection between Gary's car, his presence... and his cock. I found myself chuckling as I realised how easily my sex organs could lead me astray.

Ten minutes later and I was jogging on the treadmill alongside Gary, exchanging pleasantries and small-talk until finally we both stopped for a breather.

"So how did the other night go?" I eventually asked, knowing immediately by the look on Gary's face that it hadn't gone as planned.

"Bloody woman," he said, "She invited me in and gave me a drink but she said she had to cancel her dinner date because her mother was due down for a visit. I mean, surely she knew her mother was coming, so why didn't she cancel beforehand?"

"Ah, tough mate," I empathised before realising that I was actually delighted.

"So you didn't, ummm, get your end away then?" I added crudely.

"No way," replied Gary, "Got a kiss and a cuddle and that was it – complete waste of a night."

It seemed appropriate to show my hand at this moment.

"You're not going to like this, but I'm pretty certain she cancelled because she had someone else over for the night," I said and as I explained about my visit at lunchtime, Gary's face looked as if it would explode.

"The fucking lying bitch!" he blasted, "The two-faced fucking cow!"

It was just as well that Karen wasn't in the gym office that evening...

I didn't really want him creating a scene out in the main room so I guided him to the changing room. I could see that he wanted to punch the living daylights out of something or someone and I felt really sorry for him for some reason... but all I could do was to drape my arm over his shoulders and squeeze him against me.

"Worse things have happened," I said as I patted his shoulder, "Perhaps its better this way – if you'd found out after you'd become a pair then it would have been worse, wouldn't it?"

"Yeah, guess so," said Gary, now calming quickly and looking very dejected, "Bloody nuisance though, I booked seats for dinner on Friday night and I've paid a table deposit... very exclusive place. Oh fuck it."

His face drooped along with his shoulders – then he brightened somewhat.

"Suppose I ought to ring her anyway – just to see if you're right," he said, digging out his mobile from his pile of clothes.

I moved away to allow him some privacy, but the conversation was remarkably brief anyway.

"Ok – some other time then," I heard him say, then he put his phone down.

"Turned me down flat – and for Friday night," he said as he turned back towards me, "I think you're right – she sounded as if she already had company lined up for tonight as well."

He shook his head sadly and I really wanted to cuddle him, such was his distress.

"Bloody waste of planning and money and effort," he moaned, "Unless... no."

"What?" I asked, curious to know what he was thinking.

"Unless you'd like to come along instead?" he blurted out, his eyes lowering.

"Eh?" I replied, somewhat taken aback by the idea, "Hah, I suppose that depends on where you were going."

Gary named a very well-known and extremely smart restaurant; one at which only the well-heeled and relatively wealthy dined; a restaurant whose menu was well coveted by many and whose reservation list was even longer than the menu.

"Wow – that's a bit posh! Guess I could keep you company if you like," I replied, thinking solely of the kudos of being seen in such a place, "Nice of you to ask."

"Well I guess you're my best friend," he said, "So if she's not going to be interested then who else would I ask? I'm probably a bit short of time to find another suitable female."

Then Gary's face broke into a smile at last. "Besides, I like eating at that place and I'm not going to waste that booking."

Friday came and dolled up in my finest suit, I met Gary at the gym. Not only was it a handy meeting place but being members, we could park there free and we could easily walk the rest of the way to the restaurant. Gary too was looking his best; all complete with tuxedo – something I didn't even possess!

"Hey man – you look hot!" I exclaimed, putting on an appropriate accent and Gary laughed happily.

"You don't look too shabby yourself," he returned, his hand smoothing down my lapel, "Best I've ever seen you – dressed, that is!"

We both laughed and bantered lightly as we set out on the short walk.

Something like two hours later and we were sitting back replete and watching the show that accompanied Friday evening diners; a steady diet of beautifully plumed and attired exotic dancers, both male and female. But despite the overt sexuality of the show it was done so tastefully that it was captivating and lovely to watch, serving only to titivate appetites for whatever might follow dinner, once the diners returned home. And certainly, both Gary and I felt that way after our evening out; really highly aroused and both seemingly eager to find some sexual partners.

Gary stood up at the end of the evening and pulled some of the creases and folds out of his clothes and as I looked at him it was clear that his penis was at least partially aroused – an observation that reminded me that mine too was quite considerably stiffened. We'd enjoyed an amazing evening full of chatter and laughter along with the floor show and it had been an enjoyable, sexy and wonderful experience, enough to arouse anyone.

We said little as we left the restaurant however and together we walked back towards the gym car park, almost in silence, until Gary suddenly stopped and turned to me.

"I don't mean this to sound the way it does," he said, looking quite coy, "But do you fancy coming back to my place for a while? Have a few drinks and you could even stay over if you like?"

"Yeah, what a great idea – that's nice of you," I replied, "How could I say no? Anyway, it's much too early to shut down, isn't it?"

"Cheers Chris," said Gary, "It'll be nice to have a bit of company – even if you're not quite the same shape I was expecting!"

I aimed a light punch at him as we laughed together, then began happy play-fighting as we ambled along.

"I'll be better company than that two-timing piece of shit," I said, laughing loudly as I dodged his arms, "And I promise I'll be faithful!"

I stuck my tongue out at him as we larked around like a couple of kids, wrestling, play-fighting and joking as we walked on.

The banter continued until we reached our cars and I followed Gary out of the car park and headed off to his place, which turned out to be a couple of miles out of town; a substantial three- or four-bedroom detached house. My eyes naturally swept over his garden, which definitely needed some attention and then over his house, which looked in far better shape.

Soon we were entering into a spatial entrance hall then Gary ushered me into his lounge, a generous L-shaped room, all complete with patio doors and a large fireplace. It looked cosy and yet airy; inviting and welcoming and I immediately felt at home – not that I'd felt the least bit tensed up anyway.

The last glow of the late evening dusk applied a warm hue to the room that made it almost erotic in it's appeal.

"Lovely room," I commented, "Love the décor; the aspect – look at the way those bay windows capture the light – brilliant!"

"Always been my favourite room," said Gary as he stood looking down the garden, "Apart from my bedroom, of course!"

We chuckled together light-heartedly, but I could feel there was still an air of sexual excitement between us, which Gary unintentionally defused by asking about drinks. We both chose Southern Comfort on ice which Gary poured with a generous hand before we both plonked ourselves down on the big settee, both seemingly perhaps looking for an opening – perhaps to discuss the assorted sexual activity at the gym, I wondered. All kinds of questions flitted through my brain – I had no idea what would happen were I to broach any of them but somehow the subject needed discussing.

We bantered for a while on many a subject until there was a moment of silence, then...

"Chris, did you mean..."

"Gary, did you really..."

We both spoke at once, suddenly and almost explosively, such was the tension that our words released.

We stopped and laughed at each other, before high-fiving with one hand each and waving the other to speak first – and Gary got the go-ahead.

"I was going to ask if you meant what you said," Gary said, his hands sliding up and down his thighs as if to wipe the sweat off his palms, "Do you remember when we showered together and you tossed me off and asked me if I'd cum for you?"

I nodded, remembering the conversation clearly, remembering the action even more clearly as I'd offered to 'do anything' for him.

"You wouldn't do it again, would you," asked Gary, breathlessly, "You were great last time..."

Suddenly I found myself laughing because the same topic had been on my lips.

"You know what Gary," I replied, "I was about to ask you if you'd really enjoyed what we did – and now you've more or less answered my question."

"Why, were you interested?" asked Gary, his words quick and eager, "Was it because you enjoyed doing it?"

I found myself nodding again, knowing somehow that this moment signalled the start of something new; perhaps something more than 'just' a bit of sex.

"Yeah," I breathed, feeling things stirring down below, "Yeah, I wanted to do it again – and more, I think."

"Really – you're interested in doing other things too?" asked Gary, his eyes wide open, "I thought that perhaps that when you did that it was a one-off, just to release the pressure, so to speak."

"No – I enjoyed you wanking me and doing 'that other thing' too," I said, now knowing that my cock was at full stretch but still unable to say the real words, "And since we're lacking a woman – perhaps we can find other ways to make ourselves feel better as well..."

I just couldn't say the proper words; the words I really wanted to say – like suck and fuck and cock. Much as I wanted to be able to do so, they just wouldn't come out...

In all truthfulness I was quivering inside with pent up excitement at the thought of enjoying Gary's body and of him enjoying mine too – I so much wanted things to develop and to carry on that I almost felt sick inside. I was like a love-lost youth; ham-fisted and word-shy!

I turned towards Gary and put down my brandy glass, my hands now reaching out towards him. Gary slid down the settee towards me and suddenly we were in each other's arms, our mouths locking together, our tongues twisting and turning together wetly and excitedly.

My hands fell to Gary's lap and I immediately encountered his erection – a solid length of muscle down his trouser leg. I scrabbled around until I found his zip which I dragged down as quickly as I could, my hand sliding inside his underpants and soon finding his penis, his warm, stiff, throbbing penis, which I pulled out into the open air.

"Oooh Chris – yessss, do that, play with him for me," moaned Gary, thrusting his cock up through my fist, "God – I need that!"

As he spoke and as I explored, so did Gary's hands, his nimble fingers quickly undoing my belt and trousers before working my trousers and underpants down, right down to my ankles.

Immediately his hands were there, grasping my penis, sliding my foreskin back, squeezing and fondling my cock until I had to stop him.

He stood up, panting heavily.

"Come on – let's go to the bedroom," he said, and I followed him as he led the way, "Let's get undressed properly."

I joined him and pulling up my trousers again I wordlessly followed him upstairs, the pair of us both taking two steps at a time in our haste. In the big spacious bedroom, I tore off my clothes and stood there, my cock quivering with excitement and desire as Gary did the same, before flinging himself down onto the bed, his hands outstretched.

"Come on Chris, come here and join me!" he said.

Hardly hearing the words, I climbed onto the bed beside him and we rolled together, our mouths once again melding tightly, our slippery kisses sending waves of pleasure all through my body. I could feel Gary's cock pressing stiffly against my abdomen and I reached down to hold it, the tip now slippery with warm precum as I slid my thumbs over it, my own erection sliding against my hand as I played around.

Gary sucked in a quick breath as I thrilled him, his whole body shuddering with excitement.

His hands moved around me, one under and the other over me to hold and massage my buttocks, squeezing them together and pulling them apart, each movement bringing his fingers that little bit closer to my anus. My own breath was quivering as I felt him explore my bottom while I explored his penis until he pushed us apart.

"I don't want you to wank me, I want to suck you instead," said Gary as he scrambled onto his knees and pushed me down onto my back and as he spoke his own hands found and held my rampant penis.

"You will let me suck you, won't you? Please let me suck you, please?" asked Gary and I nodded, too far removed from reality to be able to form words.

Gary moved around and I watched as his head dipped steadily towards my groin where his hands now held my cock upright for his mouth.

There was a moment when I thought he'd licked me but it was just his fingers sliding over my now exposed knob – and then there it was; that moment of contact as his wet tongue found my sensitive flesh.

"Ooooh fuck," I moaned, sucking in a tight breath, "Noooooo, ohhhh god!"

"What's the matter?" asked Gary, lifting his head.

"Nothing – I've never been sucked before... well, not by a bloke," I said, "It just shocked me."

"Nothing odd about my mouth!" said Gary, "Just wait until I get going!"

Oh yes, I was prepared to wait for that; it had just been unexpected to be sucked, but even that first little touch was lovely, and no way was I going to complain now.

"Yessss, get going Gary, give me some more!" I cried happily, my hips pushing my erection back towards his face, "Suck me off!"

"Mmmmmmm, going to," came the reply from Gary, his mouth now firmly closed around my cock, "Mmmmm, you taste delicious!"

The position Gary was in meant that he was kneeling near my chest and was bent down towards my legs and so my arm almost naturally slid between his legs to allow my hand to hold and caress his muscular thighs. I worked my hand up and down until suddenly I felt my hand brush against some hanging meat.

I explored – and soon found a large pair of balls and then his erect penis which I grasped firmly. I felt down the length of his cock until I was able to pull back his foreskin to uncover his still-slippery knob then I moved away and cupped his balls, the hairy pair filling my hand completely as I felt the spongy sacs inside. I followed their root back up until I found his cock once more and then settled into contentedly rubbing up and down his penis as Gary worked away on my cock with his mouth.

Now that we'd broken the ice, we seemed to have lost our original huge sense of urgency and now we were both content to simply explore and enjoy each other and time slowed down to a crawl. I felt content and relaxed even as my penis quivered under his touch and I felt Gary's cock ooze precum copiously. Despite my contented feeling I wanted more and just as I was about to raise the subject when Gary stopped his sucking and licking, and I paused my exploration.

It was time things moved along...

Gary lifted his head and looked up at me, my moistened instrument in his hands now.

"Chris," he said, "You know you fucked me in the toilet the other week – could you do it again? I've got some lube here – please, I'd like you to... it was so damned good to feel you inside me."

I think that the way my cock jumped told Gary that I would agree.

Taking control Gary now knelt up and reached for the little tube which he'd located in moments and now he applied some of the lube to his arsehole, before bringing a blob of the stuff to my cock. His hand smeared it over my length – then he got on his hands and knees on the bed and beckoned me into place.

"Come on Chris, please, fuck me," he asked as he wiggled his arse at me, "Come and put him in me!"

Well and truly aroused by Gary's expert mouth work I was up and into position in moments, my slippery dick held out to line up with his equally slippery hole.

"Just push him in," said Gary as his hands stretched his cheeks apart, "Not hard though – be gentle to start."

Kneeling behind him I moved my hips forward and my cock touched his hole, the puckered flesh stretching as my tip sank in slightly. I moved him away as I adjusted my knees before bringing my cock back into place. And now I pushed a little harder, hearing Gary breathe deeply as my knob began to disappear inside his body. His whole anus moved inwards with pressure at first, until it allowed my cock to enter his body, upon which his flesh recoiled as if to absorb my length.

There's a special feel to entering into a person's anus – firstly the stretching of the anal entry itself, then the easing of the sphincter muscles; then the comfortable sliding, penetrating feeling as all obstacles are cleared. But before penetration is complete there are what feel like several rings of muscles to pass, multiple gaskets that lead to the main cavity. And it's as you penetrate that last barrier that the pain peaks and then the pleasure starts...

We'd now reached that point – and Gary cried out briefly before uttering a long sigh of contentment as my penis began to slide inside.

"Ooooh that's better," he said, his arse squirming slightly, "It's lovely once you're inside!"

147

"Mmmmmm," I responded, it being my turn to be speechless, "Mmmmmm!"

Gently I moved my penis in and out then I applied another blob of gel to the ring of his arsehole and my cock seemed to slide in and out that much more easily. Inside, Gary was warm and moist and I could feel his prostate gland against my knob as I slid past it; his internal muscles now pulsating and squeezing around my cock; his anus tight around my shaft as I began to fuck him properly.

"That's it, like that," said Gary, "Ohhhh lovely – keep doing that Chris."

And so I did – my penis happily enjoying the feelings surrounding it as I slowly worked myself up towards my orgasm, until I realised that Gary's cock was being left out.

I reached underneath him and soon found my target; his gloriously stiff and slippery lengthy cock, perfect to hold and rub in time with my thrusts. His knob was almost dripping with precum which I spread all over his penis as I stroked it.

"How's it going?" I asked and Gary moaned his reply.

"Wonderful Chris, just wonderful – you feel so good," he said, his hips writhing beneath me, "Oh god – Karen would never have been able to do this for me!"

I laughed, realising that Gary had originally been expecting to take her out; to take her home afterwards to fuck – and instead it was he who was being fucked! And I'd more or less given up on the chase for Karen and hadn't expected anything to be happening – and yet here was I having a damn good fuck too!

Gary's laughter had caused his arsehole to flutter around my cock and the extra sensations were sending me ever closer to my orgasm now I realised, so I slowed down.

"I'm getting close," I told him, "What do you want me to do?"

"Don't cum Chris, save it for a bit," said Gary, "Let's stop for a moment."

As he spoke, he pulled his hips from my clutches and my cock slid easily from his hole, bouncing upwards against my abdomen.

"Hey – that's not fair!" I cried, "I was getting all ready!"

Gary and I were now kneeling on the bed, face to face, cock to slippery cock and Gary reached down and took hold of my shivering length.

"You're getting all excited, are you?" he asked, his tongue licking his lips, his eyes sparkling, "Nearly there, eh?"

He smiled broadly as my answer consisted of a somewhat pained smile – I had indeed been about to cum and he'd stopped me in my tracks!

"I'll get you off, don't worry, but I want to play with your arsehole while you cum," Gary now said and I felt a shudder of fright and excitement pass through me as I nodded my approval.

"Go on then, take it easy – just your fingers," I said, unused to any activity around my arsehole, "Use some lube too."

"Course I will. Get on your hands and knees then," said Gary and like a lamb I turned and settled, my head on my hands on his pillow while Gary moved behind me and his hands descended onto my arse.

I felt the chill of the lube as he touched it to my flesh; the slight pressure as he pushed the tip of one finger inside me; the thrill of something illicit, exciting, new, frightening and wild happening.

Gary pushed a little more and I felt his finger slide easily through my sphincter muscles until he was obviously embedded up to the knuckle inside me. It was weird, perverted, kinky and strange and yet his actions excited me beyond all normal levels as I felt his finger moving around inside my body.

He pushed his finger in and out a few times before he pulled it out. Then suddenly there was a little more pressure and I realised that Gary was now using two fingers inside me – but they'd been able to penetrate my hole without a problem – so what was I worrying about?

But Gary spoke for me, asking me to air my concerns and feelings.

"How're you going? Feels odd, does it?" he asked and I wondered what to say.

"Fine really," I replied, "I'll agree that it's a bit strange but it's not really painful and actually it's starting to feel pretty good, that's all."

"That's great, ok, I'm going to push a bit deeper now," said Gary and I felt his fingers probing around inside me, suddenly discovering my prostate in the process.

His other hand came around me and grasped my cock and with just a few wanks it was leaking precum generously; his other fingers now massaging me internally. I was getting closer and closer!

"You still ok?" came Gary's voice.

"Yeah, fine, I think," I said, still not entirely comfy with his slippery fingers.

"Can I try stretching you a little bit more?" asked Gary, "Don't worry – I'll use some more lube!"

I laughed a bit uncomfortably but when Gary pulled his fingers from my hole I felt that I was missing something, something I was already coming to enjoy. But moments later and he was back, his fingers now feeling larger again – I felt myself relax my breath as the feelings returned.

'That's three fingers,' I thought to myself, wincing softly, 'Phew – that's a stretch!'

"Careful!" I called out softly although the pain wasn't all THAT bad.

Gary seemed to be stretching me quite considerably now – not to the point of painfulness but definitely stretching beyond anything normal then he held still to allow me to become more accustomed to the pressure.

"I'm being gentle," Gary breathed from behind me, "You still ok?"

Instead of answering, my mind was now focussed on his hand which was working harder and faster on my cock, working me off, bringing me ever closer to cumming; taking my mind off the other pain; transferring my feelings temporarily.

Then, as my mind became distracted, he pushed a bit more and as a final sharp feeling inside me brought me back to reality, the tension in my arse suddenly eased off and now I realised that I felt very full – and yet it felt amazing! But my thoughts were dragged back to my cock as Gary's hands was working harder and faster – then I felt myself spasm and shudder as my orgasm arrived.

"Ooooh Gary – I'm cumming! Cumming!" I cried, "Gonna cum Gary – gonna cum!"

And as I erupted, so Gary pushed at my arse – and suddenly I understood that what was inside me wasn't his fingers – it was his cock!

But I was so engrossed in my own orgasm that I hardly cared; instead I was pumping jet after jet of cum way up the bed, splattering over his pillows and his headboard as I came like never before!

Then suddenly reality returned, along with the sudden feeling of wiry pubes rubbing against my buttocks!

"Gary – you've got your fucking cock up my arse!" I said, frozen and stiff, not really knowing what to do next, "What the fuck?"

"You liked one finger; then you enjoyed two and three fingers and you needed something larger!" he said, "I knew you'd enjoy my cock!"

"But, but..." I stuttered, my frozen arse quivering around his cock, "You're fucking me!"

"So? You've fucked me!" he replied, his penis now starting to slide in and out of my hole again, "Aren't you enjoying it?"

151

"Yeah, I am – I mean, no, oh fuck – I don't know what I mean!" I replied, my mind unable to form suitable words as my arsehole slowly absorbed the immensity of our situation.

"Put it this way – did you enjoy your orgasm?" asked Gary and I had to nod my approval.

"See – you came off better when I was inside you, didn't you?" he continued, his penis slowly moving in and out of my hole, "You're enjoying it, aren't you?"

"Yeah, I can't help it," I moaned, "You're just doing something inside me... it's wonderful..."

And now his penis was indeed doing something wonderful – it was arousing me once more as it slid steadily into my anus and then out again until just his knob was still inside me. But it wasn't nasty now – instead it felt exciting and stimulating and wildly erotic and it was starting to feel as if it was something I couldn't do without.

I felt myself unintentionally pushing back at his driving cock; helping him to penetrate me deeper and more easily. I was shaking and shivering with excitement as the newly-found feelings sent my brain into orbit and my cock skywards once more as I felt another orgasm beginning to form...

"Ohhhh Gary, you're gonna make me cum again," I moaned, my hips pushing and moving lewdly as his cock penetrated me, "You keep doing that and I think you'll make me cum!"

"What – again? Already? Do you want me to keep going?" asked Gary, his penis now moving faster, "You want to cum again, do you? Do you think you can?"

"Yeah – yeah!" I moaned, "Ohhh fucking right I can!"

"I'll make sure you get off," said Gary and moments later his hand was around my shaft with his thumb playing in the small stream of oozing precum which blended with the remains of my recent eruption.

"You're so stiff already!" he said, "Feel so hard and hot – just like your arse is so hot and tight! Oooooh yes, you're gonna cum very soon, aren't you?"

I felt his fingers sliding in some remnants of my last orgasm, some of my spunk, that made his actions feel even more exciting.

"Yeahhhhh, definitely – any minute now," I cried, "Yeah, do that – fuck me, rub me – ooooh fuuuuuck – do me!"

It was all action now – Gary's hand was sliding quickly up and down my spunk-slick penis while his cock slid equally quickly in and out of my arsehole. On my part I was panting hard, quivering with pent-up desire and shaking with unknown feelings. It wasn't just that I was about to cum for the second time in ten minutes – not an entirely unknown event – but it was that I was going to do so at the bidding of his penis as it stimulated me from the inside.

"Here it cums!" I cried, "It's cumming!"

"Let it go then!" said Gary, his hips now driving his cock into me even faster and harder; his hand working fast, "Let it cum!"

I froze and bellowed and erupted – my anus squeezing tightly around Gary's penis; my cock driving hard through his fist as the first of my sprays of cum erupted, splattering more white stickiness onto the already wetted bed spread and pillow.

"Ooooh fuck!" I cried, panting heavily, "Oh god – that was hot!"

"Oooh fuck – and this'll make you even hotter," moaned Gary as his thrusting came faster than ever, "Here I cum – ooooh fuck – yeahhhhhh! Yeahhhh!"

With his sudden cries I came back to reality and immediately and shockingly realised that Gary was cumming; his spunk squirting from his cock up inside my welcoming cavity; his warm sperm flooding out and sending waves of comforting and unexpected pleasure through the depths of my bowels; the pleasure compounded as Gary's penis lodged itself deep within me and stayed there, jerking slowly as it unloaded.

I just didn't know what to feel – revulsion, delight, shock or pleasure but as my mind strove to get round all the sensations I finally realised that I'd loved it – the pressure, the fullness, the way he thrust into me... and now the way he'd squirted hot spunk into my depths.

"Bloody hell, that was excellent!" said Gary, his slowly softening penis now beginning to slide from me, "That was so good – your arse felt as if it was just made for me!"

"I can't understand how good it felt either," I replied, "God – it was strange and yet when you came off, I just wanted you to keep cumming and cumming! I couldn't get enough of you!"

"There's plenty more where that came from," quipped Gary as his penis slid from my hole, "Bit later though – we need some time to recover I think."

He rolled sideways from me and collapsed onto the bed on his back, then he looked at me, still on my hands and knees. His face was all smiles and happiness beyond the sweat and exhaustion; I guess he felt and looked very much like I did...

Gary's arms reached up to me and I edged across the bed and gently eased myself down on top of him, our hot steaming bodies melding together comfortably, our lips soon joining together as we kissed.

"Mmmmmm," we both moaned, and I felt Gary's cock stiffening once more against my abdomen.

I squirmed around to enjoy the feeling of his hardening length rubbing over my body, soon finding that my own cock was also becoming harder. But I needed a rest before I performed again – the body might be willing, but my balls were empty!

Eventually we parted and sat up, both of us still smiling and giggling at the other like a pair of childish girls as the reality of what we'd just done sank in.

"Come on – let's get a drink," said Gary sensibly at last, "Come back down to the lounge for a while."

Together, without bothering to get dressed, we went downstairs and I settled once more on his settee as he made us some drinks and then came and joined me.

"Quite a night," said Gary as he sipped his Southern Comfort, "Not exactly what I expected but I'm not complaining!"

"Nor me," I replied, the ice rattling in my glass, "Certainly wasn't – but it was fun."

"You enjoyed it, did you?" asked Gary and I nodded happily.

"Feel empty now though," I said, my arse squirming, "Feels odd without your cock up there!"

Gary's eyebrows lifted as did his smile.

"Can't do without me, eh?" he quipped, "We'll have to see about that."

He ran his hand down his penis, his already rising and eager penis. He slid back his foreskin to reveal his lovely purpled plum-sized knob atop his lengthy and thick shaft.

"He's all yours," said Gary, "And I mean that."

"Eh?" I replied, wondering exactly what he meant.

"You and I could stick together," said Gary, "Partners, friends... good friends perhaps... I could make you happy and your cock would suit me just fine..."

"What – you mean like lovers?" I asked, wondering if I was hearing things right and Gary nodded and smiled.

"Yeah – lovers, if you prefer it that way," he said as he reached and stroked my own rising penis, "Be good if we could try it and if we get on then..."

My cock obviously knew what it preferred and what it wanted and now stood up once more, jerking steadily as it rose to full hardness. Gary's penis had been hard for a while and I reached out to hold it. A long trickle of precum oozed down and over my hand as I held him, before I slid my hand back up his shaft to spread the slippery fluid everywhere.

Gary moaned softly and edged himself closer to me so that he too could hold my cock – the pair of us now gently pleasing the other's rampant, recovering, eager penis.

He leaned towards me and our mouths reached out to each other and suddenly we were into a really tight embrace; our bodies had squirmed around until our chests were rubbing together while our lips meshed and slid and tasted each other.

"Ooooh Chris," moaned Gary, moving away for a moment or two, "I love you, I do!"

"Love you too!" I replied, the words coming so easily now, "Love you Gary!"

We slid together like a pair of mating slugs wrapping around each other in their lust until I pushed Gary away a little.

"What's going to happen about Karen?" I asked, "Are you still after her?"

Gary raised his eyebrows high and sighed.

"You're joking Chris – after all she put us through – wouldn't touch her with... with a plastic dick, never mind with mine!" he said, "She's history. What about you though – thought you were interested as well?"

"Same thoughts now," I replied, quite happy to admit that I'd gone off her, "I want someone who'll stick by me, who'll be true and honest and who I can love, not a two-timing bitch."

"Will I do?" asked Gary coquettishly and I reached out my hands to him.

"I've a funny feeling that you might!" I answered with a huge grin.

Gary smiled, grasped my hands and stood up, pulling me to him.

"Perfect! Back to bed then," he said, turning to lead the way, "I want some more of you!"

His actions pulled me up against his back as we wriggled around and my erection slid between his cheeks, Gary helping him to slide in by spreading his buttocks apart.

"Yes Chris – that's what I want – your cock!" he said, squirming his arse around on my cock, "I want you inside me – quick!"

We almost sprinted up the stairs and into the bedroom; Gary stripping the wetted covers off the bed and diving onto it, his penis now standing proudly above him. I too leapt onto the bed and moments later I was beside him, the pair of us rolling together to kiss, caress and fondle each other's bodies, our two cocks rubbing hard and eagerly against each other.

"Stay there," said Gary, "I want to ride you – let me get the KY first though."

Moments later and he was squeezing gel onto my extremely hard penis, my full length rearing above my body while he held and anointed it as I lay on the bed.

"Ok – can I come aboard?" he asked as he straddled me and rubbed the remainder of the gel over his hole, "This is going to feel so good!"

I was shaking with excitement and fear in equal quantities as Gary gripped my penis and guided it to his target. I felt the pressure of his flesh against my tip as Gary slowly lowered himself downwards, Gary's mouth now held open as he let the pressure build up.

Then suddenly he sucked in a breath as his hole stretched to accommodate me.

"Aaahhhh – oooohhh," he grunted, "Big! Stretching me... ooooh fuck! Ahhh yesssss, that's getting better now."

I felt his body falling towards me, my penis now sliding smoothly into its home; the warm, slippery tight space that Gary was providing for my cock. It felt sublime to have the warmth and tightness of his arsehole surround my cock, massaging and stimulating me as Gary's hips moved and swayed above me.

"Is that nice?" he asked and I hummed my approval, my eyes shut.

He moved up and down a bit, pumping my cock into his hole until I joined in and began using my hips too.

"Better..." he said dreamily, "That's good, keep doing that!"

The pair of us were now both involved, both of us working to enjoy this fuck; our bodies actively moving together; my hips pushing upwards while Gary's arsehole was busy squeezing and sucking at my cock, steadily bringing me to a climax. Facing me, Gary's cock was hard and erect and bouncing up and down – I reached up and took hold of him, feeling the slipperiness of his precum on his knob. I held him as I spread the lubricant around, then began to slide his foreskin up and down his lengthy tool, just loving the firm yet soft feel of his instrument.

Busy together we fucked on and on until I heard Gary grunting.

"Keep doing that Chris – you'll make me cum," he grunted, "Every time your cock goes up inside me and every time you rub me I'm getting a bit closer – and closer."

I began thrusting my hips faster, driving my rigid penis deep into Gary's body while continuing to rub his erection, his glowing knob jutting over my body as I did so.

"Come on then, cum if you want to," I said, "Let it go when you're ready."

"I want you to cum too," said Gary, his buttocks crashing down onto my hips, driving his cock ever deeper into his hole, "Please cum with me!"

I stilled my hand on his cock as I concentrated on my own penis. I wasn't all that far from an orgasm but I needed to concentrate first; to get closer...

And then I felt that 'something'; that feeling that you've passed a tipping point, a trigger point that sets off your orgasm – suddenly it was I who had to hold back.

Gary realised my situation and urged me on...

"You ready?" he asked, knowing that I was, "Come on then – let's do it together!"

"Yesss, yessss!" I muttered as I powered my cock into him, now feeling those tingles of an imminent eruption stirring, "I'm just about there now – come on Gary – cum for me!"

My hand was working quickly on his erection and now I felt his cock stiffening even more and swelling in my fist as Gary groaned and stiffened.

His hole tightened around my cock, sending thrills to my balls – which immediately responded. Sudden muscular contractions in my groin powered a heavy bolt of cum up my penis and into Gary's rectum just as I saw his little hole open and eject a long streamer of white spunk, straight at my face!

And with my mouth open as I released lungfuls of air as my orgasm hit me, so Gary's spunk splattered wetly and stickily across my face, anointing my lips and wetting my tongue.

"Oooooh!" I found myself crying, "Ooooh fuck – yeahhhhh!"

Quickly my mouth opened wider and my head lifted to be closer to Gary's penis – a penis that was now ejecting another gusher of cum. With both eyes focussed on his penis I caught his cum almost perfectly, his generous offering splashing deep into my mouth!

I swallowed immediately, finding myself loving the texture and taste of his sperm in my throat; then quickly opening my mouth in case there was any more! And there was – Gary produced two more eruptions, one of which I caught, this time to savour in my mouth before swallowing.

And in the meanwhile, my cock and balls hadn't been idle – I'd pumped at least four bolts of cum into Gary's interior, each squirt causing Gary's eyes to flash open anew, before the warm cum gathered around my cock inside his anus.

Eventually I let go of the slowly softening penis before me, my arms falling to the bed, my hips also now quiescent beneath Gary.

Gary in turn had slumped, still breathing hard and fast, but at last his hips too were stilled as my cum soaked into his cavity, as my own penis gradually deflated.

We smiled at each other and our hands linked, our fingers interlocking contentedly.

"That was bloody fantastic!" said Gary, "I'd never have thought we could have done it again – incredible!"

"I'm knackered!" I replied, "Not use to all this excitement! But oh god – it was good, wasn't it?"

We laughed together and slowly disengaged until we were both lying back on the bed.

We rolled together and kissed again, gently at first and then more ardently, our rubbery almost prehensile tongues meeting and melding, our lips sliding wetly around, our love almost palpable.

Our post-cotial loving continued for a while until we parted, both of us now breathing more easily, both of us now comfortable together as we looked into each other's eyes.

I opened my mouth to speak but Gary got there first, so I let him...

"Chris, how do you feel about what we're doing?" he asked, hope sounding in his voice.

"It was... strange... weird at first," I said, "But I think I'm getting used to it and it's really been excellent tonight."

"Do you really think we could get on together?" he asked, causing my eyebrows to shoot upwards, even though we'd vaguely discussed this matter a little earlier.

"Ummmm, ummmm, I don't know," I said, still rather uncertain, "Might be fun to try!"

"It doesn't have to be in public, does it," continued Gary and once again my eyebrows shot up.

I hadn't thought of such ramifications...

"You do mean us as a pair?" I said, not entirely sure what to say next, "Like boyfriends?"

"Yeah!" said Gary, "Couldn't we?"

I returned to a subject we'd covered, but I wanted to check things out again.

"And Karen? She's definitely gone, isn't she," I suggested, because in my mind I knew that she was history, "Well, at least that's what you said a little while ago."

"Yeah, absolutely history," agreed Gary, "Just like you said, I'd much rather have someone I can trust. A real friend... like you."

He leaned forward and kissed me before pulling back again.

Suddenly it hit me – although just how I hadn't cottoned on much earlier I don't know. Suddenly I comprehended that Gary was suggesting a gay relationship with me – us two together as partners in love and in bed!

"Oh God – I dunno!" I replied, lost for words for a moment, "Ummmm yeah, I guess!"

"Really – honestly?" replied Gary, lifting up off the bed, "Do you mean it?"

"Guess we could give it a try," I proffered, searching for words, "It's certainly been good having sex with you – I mean it was good with Karen, it used to be good with girls but somehow this feels better and stronger."

"And safer – I won't two-time you or get pregnant!" said Gary with a laugh, "Say yes... please."

I pondered the matter for a few moments, but my mind was already made up.

"Of course!" I said, "Let's give it a go!"

"Oh Chris!" cried Gary as he flung himself on top of me, "I love you, you're wonderful!"

"And you," I replied quickly before Gary's mouth engulfed mine; before his body covered mine with his.

I felt his penis hardening against my abdomen and I knew that if I wanted him he'd be ready for me, just as I would be ready for him too.

This was going to be quite a partnership, I realised, two sex-hungry men in their prime. We'd find it hard to get any work done, but so what!

And so it came to pass. Gary and I remained, for now, as independent single men during the day but at night we'd both end up at the same house, in the same bed, as closely woven as threads of wool in a jumper.

Karen was simply ignored now but it was at the gym a few days later that we finally got our own back on her.

We'd both arrived for our work-out one evening, separately and a few minutes apart and we'd both begun our exercises when Karen appeared, her looks as perfect as ever; her dress as enticing and stylish as a model, her face wreathed with smiles for everyone around... until she saw Don.

Don was sitting in his office and remained there, despite his usually polite habit of standing to welcome visitors and one look at his face told us that trouble was brewing and that Karen was his target. Something was wrong – something deadly serious apparently.

We heard his terse "Come in – sit down Karen" and we froze, silently listening for the bombshell that seemed suddenly inevitable...

We saw Don thrust a pile of papers at her with another terse outburst.

"What's this?" he demanded, loudly enough for us all to hear and we saw Karen's pretty face crumple but there was no other response.

"Come on, explain yourself," Don continued yelling, "Before I phone the police."

A handkerchief appeared in Karen's hand, dabbing at her face as she spluttered to speak.

"I can explain everything..." she said unconvincingly, but Don now stood up, shook his head and held his hands up, palms outwards towards Karen.

"On second thoughts, don't bother, I've got all the information I need right here," he shouted, "So all I can say is GET OUT and don't come back! You're fired, as if I need tell you."

Karen slouched away, her head in her hands, her beautiful body defeated for once and we listened until the sound of her dragging heels died away down the corridor before Gary and I turned to each other.

"Phew – what was that all about?" said Gary and just as he spoke Don came out of his office, a cloud of paper in his wake.

"Fuckin' woman!" he said vehemently, "Tried to take me for a ride."

"What's up Don – come on, tell us the story," I found myself saying and Don obligingly joined us and the few others who'd gathered around.

"Said she was qualified; gave me a pile of references; tried to come over as little Miss Perfect, but she wasn't," he said, "They were all fake – she was kicked out of her last job for fraud but she was still trying it on, stupid cow!"

Don looked at us as we stared at him in something resembling shock, then he continued...

"And what's more, she's due in court on a charge of theft from an earlier employer," he said, "I reckon she's one of nature's mistakes."

He turned and stomped back toward his office.

"Oh well, better start hunting for another manager," he muttered as he pulled his door closed behind him.

The other observers headed back to their bits of equipment, leaving Gary and I alone together by the treadmills, both of us keenly looking at the other.

"Near miss?" asked Gary quizzically and I nodded.

"Yeah, I reckon we got lucky," I answered, "And we both got a good ride out of her!"

"And then we got even luckier," added Gary, "We discovered each other!"

"Wonder who he'll get in this time?" I asked but now I knew that things would be different.

No matter how pretty, how talented, how sexy Don's new manager would turn out to be I wouldn't be chasing her and nor would Gary. Gary was the man for me now and I knew he felt the same about me.

"Don't care who he gets!" said Gary, confirming my thoughts, "But all that excitement has made me quite horny – fancy a bit of fun? Come on, a quickie in the toilets, eh?"

His cock was clearly visible in his shorts now, a big hard bar standing upright and ready for me.

"Yeah – come on, let's get down and dirty!" I replied crudely and happily as I rubbed my hand over his cock, "Your turn; you can fuck me this time!"

My own penis was hard and throbbed in eager readiness – a nice quickie would be just right. And then next week we were planning to move in together; then we'd be able to enjoy each other to the full – and no woman would get in our way again!

What a Difference a Gay Made

To our mutual annoyance our relationship foundered after less than a year. We both proved to be too dominant and headstrong and while we thoroughly enjoyed each other's bodies we both also entertained a lust for the flesh beyond our relationship. We soon found that each of us had been unfaithful and we eventually admitted that we both needed freedom to explore the sexual world – both male and female. Our parting was amicably enough but that was that – a most energetic and erotic phase of our lives that quickly became consigned to history. Soon I was back enjoying female company and it wasn't long before I spotted Gary with a girl on his arm too, then we both changed to male partners and then back to new girlfriends again. We were both truly versatile, it seemed.

In addition to parting from Gary I also changed my lifestyle, selling off my garden maintenance business to return to writing. Writing was something I missed – my editor apparently missed me too and combining that with my IT activity was far easier than mixing my gardening with anything else.

I woke up and rolled over to glance blearily at the alarm clock. It told me it was 9:41 AM – so today must be Saturday or Sunday – otherwise I'd be up and out at work by now. Well, I hoped that was the case!

I rolled back and came face to face with an elfin female face, sleeping contentedly on the pillow, a happy smile playing on her countenance. And it started coming back to me...

Oh god yes – I'd finally invited my new girlfriend to stay the night – with thoughts of getting her to come and live with me one day – and here she was! My wandering eyes also took in two part empty glasses – oh yes, we'd downed more than a few last night too, hadn't we?

My gaze fell back to the gorgeous Casey, still blissfully asleep with her upper body partially uncovered. My eyes almost naturally dropped to her breasts, plump and firm and nicely bronzed and tipped with her cute little brown nipples. I remembered sucking on them last night; running my hands over her warm invitingly soft flesh as I filled my hands with her breasts.

I remembered working my way down her body, kissing her between her quivering breasts in the valley where I'd hopefully slide my rampant cock, sliding further down to poke my tongue into her navel and twiddle her little gold belly bar with my lips.

I remembered working my way further down, my hands now leaving her breasts to caress the smooth, sleek flesh of her waist and hips. I remembered her wiry patch of trimmed pubic hair tickling my chin before I lowered my mouth into the forest and onto her clitoris.

She tasted so sweet, so erotically sexy, so desirable – I couldn't help but work my tongue between her hot lips to explore the source of her delicious fluids.

I remember Casey's body jerking violently as I sucked at her pussy, licking up her copious lubrication before slithering upwards and back to her clitoris – her little penis, an organ that when erect, as it was then, must have been over an inch long – and truthfully, I just loved to suck on it! I sank my mouth over her mini-erection and sucked away, my tongue sliding and dancing over the tumescent flesh while beneath me her whole body seemed to be in motion – waves of excitement were rippling through her as I brought her towards her climax. Then Casey was crying out, groaning and gasping in ecstasy as her orgasm peaked – her hips thrusting her pussy hard at my mouth as I continued to stimulate her until she could take no more.

For a little while all was quiet, except for Casey's breathing – well, panting, as she came back to earth. I raised my mouth from her sex, the taste of her orgasm strong in my mouth – strong but delicious and I looked down at her exposed cunt.

Her lips were splayed apart and her little forest was shiny with sprayed dampness from her frantic climax – and above it all, her lovely clitoris still stood as if awaiting more action.

And there was definitely more to come – my rampant seven-or-so inch erection was drooling with desire and eagerness to sink itself into her hot hole and it wasn't long before he was poised to do just that.

Once I too had recovered, I leaned forward over Casey's sun-tanned body and lowered my cock towards her pussy. I felt her hips come up to greet me – to welcome me into her body and moments later we connected. A slight adjustment and my penis was seated in the slot, sliding up and down to gather some additional lubrication before beginning the act of penetration.

Some more adjustments and he was there, pushing into her hot slippery flesh like a knife into butter – sliding, sliding, deeper and deeper – his descent only brought to a halt as my pubes met hers.

I stopped – holding still while Casey's vagina got used to my length but soon impatience overtook me and I began to thrust. Slowly at first; small strokes to excite her G-spot then longer deeper strokes to excite my penis and soon we were rutting – our bodies slapping together, our breaths now coming in faster, our scents rising from us in waves of sexual excitement.

Faster and harder we fucked, on and on, until excitedly we both cried out as our bodies climaxed – Casey's once again shuddering and shaking all over, while my body just stiffened and thrust – pumping cascades of scalding hot cum from my straining penis to fill and overfill her grasping, squeezing vagina.

As we wound down and our actions eased off, I could feel our juices all around her pussy; her excited slippery fluids and my hot sticky overflowing cum combining to create a wet, highly-aromatic swamp where our sex organs met.

Gradually I eased my cock from her hole, a gush of whitish bodily fluids slowly flowing from her vagina as I departed, then slowly her hole closed, my cock deflated, and Casey's body stopped quivering. We were both still panting steadily as we now reclined side by side on the bed in post-coital relaxation mode and we were content. That had been a good quick late-night fuck – a short solid sex session that had satisfied us both.

I remember getting up to have a pee and Casey doing the same and then we just crashed out again; sleeping the sleep of the just-after, until morning had woken me. Well, it was the need for another pee that woke me, so I got up.

When I came back, my bladder now empty, Casey had woken too and with a quick smile she too had headed to the toilet.

"You coming to share a shower?" I asked hopefully as she rejoined me.

"No – not right now," she answered, "It's too early and anyway I'll get my hair all wet."

"Ok then – but I'm going to have one," I said, preferring to rise early and to feel and smell fresh, "Won't be long."

And I was quick – just a good once over, a shave and a tooth wash and I was back, feeling much better. Casey had collapsed back into bed once more.

"Come on then, sleepyhead," I said, lightly patting her bottom, "Come and have some breakfast."

"Nah – it's alright – I don't eat breakfast," she said, her face remaining buried in the pillow, "I'll stay here for a bit longer."

"Fine, fine – I'll leave you to it," I said feeling a tiny bit peeved as I pulled my shorts and a t-shirt on and headed down to the kitchen.

Soon I had some fruit juice, some cereal and some toast inside me and I was ready to face the world. A quick half an hour run around the area each morning got me going and kept me fit and now I felt I needed to be up and away – and I was about to depart when Casey appeared, still looking half asleep, now wrapped in my dressing gown.

"I'm just off out for a run – don't suppose you fancy coming, do you?" I asked, not really expecting a positive answer... and I didn't get one either!

"No way!" said Casey, her face wrinkling with distaste, "I don't like running anyway. Don't fancy that at all."

"No problem – hey, just make yourself at home – I'll be about half an hour," I said as Casey headed towards the lounge.

She didn't reply, so I just opened the door, shut it behind me and started out.

Steadily I jogged along, not rushing, just keeping up my usual pace – and that gave me time to think. I found myself wondering, as I jogged, if I was doing the right thing with Casey? She was nice enough, but already we'd found several differences in our lifestyles. Would that matter?

I jogged on and on, my mind elsewhere.

'I wonder what else she doesn't like,' I thought, *'Oh well, I'll soon find out I suppose.'*

Interrupted only by the occasional dog-walker and other morning people I was home pretty well 'on time', having had what I always felt was a good beneficial bit of work-out; then I did a few cooling-down exercises before I went indoors.

The sound of the TV alerted me to where Casey would presumably be – and there she was, glued to some vapid and banal show, the theme of which had no idea. I found myself taking a deep breath and then blowing out a long exhale before I spoke to her.

"You really don't want any breakfast?" I asked again and Casey shook her head firmly.

"I said no," she answered, "I hate breakfast."

"So are you going to sit and watch that all day?" I asked, perhaps a bit sharply.

"Why not," she said, not looking at me, her eyes still locked on the TV, "Why – what else is there to do?"

"What would you fancy then?" I asked, trying to remain bright and sociable, "How about a wander around the shops? Or perhaps we could go for a look around somewhere or even just a drive..."

"Nah – I'm ok," she said, "You go – I'll be fine here."

"Well how about heading down to the beach – Sandy Bay isn't far from here and you could top up your tan," I suggested, pretty well knowing by now what kind of answer I'd get back – and I was right.

"No – I like to get my tan done properly," she said – really meaning that the sun wasn't good enough for her!

"Oh come on, for fuck sake," I said somewhat exasperatedly, "Let's do something."

"Like what?" she replied quickly.

'Like take you home' I thought, but I held my tongue, for now.

"I've made some suggestions," I said, "So what do you like to do all day?"

"Not much," she said, "Unless you want to get back to bed?"

Now normally the idea of taking a voluptuous young lady back to bed would have raised my flagpole in moments but today he remained still – she'd totally dampened my ardour.

"No – I just don't feel like it now," I said, almost feeling that I'd got my own back, "Look, let's go out and do something, for god's sake."

171

"Alright then – take me somewhere," Casey said as she turned off the TV, "And it had better be good!"

'Oh fuck – like what?' I thought, *'No, sod you, we're going down to the park whether you like it or not.'*

At least the park was always full of activity – children playing; a band would be blasting away in the bandstand; ducks were there waiting to be fed; flowers and trees to be admired; the model steam railway; golfers; tennis players... and more...

We left the house eventually, after Casey had spent half an hour doing her make-up, only for her to stop at the gate.

"Aren't we taking the car?" she said.

"No way – it's only a short walk to the park," I said, "Parking's not free you know."

"Oh what!" she exclaimed, "I'll ruin my heels."

I'd had enough.

"Ok – ok – we'll go in the car," I said, stepping back indoors to get my car keys, "Have you got all your things?"

"Yes – didn't bring anything much with me," Casey said.

"Good," I answered harshly as I closed the door and pressed the key to unlock the car doors.

Casey got in and I did too and I reversed out of the driveway, pulled away and headed across town.

"So, which park are we going to then?" she sullenly asked after a while.

"We're not going to a park at all," I replied, "I'm taking you back home."

She said nothing but just looked straight ahead.

"Casey," I said, "You're beautiful and you're a wonderful fuck, but we're just so different. What's the betting you're a vegetarian while I eat meat and everything?"

"Yeah – I am," she nodded.

"See – we couldn't even have dinner together!" I replied somewhat caustically, because by now I'd made my mind up.

"Casey – I'll let you go home for now. Perhaps we'll meet again and it's been lovely to know you, but we're completely chalk and cheese. Sex is about all we have in common," I said as we pulled up outside her parent's house.

"You were really good last night, sweet girl," I said as Casey got out of the car, "But that's about as far as we go, thank you."

She said nothing but slammed the car door in my face as she walked away and quite honestly, I didn't care – I was free again!

Normally after I'd broken up with a girl I'd mope around for a while; perhaps get drunk and generally behave badly – but today I felt fine – relieved!

Well – relieved but very horny! Casey's body had turned me on as usual and inside me there was now a chamber of sexual need building up again... not manifested by an erection but by this feeling that I just needed more sex – and soon. Never mind – it would have to wait, so I shut the mental door on it and concentrated on relaxing instead.

I motored home with the radio blaring, almost enjoying for once the rattle of some local pop station's selection of somewhat insipid records. I pulled into my driveway and sat in the car for a few moments while I considered what to do next. I tapped the wheel as I thought but few inspirations came to mind until the idea of washing the car surfaced. I usually took it to the local car-wash but since it was a nice enough day, I couldn't now think of a reason not to wash it – and anyway I needed something to do to take my mind off girls and sex.

Soon I'd gathered all the necessary bits and pieces; hose, sponge, cleaner, etc and just minutes later I was wetting the paintwork and humming happily to myself.

173

At least car washing wasn't exactly serious brain work so I had time to think what to do next; whether to go out and get pissed; to go out and find another lay; or just to stay in – home alone? I eventually decided that a bit of company would be good so after the car was washed, I'd head down to the pub for a few pints.

With the water splashing around and some exercise I soon stripped off my t-shirt, enjoying the feeling of the warm sun on my back. The warmth made me flex my muscles and that reminded me that I hadn't been to the gym for a few days – all my exercise had been in bed! And that thought made my penis stir and start to fill out even though I did my best to will it to go away. I chuckled at the way sex had popped to the surface so easily and then became serious for a moment as I realised that I'd been sleeping alone tonight.

"Damn, that's fucked that up," I muttered as I ruefully thought back on the pleasure I'd enjoyed last night.

I liked sleeping with my partner especially after a good fuck – and at that moment I was startled out of my reverie by a voice from nearby. It was my neighbour, John, standing the other side of the low hedge.

"Hi Chris," he yelled, "Nice to see someone using a bit of energy."

"Forgotten what colour the car was!" I joked as I stood up from my work and stretched my back.

"Wowee!" said John, "Hey Chris – you've got some great muscles, man – don't you look good!"

Yeah – well I admit to being fairly muscular but although I spent some time at the gym I'd actually cut back considerably once Gary and I had split up but even so I continued to do workouts and plenty of running and it all helped.

I looked down at myself and smiled happily then I stretched my chest muscles and then, showing off in a cheerful way I raised both arms to show off my biceps. Stupidly however I completely forgetting that I was still holding the hose, complete with running water and three seconds after I assumed the pose I threw the hose away as water cascaded down all over me!

"Bloody hell; stupid idiot!" I exclaimed, laughing but totally embarrassed, "It's the car I'm supposed to be washing! Sod it!"

But John wasn't laughing; instead his eyes were riveted on me. I frowned, wondering why he was looking at me so intently.

"Bloody hell Chris, you could win a talent contest looking like that," he said, "You look so hot – look at you! Your hair all spiky and wet; your body all glistening with water – and you ought to see your shorts!"

"Ah piss off!" I said cheerfully, "I'm not hot – wet maybe but not hot."

"You wanna bet!" laughed John, his outstretched arm pointing at my lower half.

The cascade of water seemed to have mainly run down my front and now I looked down – and immediately understood what John was on about. My soaked shorts had gone almost see-through and with no underpants on, I was showing off somewhat, my visibly inflated cock hanging to one side!

"Oh for heaven's sake," I groaned as I turned off the water, "Sorry John. I'll just nip inside and change."

"Don't bother on my account!" said John, "That looks good! Who have you been thinking about then?"

"Not you for a start! "I said, laughing, "Why, do you fancy me?"

I turned around and wiggled my bum at him and he wolf-whistled at me.

"Fuck off – I don't fancy being a pin-up for men!" I said.

John laughed happily and struck his own pose to make me laugh as well – then he turned away. It was a typical bit of male banter that made me happy... it was great that we got on so well.

"Anyway, got to go – things to do," he said as he opened his car door, "You busy today?"

"Apart from the car, no," I said, returning to my task.

"Where's the girlfriend then?" he asked, "She was with you last night – I saw you come in."

Not that it was any of his business, but I didn't mind telling him somehow...

"Dumped her, mate," I said, "She looked good and she was fun in bed – pity that's all she was."

"Hard luck. Another one bites the dust, I guess," answered John, "Hey – if you get bored this evening you can always pop round. I've asked some friends over for the evening. Come and join us if you like."

"Yeah could do," I replied offhandedly as John waved his goodbye, then he puckered his lips as if to blow me a kiss.

I threatened him with the hosepipe, and he laughed and disappeared inside his car, soon reversing away down his driveway.

I didn't really mind the sexist banter coming from John because we were often teasing one another about one thing or another, our sex lives included. Having said that, although I was often bringing girlfriends home I seldom if ever saw John with a girl – I couldn't remember when, now I thought about it. Still, he was probably just more secretive than me, I concluded.

He was a lot like me actually – we seemed to have the same kind of humorous ways and approach to life. And we were of a similar build as well – he too was tall and quite well-built though not as muscular as I was. He too had short, light-coloured hair that he spiked to some extent – actually more of a bed-head look, I think. And he was always bright and cheerful; I often felt thankful that I had him as a neighbour as opposed to some old trout or miserable git, but today he'd been exceptionally amusing, even though I'd felt a bit embarrassed.

"What the fuck's going on though?" I muttered to myself, "Just because my cock showed through my shorts, I've got a bloody bloke after me now!"

I glanced down my body, noting my firm smooth belly and the bulge of my pecs.

"Oh well, I suppose everyone likes a man with muscles," I concluded with a chuckle.

I smiled smugly – then I settled back to finishing off the car.

With John gone and no other distraction, my penis soon returned to a relaxed state and I forgot about the wetness on me. Half an hour later the car was all done – washed and wiped dry, the paint and chrome all now shining nicely. Even I had dried out as I'd worked steadily and now I went indoors to get myself a snack and to sit down for a break. I headed out onto my patio where I relaxed in the sun and pondered on my actions for the next few hours.

No way was I going back to my regular pub – Casey would be sure to be there – no, I'd have to drink elsewhere for a little while. I mulled over my choice of pubs then let my mind debate whether to drink that afternoon or that evening, eventually deciding enjoy a pint or two at a different pub a bit later on – I'd nothing better to do, so why not.

I ate my bit of lunch; then put some clothes in the washing machine and set it going and then found myself wandering around listlessly. Finally, I sat down and decided to try to deal with one of my customer's problems but my heart wasn't in it – it was busy chewing over John's words.

"What's all this with John – what the fuck was he up to?" I asked myself, "He's not gay – I'd know it if he was."

I shook my head as I concluded that he'd just been taking the piss and making cheerful conversation – anyway, perhaps I'd deserved it, I decided.

Eventually I just couldn't sit around any longer, so pulling on some cleaner clothes I locked up and headed out to the pub in the opposite direction to my regular watering hole – fortunately still within walking distance.

Ten minutes or so later I was at the bar ordering a pint of lager which I took out into the almost unpopulated beer garden which overlooked the river and there I sat, just relaxing and watching the world go past on the river – it was very peaceful.

And then, as a moment of almost complete silence arrived, I overheard some conversation coming from another table a little way away.

"...turning me on something rotten," a man's voice said.

Something must have clicked in my brain because now I seemed to tune in on the conversation and at that point, I picked up the thread.

"Ooh, I agree. He look's gorgeous; all those lovely muscles," another male voice said, "He could have me any day!"

"Not if I get there first!" the first male voice answered, "He looks so hunky!"

"I'd love him to give me a good going over!" the second voice replied, "Oooooh, I bet he's well hung too!"

"I bet he's not gay though," said the other voice, "Do you think we could ask him?"

I looked cautiously around and there, some twenty yards away two young guys were sat side by side, both obviously looking my way. Ok – they might have been talking about someone else but the way they both looked aside as I looked at them meant only one thing – they'd been talking about me!

'Fuckin' hell!' I thought, 'All these gay people everywhere! Why are they all after me? Have I got the wrong aftershave on or something?'

The two young men seemed to realise that they'd been rumbled, and both coyly looked at me and smiled.

"Hi," they said together, one of them cautiously waving a hand at me.

"Were you talking about me just now?" I asked gently, "I didn't mean to overhear you, but I was fascinated. What were you saying?"

"Sorry mate – yeah, we were talking about you," the one with the deeper voice said, "We just thought you looked really hot."

"So we just wondered if you were gay or not," continued the other one bravely.

"Ha – you wish!" I said with derision in my voice, "No way am I bent, thank you."

The last thing I intended to do was to reveal my bisexual nature, especially not to strangers.

"I'm really sorry mate," the first man said, "We don't get many straight blokes in here now, so we just thought…"

"Why, what's happened – why don't straight blokes come here then?" I asked.

"New management," the first guy continued, "This place is almost entirely full of gays now!"

Damn – I'd wandered into a gay bar without noticing it! My Gaydar must have been defective today! I downed my pint quickly and stood up.

"Sorry to disappoint you both," I said, "Cheerio!"

And I was off, as fast as I could get out of the place. Despite my history of gay sex, my world was full of females nowadays, not gay men!

"Fucking shit," I said quietly, banging my heels down as I walked home, "That place has changed, and I didn't even notice – serves me bloody right I guess!"

Soon back home I gradually relaxed, eventually feeling comfortable again. The washing machine had done its work, so I hung out the laundry

– I was quite a good house-husband really. I could even cook quite well although tonight I'd slum it – a microwave dinner would do today because I couldn't be bothered with cooking for once.

Being summer I was still out on the patio at eight, having just polished off my dinner, when I heard voices chattering away next door.

"Oh yes – that's John and his guests...wonder if I might join them..." I muttered to myself and then I remembered how John had made comments about me.

"Huh – what if he was gay? No – he wasn't, surely; not John," I said, talking to myself, "But if he is then I think I'd rather stay at home."

I just wasn't in the mood to delve back into the gay side of life right now even though I felt my penis starting to fill out somewhat at the thought. I sat there unwinding and as I did so the voices drifted over to me again and I recognised one of them. It was Pete from the office.

"Well sod me, what a coincidence!" I said, "Be nice to have a chat and a drink with him – he's safe anyway, a big guy like him."

So instead of staying at home alone – or heading out to some other unknown pub, I decided to accept John's offer. It was a warm evening so shorts and a t-shirt would be quite adequate although I made sure I was wearing underpants! I didn't want any chance of a repeat of this afternoon's episode!

I spiked my hair up; sprayed briefly under each arm; checked myself in the mirror and went outside once again. Moments later I was pressing John's doorbell...

"Chris – great to see you!" said John cheerfully as he opened the door, "Come on in – so glad you decided to pop round."

He guided me down the hall to the lounge and waved his arm to the two men who were seated there...

"People – I'd like you to meet my neighbour, Chris," he said and there was a deep roar of laughter. John looked startled.

"Well, if it isn't my workmate! Hello Chris!" boomed Pete as he stood up and advanced towards me, his huge arms outstretched.

He was a big bear of a man complete with a big bushy beard, who made me look small. He must have been six foot six if he was an inch and probably weighed the best part of 300 pounds; very little of it being fat, I reckoned.

"Good to see you buddy," he said, wrapping his big arm round my shoulders and dragging me towards the settee, "Didn't know you were John's neighbour. John – this guy works in the same office as I do. Come on Chris – come and sit down; let him sit down with you John."

John looked a little shaken by this and the way that Pete had taken control, but he had no option as I was plonked onto the settee beside him. He shrugged and looked apologetically at me and we smiled carefully together.

Pete, as the only one still standing then imperiously waved his hand to John.

"Come on John – get your guest a drink!" he said jovially, then he held out a hand and pointed, "Oh Chris – this is Neil by the way."

"Hi Neil," I said, not knowing what else to do or say, because Pete had obviously taken over and Neil responded with a small and perhaps embarrassed finger wave.

Neil was just the opposite to Pete and being seated made him look even smaller. He wasn't weedy; he was just small; compact perhaps might be a better description because his arms were quite solid and his shoulders implied that he'd got some muscles... not that I really cared about such things on other men. John had disappeared and now returned with a can of lager for me, then picked up his own can. For a few moments it all went quiet as we drank and settled down but then I thought I'd start the conversation.

"I heard your voice Pete – couldn't mistake it," I said, "I wasn't sure if I felt like socialising tonight but when I heard you, I just had to pop round."

When John rejoined us he'd settled into one of the armchairs and now the conversation meandered back and forth, covering whatever seemed to come to mind. We drank – wine, lager, beer – whatever we fancied, and we were a happy and chattery bunch.

Eventually Pete stood up.

"Got to take a leak – John, go and sit beside Chris; I thought that's where I told you to sit," he boomed as he disappeared down the hall.

John duly rose from his chair and came and sat beside me, raising his eyebrows at Pete's comment.

"He always takes over," said John, "Very dominant sort of guy."

"Like that in the office too," I said as I chuckled, "Nice bloke and all that but I'm glad he works in a different department to me."

Pete returned, still pulling up the zip of his jeans.

"Dominant, did I hear you say?" he crowed, "Ooh yes – especially with Neil!"

"Eh? Do what? Dominant, as in sexually dominant?" I squeaked, "You're not gay are you?"

Pete smiled benevolently at the two others before replying.

"Didn't you know?" he said, "Neil's my sub – I'm his master."

I just looked totally confounded, so Pete continued.

"You're right, I am gay – well we all are actually, except possibly you Chris," said Pete, "Neil and I are partners – we live together and every so often we come and visit our good friend John. He's just plain gay – he just likes men, so we come over here for a bit of fuc...fu...fun."

"John's never gay too, is he?" I questioned, convinced that Pete was wrong, but John nodded to confirm his statement.

"You don't have to be a poufter to be gay," he said, "You don't have to act all soft. Gays are quite normal really – like me."

I was gobsmacked until John spoke again and as he did so he firmly grabbed hold of my hand just as I was about to wave it to make a point... and held on.

"Look – I'm touching you and you haven't turned into a limp-wristed pouf, have you. I'm not different – I'm just your neighbour, I'm just another bloke," he said, "And I just happen to like men, not women."

Actually, after my recent experience with Casey I tended to agree with him about women, although I didn't dare mention about liking men, so I just laughed.

"That's better," said John, squeezing my hand before releasing it, "Relax!"

Then Pete spoke up again.

"You still got those DVDs, John?" he asked, "Especially that one – you know which one I mean."

John nodded then pointed to a niche beside the TV, then he stood up, moved to the TV turned it on and soon popped a DVD into the slot.

"Watch this Chris, see if it doesn't make you horny!" he laughed, as he settled back into his chair.

I wasn't at all in the mood for anything gay and truthfully I really wanted to get up and go but not only would that be rude but Pete would probably make sure I suffered at work somehow – so I stayed...and soon the screen lit up with the credits.

"Ah," said John, the remote control in his hand, "Think I've got the right one. This is the one with those five short films on, isn't it? Where shall we start?"

"Second one in," said Pete and John made the selection and pressed play before I could register the title.

"See if you like this!" said John as he sat back in his chair, "Bet you will."

How could I not like it! There before me was a tall curvy big-breasted blonde in a shimmering mini dress that all but showed her knickers and her tits. She paraded around the room gradually displaying more and more of her delicious body, while my own body absorbed the sight with enthusiasm.

"Bit tasty?" asked John and I nodded

She certainly was worth looking at and I just couldn't wait for her to show her tits... which she was obviously about to do. Soon she bent over to show off her tight bum; her soft blue knickers pulled into her crack, then turned once more and just slid her dress down from her breasts.

I felt my cock lurch upwards as her magnificent mammaries sprang into view and I looked around me. All the other guys were watching avidly too; Pete with his hand in his lap obviously massaging his cock and the other two guys squirming around in their seats.

She was enough to wake up even the sleepiest gayest penis it seemed!

"Just wait," said Pete thickly, "Won't be long before she gets her dress off – wait and see!"

A few minutes of posturing and squeezing of her breasts and she began wriggling out of her dress – eventually it fell to her feet and she stepped out of it, squeezing her breasts together as she stood up. And now she was dressed only in her tiny knickers; her generous breasts a lovely contrast to her slim waist and smooth flat tummy – I was captivated, and I could feel my cock starting to swell and drool with pleasure.

"Here she goes!" said Pete breathlessly, having obviously seen the film before, "Watch..."

The blonde bent over, her free-hanging breasts close to the camera and in the background you could see her hands sliding her knickers down over her hips; then she stood up, her hand over her crotch. Slowly she moved her hand down, revealing that she was shaved... and as her hand went further, I suddenly found myself wondering where her slit started.

Then all was revealed to me as her hand reached between her legs – and pulled out a penis that any man would be proud of! A few quick tugs and it stood up, some seven inches or maybe even eight inches of definitely masculine flesh!

"Fuck!" I exclaimed, never having ever seen a shemale before, "What the...?"

My browsing and sexual preferences had seldom led me from the path of 'normal' heterosexual sex and there was more than enough to enjoy in that category alone of course, so this was a huge leap into the unknown for me.

Around me a selection of laughs echoed around the room and I just had to join in, even though the laugh was on me!

"What's she doing with a dick?" I asked naively, "Is that a bloke or a woman?"

"She's a shemale – a tranny – a bloke who's had hormone treatment and implants," said John, "Best of both worlds! She can fuck or be fucked."

"Eh?" I queried, my eyes unable to look away from the screen, "Oh yeah – oh yes, I see, of course."

"She'll be doing both in a few minutes," said John and sure enough, on screen a hunky guy appeared, already busy stripping off his clothes.

Soon he too was naked, and the pair embraced, their two big hard cocks rubbing against each other.

"Look at those cocks! Almost as big as mine!" enthused Pete, his comment causing me to sharply check out his groin.

For the next ten minutes we watched, almost in silence, as the pair made out – he sucked her; she sucked him; he fucked her; she fucked him and then they both wanked off over her abdomen and tits – the movie playing out as it closed in on the strands and pools of white and sticky cum on her breasts and belly. The basic theme for any fuck movie – but with a difference I'd never seen before!

"Phewwwww!" I heard from Pete and I looked at him.

His hand was still at his groin where it was now clear that he'd been rubbing what looked to be quite a considerable erection – well actually I could see he was still holding it... He looked at me unashamedly.

"So – what did you think of that then? Was she hot or not?" he asked, his hand still moving slowly, "Could you take that home with you?"

"Suppose that if I met her in a bar and she came on to me, then I would," I said feeling my penis stretching out down my leg, "She looked pretty amazing actually and I'd never have known she was a he until it was too late, I guess."

"Ok – then is she gay?" John added and damn me, I could see that he too was holding his hard cock in his shorts, next to me.

"Yeah, I guess so, I guess she is," I replied.

"Ok. So if you'd taken her home and when you took her to bed you found her cock, what would you do then?" asked Pete, his hand still moving on his penis, "Would you have fucked her – in the arse of course?"

"Perhaps I would – well probably," said, feeling a bit uncomfortable, "I suppose if I took her from behind it would hardly be any different from fucking a woman in the arse."

"Exactly, and what if she wanted to suck you?" asked John, "Would you have let her?"

A blow job was a blow job, so I nodded happily!

"So what about the leading question," said Pete, "Would you want to suck her?"

"Ummmmm – I guess I might have been able to," I said, remembering Casey's delectable mini-penis but still reluctant to reveal my gay side and Pete chuckled.

"So, using some bent and illogical deductions, that would mean you'd be willing to suck a man and fuck him too!" said Pete with a grin.

"I didn't say that!" I replied, a bit flustered, "Uh – I suppose I did really, didn't I?"

"Got you then!" said Pete, "Therefore, welcome to the club! Because we all like to suck and fuck men too!"

It went quiet as the statement hung in the air – then Pete spoke up once more.

"Let's show him the next one, eh?" he said, pressing the button and this time there was no ambiguity – this time there were just two guys getting to grips with each other.

And somehow I was now able to sit there and enjoy watching as they sucked and fucked each other – and even swallowed each other's cum at the end.

"Wasn't so bad, was it?" asked Pete, now displaying a prominent damp patch on his jeans as well a very long stiff ridge.

I wasn't sure what to say or do, partially because I now realised that my own penis had remained completely hard throughout the ten-minute film and it was still throbbing now. But Pete had spotted my predicament and he laughed.

"Didn't turn you off then?" he asked, and I found myself blushing.

I looked down in embarrassment – and was completely shaken to see that next to me, John, who was also wearing shorts, had some two or three inches of penis showing beyond the leg of his shorts! And it was obviously hard and excited – it was dripping precum onto his leg even as I watched.

It was then that John nudged my side with his elbow.

"Do you want to feel it?" he asked, sliding his shorts up so that even more of his erection was on display, "It won't bite! Come on – have a feel."

He grasped my hand and pulled it to his cock and the next moment my hand was wrapped round his shaft – and I'd just let him do it!

"Come on – hold it – squeeze it!" he said, holding my hand in position and once again I just did as he asked – he'd taken over my mind!

The next story was already unrolling on the screen – more men sucking and fucking each other – but none of us were concentrating on the screen now.

I looked down at where my hand was now sliding up and down his cock – my hand was on auto-pilot – it had nothing to do with me! And yet it did, because my actions were causing my own penis to stiffen even more and to pulse up and down – I could feel the way it strained and jerked from impulses from my brain.

As I looked down, I saw John's hand move onto my cock; sliding the material of my shorts out of the way and then grasping my own tower of flesh.

"Ohhhhh god," I cried somehow unable to brush his hand away, "Quit it will you!"

"Just helping you to relax," said John beside me, "Let it go – enjoy it."

And I was – his hand felt great as it rubbed my cock and I just couldn't help but do the same to him – he didn't need to hold his hand over mine now.

I leaned back as John began to work me up and I too increased my actions on his penis.

"Get some clothes off," breathed John in my ear and we both stood up, dropping our shorts and underpants, then stepping out of them.

It felt amazingly good to stand there with John, our two cocks both glistening with precum.

"Oh wow – look at that damn great thing!" I heard John say, "Now that's what I call a real cock!"

For a moment I thought he was talking about my penis but he couldn't have been – I was no bigger than he was but then I looked up and there, not more than a few feet away, Neil was on his knees between Pete's legs; Pete's jeans were around his ankles and his cock was well and truly buried in Neil's mouth.

From what I could see, Pete's penis was indeed a monster – I reckoned there must have been seven or eight inches still visible – and I had no idea how much was in Neil's mouth.

"Ooooohhh yeah," groaned Pete, putting his hand on Neil's head, "You're good, you suck me so well."

"Mmmmmm – love to suck you," said Neil, "You taste so nice."

And as he spoke, he took Pete's cock from his mouth and I saw the whole thing – the best part of what had to be ten inches of thick rod, topped with a knob like a large plum, which glistened with saliva. Moments later Neil let the giant rod slide back into his mouth, and I could have sworn that he managed to engulf a generous eight inches of it somehow!

John and I had already sat down again, and I returned my gaze to John's hand which was now able to slide more freely up and down my penis. I looked over at his groin and John's cock was now entirely on view to me – it was probably a bit over seven inches long and was uncut like mine, and as I watched, I saw my hand moving up down his shaft – it was almost as if I was watching someone else's hand...

On the next upstroke a bubble of clear slippery precum oozed from his tip and, conscious now that it was my hand and that I was stroking him, I caught the little bubble and spread it around his knob. Soon it glistened and shone, and my fingers slid easily over the smooth surface.

"Chris," John's voice interrupted my watching, "Could I suck you... please?"

Of course I'd had my cock sucked by a man before – by several in fact, but I'd done my best to suppress all such gay thoughts in recent years but now they were rising quickly again. I'd wanted to open up to John a long time ago but, having presented myself as a hetero guy I couldn't just suddenly turn around and release my bisexuality. I just didn't know what to do or say so John just continued.

"Your cock looks so gorgeous," he said, "I just need to get it in my mouth – you'll love it – I'll make you feel so good."

Whatever I might have replied was shut off as John moved to squat in front of me and in seconds I felt the tightness of his lips clamped round my penis and all I could do was to groan with pleasure.

"Oooooh fuuuuuuck," I groaned, "Fuckin' hell – where'd you learn to do that?"

His hand movements on my cock speeded up as wild feelings shot all through my body... he was reaching parts that no-one else had reached for several years and I felt my desire for cock surfacing once again.

John's mouth was alive; his tongue prehensile as it wrapped itself around my knob and tried to insinuate itself into the little slit at the tip. His hand was rubbing up and down my shaft as he sucked me and I found myself putting my hand on his head to push him down on my cock – he was good!

I saw movement ahead of me through my half-closed eyes and watched as Neil stood up, dropped his trousers and revealed his own solid erection. I watched as he moved closer to Pete who grasped his cock and sucked it deep into his mouth, making Neil hum with pleasure. But soon their scenario changed – Neil pulled his penis away and knelt down, while Pete dropped his jeans and stepped out of them.

His enormous cock now stood proudly from his groin – like a baby's arm it stood – drooling precum and jerking in time with his heartbeat. He spat in his hand and spread his saliva over his penis making it shine with moisture, then got onto his knees behind Neil.

'He'll never get that in his arse, surely!' I thought, my eyes now wide open, but I was wrong!

Pete leaned forward, bringing his penis in line with Neil's arsehole and put one hand on Neil's back. And then Neil's body pushed backwards and Pete's moved forwards... and within moments at least half of Pete's monster had disappeared.

I heard Neil suck in a big breath but there was no scream of pain or distress – I was staggered!

"Done it lots of times before, haven't they," explained John, lifting his head from my cock, "Do you want to try that?"

Inside me my buried desire was growing although whether or not I'd enjoy anything as big as Pete's monster was another matter. But John's cock looked simply delicious and I just knew that, given the right nudge, I'd welcome it inside me. My eyes though were locked onto the scene before me as Pete began to saw his cock in and out of Neil's hole, seemingly gradually probing deeper and deeper into the man's body.

I couldn't even answer John, who'd now returned to my penis; all I could do was to watch, with my mouth open, I suddenly realised. I shut it quickly, instantly worried that someone might see the opening as a place to shove their cock – then felt stupid about doing so. But down below it didn't feel stupid; in fact things were heating up and it felt wonderful. Automatically now, my hips were thrusting upwards to drive my penis into John's mouth; shivers and shakes were running through me; incredible sensations were firing off through my brain – and John was sucking harder...

Then he stopped again.

"You didn't answer," he said, leaving me hanging, teetering and urgently needing him to complete his task, "Do you want to try that?"

"I want to cum!" I cried, shivering with pent-up excitement, "Don't care where – just want to cum!"

"Come on then – try me!" said John, relinquishing my cock and getting onto his hands and knees, "I want you to cum in my arse then!"

As if in a daze I moved down behind him while John held his arse cheeks apart for me and without thinking I lined up my saliva-soaked erection with his hole and pushed gently. Frantic feelings ran through my cock as it began to penetrate his arsehole; fear, trepidation, panic even but above all a feeling of excitement as I realised that I was now about to fuck a man once again!

Easily I slid inside, John's hips pushing back at me as I penetrated a man for the first time in several years. Easily I began to move in and out, feeling my sperm practically bubbling like lava building up in a volcano and quickly I found myself nearing my climax.

For a moment a feeling of panic swept through me as I realised that I was going to unload my sperm inside John, but the need to cum was so great that I didn't care – all I cared about was having a place in which to empty my balls – and it wouldn't take long to do that!

Furthermore, my excitement was heightened as right beside me Pete was nearing his own climax inside Neil's hole. Pete's powerful penis was slamming into Neil's body; almost disappearing with each stroke, although just how Neil could accommodate all that length inside him was beyond me – but it was so exciting to watch that I didn't care and Pete was panting hard as he powered in and out, faster and faster.

"Yeah – yeah – yeahhhhh" he growled as he thrust, "Here it cums! Oh fuck – yeah – here it cums! Oooooooh! Oooooooh! Oooooooh!"

Pete was shaking all over; his hips now slowly thrusting in jerks as each surge of his hot cum emptied into Neil's body and suddenly I was doing the same!

"Ooooh damn John – you've made me cum!" I cried as vast tremors made my legs shake, "Aaaaaahhh! Yesssss – fuckin' cummming!"

"Come on then, let it go! Let it all go!" cried John, his arse squeezing my penis; pulsating around my flesh as each jet of cum left my cock.

"Oh yessss – ooooooh god!" I moaned, "Uuuuuuhh! Oooooooh! Fuck – oh fuck, oh fuck!"

"Ohh Chris, I'm sure I felt that," groaned John, his body quivering as I pumped him full, "Ohh, that felt so good!"

I could feel my sperm pooling around my cock deep up inside John's body, helping to smooth out the friction as I continued to slide in and out, my movements now languid and relaxing as I came down from my orgasm and slowly my thrusts became just twitches and shudders before I collapsed down onto John's back.

I was panting as heavily as if I'd been fucking for hours, such was the degree of illicit excitement in me but finally I was able to kneel upright behind John, my penis still embedded in his arse.

"Fuckin' hell," I said as I shook my head, "Never expected to do that tonight!"

"Never expected it to be you who fucked me tonight either!" answered John as he smiled at me over his shoulder.

A small towel landed on John's back, thrown by Pete who was now standing up, his still huge penis drooping from his groin.

"Here you go – you can take it out now," he said.

I gently slid my penis from John's hole, watching as his arse fluttered closed and open again, letting a little stream of spunk slide out. I caught it on the towel, wiped my cock on the towel too and then put it into John's waiting hands as I moved away and sat down on the settee once more.

A little while later John came and sat by me once more, this time on the folded towel however.

He smiled at me – a happy smile...

"Did you enjoy that?" he asked, "You were so hot – I loved the feel of your spunk inside me – wow, didn't you cum hard!"

I nodded contentedly, looking down at my now flaccid penis and then at John's still hard cock.

"Yeah – that was good – never thought I'd do that to you!" I exclaimed, blowing out a deep breath.

I paused as I realised that I ought to confirm my heterosexuality. I might well have been quite enjoying myself, but I'd come here as a 'normal' man and needed to retain that bit of comfort.

"Hey, I just fucked a man!" I exclaimed as if it had been my first time.

"Was it any different to fucking a woman's arse then?" asked Pete who now stood beside me, his huge half-hard organ mere feet from my face.

I shook my head, immediately realising that actually, John's arsehole had been better and tighter than the last female's arsehole I'd fucked. It hadn't been Casey's – she hadn't been willing to let me use that access to her body.

"Better actually," I said, being honest, "Thanks buddy."

I put my hand on John's thigh; precarious inches from his erection and smiled at him.

"Honestly, thanks," I said, "You were good – I needed that!"

"Could you do it again some time?" John asked and without hesitation I answered.

"Yes – definitely!" I said cheerfully, suddenly realising that some gay sex would be great, "Sure I could."

John smiled back at me and put his hand on top of my hand on his thigh.

"Oh that's great because actually there's something else I want you to do," he said.

"What's that then?" I asked innocently, my mind not concentrating.

"Get me off!" he said, grasping my hand and moving it onto his erection, "I need to cum too!"

His cock stood hard and slippery in my grasp as I held it, then I began stroking it gently as I settled my mind.

"Umm, ok," I said, rather surprised at my own enthusiasm, "Here – now?"

"Yeah," said John as he moved his arse forward and leaned back, "Can you do it from there?"

"Yeah, course I can!" I said, my hand now moving up and down his shaft.

'Hah – he's not as big as Gary was,' I thought as I worked up a bit of speed, *'Feels good though.'*

"Take it easy Chris," groaned John, "Slower..."

I hadn't realised that I'd been rubbing him just as fast as Gary had liked me to do so I practically stopped my movements; now just caressing his penis, squeezing it and feeling the texture of his flesh and skin in my hand; sliding my thumb and then my fingers too in the ever increasing dribble of precum that was issuing from his tip and spreading the lubrication over both his knob and his shaft.

John began groaning from time to time as I manipulated his fine upstanding erection, his hips too working in time with my hand as I began to move more actively.

"Getting there," he moaned, his hips lifting upwards with each stroke, "You're doing fine, keep it like that – yeah, just like that!"

I was leaning partially over his body now as I concentrated on wanking him and John now had his arm draped over my back, squeezing me from time to time. My face was not all that far from his cock as I closely observed the way his foreskin slid over his purpling knob; the way small oozes of precum kept leaking out; the way my fingers pushed little waves of precum up and down his cock – I was well into it and so was John.

"Oooooh yessssss!" he hissed, "Nearly there – keep going – keep going..."

Inside me my gay feelings were now growing fast and I was sorely tempted to take John in my mouth but I held off. Nevertheless, I was eager to see him shoot off and I leaned even closer, my hand keeping up a steady rhythm, until John shuddered all over.

"Here it cums!" he cried, "Here it cums!"

And as he spoke a rapid shot of white cum squirted from his cock straight into my face! I didn't even have time to move before a second jet hit me and when I tried to move away John's hand behind my back tightened and held me down and a third and fourth belch of cum erupted all over my hand. Then, just as I opened my mouth to complain a last big spurt of cum shot from his cock, straight into my mouth and as it entered, I closed my mouth reflexively. Then I felt his arm relax but despite that I just continued to wank him, bringing forth some small dribbles of cum, until he stopped my hand from moving.

"No more – no more – too sensitive," he said, and I took my hand away and sat up straight.

I must have looked a proper sight – I could only see out of one eye and I could feel sticky cum on my lips – I could even taste it.

"Did you get some in your mouth?" John asked and I nodded and managed a grin.

"Sorry," he added, "Hope it tasted ok."

"Do you eat your own cum?" said Pete from beside me obviously having noticed me licking my lips.

His huge and newly erect penis strained from his busy hand and I nodded again.

"Well, now you've sampled John's as well, try some more – bet you'll think its lovely," he said, "Go on – you might as well clean him up."

I stuck my tongue out and immediately encountered a big blob of the stuff – which stuck to my tongue as I withdrew it. The taste of the not-inconsiderable load on my tongue wasn't any different to my own cum really and it seemed tastier than I remembered Gary's had been. I knew then that my gay side was returning eagerly.

Then I felt fingers move on my face and moments later they were pushed into my mouth, together with more of John's ejaculated cum which I sucked off and swallowed. A moment later another finger-load was pushed into my mouth and then another.

"See – you can do it!" Pete said, his hand now moving quickly on his cock, "Nearly all gone!"

Then John wiped a towel over my face, clearing my vision and my nose and I could see and breath properly now – just for now because beside me Pete was panting as he worked hard on his erection and now he spoke.

"Chris – this way... I've got some more for you!" he said and as I turned towards him, my mouth open to speak, at that very moment his cock jerked and splashed a huge squirt of very hot cum right in my mouth!

I almost blew it out again but moments later I couldn't – Pete had pushed the end of his penis into my mouth where another flood of cum splashed! Just the two squirts in my mouth – it tasted simply hot and delicious – then he pulled his cock out and sprayed my face with several more generous gushes of spunk before he turned aside to strip out the last lesser dribbles.

I was back to where I'd just come from – covered in cum once more – even my t-shirt was liberally splashed! John pulled me to him and pliantly I allowed him to attend to the mess. But this time instead of using his fingers I felt John come closer and the next thing I knew, his tongue and lips were licking and sucking the sticky blobs and streaks of cum from my face.

Although initially I wanted to recoil from his touch it actually felt good and not a little erotic – even when his lips settled briefly on mine. It even felt good when his tongue slid between my lips – I actually pushed back with my tongue, making our contact wet and slippery with saliva and with Pete's spunk.

Then he was finished and, handing me the towel once more, he sat back, sated.

I cleaned what was left of any stickiness from my face and just sat there, too shaken to speak. Part of me wanted to run away – part of me loved it – part of me just didn't know what to do but Pete soon pointed out where my priorities lay.

"Your cock!" he laughed, "Ever since I sprayed your face it's been hard as fucking iron – look at it!"

Actually I didn't need to look because I'd known all along that my penis had just loved all the action – he at least had no qualms about who he had sex with! And slowly I had to admit that I'd thoroughly enjoyed it all – even the mouthfuls of cum; even being wanked and sucked by another bloke. It was good sex – good wholesome sex – no posturing and preening and female histrionics – just plain excellently good gay sex.

John got up, his own already-returned erection swaying before him and wandered off to the kitchen, returning with some more wine and some cans and we refreshed ourselves as we recovered. Somehow the talk avoided sex – we were all contented for now at least and despite our part-dressed bodies, we didn't need to get intimate for now... and slowly our tumescent organs relaxed – which was just as well, as Neil's phone suddenly went off.

He got up and moved away to answer it and I heard him say a loud "Damn!"

He came back looking a bit crestfallen.

"Bloody typical – of all nights!" he moaned, "They're short of drivers at the depot and they want me to come and fill in – it's urgent – right now. Shit!"

Pete stood up too.

"That means I've got to go too – Neil drove us here and I'm not walking home!" he said, "Sorry John, Chris – fuckin' nuisance but that's life."

"Would happen tonight, wouldn't it? Oh well, see you again soon?" asked John and Pete put his thumbs up.

"Definitely!" he said, looping his arm over Neil's shoulder, "Sooner the better. But we'd better be off – I'll catch you in the office Chris!"

"See you Monday," I said, not knowing if I was saying the right thing, but also knowing that I'd have to be there anyway, "Bye Neil, bye Pete."

Soon the door slammed, and John and I were left there – the pair of us still wearing only our t-shirts. We looked at each other and just burst out laughing at the incongruity of the situation, then both sat down on the settee. On the screen before us yet another gay suck and fuck film was running – we both absentmindedly looked at it for a while before John turned to me.

"I'm sorry Chris – I didn't know it would turn out the way it did," he said, "I asked you round for a bit of a social evening, but Pete – he's a bit of a handful – I never expected him to..."

"Did you mean that?" I asked John playfully, "That Pete's a bit of a handful? I'd say he's a damn sight more than that!"

"Dirty bastard!" said John cheerfully, "No – I was being honest – but yes, I go along with your thinking! Two hands full actually!"

Then somehow I just had to ask...

"Has he ever fucked you?" I said, feeling my cock jerking back into life and John nodded.

"Twice," he said, "I was pissed otherwise I'm not sure I could have taken him. Stretched me like anything – couldn't shit straight for a week!"

I laughed like a drain – but inside me something was asking me if I wouldn't actually like to feel something like that being shoved up inside me... and I looked down at John's erection.

'I bet this one would feel great,' I thought as I let out a long breath, 'Gary's was bigger – this one would fit easily.'

John must have thought that I was thinking of Pete's cock inside me and he put his hand on my arm.

"Don't even think about it!" he said, "You're not up to getting Pete's cock up you yet – you need some training first."

My head span round from the screen to look at John beside me.

"You what!" I exclaimed, horrified, "No way! Pete could do some damage with that! You're more... I mean – oh ooops!"

"I'm more your size? Is that what you were trying to say?" said John and I found myself nodding.

"Do you want to try it? I'll be gentle," asked John, putting his fist round his erection and sliding it up and down.

Once again, part of me wanted to say 'yes' but lots of me wanted to say 'no'. I was still in limbo about being in any way gay and yet...

"Think about it," said John, "Think how easily you got your cock inside me. Think how smoothly you slid inside – and I can tell you, I loved it – I reckon you will too. I've got plenty of lubricant around."

I just couldn't bring myself to answer him or to tell him about my past so I just shook my head, although my cock obviously thought it was a great idea, as he stood up and nodded at me as I tried to will him to go down again.

John interrupted my indecisive moment... and took some pressure off my mind.

"Tell you what – let's forget that idea for now. Come and have a shower – let's get cleaned up," he said, stripping off his t-shirt, "There's plenty of room – I had a posh new shower fitted a few months ago – come and try it."

"Yeah ok," I said, feeling easier as I stripped my t-shirt off too. I'd shared many a shower with other men at the gym – this was known territory.

And it sounded like a good idea too – I was covered in the stickiness and smell of man-cum and of hot sex and much as I liked it I wanted to feel fresher.

John led me through the house and up the stairs, his remarkably hair-free bum moving tightly before me. He opened the door into what in my house was the bathroom and as we had similar style houses – just two of a row of a development – I knew what to expect. But instead there was a completely tiled room; subdivided into what I think is known as a wet room and a dry room; perhaps half and half – with room for several people under the shower at once and even seats. The rest of the room was fitted out with all the usual bathroom furniture...

"Hey – that's smart!" I said, impressed, "Beats my bathroom hollow."

"Cost more than your bathroom though," said John as he turned to a type of control panel.

He began pressing buttons and entering figures and soon the place was lit up like a spaceship with water firing out from orifices from floor to ceiling.

"That's really nice," I exclaimed as I admired the place, "Definitely must have cost more..."

"Come on then – the water's fine, as they say," said John and together we entered the shower room. Sensors somewhere realised we were there, and the water pressure increased at once, jetting hard against my skin. For a little while we both just luxuriated in the pressurised jets almost tingling as the water hissed against our bodies. Eventually the water turned itself off and from somewhere John produced a large sponge and some gel soap...

"I'll do you," he said, "Turn around."

Compliantly I turned away from him and soon I felt the sponge rubbing over my shoulders and up and down my back. I squirmed with enjoyment – John had a nice touch – firm but not vicious and pleasurable, that was for sure. His movements worked their way down my back and onto my buttocks. I felt his hand push the soapy sponge between my cheeks and I just naturally relaxed, allowing him to slide his hand down and then underneath me, finally reaching my balls. My cock, flaccid for once, immediately rose once more, obviously enjoying all the attention his root was getting. I felt John's fingers rubbing up and down my arse crack and it was that relaxing that I simply opened up to him with his slippery fingers and soft sponge.

'Oh my, this is bringing back memories!' I thought, closing my eyes better to enjoy the feelings.

And then John centred his touch around my arsehole – his fingers sliding around my hole, rubbing over the crinkled flesh and then pushing into my hole itself. It was so enjoyable that I actually pushed my arse out towards John, and I felt what had to be a finger slide inside me, just for a moment, stirring long forgotten feelings in my brain and my balls.

John looked at me to see my reaction, but I still had my eyes shut, blissfully enjoying the feeling.

"Is that good? I'm just making sure you're nice and clean." he said and I hummed my approval.

"Yeah – go ahead!" I answered innocently, "It's nice. Feels amazing actually..."

A moment later John's finger slid inside me again, deeper this time – it felt as if he was in up to his knuckle and far from finding it to be unpleasant, I was loving every moment. My cock was jerking as he probed around inside, leaking precum from time to time as John slid his finger over what I knew to be my prostate.

"Ooooh my god," I groaned, feeling my cock straining from the stimulation, "What are you doing to me?"

"Just cleaning you up," John said once more, "Hang on..."

I felt my arsehole being stretched and I drew in a sharp breath as a spasm of pain erupted – but it was soon gone.

"Still ok?" asked John, his other hand now reaching round me to grasp my stiff penis.

His soapy hand slid easily up and down my shaft while his other hand worked away at my arse.

"I've got two fingers up you now – do you like it?" he asked.

"Oooohhh – yessss, its nice – I'm ok," I groaned, "You're going to make me cum!"

"Let's have your hand," said John and I held it out for him to grasp.

He pulled me a bit and suddenly his penis was in my grasp and I was so turned on that I just had to wank him as he wanked me.

"Oh god – I like it," I moaned, my arse wriggling around on his fingers, "Oh god – I'm getting close John, getting close."

"Ooooh," I groaned, sucking air in through tight lips, "Keep going – gonna cum – gonna cum!"

I felt John's fingers rubbing against my prostate inside me while his hand worked rapidly up and down my shaft – and I was there!

"Oh yesssss – here it comes – cummmming!" I cried, feeling my arse clenching tight around his fingers and my penis jerking hard.

A big thick jet of white cum shot from me, splashing against the shower room wall; another one followed and a third and a fourth before I was left with mere dribbles that slid over John's soapy hand.

Slowly and gently he eased his fingers from my hole and I felt myself pulling my hole closed again – there was a strange feeling of loss somehow. I was still holding his erection in my hand but I'd forgotten to wank him and now I let go.

I turned and looked into John's eyes.

"I ought to be fucking mad at you," I said, "But I can't because I actually enjoyed that. I know you're trying to turn me gay but I'll let you off for now – you and your fingers! Anyway, who said you could stick your fingers up there?"

"Told you, I was cleaning you," said John, "I like a man to be nice and clean."

"Well, I'm bloody well clean now or at least my arse is but I haven't done the rest of me – or you, so let's finish our shower," I said, "You finish off soaping me and then I'll do you."

With a wave of his hand John powered up the water for a while and then set to work with his sponge, cleaning me from head to toe. I'd shared an intimate shower with a girl recently but it had been several years since I'd showered with a man but now it was all coming back. Somehow John knew just how to apply pressure; how to smooth the sponge, or his bare hands across my body; how to make me feel good. I was positively purring by the time he'd soaped me all over.

I gave him a big smile as I took over with the sponge and now I tried to return the compliment, reaching every part of his body until he was glowing with cleanliness.

"You going to do my arse too?" John asked and I found myself smiling at him.

"Well if you can do mine then I'd better do yours too!" I said with a laugh, "Anyway, I've already had my cock in there so why not my fingers?"

I pulled John closer to me and reached my soapy hands round him. As we got closer his erection bumped against my abdomen and I couldn't help but wriggle myself against the rod of hot slippery flesh.

I began feeling around behind him and soon located his arsehole then felt John pushing against my fingers.

"Come on then, it should be easy," he said, "Start with one finger..."

Using that one finger I felt around his hole, discovering his own ring of crinkled flesh and the small indentation in the centre that was his hole.

"Ok – I'm pushing out – try now," John said and with no hint of pain or hindrance, my finger slid right up inside.

"Oh yessss, oh yessss – that went in so easily – you can try two now!" he said.

My second finger also slid in easily and I moved them around inside, feeling the walls of his anus sliding against my fingers. I located his prostate and rubbed it for a while making John's very stiff cock jerk and thrust. I played around for a while before I gently pulled my fingers out and slapped his arse lightly.

"Come on – let's get this shower finished – we'll get all wrinkled!" I said.

"Don't you want to put your cock up me," said John, pushing his arse out towards me, "Oh please – you've got me all ready!"

No – no – and not in here," I said, gently pushing him away, "Not sure I really want to do that and anyway I've just cum; who do you think I am, Superman?"

"You fucked me earlier – can't you do it again?" he asked, "Please!"

But this was going too far right now. I was still getting used to the idea of having sex with a man again and I was trying to avoid it for some reason. What we did earlier was something like bravado in front of Pete, I decided – what we were doing now was rather different. It felt more like making love... and I didn't feel ready for that.

With some light banter we finished our showers and towelled dry before he pulled me across the landing to his bedroom. His bedroom...

"Why are we in here?" I asked, "My clothes are downstairs."

"I wanted to get some deodorant, but there's something else I want to do too," said John, moving close to me, "I want to thank you for being so good – for letting it all happen."

And he wrapped his arms around me and just kissed me – his wet lips sliding across mine, his tongue already probing between my now parted lips. Somehow I just let him explore and then I discovered that my own tongue was joining in, sliding around over his tongue and lips and pushing into his mouth to feel the smooth enamel of his teeth.

Moments later John sort of leaned on me or pushed me and together we lost our balance and fell onto the bed.

"Uuuuuufff!" I grunted and John too let out a puff of air as we hit the mattress together.

He looked at me, his eyes shining and his mouth smiling, before once again we locked lips and continued our courtship.

And now two hard cocks jostled for position between us, John's now finding a home between my legs. Together we kissed and dry humped each other, my penis sliding up and down his abdomen while John's cock slid excitedly against my anus, sending erotic feelings through me.

"Do you want to let me in?" he asked after a little while, "I'd love to be inside you!"

"I think I do," I finally admitted, "You sure though?"

"I'd love to," he breathed quickly, "It'll be wonderful."

John reached out and his hand came back with a small tube – lubrication, obviously.

I knew what was to come and now I found myself almost straining to allow him access, now desiring nothing less than to feel a cock inside me again. I felt John's fingers slide over my hole – and in a few seconds his slippery digit was inside me once more, sending hot vibrations all through me.

'Oooooh yeahhh!' I groaned as a second finger joined the first – but there was no more than a tiny sensation of pain and then it was gone, to be replaced by a needy feeling – a need to be filled, properly!

John's fingers were making my hips thrust back at him and I was hardly aware that he'd withdrawn them until I felt some more pressure on my arsehole.

"Relax – push out," he said, and I did so, willing his penis to slide inside.

And he was in me – way inside, so easily!

"Oh god, that's great!" I groaned as I felt his penis moving around, "That's brilliant. Ohhh fuck, I can feel you – I like it."

"Knew you would," said John as he began sliding his cock in and out more quickly, "Always feels good to me, especially when your prostate gets rubbed."

"Oooooooohhh," my voice quivered as his cock stimulated my internal organs, "Ooohhh yeahhhh!"

"More?" asked John and I nodded rapidly.

He increased his pace and I could hear and feel his thighs slapping against my buttocks as we twisted around and fucked wildly. This was getting good – and I realised that it was so amazingly stimulating just as I realised that I'd been missing this kind of loving. John was panting now and thrusting harder, his entire penis jamming itself hard up into my bowels, skewering me on his shaft of solid flesh. My cock was leaking profusely too, threads of precum drooling onto my thigh almost as if I was cumming.

"I'm going to cum inside you," said John, not giving me an option and I realised that was exactly what I wanted.

"Yes – yes – fill me up!" I cried, "Give me your sperm – right up inside me!"

"Any minute," groaned John, still hammering his rigid erection into my hole, "Nearly – nearly! Oh fuck – here I cum!"

Suddenly I felt a warm pressure inside me – his powerful thrust driving his spunk up into my anus; spraying into my bowels; heating my insides as his cock gushed his cum time after time.

"Fuck – fuck!" cried John as his final thrusts sent the last waves of cum into me, "Oh yeahhhhh – oooh fuck, that's lovely! Oh Chris I needed that – that felt so good!"

I pulled John to me and kissed him – I think he was so shocked that for a moment he didn't respond but soon we were once again exchanging more bodily fluids as our mouths made love to each other. Eventually we parted, although John's penis was still firmly inside me.

"Ok to come out?" he asked, "Put your hand there – feel me slide out and then put your hand over your hole to catch anything that leaks while I find a towel."

I reached down and wrapped my fingers round his still hard, very slippery penis, feeling him sliding through my fingers and out of my body. A moment of emptiness came over me before I remembered to move my hand and I felt wetness on my hand as I covered my hole.

Very quickly however John gave me a towel and I replaced my hand – a hand that I now saw was smeared in his sticky white cum. I nearly licked it off but chose instead to use the towel as intended.

I scrambled up the bed until I lay alongside John, the pair of us breathing hard and glowing with sexual satisfaction – although my erection said that there was unfinished business about. I looked at John and raised my eyebrows to indicate my total surprise.

"Wowww – I can't believe we just did that," I said, genuinely shocked at the way I'd just allowed him to fuck me, "Liked it though – that was excellent – you were good."

John was smiling at me and now he laid one hand on my chest.

"You're shocked!" he said, laughing quietly, "How do you think I feel? Never ever thought you'd be in here with me having just had a good fuck!"

My mind was a turmoil of strange thoughts; visions of rampant cocks, sprays of cum, clenching arseholes and hairy bodies mixing and sliding past my mental viewing screen and then I was brought back to reality as I felt John's hand sliding down my body. Soon it grasped my erect penis and started wanking it and my mind began to concentrate on the feelings he was bringing.

"Hey, I'd nearly forgotten you," said John, releasing my cock and sitting up beside me, "You still need to cum again don't you... would you like me to suck you off like I did earlier?"

Without waiting for my answer John slid down the bed until his head was at my groin – his warm breath on my belly, his hands on my thighs. Then I could feel him as he closed in on my throbbing erection and in moments, he was grasping it again then seconds later I felt the hotness of his mouth as it closed around my knob.

"Uuuuuhhh!" I gasped with pleasure, John's lips and tongue already working away at the sensitive parts of my penis, "Oooh that's nice!"

I shut my eyes and squirmed with pleasure as John stimulated my excited penis, his active mouth, lips and tongue working hard to excite me, to extract my sperm – to make me erupt. And erupt was what I was soon going to do – because although I'd had my share of orgasms already, my penis was still incredibly sensitive. Perhaps it was because of all the action that it was sensitive but whatever, John had already set off my system and now his energetic mouth and lips were quickly sending me towards another climax.

"John – John," I groaned as I urgently patted his arm to warn him, "I'm going to cum – ever so soon, I just know it!"

He lifted his mouth briefly and looked at me.

"Yes Chris, you cum when you're ready mate," he said and he lowered his head once more, his hand now assisting his mouth to bring me off.

I managed to hold out for a little while longer; my body increasingly out of my control before I cried out.

"Aaaaahhh – cumming – cumming!" I howled as John's hand and sucking mouth drove me over the top, "Yessssss! Oh shiiiiit – ooooo, ooooo, oooohhh!"

My hips were thrusting up into John's mouth, firing off energetic blasts of hot cum; filling his mouth – even overfilling it so that small rivers of cum oozed back down my shaft.

"Aaaaaahh!" I groaned again as yet another pulse of cum left my cock, "Oh god – I'm out of practice!"

Suddenly all feeling left me and I sank back flat on the bed – my body drained of all my energy, emotion and spunk too. John sat up and looked down at my rapidly wilting penis – his mouth glistening with slippery juices and turned towards me. He opened his mouth to show me that it was almost completely filled with my offering; strands of spunk hung down and pools of cum puddled on his tongue... He shut his mouth and I saw his throat work as he swallowed it, a look of pleasure sliding over his face then he opened his mouth once more to let me see his tongue now cleaning up the last of my spunk; then he closed it once more and swallowed again.

"Delicious mate," he said happily, "Nectar – bloody nectar!"

I slapped his leg gently to cover my embarrassment at his praise of something, which for the past few years had been only of interest to my girlfriends and me.

"Can't be that good!" I exclaimed.

"Well I thought so," he answered with a chuckle, "Perhaps I need some more samples then. Might taste better still tomorrow."

"What you mean, tomorrow?" I replied, a bit worried about the implications and realising that my life was spiralling out of control...

"You mean to tell me that after everything we've done today, you won't want to do it again?" asked John, his face looking hard at mine, "I thought you enjoyed yourself... you even had eyes for Pete's cock, didn't you?"

Now I felt totally embarrassed – he'd got me!

"No – no, I mean yes, oh I don't know!" I blundered about, feeling in my mind for the right response, "Look, it's been a bit of a trip for me – don't know if I'm coming or going!"

"Definitely been coming! Lots of that!" said John with a wink, "But I know how you feel – all shaken up mentally. So let's calm it all down for a bit, eh."

"Yeah – I'd like that," I said, feeling relieved that the conversation was ending, "Anyway, I ought to get home."

"What's the rush – what for?" John said, using more logic than I possessed at this moment, "There's no-one there now your girlfriend's gone; the house will be lonely and boring and I've got some nice thick steaks for the barbeque we'd been planning to enjoy – so stay!"

The mention of food and especially barbequed steaks focussed my mind on the important things in life – getting my belly filled.

"Mushrooms, tomatoes, salad, beer, wine... the steaks have been marinating..." said John seemingly realising that this was the way to my heart – the way to keep me, "Stay then?"

"Yeah – ok, you're on!" I said and with a quick high-five between us we rose from the bed; shot in and out of the shower and padded downstairs to find our clothes.

And now that I was back in more 'domestic' surroundings and with some clothes on I felt fine again.

'What's wrong with staying for a meal?' I thought, *'What was I going to have – a microwave dinner – yuk! A steak sounds a lot nicer – and some company!'*

"Ok John," I said, "Find me a lager and I'll be fine! And then I'll help with the barbie, if you want."

"You just relax," said John already with two chilly cans in his hands, "Enjoy yourself. It's a gas-fired barbeque so it won't take much to get it up and running – you just enjoy your drink."

Before long John was bustling around with plates and utensils and was fetching the food from the fridge.

"There's loads more cans in the fridge – help yourself when you need to," he said as he breezed in and out of the patio doors.

I sank back into the settee once more, now feeling totally relaxed. Ok – there was still the worry that I'd been having gay sex – but had I hated it? No way – I'd had a fucking good time, I decided!

Soon a second can was needed, and I took one outside for John who accepted it cheerfully. Delicious smells of cooking and all kinds of other things were now filling the still evening air around us, making my tummy rumble.

"Could eat a horse!" I said to John and he laughed.

"No mate, this is prime beef – Scottish beef – no way did it have reins on it!" he laughed, "Won't be too long now. How do you like it, by the way?"

"Bit rare please," I said, my mouth now watering, "Anything I can do?"

"Yeah – get two more cans and then go and sit at the table and wait!" he said as more sizzling noises filled the air, "It's coming on nicely."

To be honest I'd make a lousy food critic – I just like tasty food – full stop – and plenty of it! And that's what John served up – a massive steak with all kinds of 'extras' and with exotic fragrances filling my mouth and nose I just plain tucked in – John joining me moments later.

I'm not going to go into exactly what we ate or just what it tasted of – suffice to say that it was delicious and it wasn't long before we'd both finished, then we sat side by side wiping our grease-smeared faces and exchanging happy grins.

"Good?" he asked, and I raised my can to toast the meal.

"Bloody good!" I replied, "Best steak I've had in years – well, ever, perhaps! Well done!"

"Cheers!" said John draining his third can, "Phew! I'm full."

"And me!" I replied, "Bet there's still room for a few more beers though!"

"There's another twelve-pack in the cupboard," said John, "I'll top up the fridge now."

We both rose and began clearing away the debris of the meal and it wasn't long before everything was done and tidied away and we stood side by side to survey the tidy scene. I turned towards John and put my arm around his waist to give him a quick 'thank you' hug but as I did so, John turned towards me and his own arms closed around me too.

And face to face, chest to chest, belly to belly we looked into each other's eyes.

"I've had a lovely evening," I said, "Thank you so much!"

"Want to thank me properly?" asked John, "Come and kiss me then."

He puckered up his lips and held them out theatrically to me and somehow I just had to do it. I leaned closer and touched my lips to his, instantly feeling his tongue pushing between my lips. But rather than be horrified I found myself responding by sucking it into my mouth; then my lips relaxed and in moments we were into a full-blown snog! Our arms and hands were holding and exploring each other's backs as our mouths explored each other and I'd forgotten just how prehensile a tongue could be... until we eventually came up for air.

"Phew – that was intense!" I said, still holding John in my arms, "Let's sit down."

John was sensible and didn't push for more and then, with new cans in our hands we sat in the two armchairs, me at least feeling buzzed and a bit light-headed, but happy and relaxed once again. Slowly our conversation meandered round, carefully avoiding anything sexual – the cricket, football, the weather – even politics and the pile of empty cans grew.

It was after we'd chatted for a while that John face began to change. It looked as if he was trying to find the right words to say, then he began.

"Chris," he started somewhat reluctantly, "I want to check on something please?"

"Yeah sure," I agreed amicably.

"It was earlier," he said, "You said "I'm out of practice" or something like that, didn't you?"

I nodded, realising that I'd blown my cover and John continued.

"So you've done all this before, have you?" he asked.

I nodded, knowing that it was time to come clean.

"I used to have a boyfriend," I said, "Actually I've had several now, so yeah, I've been there, done that."

"I thought you seemed a bit too eager!" he said with a laugh, "Good for you Chris – I'm so pleased."

"I wasn't sure if I wanted to try gay sex again," I said, "But now I have I realise what I've been missing. It was fun wasn't it!"

"You dark horse you!" laughed John as he stretched across and patted my cheek, "Come on then, tell me the story."

So I did, recounting my time with Gary and my earlier years with Peter, eventually feeling far better now that I'd come clean. Finally, I reached the end and John stood up.

"Wow, that was an amazing story," he said, "Thank you for telling me."

"Glad I did actually," I admitted, "Perhaps I'm at peace with myself now."

"That's good, now, time to shut up shop, I think, I'm a bit pissed," he said as he swayed a bit unsteadily.

I looked at him through somewhat hazy eyes and grinned back at him.

"Me too!" I said, "Not complaining though!"

I remained seated while John busied himself around the house before he returned.

"Come on then, up you come," he said, pulling me to my feet.

"Where we goin'?" I mumbled.

"Up to bed – time for some sleep," John said.

"Yeah – good idea!" I agreed with him and arm in arm we helped each other to mount the stairs.

John guided me to the toilet where I gratefully began to unload several gallons of used lager and a few minutes later John joined me.

"Finished?" he asked as I moved a bit unsteadily aside, "Good."

With that he pulled his penis out and began pissing – leaving me leaning against the wall beside him and soon he too had finished.

"Come on then," he said, pulling me across the hall to his bedroom, "Get your clothes off and get in."

"I ought to be goin' home," I said, my befuddled brain hardly working at all now.

"Plenty of room here!" said John, pushing my shorts down for me and soon leaving me naked.

He pushed me backwards gently and I just fell onto the bed and a few moments later I felt the bed move as John got in too.

"Why am I here?" I managed to ask.

"'Cos you're not fit to go home," said John, "Now roll over and go to sleep!"

"Yeah – alright – good night," I mumbled and that was the last I remembered...

I woke up and rolled over to blearily glance at the alarm clock – it was a different one – oh so what. It told me it was 8:53 AM – so today must be Saturday or Sunday – otherwise I'd be up and out at work by now. Well, I hoped that was the case!

I rolled back and came face to face with a gently relaxed masculine face, sleeping contentedly on the pillow, a happy smile playing on his countenance. Oh god yes – I'd spent the night with John – in John's bed – with him. In the nude too! Did I do anything stupid in the night – I can't remember...

My wandering eyes also took in two cans of lager by the bed – oh yes, we'd downed more than a few last night too, hadn't we?

My gaze fell back to John, still blissfully asleep with his upper body partially uncovered. My eyes almost naturally dropped to his chest, firm and nicely bronzed and tipped with his little brown nipples.

And then it all started coming back to me...

I remembered sucking on those nipples last night; running my hands over his warm invitingly hard flesh as I filled my hands with his muscles.

I remembered working my way down his body, rolling him over and kissing him between his quivering buttocks in the valley where, some time, soon I'd slide my rampant cock. I remembered sliding further down to poke my tongue into his anus and kiss his puckered skin with my lips.

I remembered working my way back around, my hands now leaving his buttocks to caress the smooth, sleek flesh of his waist and hips. I remembered his wiry patch of trimmed pubic hair tickling my chin before I lowered my mouth onto his upstanding erection.

He tasted so delicious, so erotically sexy, so desirable – I couldn't help but work my tongue into the little hole at the tip to explore the source of his delicious fluids.

I remember John's body jerking violently as I sucked at his cock, licking up his copious lubrication before slithering down to allow more of his penis into my mouth. It felt huge in my mouth but truthfully, I was just loving being able to suck on it!

I remember that I sank my mouth over his erection and sucked away, my tongue sliding and dancing over the tumescent flesh while beneath me his whole body seemed to be in motion – waves of excitement were rippling through him as I brought him towards his climax.

Then John was crying out, groaning and gasping in ecstasy as his orgasm peaked – his hips thrusting his cock hard into my mouth as I continued to stimulate him until he could take no more.

And now I remembered the feeling of sperm being ejected into my mouth; the feeling of warm slippery spunk sliding down my throat; the glow inside me as I accepted his offering.

I shook my head in wonderment...

'Wow,' I thought, 'What a difference a day made!'

Sittin' On The Cock Of The Boy

As far back into my life as I can remember I've always loved fishing. I think my granddad started my interest because he had his own boat – only about 18 feet long with a small cabin on – but to me as a child it was as good as a pirate ship! And so, whenever we stayed with my grandparents, namely every Easter for a couple of weeks and each summer for six weeks I'd hanker after going out on his boat. If granddad wouldn't give in to my entreaties, I'd go and just sit in the boat, whether it was in the water or out of it and make-believe, because in the boat on my own I could be anyone and do anything. Heck – the boat could even be my own spaceship if I chose!

But when granddad did take me fishing in his boat I was in heaven – the feeling of being out there among the waves and other craft made me feel strangely grown-up even though I wasn't. And when I caught a fish, I definitely was grown-up! But times passed and granddad passed on too, but the memories lingered...

Therefore, many years later I inevitably bought my own boat.

I was now in my latter 30's and I'd settled down comfortably. My work as a writer and computer man had grown and with no partner, I was able to enjoy a bit more free time and I was financially well placed. I'd bought myself a slightly larger house nearer the coast; I had a decent car – and now I owned a boat too. And I didn't even have a wife or kids to muck up my weekends either. I'd actually bought the boat using a tax refund – my life seemed to be filled with such bits of good fortune – so it was a 'luxury' that hadn't even hurt my pocket.

Needless to say, my boat was somewhat more sophisticated than my granddad's had been. This one had a proper cabin; it was 36 feet long and had a built-in diesel engine and I kept it in a marina on the south coast of England, not far from my new home. I always seemed to be pottering around in it with small trips up and down the coast, occasionally taking a few friends fishing or just heading out alone for pleasure – it was an amazing way to escape from the 'normal' rigours of life. Naturally it was also rigged up to sleep and eat in, even if the accommodation was a bit primitive really.

To be honest, just why I fished, I don't know – presumably just for the pleasure of it; just for the enjoyment of pitting myself against nature; of braving the elements on occasions and of enjoying the peace. Perhaps I needed to fish to justify going out in my boat. There wasn't a whole lot of sense in bringing piles of fish home – there was only me to feed, so I used to put my catch back alive except for the occasional decent cod which I'd bring home, fillet and then freeze.

I'd never got around to settling down. Every woman I'd met seemed to be lacking something. Somehow we never clicked; somehow we always parted with one or other of us saying "I'll give you a call" – which never happened... Every guy seemed to be much the same and although I'd had some deep and meaningful relationships with both sexes, I seemed to be happier on my own and quite honestly, I'd become quite contented as a kind of loner. I still had quite a few friends; but they weren't 'in' my life – they were more like passing acquaintances on the whole. I could always round up someone if I wanted a dinner or bed companion – male or female, so I was happy enough. And I suppose I had more male friends than female, but that was hardly surprising – what woman wants to spend an evening talking about boats or computers!

I often wondered if I was totally gay but although I was happy to spend time in bed with men or women my real love was for freedom – and now my boat!

It had been several years since I'd last had a male partner – it had been John actually, but we'd parted company when I sold up and moved. I'd enjoyed sharing my bed with a small assortment of women since then and of late I seemed to feel that I really preferred the company of a woman, so I'd gone out of my way to avoid talking about either my boat or my computers. Instead I'd done my best to cultivate a more heterosexual and suitable range of interests for the ladies to enjoy – but it all came unravelled as I'll explain.

It was in early May if I remember correctly and we were having one of those spells of mid-spring warm dry sunny weather. I was at the marina and I'd had the boat hauled out so I could clean the hull, give it some coats of paint and varnish and spruce up the deck too when I realised I was being watched. That actually wasn't all that uncommon – it's amazing how many people just come and watch a man tinkering with his boat, but this felt different, I could tell.

Eventually, having reached the end of a section of hull I stood upright, stretching my back after having been bent awkwardly for too long and pulled my shoulders back. I took a deep breath – and relaxed.

"Must be time for a break," I said to myself as I worked to relax my muscles.

"I think you deserve one – you've been working really hard," a male voice said, and I looked to see who it was.

The owner of the voice was a young man; I'd have guessed he was a fair bit younger than me because quite honestly, he looked more like an overgrown boy than a man. He was sitting on the upturned hull of a small dinghy just nearby but now he levered himself up and sauntered over to stand nearer.

"Been watching you working – it's good to see someone working so diligently," he said, "Sorry – I ought to introduce myself, shouldn't I – I'm Andy."

"Oh hi," I said, not sticking out my hand, because it was covered in muck, "Nice to meet you. I'm Chris."

"Nice to meet you too then, Chris," he replied, "I hope you didn't mind me watching... my dad's got his boat over there and I'm stuck here for the day."

"Could be a worse situation for you," I answered amicably, "I don't mind you watching but why on earth are you watching me then?"

"Got bored over on our boat," he said as he waved his hand across the marina, "And dad's a grumpy old fart, so I've left him to it! Anyway, you're a pretty good-looking guy."

I laughed at his predicament and let my eyes scan him while wondering what he saw in me. He too was in shorts and a t-shirt, but they looked a lot nicer than my own clothes.

'They're probably cleaner too,' I thought, my mind imagining my own appearance.

He may have looked boyish but his muscular legs gave his age away a bit, I reckoned – that and the fact that he was over six feet tall and he had a nice happy smiling face, so I mentally accepted the idea that chatting with him wouldn't just be a load of childish questions and answers.

"Don't blame you giving your dad a wide berth then, errrrmm, Andy," I said, eventually remembering his name, "And no, I don't mind you watching but don't let this anti-fouling stuff get on you though."

He stepped back carefully and looked at where I'd been working.

"Horrible stuff isn't it – still so long as it does what it's supposed to," he said, "Personally I prefer to paint the nice bits of the boat – above deck."

I laughed at him and then, as I was not a little sweaty, I stripped off my t-shirt.

"Wow!" said Andy suddenly, "Where'd you get those muscles? Don't you look good! Looks like you've been working out!"

"I used to go to the gym a lot," I said as I did some gentle stretching exercises, "Nowadays I only go twice a week for a quick work-out – well, more of a keep fit thing really, I'm not dedicated to it, not like I used to be. Mind you, I tend to be stuck in my office, so I need the exercise or I'd probably get fat!"

"It works for you then," said Andy, "Wish I had more muscles."

It was then that something caught my eye. He'd developed a bulge in his shorts that hadn't been there before and suddenly I found that I had to turn around because as soon as I'd spotted the bulge I too had immediately been struck with the same affliction.

I busied myself with cleaning off what muck had found me while I pondered the situation.

Here was me showing off some muscles and Andy was getting turned on by them! Was he gay? I guessed he had to be... but since I'd stiffened too, what did that make me? Oh yes, I'd been with John and with Peter and several others before and since them but since those days I'd tried to cultivate a more hetero way of life, fearful of upsetting any homophobic customers so this was causing something of an unwelcome stirring of my inner feelings. Fortunately my cock subsided enough for me to turn round again and immediately my eyes clamped onto his groin once more... and sure enough, there was his bulge, only decidedly bigger than before!

I was about to make some excuse as to why I couldn't keep on chatting when Andy spoke.

"Chris – I know I've only just met you, but I was planning to get some lunch soon so would you care to have a beer with me and perhaps a bite to eat? The clubhouse bar isn't too bad," he said, his words tumbling out quickly, "Once you've cleared up, that is?"

Since there were two main things on my mind – a cool drink and something to eat, I could hardly say no – anyway, he'd be company for me regardless of his bulge.

"Yeah, sure, be glad to," I replied, "Let me get cleaned up a bit then."

"Oh that's brilliant – thanks everso," said Andy, "There's usually such a load of old stuffed shirts here – it's nice to meet someone who isn't! I'll wait for you."

"Agreed! Ok – won't be long," I said as I worked hand cleaner into my skin, "Clean t-shirt and I'll do, I guess."

I was still a little worried that I'd be having lunch with a "gay" person – but then I realised that he was right – we were some of the few younger people here so lunching with him, whatever his sexual orientation, was better than getting lumbered with some old crust or eating alone.

Five minutes later I was relatively clean and presentable, and we sauntered over to the marina clubhouse – and as we walked, I realised that we made a quite reasonable looking pair. Andy was of very similar build to me if not quite so muscular. We both had fair curly hair and narrowish faces; smiling eyes and mouths and we were about the same in height – a little over six feet – only our ages were different. I was feeling quite contented as we idly chatted as we walked to the bar.

"Are you old enough to be in here?" I asked as we approached the bar.

"Yeah – I'm 20 but I'm always having to dig out my ID," Andy said, "Cor – it was great once I left my teens. I thought I was properly grown up!"

"Still just a big kid though!" I quipped, as the barman came to us – and sure enough, Andy had to produce his ID, even though he'd been at this bar many times before.

He raised his eyebrows and pulled a face at me as he pocketed his little card...

For once the place was quite busy, so we got our pints and ordered a steak pie and chips each and then took ourselves out onto their outdoor decking where almost no-one else seemed to have ventured today. We sat at a table at one end, out of the way and supped our beers while we waited for lunch to appear then before long we were tucking in and also working our way through our second pint each...

"Won't get much work done this afternoon at this rate," I grumbled light-heartedly.

"I can help if you like," said Andy as he finished his lunch, "Got nothing better to do this afternoon. In fact I'll probably be here all the weekend, so I could help you tomorrow too if that would be ok."

"Hmmmm," I pondered, because I did like to do things myself, "Suppose you could."

Andy put his hand on my arm and squeezed it.

"Go on – please," he said, looking me straight in the eyes, "I like being with you – you're nice!"

My eyebrows lifted at that comment – what exactly did he mean? Nice, indeed!

I pushed myself back from the table just as Andy did and we both leaned back in our chairs to gather as much of the sunshine as we could and to let our meals go down and as Andy pushed back I happened to glance at his lap and there it was again! His bulge! But now it was stretched out over his thigh pointing towards me and I realised that while he didn't have a full-blown erection, his cock was aroused and had uncoiled itself.

'I wonder how big he is?' I pondered; then stopped.

'Quit thinking like that!' I told myself as I dragged my eyes away from his lap.

But Andy must have seen me looking...

"Sorry Chris," he said, "My thingy got all excited over something. He does that – well, he's always doing that!"

I was a bit curious now, but I hardly knew what to do or say next – but suddenly I found myself responding.

"Come on then, tell me what excited you," I asked, taking myself by surprise with my audacity!

"You want me to be completely honest," said Andy, "It was you – when I touched you it just set me off!"

"Really?" I queried, "I'm not that exciting, am I?"

"To me you are," said Andy, putting his hand back on my arm, "I guess you realise that I'm gay, well I think I am and you just turned me on – you're just so sexy. The way you look – even the way you talk. I'm sorry."

"How do you know you're gay then?" I asked, curious to know how he felt.

"I just don't fancy girls," he said, "Only blokes, but I haven't been brave enough to chat any of them up until now. But I just couldn't help it with you."

His eyes fell contritely downwards, as did his hand.

Quickly I reached out and grabbed his hand, just as it landed on his thigh and there our hands rested, just inches from his penis.

"Hey – don't worry!" I replied, squeezing his hand, "I'm not offended; just surprised, that's all. I'm not used to being told that by a bloke."

"It's not something I go around saying all the time either," said Andy, "But there's just something special about you."

I smiled at him before choosing to look down at our hands. And there, not two inches away, his cock was now a long hard ridge in his shorts and already there was a little damp spot at the tip.

"Wow!" I said, rather unintentionally declaring my interest, "Looks as if you're right! And it looks as if you need to do something with him, doesn't it?"

"Oh fuck!" exclaimed Andy covering his bulge with his other hand, "Seriously I can't help it! He just does what he wants to."

"He definitely can't do what he wants to here," I said, "You'd better come back to my boat – you can get in the cabin and have a quiet wank if it'll help."

"Really?" said Andy, "Oh god – thanks for the offer! Think I'd better take you up on it."

We managed to exit the club without anyone arresting Andy for public indecency and quickly made it back to my boat. Andy swarmed up the little ladder and climbed into the boat and I did likewise, getting a good view of his tight arse and strong legs as I followed him.

We went into the cabin where I pulled all the curtains across the windows and searched out an old towel.

"Here you are, buddy, wank into this," I said slapping him gently on the back as I turned to walk out.

"Could you stay?" asked Andy plaintively, "It's you who caused this and if you go he might lose interest. Stay please – you can watch if you like!"

Wow! I'd almost forgotten what it was like to watch a man other than myself having a wank – this might be interesting!

"Oh ok," I said rather offhandedly but sort of curiously, "Get 'em off then and get started!"

"You sure?" he asked as he fiddled with the catch of his shorts.

"No – not really but get on with it anyway and perhaps I'll feel better about it," I said, now rather hoping to see his cock.

A moment later Andy's shorts hit the deck; a moment after that his underpants did too and there it was – his penis in all its erect and pulsating glory!

I just had to look. He was uncut, as was I but unlike mine, his penis was quite slim – but it was long; definitely very long! I gasped quietly as he held it and slowly pulled back his foreskin. His glistening purple knob appeared, tipped with a small drop of seminal fluid. He rubbed his cock slowly, bringing forth another streak of fluid which he smeared over his knob.

"What do you think then?" asked Andy as he began rubbing his shaft, "Any good?"

"Don't know," I replied as I realised that my own penis was now rock hard, "Looks alright to me. Looks so long though! What is it – ten inches or about that?"

"Spot on!" chuckled Andy, looking pointedly at the large tent in my shorts, "Could you get yours out too – you might as well; then we can both have a wank. Perhaps you can turn me on while I turn you on!"

Hardly comprehending what I was doing I undid my shorts and let them drop to the floor. They had a built-in mesh lining that doubled as underpants, so now I was bare – my own erection now thrusting out mere feet from where Andy was stropping his penis.

"Hey Chris – that's a decent cock. I love the way it's so nice and thick," said Andy as my seven or so inch penis swayed as I moved, "Oooh – that looks really lovely to me!"

Together we started wanking; each watching the other at work. For a while there was comparative silence, only punctured by our breathing and the steady slapping of our hands as we wanked together but despite the newly thrilling feelings in me things were slow and I suddenly remembered that I had a small pile of wank mags in one of the lockers.

"Fancy a bit of a help?" I asked, interrupting my own wanking to fetch out the magazines, "See if these help at all."

Andy scanned through them and pulled out two of them.

"Hey, you've got some all male ones!" he said, "Brilliant!"

"Oh shit yeah," I said somewhat shamefacedly, "They were just to see what they were like."

"Well then – did you enjoy them?" asked Andy, picking up his wanking again.

"I guess you could say so," I said, "I'll be honest – I liked looking at them and the cocks in them turned me on, but I always felt ashamed to wank off over them."

"Well now's the time to break your inhibitions then," said Andy with a laugh, "Let's look at them together and wank together. Ok?"

"Come on then!" I said bravely and with that we settled to our task, Andy turning the pages and both of us making comments.

"Fuck me!" said Andy as we found a double page spread of three men – the guy in the middle being fucked at one end and sucking a cock at the other, "Oh that's hot! What does it do for you?"

"Makes me harder, that much I know," I said, wanking quicker, "Oh look at this one though!"

I'd turned the page and there was a series of photos; the first depicting a young man sitting naked with an incredibly long cock rearing from his groin and another man, also with an erection, approaching him.

"Hey – that could be us!" said Andy, because the young man did indeed look quite like him.

The series went on to show him kneeling down; grasping the upright penis; sucking it (from various angles) and finally several cum-shots with the head of the penis trapped inside the man's mouth while dribbles of white sperm ran out of the corners of his mouth and back down the shaft of the long muscle.

"I DO like that," said Andy with emphasis, "Now that is hot!"

I saw Andy looking hard at me as he spoke, but I was too carried away with my wanking because now I could feel the start of my orgasm. Oh, it wasn't there yet but you know those spasms that jerk through you as you wank when you're nearly there; well, they'd started.

Then Andy turned the page again and there was another two-page story – with the same two men in it. Obviously it had been taken on a different day or earlier than the first photos because the man that looked like Andy still had his erection and was still seated, but this time the other guy was lowering his arse onto the fine pole! By the third photo he'd sunk right down on it – all of that nine- or ten-inch cock was now up inside him! And even before I'd properly looked at the next photos, I just couldn't help it – I just erupted!

"Aaaaaagh!" I cried, "Oh fuck – sod it! Cummming! Uhhh! Cummmming!"

Without any further ado a huge gush of spunk hosed from my cock right across the magazine!

"Ooooh – ooooh!" I groaned as more lava erupted and splashed onto the photos.

A few moments later Andy groaned too.

"Oh you sod – you've made me come!" he cried, "Ooooooh yeahhhh, yeah!"

And his lengthy tool jerked violently and sprayed energetic jets of cum; the first squirted massively and powerfully across my cock then up the side of the cabin; the second, third, fourth and fifth splashed across the magazine and the mattress!

"Sorry – sorry!" he groaned as he stripped the last of his cum from his cock, "You set me off – oh fuuuuck! Oh that's better!"

We both stood there panting with sperm drooling from our penises; both with that wild-eyed look that follows an event that's really exciting.

"Wow," I exclaimed as I picked up the towel and cleaned my cock, "Didn't you enjoy that!"

I laughed as I followed the deposits of cum across the cabin and Andy laughed too.

"I didn't expect I'd do that!" he said as he shook the remaining drops of cum onto the towel.

"What – cum?" I asked with a silly grin.

"No – cum so much – that was amazing!" he chuckled, "But those pictures just got me going – that and the fact that you were wanking right beside me."

I began using the towel to clean up at least some of the mess then had to find another one to finish the job.

"Do you always make so much?" I asked as I dumped the towels in a bag to take home to clean.

"Not usually as much as that but I'm always generous! Hey, you pumped out a fair bit too, didn't you!" he said with a laugh, "And did you notice that the guy in the photo looked like me?"

"Is that what turned you on so much?" I asked and Andy nodded.

"I think so," he said. "Perhaps it was just the whole thing but yes, I think you're right."

"Did you like the idea of sucking a penis and being fucked by one then?" I asked and Andy's head nodded firmly.

"So – could you do that?" I enquired as I finished cleaning my cock...

"Dunno, honestly," he said, "Perhaps given enough alcohol!"

"Hmmmm, I'll remember that!" I answered with a smile.

With the evidence of our substantial loads cleaned away and the cabin returned to it's normal state we both dressed again, then climbed out of the cabin and into the fresh air once more.

"Come on, I'm getting back to work," I said, putting my arm round Andy's shoulders, "Or it'll never get done."

"Hey, I said I'd help," said Andy, "I know what I'm doing. Give me a scraper and I'll get the hull cleaned down over here."

"Cheers – that's good – that's the worst part, I reckon," I said with relief, "There isn't all that much left to do anyway... might even finish it tonight if we get on with it."

We climbed down out of the boat and stood there facing one another when suddenly Andy reached out and hugged me to him. And for some happy reason I responded by hugging him too!

"Thanks Chris, I so enjoyed that, and I really needed it!" Andy said, "Thank you, thank you!"

He hugged me tighter until I pushed him away gently.

"Hey, come on, don't get all sloppy!" I said, "It's not as if you're saying goodbye, is it?"

Andy held me at arm's length and beamed a huge smile.

"Really – will I see you again?" he gushed.

We'd still be 'together' as we finished off painting the hull, but I knew what he meant.

"Yeah – of course!" I said happily, because even putting aside the sexy bits, he seemed just the kind of guy that I could get on with – the unexpected sex was just a bonus!

"Yeah!!!" crowed Andy with delight, "Ok – let's get to work!"

And much as forecast, with the two of us hard at it, the job was completed that evening just as the sun was going down – I was well pleased because the hull was now clean and fit for the water. There was just the upper deck-work to sort out.

As we stood and cleaned up beside my now much better looking boat the subject of tomorrow came up.

"You're down here again tomorrow?" Andy asked, "I told you I'd be here tomorrow – are you coming down too?"

"Yep," I said, "I'd like to get the boat back in the water next weekend and there's a lot to do that's easier to do while it's up here. I don't suppose you'd be willing to help again would you?"

"Love to!" said Andy, "Better than being stuck with my dad – I much prefer your company!"

"So it seems!" I said, laughing, "Ok – well, you know where to find me... I'll be down before lunch again – probably about tennish."

"Look forward to helping you again," said Andy, sticking out his hand.

I reached mine out too and shook his but he turned it into a clasp of hands instead and pulled me towards him. Our bodies touched and I could have sworn I felt his cock hard against me... but somehow I wasn't repulsed now as Andy squashed us together in a parting hug.

"You don't know how happy you've made me," he said, "I never thought..."

"Shhhh!" I said, "Don't go all soft on me!"

Andy pushed us apart and looked down.

"No chance of that!" he replied, outlining his newly sprung erection with his hand.

I shook my head as I put the small ladder away and then climbed into my MG.

"Incorrigible!" I yelled, as I gunned the motor, "Look after it!"

My evening at home was quiet but somehow, despite the loneliness of home, I felt happy. Had I rediscovered my sexual orientation? Had I found someone to share my time with? Or was it just lust and hormones?

Whatever, as soon as I thought back to the day's events, my cock would stiffen and I feel tingles coursing through my body as the action re-ran in my brain. And whatever my true orientation, my brain and my cock had obviously enjoyed themselves! I spent the evening cheerfully humming to myself as I did my chores and finally, when it was time for bed, I found that my cock was once again hard and demanding. For a short while I played with it but tiredness overcame me and I drifted off to sleep, for all I knew, still with a hard-on!

I woke in the morning refreshed and somehow eager to meet Andy again. Ok – we'd crossed a line somewhere that wasn't in my usual life, but I'd really enjoyed it – the daring and excitement of what we'd done had fired my gay sex life up again! Perhaps I'd been somewhat jaded by a succession of ineffectual affairs and meetings I'd had of late, but now, this was something fresh!

So it wasn't all that long before I was roaring off down the road to the marina, happily singing some inane ditty as I went and feeling young again. I'd obviously become set in my ways even at 36 and yet this sexy young man had done something that no-one else had managed for some time!

And at just after nine I was crawling (speed limit 5 mph!) into the marina and parking up by the slipway. I soon had my ladder back in place, my scrapers, sandpaper, paint and brushes at the ready – hell, I was setting out my shop, I suddenly realised! Getting all my goodies ready for my first customer – my Andy!

'MY Andy' did I say?

"Wake up – come on, stop dreaming! What are you on?" I muttered to myself.

Despite my desires there was no Andy in the morning. Perhaps it should have been another one of those "I'll give you a call" moments last evening...

I mooched around for a bit and then realised that I had to get on with my work regardless, so I climbed into the boat and settled down to my task. In the confines of the decking it soon became quite warm, so I stripped off my t-shirt and worked on in shorts, enjoying the sun on my back. I won't say that steam was rising from me – it wasn't that hot, but I soon found myself sweating as I scraped and sandpapered some rough areas... but I was happy enough.

And then I felt the boat tremble slightly as some weight was put on the ladder and suddenly Andy's head popped over the rail. Instantly I felt a thrill run through me and a smile form on my lips.

"Bloody dad," said Andy with feeling as he vaulted over the rail, "Wanted me to get some stuff in town. Could have done it himself if he'd wanted to. Old bastard!"

"Fine way to speak of your father!" I said, standing up from my chores, "You obviously don't think much of him."

"Oh, he's ok when he's at home I suppose – a bit bossy, but down here he acts like he owns the place. Just 'cos he's got a fucking' boat!" he said as he dumped his bag in the cabin.

Andy continued talking... unloading his irritations.

"Can't wait to leave home really. I've just landed a nice job so I'm going to save up some cash to rent a place – then I'm off!" he said as he sat down on one of the transom seats.

"What do you do then?" I asked, genuinely interested.

"I'm a male model," he said, standing up again, "Or at least I will be when I start work – it's only a provincial company but the money's going to be ok and I like that kind of work. Actually I think I'm pretty good at it!"

He twirled around like a drunken ballet dancer and almost lost his footing as he tripped over some of the junk on the deck. I grabbed him before he fell.

"Oooops!" he said, laughing gaily, "Normally the stage is clear...!"

But do you know what? For some reason I didn't want to let him go – for some reason I wanted to be able to hold onto him, to feel him in my arms. I could have sworn that I'd never felt like this before. My hands were still holding Andy's waist when he spun around until he was facing me, his eyes twinkling.

"Thanks Chris, thanks for saving me," he said, and his hands came up and grasped my waist too.

"I'd have hated to see you fall overboard," I said, "The concrete's a lot harder than water."

"No – no – not that – thanks for saving me from my old man," he said, "I would have died of boredom and I wouldn't have had half as much fun without you."

Simultaneously we pulled each other closer together and this time I definitely felt his erection digging into my groin. My own penis rose and began filling out as we clinched, and I began to think about yesterday's bit of fun.

'Could we do it again?' I found myself wondering, *'I know I feel like it.'*

But sanity took over once more and I pulled myself from his (my) clutches.

"Come on – less of the fashion show and more of the painting," I said cheerfully, "You promised to help and this isn't helping at all."

"Oh!" groaned Andy playfully, "Ok then, where do I start?"

For the next few hours we both put our backs into it and we really made some good progress, but there's a lot of boat in a 36-footer – and a lot of it needed repainting.

Eventually it was well past midday; actually almost two o'clock. I stood up to stretch my limbs and soon Andy did likewise.

"Hey, that's some good work we've done," I said as I surveyed our work, "I'm well pleased – thanks!"

"Glad to be helping you Chris," said Andy, "You ready for some lunch?"

"Starving already," I groaned, "Breakfast seems too long ago. Clubhouse again if we're not too late?"

"Actually, I hope you don't think I'm too forward," said Andy, a bit hesitantly, "But when dad sent me off to the shops, I bought us some bits and pieces – could we eat here?"

"Excellent! Great idea!" I said, not considering anything but the thought of food in my stomach, "I'll pay you back."

"Don't have to – dad paid on his account, although he won't know until he gets his statement – and then I don't suppose he'll think to check it!" said Andy as he hopped over the rail and trotted over to his car.

He was driving an oldish VW convertible which was parked beside my MG. He picked up a large bag and loped back to the boat on his long legs and climbed back aboard.

I went into the cabin and Andy began spreading out his wares on the table. Quite honestly I'd have eaten anything but his offerings looked plentiful and mouth-watering and by the time I'd found some old but cleanish glasses for the wine he'd brought, we were well set for a feast.

Contentedly we munched away, and we'd also soon emptied the first bottle – something that Andy had obviously anticipated because, wearing a big smile, he pulled a second bottle from his bag and opened it.

"You're not aiming to get much work done this afternoon, are you?" I commented but Andy just raised his glass in salute and carried on scoffing.

'Fair enough,' I thought to myself as I ate, 'All work and no play can't be good... might as well take some part of the weekend to relax. With two of us we can probably finish the job before next weekend. Guess it might mean coming down after work, but so what!'

Together we cleared our lunch and also finished the second bottle. I stood up to stretch and almost overbalanced, noting that the rather heady wine, the hot sun and the good food had combined to cook my brain. I shook my head as we walked out onto the deck to stand in the sun.

"Thanks Andy – that was good, mate," I exclaimed, realising that I was a bit pissed, "So if you're not aiming at working this afternoon, what are you planning to do?"

"You!" he said as he finished disposing of the rubbish.

"Eh?" I exclaimed, not really catching on yet.

"Well," he said, now coming to stand near me, "Since we can't really paint while we're in this condition, we can at least get to know one another better – eh? And then we can play, perhaps..."

He ran his hand down over my penis making both me and my cock jerk at his touch and I felt it began to stiffen.

"Is that what you're after?" I asked, sitting rather clumsily on one of the bench seats.

Andy nodded happily and smoothed his hand down over his own groin.

"Ok – let's get back to the getting to know one another bit," I said, realising that my cock had started to fill out quite considerably, "So what do you want to know?"

"Isn't so much about knowing as about finding out," said Andy, mysteriously, "I'm not worried about your background – what I'd like to find out is where you're heading."

"Oh – ummm – dunno – really don't know!" I blustered, not entirely sure how to answer that.

"Well, for a start," said Andy, his hand still gently rubbing across his groin, "Could we pick up from where we left off yesterday, please. I

238

want to know you better and I'd love to, well, go a bit further if we could."

Immediately my partial erection jerked and throbbed because I'd really enjoyed our mutual wank which I'd found it to be both exciting and a big turn-on.

"Could do," I replied, feeling my penis moving inside my shorts, "What are you planning then?"

"Let's just start again," said Andy, his hand still over his groin, "You know – strip off and then go from there."

"Seriously?" I asked, not really expecting this kind of thing, "Then what?"

"Well, ummm, just wank together for now," said Andy, removing his hand from his groin and undoing the clasp on his shorts, "Ok – yeah?"

"Whoa – not so fast" I hissed quietly as I stopped him disrobing, "Not out here! Come into the cabin."

It wasn't as if there were other people nearby, but my natural shyness took over and a few moments later we were out of sight standing close together in the cabin.

"Alright now," I said.

Andy took his hand away and his already undone shorts fell down, his erect penis springing out and up before me!

"Fuck me," I said, "That definitely is one long penis – wow!"

Automatically I undid my shorts too and moments later we were both bare from the waist down but somehow that just made me feel silly, so we both pulled off our t-shirts as well. All that remained to deal with were our two penises which stood up hard and eager before us – less than two feet apart.

"Can I see those mags again?" Andy asked and in a few moments I had them spread out on the table.

"Yeah – these are the good ones," he said as he pulled the men only ones off the top of the pile, "Come on then, let's get into it."

Caught up in the moment I couldn't do much but follow his example – this was almost forgotten territory to me, but I was enjoying it!

Side by side we began to wank – both of us stropping our shafts slowly and gently as we perused the erotic flesh on display. We were almost silent apart from the occasional slap as flesh met flesh and the sound of our breathing, which was gradually becoming faster. And then, out of the blue, Andy said something that changed everything.

"Can I suck you?" he said, "Can you put your cock in my mouth, please?"

The blurriness from the wine disappeared in seconds as I registered his request.

'Yeah – a blow job! At last! Yeah mate – come on!' I thought.

"Yes please," I groaned, "Suck me – please suck me!"

Moments later I felt Andy's hand grasp my erection – and that alone was so good! And then I felt his lips tight around my cock...and that was even better!

"Oh fuck – oh my god – this is brilliant!" I gasped as I looked down.

It was amazing to look down to see a man's head again and especially one who was very busy sucking my penis.

"Oooooh fuck Andy – your mouth feels good," I groaned, "Oh, this is brilliant!"

Andy was on his knees before me, at least half of my cock inside his mouth as he gently moved back and forward while he slid his lips up and down my shaft.

"Why aren't women this good?" I groaned, "Oh fuck – this is so, so fucking brilliant."

I could feel my hips jerking upwards, driving my cock into his mouth, harder and harder.

"Oooh yeah, yeah! I like it! Oooooh fuuuuck!" I moaned as Andy began wanking me as he sucked me.

For some minutes he just kept on sucking and wanking me and it was fantastic! Without a doubt this was the best blowjob I'd ever enjoyed! And now I felt something different... I could feel Andy's mouth accommodating my cock – all of it – as he let my length slide down his throat – he was taking all of me! I felt the pressure of his throat around my knob as he swallowed my entire seven-inch length, then the pressure of his nose against my belly.

I heard Andy cough lightly as he lifted off before he once again engulfed my penis – this time concentrating on my knob. His active tongue was swirling and twisting over and around my knob and really stirring up my feelings – in a relatively short time he'd brought me almost to an orgasm.

Collecting my senses, I pulled him off me.

"You'll make me cum" I said, somewhat worried about my generous offering, "Stop it!"

"No way," he said, redoubling his efforts on my penis, "I want you to cum in my mouth, please."

And now my orgasm was very close. I could feel my hips jerking involuntarily as my orgasm neared – my breath was coming in uneven intakes, my knees were trembling...

"Oh fuck – oh fuck! I'm cummming! Ohhhh yeah!" I cried as my cock began erupting its load into Andy's eager mouth.

"Uuuuuh – uuuuuugh!" I cried as more sperm was ejected into his mouth, "Oh god, that's good!"

Andy seemed to be enjoying it too but after my first four eruptions had filled his mouth, a small squirt of cum slipped from the corner of his mouth – then he pulled his mouth from my penis. As he did so, my final jet, admittedly fairly feeble, squirted out and slashed across his nose and made an amazingly erotic sight! Finally, once my penis has stopped providing Andy with any more liquid offerings, I was able to recover and sit down on the bench seat in the cabin.

"Fuckin' hell!" I said shaking my head, "That was good! What on earth made you want to do that?"

"Chris, don't forget that I think I'm gay," said Andy, "I love cocks – well, I would if I knew any and as for cum there's nothing I enjoy more than licking my spunk up after I've cum. Yours was only the second one I've sucked and it was such a good cock to suck! Not only that you gave me a huge load didn't you?"

"Ummm – only one day's supply!" I said, bragging, "That's all."

"Can't be bad!" said Andy, wiping my cum from his face and licking it from his finger, "Mmmm – tasty!"

He laughed when I pulled a face as I tried to disguise my feelings.

"It's not nasty," he said, "Perhaps it's a strange taste at first but you soon get to like it. Haven't you tasted your own then?"

Somehow, against my intended wording I shook my head, refusing to admit my gay past.

"Not really," I said, "Wondered about it sometimes but bothered to try it."

"Hmmm – too late now to taste yours right now, so how about trying mine then?" he asked, holding his erect cock towards me.

It looked so inviting and I found myself feeling for him, so much so that while I couldn't reveal my desire, I still had to answer.

"Oh I'm sorry Andy – quite forgot about you – you haven't cum yet, have you," I said, "Do you want to rub one out?"

"I'd much rather you did it for me," said Andy, moving closer to me, "Could you help me and rub it for me, please."

I was still sitting as Andy brought his cock closer to me and while I wasn't entirely certain that I wanted to do this I just had to. I'd almost fought to stay away from my gay side and now I could rapidly feel myself losing the battle. His erection was now just inches from my hand, so it seemed almost natural to raise my hand and grasp his cock. Inside me I just had to do it – something just made me, despite my initial uncertainty.

Wow – it felt so incredible as I wrapped my fingers round his shaft! The same skin, tissue, sinew and blood as mine but totally different! His cock was slimmer than mine but there seemed to be feet of it to play with... well, many inches anyway! And it felt hot, ridiculously hot!

Above me Andy groaned with pleasure as I began moving my hand up and down his long shaft.

His foreskin felt thinner than mine and slid that much more easily but there was still that lovely ridge full of nerve endings around the knob that needed passing with each stroke and I could feel it easily under my fingers. And I knew that he'd be enjoying the feelings because that's where my best pleasure lay...

"Rub me a bit faster," Andy said, groaning from time to time, "Squeeze a bit harder too while you're doing it."

I complied, feeling the stiffness of his cock as it pulsed under my fingers. He was leaking precum copiously and it was getting everywhere as I wanked him. Well, mainly it was getting on his thighs and my hand and every drop seemed to make me tingle with desire!

He was facing me well within arm's reach as I tossed him off, so I was moving my hand towards myself and then away with each stroke – and with each up-stroke a little spray of precum now splattered onto my body. I kind of ignored it and yet at the same time I was enjoying it – it was the height of eroticism to me! It was certainly making me harder than ever once again, despite having had a wonderful orgasm not ten minutes before.

Eventually my efforts began working on him – Andy was actually getting there – I could tell! His breathing was faster and ragged; his body was jerking and quivering; his cock was pulsating and jumping as he neared his orgasm.

"Oh fuck, this is good, feels so good!" I muttered, knowing that I'd lost control of myself, "You feel amazing, I love doing this!"

Andy's body suddenly stiffened and if I'd been him that would have said that I was about to come... and I was right – he was!

"Aaaaaahhh!" he cried, "Oooooh yeahhhh – that's good – cumming – cumming!"

And not a second later his cock erupted – I felt the bolts of fluid pass down his long shaft and exit – straight at my chest!

"Oh fuck!" I cried, although there wasn't a lot I could do – I was a sitting target, so I just carried on wanking him!

"Shiiiiiiiit" cried Andy as a long streamer of spunk splattered onto my chest, "Oh fuuuuck!"

Another big blast of sperm squirted up almost to my neck – rapidly followed by another in the same area; then a lesser squirt that landed on my groin; a few more spits of sperm – and then, apart from a small dribble of cum, it was all over.

"Phew!" said Andy, still breathing fast, "Not bad – you did well, for a beginner!"

I was panting too from my exertion – and partially from the excitement, I think.

I gave Andy a big smile and then looked down at my body and from neck to groin I was splattered with streaks and globules of whitish cum.

"I'm not a beginner actually," I admitted, "I've done this before – many times!"

"I knew it – I just knew it!" answered Andy happily, "I could tell; you just seemed to know your way around, you knew how to do it so well."

For a minute or two I told him a fair bit about my past while also including that I'd tried to keep away from gay sex.

244

"But why?" he asked, "You've just shown me that there's nothing wrong with it, haven't you?"

I grinned back, knowing that he was right, then glanced down at my chest.

"Hey, let's get all this cleaned up," I said, "It's getting cold!"

I reached out for a towel, but Andy stopped me.

"Can't you lick it off, I mean, with your fingers?" he asked, then he did it for me.

He reached down and gathered a generous blob onto his fingers and then, before I could think, he pushed his fingers into my mouth. It helped that my mouth was partially open at the time – I was about to say something – and in went his sticky spunky fingers.

"Come on, taste it!" said Andy and a moment later I'd swiped it from his fingers with my tongue.

"Mmmm, that's pretty tasty," I admitted as I gathered as much of his cum as I could onto two fingers, which I then conveyed to my mouth.

With Andy's help we gathered most of his cum and with Andy now sharing it we made quick work of it. His cum was only a little salty and had that deliciously thrilling flavour of fresh cum and by the time we resorted to the towel to dry my chest and groin off I felt almost replete.

"Well?" he asked, his head slightly askew, "Was that good?"

"Of course it was, you're tasty!" I admitted with a smile, "Makes me wish there was more!"

"In a bit if you like!" he answered as he held up his somewhat limp penis, "Give me ten minutes!"

I waved him away, my desire having eased off now that we'd both climaxed and pondered on our next move.

"Let's take a break," I suggested, and Andy nodded his approval.

I reached across the cabin to the bottle of wine that remained and was pleased to see that there was still a fair bit left. I poured it into the two glasses and handed one to Andy then sat back again, the two of us slumped on the seat, both of us still naked.

We sat and looked at each other and exchanged the smiles of two people who were content with each other as we relaxed contentedly and drank until our glasses were empty. Of course our conversation had been mainly about sex and as I put our glasses in the sink I realised that my cock was on the rise once again. One stroke and my penis stiffened and throbbed.

"Wants some more, does he?" asked Andy, smiling broadly as I nodded vigorously.

His hand wrapped itself around my cock and began moving up and down, then Andy spoke again.

"Can we lie down somewhere – have you got a bed in here?" he asked and I nodded again.

I pulled myself from his delicious grip then quickly rearranged the seats and cushions and soon there was the equivalent of a double bed across the cabin width.

"Perfect!" breathed Andy as he stretched out across the width, "Come on then!"

Andy beckoned me as he climbed onto the bed and soon we lay side by side but now with two erections between us!

"You want some more too, eh?" I asked and Andy purred his approval of the idea and together we began to work each other up once more until Andy spoke again.

"You're going to make me sore if you keep that up Chris, do you have any lotion or lubricant or something?" he asked.

For a second or two I couldn't think then an idea hit me and I reached up into one of the bulkhead sliding cupboards and brought out a big pot of Vaseline that came in handy for fishing lines, fishing reels and anything that needed protection from the salty air.

246

"Any good," I asked, "Super multi-purpose stuff!"

"Ah – not perfect but it'll do nicely!" said Andy, then he paused and put the container on the side.

"I was going to use this as a lube, but I've just changed my mind," he said with a smile, "It doesn't taste all that wonderful, does it."

"No, that's true," I answered having experienced the greasy, oily taste myself, "Why?"

"Because I've just decided that I'm going to suck you again," he answered with a big grin.

I felt the added excitement stiffen my cock even more and felt my breathing quicken too.

"Ohhh yeah!" I exclaimed gleefully, "Oh brilliant!"

We changed positions on the bed and before I knew it I felt his mouth clamp softly around my cock.

"This time I want you to cum in my mouth," he said as he lifted his head for a moment, "You ready?"

"Ooooooh wowwww!" I groaned, my body reacting to his ministrations by jerking all around, "Ooh, fuckin' hell yesss, that feels good!"

As I thrashed about, I turned my head and there before my eyes was Andy's penis, stiff as a poker and dribbling with precum.

'Dare I go this far?' I asked myself before stretching out my tongue.

Gingerly I touched the tip of his cock with the tip of my tongue; the texture of his tightly stretched knob on my tongue was incredible – I just had to have some more. Andy had jerked as I touched him with my tongue and now he looked up from his sucking.

"Please Chris – put it in your mouth," he moaned, "You know how – you told me..."

He returned his mouth to my erection and I returned my gaze to his. It was still there – not a cock's length from my mouth – twitching and dribbling and just ripe to suck!

I leaned forward again as we lay side by side and put my hand up to hold his cock. Slowly I pulled it towards my mouth, and I felt Andy move his hip to assist me, until that moment came when I felt his flesh touch my lips.

I kissed the tip, feeling my lips suddenly sliding in the small dribble of precum and I pushed my tongue out to get a taste. Memories returned quickly, memories of delicious hot juicy cocks and Andy's cock suddenly looked wonderful. I let several inches of his stiff penis slide between my lips, delighting in the feeling of having a penis in my mouth once again. The scent of his heated male organ now filled my nose and I swear that it made my own cock jerk excitedly too – it was all coming back. I sucked hard on his cock, tasting the slight twang of his juices as I did so.

"Aaaaaahhhh!" groaned Andy, "Oh Chris – oh I love it, oh yesssss!"

I could feel his penis pushing into my mouth as the largely uncontrollable twitches of his aroused body tried to get me to be more active and taking my cues from them I tightened my lips round his cock and began sawing my mouth up and down his shaft. He was oozing precum freely now, a slippery sharp emanation but it only drove me on to want to discover the source of the exciting flavour and anyway, at the other end of the bed, Andy was working on my cock with renewed vigour, both sucking and wanking me with enthusiasm. This definitely wasn't liable to last for long before at least one of us erupted!

Andy pulled my hips towards his mouth and then I could feel the tightness of his throat around my knob as he deepthroated me. I felt his chin come to rest against my abdomen as he absorbed my penis into his body.

And then I felt something different – Andy had a finger between my buttocks – sliding and pushing towards my arsehole... and as more memories flooded back, I just relaxed and let him!

Oh god – I just didn't know whether to tighten up or relax – to push back at his finger or forward into his mouth. Eventually I just quivered all over as Andy explored me.

A few moments later his finger centred on my anus; I pushed back at his finger, relaxing my hole as I did so. I held my breath...

Andy's finger seemed to slip and slither around my puckered hole, probing and feeling and then pushing right into the centre... and in it went!

"Aaaaagh!" I cried – not because of pain but because it came as so much of a shock!

"Sorry – sorry!" said Andy, but not removing his finger, "Sorry – did that hurt?"

"Bit but not really," I groaned, "Its ok now though, keep doing that!"

'Wowww! I just told him to keep his finger in my arse! I said I wasn't going to get into all this again!' I thought, but then I realised that I really liked having someone stuff their finger inside me!

But my concerns were soon forgotten as Andy renewed his oral attention on my erection and the fact that his finger was still up inside me became of secondary importance as I felt my orgasm building.

"Andy," I warned, "I'll cum in a few minutes if you keep that up."

He pulled his mouth away.

"Yes please – that's what I want. I want all of your spunk in my mouth," he said, "As soon as you're ready."

He returned his grasping, sucking, caressing mouth to my cock and I sucked his penis back into my mouth and we both settled down to bring each other to a climax. But I'd reckoned without Andy's finger – because suddenly he twisted it around inside me; touched my prostate

249

deliciously – and a second later my body went rigid as a violent eruption of cum jerked from my penis!

"Oooooh fuuuuuuck!" I cried as my body jerked again, squirting another powerful jet of cum into his mouth, "Ooooooh yeahhh!"

More sperm erupted from my cock, filling Andy's mouth and as I opened my mouth to cry out again, Andy's own cock recoiled and spat a blast of cum straight into my mouth. Instinctively I swallowed – just as well because another load was coming my way a moment later – and this time I had the end of his cock inside my mouth!

'This is so wild!' I thought, as I swallowed another load, *'What the fuck am I letting him do?'*

A minute later and it was all over – we'd both emptied our reservoirs of cum.

Undoubtedly that had been the most powerful orgasm I could ever remember having and I was left limp and exhausted as I let his cock go and sagged onto the bed. Andy too must have enjoyed it and he rolled away from me and onto his back.

I looked at him with a question on my lips...

"What the fuck did you do – how come you found my prostate?" I asked, not unkindly, "How did you know what to do? And who said you could stick your finger up there anyway?"

"The Vaseline gave me the idea," said Andy, "I was going to use it to lubricate our cocks but when I pulled you towards me I just found myself near your arsehole... and then I wondered if what they show on the internet was true. You know – prostate stimulation, they call it – and it seems to work!"

"Yeah I know – it always feels amazing to massage your prostate," I replied, "Personally I love it but I've tried not to get involved in all that stuff again."

"Why on earth not?" asked Andy, "I've had a prostate check-up too and when the doctor did mine, he made me leak all over the place! It's such good fun isn't it!"

"Yeah! You made me cum like anything, didn't you!" I said, chuckling quietly, "And I'm not complaining, that's for sure. I suppose you'll want me to do that to you as well?"

"Would be nice if you could," said Andy with a happy smile on his face, "But shall we save that for another day. I've already cum twice – let's do it when we're both fresh."

"Yeah – good idea," I said as I rolled off the bed, "Come on, let's get this place shipshape."

Andy too rolled off the bed and stood beside me. I reached out and hugged him and he returned the compliment.

"I enjoyed that," I said, "Thanks buddy!"

And no sooner had I spoken than Andy pulled me even closer and kissed me – mouth to mouth!

Somewhat taken aback, all I could do was to return his kiss – then I pushed us apart, immediately wishing that I hadn't. Tingles of excitement had coursed through my body as we touched lips and my cock had immediately risen into full erection. It had obviously affected Andy too as I felt his penis now pressing hard against my thigh.

"Mmmm – enjoyed that too, didn't you!" said Andy as we separated and pulled on our shorts.

So did you!" I retorted, grabbing his penis and giving it a few quick rubs before he hid it away.

"Ooooh," groaned Andy, dropping his shorts again, "Don't stop, don't stop!"

"Ah-ah!" I said, wagging my finger at him, "Next time...!"

Andy looked crestfallen, but it was just for show and we laughed and finished tidying the cabin while I did my best to ignore my erection. Fortunately it eventually subsided.

Soon we were back up on deck and considering our options but since it was now almost five, there weren't many left. Andy would have to get back to his dad and I needed to get home to check that I wasn't on call. I sighed.

"When's the next time you'll be here?" I asked, wishing that it would be soon.

"Next weekend I guess," said Andy as we tidied up, "That's ages ahead."

"Yeah, you'll have to come back to my place sometime," I said, "But you owe me some work here first, so you'd better be here next weekend."

"Definitely," said Andy as we worked to clear the tools, leftovers from lunch and other debris from the deck, "Dad's always down here before lunchtime on Saturday so I'll see you then."

Soon we were ready to part company – Andy back to his dad and me back to my home and with a final hug – which no longer felt an entirely strange thing to do – we went our separate ways.

Less than twenty minutes later I was back home and it wasn't long after that before I'd opened a nice cool can of lager and had settled myself into a deckchair on the still sunny patio.

My body began to relax but my mind was still in a whirl as I mentally ran back over the events of the day. Wow! I'd had my cock sucked and I'd sucked Andy – and then he'd stuffed his finger up my arse too – and then we'd kissed as well. The whole day was one of renewed explorations and discoveries and I'd loved it!

Some while later I awoke with a start as I spilled some chilly lager down my front. I'd nodded off and now I needed a towel – damn it! Not to mention a waste of good lager!

Never mind – I had to wake up, to get a meal ready; to check my emails in case any urgent work had come through (nothing had) and to get myself organised for Monday. Oh, and have a wank because every time I thought back to the events of the day my cock rose up, demanding attention. Did I say 'a wank' – what I really meant was 'another wank' because it was as necessary to me now as eating or drinking.

But I was happy – life was taking a turn for the better, it seemed!

I'm pleased to say that my week – during which I finally finished a lengthy chapter that had been bugging me and also was able to complete the set-up of a client's two computers – ran smoothly and remarkably quickly. No mad panics; no disasters – the whole week just flowed along, and I even managed to find some hard-to-get components that I'd been needing. Friday, instead of being a day of panic to get things finished, became a day to more or less unwind for once – it was brilliant!

And so I faced the weekend in a relaxed and happy mood, buoyed even more by the thought that I'd be seeing Andy again. Even the weather was in a sunny mood – we'd now had well over a week of sunshine which was perfect for my early-season suntan!

By nine o'clock on Saturday morning I was on my way to the marina and this time I'd come prepared! I'd bought a much larger selection of food items than I would usually do and some bottles of wine... and I'd also bought some KY gel – because I intended to do some exploring of my own!

To add to my pleasure, as I pulled up to park near the boat, there was Andy. He'd already stripped off the tarpaulin cover from the open deck area and had the ladder in place and he was waving madly as I pulled up.

"Hey," I said to myself, "With his help, this should be the last weekend on land – be great to get the boat back in the water."

Andy came across the small car park to greet me and we hugged as we met.

"Missed you," Andy breathed into my ear, "Been a long time without you, Chris."

"And you," I replied although I hadn't intended to reveal my eagerness to see him again.

Mind you, I think that my cock had already given away my feelings when we hugged. We walked to the boat and clambered aboard – it was already pretty warm in the partially enclosed deck and, having stowed the foodstuffs, we both stripped down to our shorts.

"So what's your plan for today?" asked Andy, standing there all tall, slim and youthful.

"Work!" I said forcefully, "Work first – play later!"

"Drat!" said Andy theatrically, "Oh well – guess there's a price to pay for everything!"

I slapped his arse and handed him a selection of suitable tools.

"There you go – you start on the port bow and I'll work towards you – then we can do the starboard side when the sun's moved round," I said, "Let's get cracking – I'm fed up with having a boat and no water!"

And we did – we worked hard and even before lunchtime we'd met and crossed to the starboard side where we split again and worked towards each other. But grumbling tummies insisted that we stop for a break and eventually we did so, both of us panting slightly from our efforts.

"Bloody brilliant!" I crowed as I clapped Andy on the back, "We've done so well – I can't believe it! Great stuff mate."

"Good to work off some energy," said Andy, "But a break is definitely needed – I'm parched and starved!"

The sun was quite warm now, so we moved into the cabin to eat and before long our mouths were full, our glasses were almost empty and our stomachs had stopped grumbling.

Soon Andy leaned back and patted his belly.

"That's better," he said, "Needed that."

"So did I," I exclaimed, blowing out a big breath, "Not going to overdo it though – we haven't finished yet!"

"Oh bugger!" said Andy cheerfully, "You bloody slave driver!"

I stuck my tongue out at him and he laughed at me.

"Right," I said, "I've been having a think. First of all, does your dad want you around?"

"Dad? Want me around? No way – he's happy in the bar with his buddies," said Andy, "I only come down with him to get out of the house and because I like being here. Why do you ask?"

"What about you and I keep working today as long as we can today and then you come back home with me," I said, "Then we can get an early start tomorrow and we might be finished by what, soon after lunch. Perhaps we can even get the boat put in the water tomorrow afternoon if we do that."

"Why not!" said Andy happily, "I'll send dad a text so he'll know. He won't worry if I want to stay at your place – he'll be ok."

"Great!" I said cheerfully, "You're fantastic!"

The great big beaming smile that lit Andy's face was worth a fortune – I'd made his day!

Andy stood up to get his phone which was in his pocket of his shorts and then sat down beside me to compose and send the message and as he did so I could see that his penis was at least partially aroused and kept jerking occasionally. Mesmerised I watched it, realising that it was still inflating and was now creating a long ridge across his thigh right beside me. The once small jerks had now become major uplifts and I also noticed that a damp spot was forming near the tip. I licked my lips and felt my own penis stiffen and then was brought back to reality as Andy moved to put his phone away.

I looked up at his face – to see him beaming back at me!

"Couldn't take your eyes off it, could you?" he said, jerking his penis violently, "Got you going too, I see!"

"Are you trying to lead me astray?" I asked as I put my hand down onto his penis, "You were doing that on purpose!"

"Couldn't help it," he said, "I got a bit excited thinking of being with you overnight and then I saw that you were looking, so I worked him up a bit more. Do you want to play then?"

Gently I moved my hand up and down his long shaft and then slid my hand down to the bottom of his shorts and reached up his leg. Very soon I was holding his hot sticky penis itself which continued to throb in my hand.

"Yeah – come on then – just for a while," I said as I realised that I just had to reacquaint myself with his lovely cock.

We both stood up and turning towards each other we rubbed our erections together briefly before we moved into the cabin. Quickly I changed the seats into a bed once more and made sure everything was to hand.

"Off with them!" I said as I slipped my shorts down and Andy was naked almost as quickly as I was.

We both climbed onto the bed and lay side by side. Almost unconsciously we both grasped the other's penis and began caressing it. As I held Andy's monster, I could feel the veins and ridges and the ripples of skin where his foreskin moved under my hand. He soon began to leak; long dribbles of precum flowed from his tip and I made sure that

I gathered them and used the viscous slippery sexy fluid to lubricate my hand as I wanked him.

Andy had obviously found my penis to be in much the same condition – I could actually feel the movement of my precum up my shaft every so often and I could confirm that I too was leaking as Andy's hand slid freely over my knob and up and down my shaft.

"Are we just going to wank?" asked Andy, "Could I suck you again Chris?"

"I want to do you first," I replied as I moved around and soon I was on my knees between Andy's legs, his erect penis only a few feet from my face.

"It won't take me long to cum," said Andy, "I've been waiting for this for ages – been holding myself on edge for so long..."

I reached out and held his cock once more and wanked him for a short while to ensure he was completely stiff and then I reached to the cupboard and brought out my tube of KY. Andy didn't see what I did because he had his eyes shut so what I did next came as a complete surprise to him.

Loading my finger with a good blob of gel I moved my hand directly down to his anus. Andy was obligingly lifting his arse up as I caressed his cock and now I was able to plant my finger almost directly onto his hole!

He jerked violently and almost dislodged my finger but my grasp on his cock held things in place.

"What the...! Ooooooh yesss – yesss – do that!" moaned Andy, now squirming with pleasure, "Please – play with me – play with my arse!"

"Gonna put my finger inside you," I said, still lubricating the general area of his hole.

His puckered flesh was firm against my finger but with my fingertip I could feel his actual opening.

"Oh yessss, please! Be gentle though!" said Andy through clenched teeth.

"Ok – will do," I said as I slowly started to insert my finger, "Coming in now!"

"Aaaagh!" groaned Andy, "Oooooooh – ooooooh!"

"Does it hurt," I asked now that half of one finger was inside him.

"Not a lot. Did for a moment at first but then I pushed out and it was easier. What you using – Vaseline?" he asked.

"KY," I said, "It's much better – I'll put a bit more on you."

So saying I added another blob to the fairly generous amount that I'd used and pushed my finger further inside. I thought it would feel horrible after so long, but it was actually amazing and totally erotic – it was making my cock throb with excitement!

"Trying two fingers now," I said as I added another one.

Andy let out another low moan, but my second finger slid inside more easily and now I was beginning to stretch his hole. I turned my hand over so I could reach upwards towards where I believed his prostate gland was and soon found the spongy mass. I rubbed at it with my fingers bringing forth more groans from Andy.

"Oooooh fuck! Look at my cock Chris – see what you're doing!" Andy cried.

There before me his erect penis was dribbling and leaking almost as if he was cumming – there was already a small pool of his liquid emission on his abdomen and more was joining it as I rubbed at his prostate.

"I feel I want to cum!" Andy groaned, "I could cum in moments if you keep doing that, I reckon."

"Not yet," I said as I slowly withdrew my fingers, "You can cum when I let you!"

I moved from between his legs and moved up to lie beside him.

"Was that nice?" I asked, somewhat unnecessarily.

"Oh wow!" he said, beaming at me, "Nice isn't the word – that was just so fucking good!"

We lay side by side as I played with two hard erections, while we recovered our composure.

"Your turn," I said eventually, and Andy looked at me.

"Your turn – I want you to use your fingers in me now. I know you did it before but I want you to use some KY on me too," I said, "That Vaseline is a bit sticky but this stuff is far more slippery – it'll feel totally different, I expect."

"Ok Chris, where's the stuff – ah, thanks," said Andy as I handed him the KY.

I rolled onto my back and spread my legs with my knees raised, to give Andy the best access to my hole. I watched as he squeezed a blob onto his fingers and approached me.

"Yeah – try this – push out a bit," said Andy as he touched my little hole.

For a few moments I could just feel him moving around and then, as I pushed outwards, I felt his finger slide effortlessly inside me, an action that made me suck in a big breath that caused Andy look up at me.

"You ok?" he asked, and I smiled at him.

"Yeah – fine," I said, "Unexpected but not painful – I'm just out of practice. You going to try two fingers now?"

Already have Chris!" he said to my surprise.

"Wow!" I said, "I'd forgotten that my arse could stretch that easily."

"Went in so easily – that lube is excellent. What now?" he asked.

"Stretch me a bit more then – try three fingers," I said, and I felt Andy fumbling around down there. Then his fingers were withdrawn.

"Come on then!" I said, "I'm waiting!"

"Actually it's not easy," said Andy, "I'm getting cramp in my fingers when I try to fold them together."

"Well, what else can you use?" I asked, my mind having gone blank, "I need you to try something bigger so I can see if I still enjoy it."

As I suddenly realised what I'd just said, there was silence for a short time which I took to be Andy mentally searching the cabin for something, but then he reached the logical answer.

"Chris," he said, somewhat quietly, "What if I stuck my cock inside you? Would you mind?"

So this was the watershed moment!

If I let him then I'd have to accept that I was gay – or at the very least bisexual and actually having proper sex with another man once again. All this playing around we'd been doing was just mutual friendship... but if he actually put his cock inside me – fucked me... then we'd really be having sex, wouldn't we? So, did I want to go down that road – did I want to renew my gay life?

Well, I'd been encouraging him to play with my arse and I'd already played inside his, so hadn't I already crossed the line? And anyway, inside my brain I really wanted him to... inside me I'd been lusting after the feel of his lengthy penis in my arse.

"Try it, try it Andy," I said at last, knowing that this was a momentous decision, "But if I tell you it hurts then stop or else!"

"Why should it hurt?" asked Andy, "My cock may be long but it's slim and it's not much wider than two fingers."

"Do it then," I said firmly, "Before I change my mind. Make sure you've got plenty of KY on you though."

"Ok, done that," said Andy and I felt him moving nearer.

The moment of truth was close!

"Here it comes!" he said and I felt what had to be the end of his penis touch my body.

Then I felt Andy move it around a bit, presumably ensuring that the lube was spread everywhere – and then I felt pressure – gentle pressure at first.

"Coming," said Andy as he pushed a little harder, "You ok?"

"Yeah – fine so far," I said, "I'm pushing out to help."

As I did so there was a slight stretching feeling that seemed to keep on and on until suddenly it eased and all I was left with, apart from a long-held breath, was a feeling of fullness.

"How you getting on?" I asked, not wanting to look – not wanting yet to see the unholy sight.

"I'm in you Chris," said Andy quietly, "No trouble, was there? Once I got my helmet inside it just slid in... my cock's probably smoother than my fingers anyway."

"How far inside me are you?" I asked.

"Got about four, maybe five inches up you," said Andy, "Have a look!"

I levered my upper body up and although I wasn't able to see my arse or the actual insertion, I was able to see just how close Andy's body was to mine; implying that a fair bit of his cock had indeed gone somewhere!

I lay back down and tried to relax. But having a cock inside you doesn't allow complete relaxation, not least because Andy's penis was now probing against my prostate. My own penis was jerking and shuddering and was now beginning to leak profusely.

'Ahhh – I knew it!' I thought to myself, 'I'm going to want more and more now!'

"I like that Andy," I said, having now got used to the feeling of something stretching me open, "Push in a bit more if you like."

"Sure?" Andy queried and I nodded my head.

I felt Andy's cock sliding further into me and I could feel how he was stretching me up inside as well as stretching my hole open. I seemed to be feeling his penis pressing against my internal organs as he slid his amazing cock deeper and deeper.

"Phew!" I groaned, "Far enough – don't go in any further."

"Can't!" said Andy, "I'm about as far up in you as I can go – didn't you feel my pubes on your arse?"

Now I came to think about it, yes, I had felt something tickling me – wow – he'd had all ten inches inside me!

"Pull out a bit," I asked Andy and his cock slid and slid, leaving my insides feeling quite empty.

"Ok – what now?" he asked, "Do you want me to move in and out?"

"Yeah – come on," I said, eager now to feel him, "And I'll try to squeeze you at the same time."

A moment later Andy was pushing his penis back inside me deeper and deeper and then sliding out once more – an action he kept up for little while, while I began to feel which muscles to use to grip him. Soon my arse was squeezing and pulsating around his cock; my own erection bouncing and dribbling as we moved.

"Hold my cock too," I asked, "Toss me off!"

Quickly Andy's hand wrapped round my shaft and he began sliding his fist up and down my cock, some residual KY on his hand helping with the lubrication. I was already close when he started and now, with his penis sliding in and out of me and his hand working on my cock, I was quickly coming to the boil.

"Oh yeah – yeah – ooooooh yeahhhhh! Don't stop – don't stop!" I cried as I arched my back and thrust my cock at his fist, "Cummmming! Cummmmming!"

A geyser of cum shot upwards and fell back onto my chest, quickly followed by another one and as Andy continued to wank me, jet after jet erupted until there was nothing left.

I could feel my whole body shivering and vibrating and I knew that I'd clamped down hard on Andy's penis as he sawed in and out – it must have been a really tight fit and would have felt good as I squeezed him. I could tell that it did because Andy's strokes became faster and I was about to try squeezing him again when suddenly his actions changed. He trembled, gasped, shook and began thrusting wildly.

"Fuck – fuck! Cumming! Ahhhhh, ahhhhh fuck!" he cried, "Can't help it! Can't stop! Aaaaahhh!"

Andy's body was slamming against mine; his cock was thudding into my bowels and his breath was hot above my chest... but inside I could feel that wonderfully erotic feeling of warmth flooding through my intestines – pulse after pulse after hot pulse. I even felt what must have been a particularly strong gush of cum as it squirted from him and painted my rectum.

Above me Andy all but collapsed.

"Oh shit – sorry, I'm sorry!" he cried, lowering his head to my chest, "I just couldn't help it. You squeezed me as I pushed in and it sent right over the top!"

"Don't worry Andy, it's done now," I said soothingly putting my arms round him, "I'm glad you did it."

"How d'you mean?" he said, lifting his head a bit.

"We would have dithered and thought it over for ages before either of us let the other one cum inside and then eventually we would probably have said 'yes' anyway, so you sort-of said 'yes' for us!" I said, "And gosh – you felt so good too! It's so amazing to know that I've got another man's sperm inside me now. So come on, buck up – that was good!"

263

Andy raised himself just long enough to locate my mouth and then he sank down, kissing me hard. I just couldn't help but respond in kind and soon we were slobbering and licking and kissing all over – and I felt so close to him.

Eventually we separated and Andy pushed himself more upright although his penis was still embedded in my arsehole. He seemed to still be quite firm inside me but Andy was uncomfy where he was now.

"Take him out," I said, "Do it gently and grab that towel too, will you."

Andy understood and, placing the towel below my arse, he slowly and gently withdrew inch after inch of sticky slimy sexy penis. One last stretch and suddenly his head popped out followed by what felt like a veritable flood of sperm. He pushed the towel in place and held it over my arse.

"You ok Chris," he asked.

"Yeah – fine; bit sore I think, but I'll live!" I said, "And you – was it good?"

"Brilliant!" said Andy, his eyes shining and his mouth smiling, "Never thought I'd do that; never thought I'd find someone I could have sex with like that."

"And there's me been trying to avoid that kind of sex!" I said, "Why on earth have I been holding back?"

We both laughed as we sat up and pulled our shorts on.

"Got to celebrate! Fancy a lager? I brought some down with me this morning," I said, "Not very cold now but better than nothing! I reckon we deserve a drink!"

"Yeah man – could just do with one," Andy replied as we moved out of the cabin, "All that work!"

"Hey – speaking of work..." I said, downing half the can in one go, "We'd better get on with it. Proper work I mean!"

And so we did. Ten minutes after we'd finished our drinks, we were both racing to complete what had been a real chore – both of us buoyed up by the amazing sex we'd just enjoyed. That though had been a true labour of love – this was just plain labour. A couple of hours later we'd finished; perhaps half a day earlier than I'd planned. All there was to do was to clean up; touch up any little bits that we'd missed and then book the crane to lift the boat back into the water the next day.

We stood up and surveyed the bright and shiny paintwork and unbidden, we slung our arms around each other's shoulders.

I shook my head in something like amazement.

"I am SO happy!" I crowed, delighted that the tedious work was done, "You've been such a help – brilliant stuff, mate!"

"Oh Chris," Andy said happily, "It's been a real pleasure. I've enjoyed myself in so many ways. Thank you so much too."

Our arms pulled us together and we embraced hard and tight – and we were happy.

"If you're coming to stay with me I think I'd better take you out to dinner tonight," I said, "I really want to thank you for all your hard work – fancy that?"

"Yeah, great, that would be amazing but..." said Andy, "Could we just have a night in instead?"

"Huh," I huffed, "Don't like the idea of a nice meal?"

"It sounds wonderful but a takeaway and a bottle of wine alone with you sounds even better," suggested Andy looking longingly at me, "Our first night together? Yeah – can we make it kind of intimate?"

"Anything then!" I said cheerfully, "Let's go. Got to pop in at the Harbourmaster's office first then the supermarket and then home. What about your car?"

"I'll leave it – it'll be safe here," said Andy, "Pick it up tomorrow."

I need hardly add that it took ages to get the crane booked and scheduled – the warm weather was bringing all the boat owner out but eventually we had our slot. It was at 11.30 in the morning, subject to all their other jobs going to plan. That was fine and meant that we didn't have to rush, which was equally good news.

We piled into my car and headed off and after we'd bought about twice what we needed we were back at my place somewhere round about half past five. I felt a bit self-conscious walking in with a man beside me instead of the usual girl but there were only a few people around and anyway, in my driveway we were more or less hidden.

I unpacked everything while Andy had a look around, expressing his pleasure at what he found and soon we were both in the kitchen, busy investigating our evening meal. In the end we opted to lay it all out and then help ourselves to whatever we fancied, along with several bottles of wine, naturally! We covered the big coffee table with the bits and pieces and settled down to pig out.

My place isn't flash – it's comfy. Probably if I'd had a wife, things would have been very different but instead, my home was more functional than ornamental and more designed for 'me' rather than a family. There was a big soft cushiony settee and a couple of matching armchairs around a large glass coffee table; all facing an imitation log-burning gas fire and a large 60" TV. A massive thick pile mat covered much of the floor near the fire. I needed the coffee table for my meals and my Playstation (and my favourite games) but otherwise the place was fairly uncluttered. Soon we were settling into our assorted foods with various contented noises arising from time to time until we gradually slowed to a finish.

"I'm done!" I said with relish, "Really enjoyed that. More than enough but not too much. How you doing, Andy?"

"Fine," he said, wiping his mouth, "Those chicken wings were really delicious, weren't they and as for that beef!"

266

I breathed out a long curry-flavoured breath as I smiled, nodded and leaned back...

"What now then; let's just sit and relax for a while," I suggested as I lifted my glass, "Let's see what's on the box."

I patted the settee next to me.

"Come over here. Come and keep me company and we can watch something for a bit," I said, "Then perhaps we can play."

Andy levered himself up and soon plonked himself down beside me as I found something to watch... and do you know, I can't even remember what it was that we watched. It can't have been very wonderful but it didn't really matter; we were just winding up for the real action in the bedroom.

After perhaps an hour of relaxing I felt desire rising inside me, desire to get back to some good loving, so I made an oblique suggestion.

"Do you want to play some games?" I asked innocently.

"Love to!" said Andy, "Here or in the bedroom?"

"You horny bastard!" I said, "I knew you'd say that!"

"Well, be honest," he answered, "I don't think you were thinking about using the Playstation, were you?"

I felt Andy squirming beside me, his thigh pressing warmly against mine and I wriggled gently to make us comfy. His arm was draped over my shoulders, but my own arm was squashed between us with my hand resting on Andy's knee – and it was now that I realised that something was nudging my elbow. I looked down and sure enough, Andy's cock had risen, and it was now announcing its presence through his shorts.

I shook my head at him.

"Forever horny, aren't you?" I said as I moved my hand, so it rested on his erection.

"Aren't you?" asked Andy, snaking his arm round my neck to tweak my nipple.

My cock responded in moments and Andy pointed downwards.

"See! You're just the same – slightest excuse for some sex and there you are!" he quipped as I continued rubbing his penis through his shorts.

Andy removed his hand from my shoulder and wove a path past my arm until he could reach my cock and soon the pair of us were sitting, blankly watching TV while we caressed each other's penis. It didn't take either of us long to extract our cocks to facilitate our enjoyment then we settled back again for a little while but we both wanted more.

"Let's get undressed," I suggested, interrupting the peace and it took just a few moments for us both to throw off our t-shirts and shorts and to settle once more – but this time naked.

"Ooooooh, that's better," groaned Andy as my hand started to rub up and down his length and I made similar noises as Andy's hand did the same on my penis.

We both leaned back, now no longer really watching TV but instead watching ourselves as our hands rose and fell on the two rigid shafts before us. Slowly we both explored our two penises; our hands sliding foreskins up and down; squeezing and smoothing the flesh; spreading the liberal quantities of precum over and around our respective knobs; slowly masturbating each other. Soon there was that fantastic scent of hot sex in the air – a pheromonal scent, so subtle as to be ethereal and yet so strong that it made your nostrils twitch with excitement. Every breath I took seemed to send cock-stiffening messages to my brain and I guessed that it was affecting Andy the same way, judging from the stiffness of his instrument. I could hear that we were both breathing more deeply now and occasionally one or other of us would twitch or jerk or otherwise spasm as sexual arousal began kicking in.

"Uuuuuuhh!" groaned Andy at one point and a long stream of super-slippery precum oozed from his slit – so much that I had to use my other hand to catch it all. The smear of precum that I collected I then spread all over my own knob, which felt like an incredibly erotic thing to do.

And it obviously was an erotic thing for Andy too because it seemed to encourage him to wank me faster, presumably in time with his degree of arousal but I seemed to be getting to him quicker. He was panting quite hard now and really jerking his penis through my fist – he just couldn't be far off cumming now...

"Do you want me to keep going?" I asked.

"Oh yes – yes – I want to cum! I need to cum!" groaned Andy, still humping my fist.

"Ok – you will," I said, holding his penis that bit tighter, "You will."

I stilled his hand on my cock so we could concentrate on his – he still had hold of my erection but now his penis was the centre of attention. It was positively glowing with arousal – it was gleaming with it's coating of precum and it was standing, long and tall; well over half of it protruding from my fist as I continued to pound away on it.

"Nearly there?" I asked, now swirling my fingers around his crown.

"Just about," said Andy through broken breaths, "Any time now – keep going – please, please!"

A few more rubs and I felt his body tighten as his orgasm began to bite.

"Yeah – yeah – Oh fuuuuuck!" said Andy, "Can't stop now – cummmmming!"

As he stiffened once more, I pointed his erection up towards me just as the first generous spurt of sperm erupted. It leapt towards me, landing on my chest; the second blast squirted me right between the eyes and down my face; the next jet fired over his chest and our arms and I managed to jerk another two smaller squirts from him which sprayed over his groin. We were liberally covered in his sticky, hot, white emission which now stuck to us or ran down our bodies like cooling candle wax. I released his penis as I wiped the sticky cum from my forehead and eagerly sucked it from my fingers, then I returned to his cock.

"Was that any good?" I asked as I gently slid my hand around in the spunk that was still oozing from his cock.

"Any good – that was just something else!" Andy said as he shuddered as the remnants of his orgasm subsided, "We need a cloth now though."

"No, leave it," I said, standing up and pulling Andy with me, "I want us to be covered with your spunk when we lie on the bed. I want to feel your stickiness all over me. I want to share your cum as I fuck you!"

Andy did a kind of double take.

"You what?" he said, startled.

"I want to fuck you," I said, suddenly galvanized into action, "I want to get my cock inside you and I want to make love to you with your cum all over me."

"Oh fuck, yeahhhhh!" cried Andy with a look of extreme happiness on his face, "Come on then – what are we waiting for!"

I almost dragged him to my bedroom and gently threw him onto my king-sized bed where he lay in all his glory with his lovely long penis erect once more. But it was my turn now and his cock would have to wait...

I made sure I had everything I needed to hand – some lube, some tissues and a towel before I joined him and by then my cock was throbbing, and Andy was almost panting with desire. He was slowly running one hand through the still slippery cum on his body while rubbing his penis with the other and at the same time he was smiling broadly and had his eyes shut. I climbed onto the bed between his legs and worked my way up until I was almost above him then I gently lowered my body onto his and immediately I felt the cool stickiness of his cum adhering to us both.

I don't know if it was the feeling or the smell that was strongest in my mind – either way, something was reinforcing my penis with steel – it was ramrod hard and more than ready for action.

But first I leaned down and kissed Andy's smiling lips, quickly before he could respond. His eyes opened and seeing me poised above him he reached up and pulled me closer again. Now that our bodies were laying flat out together his erection was a long ridge that pressing into my belly while my cock was down between his legs. We kissed again, longer and more lusciously this time, using lots more tongue and saliva until we had to break for air.

I leaned more upright; then lifted up and moved back a bit, a movement that released my cock from between his legs. I reached for the lube, unscrewed the top and squirted some onto my finger which I then placed against his arsehole. I rubbed it into his firm puckered flesh, then I placed another blob on my rigid cock and rubbed it all around – then I looked up at Andy.

"Do you want me?" I asked somewhat superfluously, "Do you want me to try?"

"Oh god yeah – yeah, please Chris, do it!" he moaned, "I've been wanting you there ever since we first played around. Don't wait, please!"

Without speaking I closed in on his arsehole. My lubed fingers ran around the rim before I gently pushed just one fingertip into the little hole. Andy groaned but he wasn't hurting, that much was apparent. I pushed a second finger in and Andy groaned again but my fingers had slid inside with no trouble at all.

"Nice?" I asked and Andy nodded.

"Be better when you use something else, I think," he said, "I'm ready any time you are."

"Ok," I said, removing my fingers and moving my body closer, "Let's have a go!"

Holding my erection in line with his hole, I moved closer and closer until the tip of my cock touched his skin then I stopped for a moment and realised that I was holding my breath... Slowly I breathed out and then quickly in again as I pushed a little bit, just making his puckered flesh move inwards slightly. I could feel the resistance of his body, but I could also feel that Andy was pushing his body at me too – he wanted this insertion as much as I did.

"Pushing a bit harder now," I said as I started applying some more pressure... and slowly his orifice opened, and the end of my gel-coated penis slid inside.

To watch it disappearing was awesome; somehow seeing my cock slide into a vagina was just 'normal' – after all, they're designed to take a penis – but an arsehole isn't, and this was always a sight worth seeing.

My knob was now inside him, although I could feel I was still slowly penetrating through his sphincter muscles, then suddenly the extreme pressure was gone, and I had to hold myself back or slide all the way into his body in one go!

I heard Andy let out a long breath and then sigh. I glanced at his face in case he was in pain but instead he was smiling happily.

"You're in, mate – you're in me!" he hissed, "Oooooh yessss that's nice!"

"Yeah, agree – are you ok?" I asked and Andy nodded once more.

"Fucking wonderful, you were so gentle," he said, "I've used dildos and vibrators, but your cock beats them all. Oh fuck – this is heavenly."

It had been ages since I'd had any pussy; I'd been making do with my fist for the past few months, so this was just what I needed and if it came to that it had been well over two years since I'd last sunk my cock into someone's arse. But it didn't feel wrong to be inside a man again –

there was no feeling inside me that I should be inside a woman instead; in fact I felt very much 'at home' fucking Andy. His man-pussy was tight, and I seemed to be sliding in and out on the same velvety cushion of lubricated slipperiness as a real pussy. If I shut my eyes, I could actually imagine a woman there beneath me – but when I opened them, there instead was a long stiffly erect penis bouncing as I repeatedly thrust with my very rigid cock.

Almost automatically I reached down; took hold of Andy's erection and began masturbating him in time with my thrusts which were slowly getting quicker. I needed to release my cum; I was full of spunk just waiting to be expelled and I knew in my heart exactly where I wanted to place it – inside my lover's body!

And I realised that Andy was now just that – my lover – and I wasn't complaining! At that moment I just wished that I could breed him, impregnate him with my sperm, totally make him mine! Andy too seemed to have had similar thoughts.

"Chris, love, don't hold back – let it go when you want to," he said as my thrusts continued to shake his body, "I might not cum when you do but I don't mind. Anyway, I can save it for your arse!"

"No you won't!" I said, my thrusting now becoming a bit ragged, "I'm going to suck you off if you don't cum with me – I won't be long now I don't think..."

"You're so sweet and considerate," said Andy, blowing me a kiss, "But this one's for you – so let it go!"

I leaned forward until I was reclining up Andy's body, his torso still sticky with his earlier offering of spunk and let my mouth fall slowly until I met his lips coming up to meet me. Together we kissed hard and deep, our tongues entwined, our lips tightly meshed, our body fluids mingling freely as we loved each other. I slowed the movements of my penis in and out of Andy's body as we kissed and caressed each other, and I just knew that I was happy now.

I'd found my direction, my orientation, my preference; I seemed to have discovered why I'd been unable to fall in love before.

Our lips parted as I lifted my body up once more; our two bodies still connected by my solid pipe of flesh. And once again I picked up the pace – now starting to pound at Andy's hole; almost slamming my cock into him... not that Andy was objecting now. His tight arsehole was gripping my penis hard and everything was intensifying...

"Yeah – yeah – yeah!" he was crying in time with my thrusts, "Keep coming – keep it coming! Yeah! You're gonna make me cum if you keep doing that!"

I realised that I still had hold of his erection and I now started to toss him off once more, trying to keep in time with my thrusts but it was becoming difficult. Difficult, because Andy was now nearing his orgasm and was jerking and heaving beneath me and I too was getting close and my thrusts were interspersed with involuntary spasms.

"You gonna cum with me?" I asked, panting now as my orgasm came closer and closer, "Try, please!"

"Keep rubbing me then!" said Andy with his eyes closed, "Don't stop – don't stop! Nearly there!"

Suddenly the world stopped spinning – time ceased – everything froze!

Then together we both let out howls of delight and pleasure as our orgasms reached their climaxes. Suddenly we were out of control – I was slamming my erupting penis into Andy's hole as hard as I could and Andy was throwing his hips back up to meet me; his own penis blasting streams of hot spunk everywhere!

"Aaaaaagh!" I cried, feeling my sperm travelling up my cock and out into Andy's body, "Oooh – uuuuhhh! Uhhhhh! Yeahhhh! Oh fuck!"

Andy wasn't so noisy – he merely grunted as his cock continued to erupt – heck, if I sprayed as much spunk as he did, his insides would be completely coated! Slowly, slowly, we came back to earth. We were still both panting hard, but the climax was past and now we could both unwind...

"Leave him there," said Andy, dreamily, "I love the feeling of him inside me – he belongs there."

Once again, I lay down on top of my lover and we kissed – this time slowly and gently and with love. We'd completed our bonding – we'd both found what we'd been looking for.

Eventually I lifted myself up and getting a towel under Andy's bum, I gently slid my gradually softening penis from his arse. A little dribble of spunk followed my cock, but his hole tightened quickly.

I moved from between his legs and came up to lie beside him, resting on one elbow. He was a mess – from head to, well, I was going to say toe, but actually from head to groin he was besplattered with cum! If nothing else he was a heavy cummer, as I'd found out before.

I leaned down and started the long job of licking him clean but not a minute into the job and Andy stopped me.

"No more – no more, please – you're making me hard again with you doing that!" he said and sure enough, there was his erection, jerking and ready for some more action.

And to my delight, my own cock began stiffening at the sight of his hard-on.

"So?" I asked, still licking at a goodly pool of spunk, "I'll want more; I want you to be hard."

"Ooh fuck Chris – with you I'll always want more!" said Andy, "Ooh – do you know what? I love you!"

I leaned towards him and threw my arms around him as his enveloped me.

"And I love you too!" I said – rather to my surprise!

Andy rolled us over until he was above me; his hard erection pressing into me.

"Do you really mean that?" he asked and with no delay, I nodded.

"Yeahhhhh!" we both exclaimed, "Whoopee!"

Much as I desired more, rather than wear ourselves out that night, we probably wisely, opted to relax and sleep, even if our two penises remained hard and demanding. We both knew that there would be many other times; many more nights of passion; perhaps many more years in which to express our love for each other. And so together in my big bed we slept; occasionally rolling together; sometimes rolling apart but both knowing that we were safe and in good company and in love.

And in the morning we both gently awoke – I've no idea who woke first but we seemed to surface together, both with stonking great hard-ons beneath the duvet! Fortunately, we both understood the nature of sex and its insistence that it be quelled and so we soon shook off the cobwebs and headed for the toilet and then my shower.

And once there and suitably soaked, we turned our attention to our two erections – Andy's wonderfully long slim flagpole and my thicker shorter masterpiece and soon we were each soaping, lathering and rubbing the other person's cock. Andy was insistent that I should cum again. He reckoned that I'd given him so much pleasure the night before that he owed me one and he was going to get it! And so, well lathered and soaked, he bent over, offering me his slippery wet arse.

"Come on Chris, get it up me, please," he said pleading for my cock.

No sooner said than done and I moved up close behind him – my erection pointing upwards whereas it needed to point forward. My hand did the trick and moments later I was effortlessly sliding into Andy's soaking wet arsehole.

"Fuuuuck!" said Andy, "You're filling me!"

"Didn't it hurt?" I asked, driving my cock deeper into his hole, "Went in so easily."

"No it didn't hurt at all, it felt lovely," said Andy, pushing his arse back at my cock, "It was even easier this time. I'm getting used to you already."

This time I was eager to unload my balls and I pushed harder and faster... quicker and deeper... and in minutes I was ready to unload!

"Uuuuh"! I groaned, "Cumming any moment."

"Yeah – let it go!" Andy cried, pushing his arse back at me, "Please – fill me!"

I reached around his hip and found his erection – I grasped it and began wanking him as I thrust my cock into him.

"Oh god – oh yessss – here it cums!" I cried as my penis drove into Andy's hole once more and began to unload its offering.

"Ooooooh yessss – oooooh fuck!" I cried, "Oooohhhh fuuuuuck!"

"Let it go! Let it go!" moaned Andy as I filled his arse with my hot sexy sperm, "Oh my god – that's lovely!"

And it was – it was just what I'd needed – a gorgeously tight arsehole in which to sink my penis. Emptied, I pulled my cock out of Andy's hole and collapsed back against the shower wall.

"Oh fuck!" I exclaimed, "I needed that. Did you cum?"

"No, not yet," said Andy, "Anyway, I wanted to save it for later..."

And 'later' came even sooner than I'd expected!

It had been fairly late when we'd woken up and now there was just enough time for us to get out of the shower, have some breakfast and then get ourselves together enough to hit the road without further excitement and we were down at the marina well before our appointed time.

We still had the best part of an hour to fill before the crane was ours and together, we busied ourselves getting the boat shipshape and suitably ready to enter its preferred medium... and then it was our time. There seems to be a certain amount of shouting and yelling required with any marina job and there was today but getting my unremarkable boat into the water was no problem today and it all went smoothly... and soon Andy and I were alone in our small cocoon of peace. We finished off packing away all the bits and pieces we'd brought down, along with a fair selection of clothing in case we got wet and then we were done. I powered up the diesel and we headed to our berth once more, with no plans of staying there for long but I had to remember to ask the harbourmaster for permission before we left the marina and it didn't take long; the radio working perfectly.

"Ok Andy," I called out as I slipped our moorings, "You ready to go sailing?"

"Aye, aye, skipper!" Andy called out, "Ready for anything!"

Under power it was easy to escape land's clutches and soon we were out amid the swells of the Channel, but neither of us had any feeling of sea-sickness – we were obviously both born sailors!

Sailors – well, we weren't real sailors – sailors used sails whereas we didn't have any! But the feeling was there as we headed out into the blue.

"Are we fishing or just cruising?" asked Andy, leaving me pondering for a bit.

"I'm just loving being out here, but do you fancy some fishing?" I offered, "Conger; Huss – possibly cod?"

"Yeah – great!" said Andy, swaying with the boat's motion, "I miss my fishing; dad seems to have given it up – he prefers to be at the bar I reckon."

I gunned the motor to take us around the point to where I knew of a wreck and some good fishing and left Andy at the wheel while I dug out a couple of rods and reels – all complete and ready to use. We'd try and catch some mackerel for bait as we sailed on.

I checked out the gear – everything was there and ready – the gaff, landing net, disgorgers, etc, etc. I also had a bolt-down fishing chair which I now hauled out and fitted into place in the hope of catching a decent sized fish. It was really for when I went shark fishing – then at least whoever was the lucky fisherman would be able to haul his catch in safely and in comfort. The chair's presence also made us look somewhat more professional!

Some forty minutes later we were moored at my spot, with a few dozen mackerel and hopes of copious catches and we settled down to fish. Regrettably however the water was still; the waves had calmed; the tide was slack and half an hour later we were still there but there were still no fish. But these things happen, so we waited and waited until Andy started it off.

"Why aren't we sunbathing?" he asked, stripping off his t-shirt.

"Fair enough," I commented, eyeing our motionless lines and the blazing sun, "Might as well."

I too took off my t-shirt and then was completely taken aback to see that Andy had stripped right off!

"Bloody hell – when you said sunbathing, you meant it!" I said, "I didn't know you were going to go that far!"

"Why not?" said Andy, "There hasn't been a boat near us since we got here and if one does arrive we can soon slip our shorts on again. Come on, join me."

"Guess you're right," I said, "Oh alright – I'll join you!"

Dropping my own shorts took seconds and we stood there, somewhat self-consciously I thought, almost wondering what to do next. Two blokes on a boat with nothing on and nothing to do! I'd never been naked in my boat before. Even our cocks seemed to be uncertain about what to do and were both just hanging at half-mast.

"How about a beer or two?" I suggested, "And I'll put the radio on to keep us company."

"Yeah – great," said Andy, settling himself down in a fold-up chair while I fetched the lager.

"Cheers matey" he said as he cracked open his can, "This is the life! But I think we ought to have some sun lotion on before we settle down – I'll do you and you can do me."

"Ok," I said, "Sensible."

Andy rummaged in his bag and came up with a bottle of sun tan oil. Soon he'd covered me and I'd reciprocated – both of us ensuring that even the hidden places were anointed!

"Hey," I said as Andy smoothed lotion between my cheeks and over my arsehole, "The sun doesn't shine there!"

He laughed and slapped my bum as he put the lotion away.

I sat back into the fishing chair and swigged at my lager and together we enjoyed the warm afternoon sun while the radio droned on in the background. I felt relaxed – sod the fish – this was just as good!

Once again Andy started things off...

"I enjoyed last night," he said, "I did things I'd always wanted to but I'd never found the right person. But with you I just felt so totally free – no hang-ups or hidden secrets. It was lovely!"

"Couldn't agree more, Andy – really enjoyed myself too," I replied, "Just goes to show I was looking in the wrong places for my partner."

He laughed and put his thumbs up.

"Me too," he said, "But at least I knew when I spotted you that you'd be my sort. Well, I hoped so!"

"I can't get over how quickly we've gone from not knowing one another to basically being lovers," I said, "Two weeks and wow!"

280

"Wow is the word!" said Andy squirming around in his chair, "We've certainly got to know each other!"

And as he spoke, I saw his penis stiffen and begin to stand up yet again. He looked at me and started to stroke it – and needless to say, my own penis rose and hardened too.

"You are a horny bastard, aren't you?" I said cheerfully, "And you always set me off too!"

"Oooh goody!" said Andy, rising from his chair.

He came and stood in front of me with his lengthy tool held in his hand.

"Will you do something for me – suck me off, please!" he asked as he held his penis towards me.

A small lurch of the boat made him stumble closer and his cock was now right in my face. I reached up and took hold of his penis. It was completely rigid and wonderfully hot – it was an incredibly enjoyable feeling now to be holding someone else's cock with no feeling of concern or wrongfulness any longer. I climbed from the seat and knelt at his feet to feel the ridges and ripples of his flesh then ran my fingers over his knob and the ridge that separated his knob from his shaft. I smoothed my fingers up and down his length and felt him twitch as I held him. A small trickle of precum oozed from his slit and I gathered it and spread it over his knob – and another larger dribble formed almost at once. I caught it in my hand and brought it to my mouth – it was so slippery and yet so tasteless – neutral would be the best word to describe it... but it was lovely!

I leaned forward and opened my mouth and pulled Andy's penis to me and with one small shuffle his cock was right there for me. Gently I let the knob slide between my lips, loving the smooth texture of his flesh, the erotic knowledge that I was taking another man's sex organ inside my body. I closed my lips and squeezed my mouth tight round his shaft as it slid into me. I let it slide until it touched the back of my throat

– I wasn't yet ready to try deep-throating, especially not a ten-inch long cock! That would come with time, but for now I just concentrated on giving Andy a good blowjob.

Soon Andy was moving his hips backwards and forwards as he added his efforts to my work – my labour of love. I wanted to taste his cum again – I wanted to feel him jerking and thrusting uncontrollably as I made him orgasm. I just plain wanted him...

And then, just as things were getting interesting Andy spotted one of the rods bending!

"Fish – fish!" he yelled as we quickly disengaged and scrambled to take up our fishing stances.

It was my rod that was in action and I gently picked it up to test the quality of the 'bite'. Something was definitely interested... I waited and waited; holding my rod firmly but with trembling limbs.

Suddenly the line drooped – and then tightened – hard. I struck! Bingo!

"Got him!" I exclaimed happily as something large began stripping line from my reel, "Shit! He's big!"

Frantically I wound back line, pumping the fish back towards the surface.

Andy had reeled in his line so as not to get in the way and now stood beside me, watching the action. And action there was – this fish wasn't going to surface without a good fight!

I kept hauling the fish up only for it to drag line from me by the mile – well, it seemed like it – and then I'd recover the line and it would do it all over again.

"Gotta be a shark," I said, beginning to pant slightly, "Blue probably – thank heavens I put a steel trace on."

"Get in the chair," said Andy and I mentally agreed that that would be sensible.

I moved across the deck and just then the boat swayed; the fish pulled hard and I headed straight towards the side! Andy grabbed me from behind and hauled me back. And the next lurch of the boat sent me the other way – backwards towards Andy and the chair. I felt Andy behind me – his erection still there and now prodding my arse as I backed towards him... then he staggered back into the fishing chair – and with his arms around me I followed him!

"Aaaaaagh!" I cried, "Shiiiiiit – oh fuck!"

I'd sat right back onto his erection and with my sun lotion covered arsehole, his long slim penis had slid straight inside me!

"Ohhh fuck!" groaned Andy, holding me tight round my waist, "Oh yeahhhhh!"

And now I was panting hard – whether from the fishing or from the sex, I didn't know. All I did know was that I now had a cock up inside me and a fish on the line in front of me... and I wondered which was most important? Almost forgetting the fish, I felt my body relax to allow Andy's entire penis to slide almost effortlessly into me as I sat back on him.

"Oooooh god – that's good!" I groaned as his penis plumbed my depth.

"Oh Chris – you've taken all of me!" Andy cried, "I'm right up inside you!"

I couldn't concentrate on both ends so, letting Andy's cock remain embedded, I worked on getting my fish to the surface. And actually it was a good combination – as I pulled on the rod so I sank back on his cock; as the fish fought back so I rose off his penis. Andy didn't need to do a thing – I was doing it all for him! Up and down I went – down as I reeled in – back up as the fish retaliated – up and down on Andy's penis until he was ready to unload.

"You'd better get that fish in soon," groaned Andy, "I'm gonna cum!"

"Do it then," I said, tightening my arsehole around his penis, "Cum in me – fill me!"

And disregarding the fish I began bouncing up and down faster and harder – I wanted his penis to empty itself inside me – I wanted his cum up me!

"Oh fuck – oh fuck!" cried Andy, "Gonna cum – gonna cum! Yeah – here it cums!"

Beneath me I felt his cock stiffen further as his sperm blasted forth inside me.

"Uuuuuuh! Yeahhhh!" groaned Andy as he unloaded, "Ooooooh fuuuuuuck!"

I could feel his spunk hitting my intestines – his energetic blasts spraying his sperm deep up inside me, time after time.

Finally he stopped moving and I too stopped my movements – letting his penis slowly wilt inside me and only then could I return my mind to my rod – it was still stiff – stiffer than Andy's rod now was but this rod had a fish on it!

I wound up some slack and pulled hard again, feeling Andy's cock still fairly hard, inside me and then the line went slack – the damn fish had escaped!

"Fuck it!" I said, throwing down the rod, "Bloody well lost it."

But what I didn't realise was that in my anger I'd clamped down on Andy's penis and that had reawakened him – and now I was once again sitting on a renewed ten inch erection.

I looked over my shoulder at Andy.

"Lost it?" he queried, thrusting his cock back up inside me, "Well I've still got it!"

"You want more?" I asked, moving my arse around, "You want to cum again?"

"Yeahhhh!" said Andy, "Love to – your arse is so fucking tight!"

I turned my head and Andy leaned forward and we kissed – happily and lovingly.

"Fuck me Andy," I said, "Love me."

"I do and I will," Andy replied.

Andy moved down off the chair and we settled on a big towel on the deck and as he began to make love to me again, peace reigned – except for the radio, which now began playing that old Otis Redding hit.

I turned my head to Andy.

"Hah, that should be *'Sitting on the cock of the boy'*!" I said as I pushed my arse down onto his cock, "And what a fucking fantastic cock it is too!"

Mr Chatterley's Lover

I freely admit that once I became aware of the novel Lady Chatterley's Lover, which appeared in public and became a best-seller long before I was born, I found myself blushing whenever the book was mentioned. That wasn't because I was shy or otherwise put off by a good racy novel – no, it was because my name is the same.

Hey, quit laughing! I'm not Connie or Constance or a cross-dresser; I'm a bloke, not a woman! Neither do I own a large manor house; I'm not Sir anything; it's just that my surname is the same – Chatterley. Nor am I confined to a wheelchair as Sir Clifford was; I'm fit and healthy...and horny too for that matter – more like the gamekeeper in fact!

But to add another similarity to the novel, my Christian name happens to be Oliver; the same name as Lady Chatterley's lover, although I tend to be known as Ollie which is far less formal. And to completely twist the image, I'm gay, or at least I'm pretty certain I am now.

All of which just makes me cringe and blush when my friends will insist on asking, using a country bumpkin voice, something like, "Have you been down to the cottage lately?"

That's usually accompanied by a wink or a nudge as well, leaving me lost for words and occasionally painfully embarrassed too.

Like I said, I'm pretty sure I'm gay, even though I used to be hetero; hell, I even used to be married. Sadly, it just didn't work out – somehow I just couldn't feel happy with her presence and although we consummated our marriage, our bedroom activities left me remarkably unmoved. Oh sure, I could fuck her perfectly well, but my heart was never in it. My reticence set the standard I think and soon she had an affair; then we had one big row after another and then she departed and I was left with an empty home and a broken heart – that was, until I met Steve.

And just in case you ponder on my income and workplace, I have two forms of employment – I'm an IT specialist who sets up customers' own computers and I'm a writer, working almost entirely from home. I've written several moderately successful stories that have helped to keep my coffers topped up and I write short stories as a pastime but I now mainly deal with technical journals wherein I review various scientific discoveries and such – generally rather dry stuff I'm afraid… and I met Steve through one of our discussions on one of those technical subjects.

Anyway, Steve was another guy who turned out to be in a very similar situation to me and he was very much like me as well. We were both in our late twenties at the time; both tall and relatively slim; both with mousey brown hair and moustaches and both in the middle of becoming divorced – and both in need of some release, it seemed. We met a couple of times to discuss our work and then we decided to meet socially and suddenly we were both eager to meet again. It only took us a few more meetings; a few drinks together at the local pub and a couple of chance meetings in town and we were firm friends soon regaling each other with lurid tales of our respective partners and their infidelities.

And then a month or so after we first met Steve came round to my place for a social evening and we found ourselves really opening up to each other, actually talking about sex itself. Not exactly describing sexual acts but discussing how we'd been unable to enjoy sex with our partners and then discussing how frustrated we both were now. In the middle of our chattering it became abundantly clear that much as we'd both wanted to enjoy sex with our women, something had been wrong; neither of us had felt comfy with the opposite sex.

Anyway, you know what happens when you're frustrated and you talk about sex – things wake up down there! Well my penis did and so did Steve's and as we sat there sharing my settee and a few drinks it was soon impossible to hide our arousal. I remember Steve's eyes sliding from mine down to my lap – then jerking back up again. I remember mine doing the same, then finding Steve grinning broadly at me and my own face creasing up too.

I remember the conversation suddenly becoming fractured and more personal and I remember squirming as I sat there, embarrassed by the rising heat inside me and my rising and dominating penis. And I remember Steve laughing; then seeing his face and understanding that he wasn't especially being put off and then us sliding closer together.

And I let him – let him stretch his hand out onto my erection; let him slide his warm hand up and down over my shaft. Let him pull my hand towards him and let him press my hand down over his own penis. I remember us both groaning and then the flurry of activity as we both began casting off clothes almost desperately until we were standing naked together, our cocks both hard and needy. A brief feel of each other's penis and then we were crushed together in a hot embrace, our mouths finding each other suddenly, our chests heaving as quick and frantic breaths came and went.

I shiver now as I remember that thrilling first evening together; as our hands explored and then his mouth went down there – and then there was me doing the same! We slumped to the floor and played a frantic and imaginary game of Twister until we'd achieved a 69 position with Steve poised above me, his knees beside my ears, his penis thrusting at my mouth. I can hardly remember the details of that first time because it was so damn quick – it seemed as if one moment we were getting comfy; a few moments later his penis was sinking into my mouth just as mine slid into his and the next moment Steve was jerking and spurting in my mouth and I was doing the same to him! And we both swallowed every last bit of our essence. The delicious shock as we both erupted still sends shivers through me whenever I think back.

But it was bloody brilliant – it was a release and a discovery and a delight, all rolled into one. Half an hour later and we were doing it again, that evening eventually emptying a year or more of pent up sex into each other until finally we were sated and once more relaxed. I don't think that either of us had planned anything; it had just happened, spurred along by some alcohol and not a little needy urgency. But we'd un-bunged that barrel; let the cat out of the bag or something and our lives now seemed to revolve around our evenings when we'd get together at his place or mine; becoming naked in minutes and horizontal within a few minutes more.

Despite being intimately together for a good six months we never progressed past a comfortable and mutual wank or a friendly blow job although I've a feeling that with a few more months of close attention then we might have done so. But fate saw otherwise as Steve was snuffed from my life one day, killed by an out-of-control car which had slammed into him as the result of a collision and I wasn't in any way related to him I only found out his fate from the local paper, the day after he hadn't turned up for our latest session. I was as heart-broken as if he'd been my brother; my closest, perhaps my only friend was gone and I was alone again, drawn back into my world of paper and of words.

Writing and remembering that made me suck in and then release a huge shuddering breath; a sigh of sadness as the memory flooded back but this story isn't about Steve and me, it's about what happened afterwards – well, not immediately afterwards because for a while I just sank back into my shell. I may have been of a quite young and resilient age but it was a tender age and a shock as deep as that sent me spiralling into depression for a while, unable to comprehend that life does have its ups and downs – until finally I realised that life had to go on regardless.

And it was around that point that I also wondered if I was gay or hetero because I still found my eyes following pretty women and yet also felt my heart leap when I saw guys who resembled Steve – but my interest remained limited by my reclusive mind. Yes, I'd been gay with Steve but only with him and only in private so far – to the rest of the world I was entirely normal.

Oh I still did my work and I still performed my chores but I was relatively lifeless and drab but then, on one early spring day things began to turn around as a new window of opportunity opened.

A neighbour of mine happened to mention, to moan actually, that he'd been supplying a local greengrocer with organic vegetables but that he'd had to stop because of ill-health, leaving his business friend without a supplier and it got me thinking – could I try to fill that gap? I loved to work the soil; I had an affinity with nature, and I needed something physical to do, so why not try? My own back garden had a vegetable patch, but I wasn't in any way set up for commercial vegetable production but perhaps I could make some changes...

The thought swirled idly around in my brain but then, when I saw my neighbour a few days later, he went on to mention that he'd also be giving up his allotment and asked if I'd like to take it over.

Suddenly things began to fall into place and within a few weeks I was there in my wellies – but with a newly-found spring in my step as I admired the seemingly huge expanse of tilled and brown soil before me, all surrounded by so much open space. It was a far cry from the reclusive hermit-like life I'd sunk into but it suddenly felt great to be out there with something to do. I became a new man, transformed remarkably quickly even to the point that people began to smile and brighten up around me once more – and I managed to smile back too.

With the healthy sunshine and warmth around me I settled to my task with huge energy and determination and suddenly I was busy again, and within a few months of excellent weather I was shifting piles of vegetables on an almost daily basis to the greengrocer, whose delight (and profit no doubt) was abundant.

And that's not to say that I didn't make something out of it, indeed, with the premium attached to the word 'organic' I did quite nicely. Neither did my paperwork suffer because my activity level seemed to have doubled and just as importantly, I'd lost the pallor of my reclusive life. I'd bronzed perfectly and developed muscles where I hadn't ever had muscles before – I'd become quite fit and healthy. I also managed to dodge the requirement not to do commercial cultivation simply by telling the local authorities that the greengrocer was a relative. Sure, that was a lie, but they never checked on it.

But I'm straying from the theme of my story, so let's get back to it...

Down at the allotment I'd erected a respectably modern if small polytunnel on my plot wherein I could grow vegetables out of season to some extent (especially early salad crops; tomatoes, lettuces, cucumbers and such) and alongside it was a somewhat ancient and dilapidated shack; a construction almost unfit for use as it stood.

Between nurturing and harvesting I worked on it, bringing it back to life with a new roof, some reinforcement, some new window glass, some paint and a bit of love and before long my little shack became my peaceful retreat – I was lord of my little manor, so to speak.

After a warm day's work I could occasionally recline under the shed canopy in a comfy old armchair I'd brought from home; overlooking my thoroughly fecund plot with a beer in my hand and a contented smile on my face and it was there that my new life began.

I didn't know the name of the guy who had the plot next to mine until we found time to properly introduce ourselves and at that point we both burst out laughing...because it turned out that his name was Cliff – well, Clifford really. It was at that moment too that we realised that we'd both read the notorious book and had immediately connected our names to the characters.

He was possibly a decade older than me but he looked fit, usually working in shorts and a vest just like me, that clearly showed off his muscular fit tanned body. He was a cheerful soul with a ready wave and smile and it wasn't all that long before we came to enjoy each other's company. We'd settle down together after our efforts, sharing a few cans of beer in the declining sunshine and we began to become quite friendly and amusingly competitive. Before too long he told me something of his background; that he'd had a nervous breakdown some while before, was now working part-time and used the allotment as occupational therapy. It was far more beneficial to him than knitting or basket making. We were competitive in the quality of what we could produce although he worked his allotment only to provide vegetables for his family, his relatives and a few neighbours so it was a pastime as much as anything else.

And it was Cliff who set things off – perhaps unintentionally, as he lugged a couple of large marrows past me one warm and sunny day.

"Hey, that's a nice crop," I said, admiring his produce, "You're doing well."

"Oooh arr!" he said using an imitation rustic voice, along with a huge wink, "I sure am! They say there's nothing like a good marrow!"

"Do what?" I asked, caught unexpectedly by his comment, "Oh yeah, marrow, mmmm, lovely. Stuffed and baked...yeah?"

"No, no – not like that! You cut a hole in one and slide your dick in so smoothly," he said, "Beats getting off with the old hand job, that's for sure!"

He creased with laughter as he dumped the pile in his wheelbarrow and then turned towards me with one remaining marrow in his hands.

"Watermelon's even better but we can't grow them so well here so marrows do the job," he continued more conventionally, his hands sliding over the vegetable's mottled green skin, "They're cool, moist – they're brilliant!"

"What – you've done that?" I answered, my question unintentionally blunt, "I mean, you've heard of people doing that?"

"Yeahhhh," grunted Cliff as he held the marrow end on to his groin and thrust his hips obscenely forwards, "Well, haven't you?"

"Ummmm, well, no, not really," I said, my words stumbling uneasily from me, "Not really me; hadn't ever thought about it."

"You want to try it some day!" replied Cliff cheerfully, stroking the marrow almost reverently, "You can have one of these if you like."

"No, go on – you can keep it," I answered but Cliff didn't answer.

Instead he was bending down to place the marrow on the ground, then standing upright again, his hands resting on his hips.

"Sorry Ollie, didn't mean to be crude. Got a bit carried away there, didn't I?" he said but now it was my turn not to respond.

Because there before me, straining the material of his trousers was the barrel of his penis as it stretched up towards his hip – hardly a pea shooter; definitely more like a carrot and a big one at that! It looked impressively long and exceptionally thick too and from its position it was evident that it was most strenuously erect. I wanted to look away and found I couldn't – my eyes were locked onto the erotic sight before me. For what seemed like minutes but was more probably just seconds I stared and imagined how his cock looked before I finally but suddenly lifted my eyes away.

And as I looked at Cliff his face was changing – his mouth falling open, his cheeks reddening, and they weren't red from the heat of the day either. Then his own eyes glanced quickly down his body then jerked upwards again until they locked onto mine. It must have all happened in seconds...

"Oh shit!" he exclaimed, his gaze falling suddenly once more, "Sorry – didn't mean that to happen."

Quickly his hands worked at his trousers, now firmly pushing his penis out of sight or at any rate, into a less visible position then his eyes lifted and found mine again.

"I'm really sorry," he said, his head now hanging somewhat contritely, "Didn't intend to show off my ummm – you know, my thing. I thought you'd find the marrow story amusing but I hadn't planned it to have that effect on me."

"Huh, don't let it worry you. Guess you're feeling a bit horny, eh? You certainly looked as if you enjoyed it but no – no problem," I hastened to assure him, "I wasn't so much offended as surprised, you know, sort of shocked."

"Just me and my little jokes," said Cliff as he came closer, "Mind if I join you?"

"Of course you can. You're welcome Cliff," I said, ignoring the sexual aspect in moments, "And if you fancy a beer there are some cans in the ice box back there..."

"Oooh brilliant!" exclaimed Cliff a few moments later as he lifted a dripping can from the box and popped the tab, "Ah, that's super. Ohhh, cold beer, cheers mate."

He plonked himself down on a wooden bench beside my easy chair and supped deeply before wiping his mouth and looking at me.

"So – how's things?" he asked, "Busy?"

"So-so," I replied, "Enough work to keep me out of trouble. And you?"

"Nah – at a bit of a loose end at present," he said, "My last contract finished a couple of months ago so I'm more or less out of work for now. That's why I've been down here a lot recently..."

"Ah – tough mate," I answered, noncommittally, "Oh well, it's a good way to spend a few hours – lots of sunshine and fresh air."

"But no sex!" added Cliff with a wry chuckle.

"What's that got to do with it?" I answered, caught unaware by his renewed interest in the matter.

"Nah nothing, it's just me," he said lightly, "Just everything makes me think of sex. You see, now I'm not working, my missus has gone off to visit her folks and I'm stuck at home."

He obviously hadn't finished his story, so I remained quiet while he took another mouthful of lager, then he continued.

"Well truthfully she's not impressed at all at me being unemployed; I mean she's really pissed off to be honest," he said, then paused to drink more deeply.

Then he continued again, "So that means no sex, no nothing..."

"You can handle that for a few months, can't you?" I asked but Cliff continued to look quite downcast and coy as he looked at me.

"Yeah, but – oh, I shouldn't tell you this but I might as well get it off my chest – the missus and I haven't been getting on too well for some time, so we haven't, you know, 'got together' for what, ummm the last four months now," said Cliff, "And now she's gone away so it's going to be even longer..."

He lifted his eyes to mine and his sadness was there to see.

"Oh fuck – I've started so I might as well tell you everything but don't tell anyone else," he said, "I'm not even sure if she'll ever come back. I think our marriage has had it to be honest."

He was actually looking almost relieved to have opened up even though his eyes still looked sad and mournful like those of a spaniel.

"Oh shit, that's bloody hard luck," I replied, "If it's any help I know how you feel then – I've been there."

I lifted my hand and held his arm for a moment or two, my comradely gesture appreciated as he managed to produce a small smile.

But it wasn't my place to ask too much about his marriage, so the subject of sex was easier to discuss.

295

"I haven't had sex in ages; I've got no-one at home either," I said as I aimed to divert his sorrow.

"Huh – so how do you deal with it?" asked Cliff as he got up and soon returned with two more of my cans, one of which he handed to me, "The old five-fingered job?"

"Case of having to, isn't it," I replied, feeling the talk of sex beginning to make things stir down below again, "What with the allotment and my writing I've hardly had time to go out hunting for a bit of crumpet."

We sat quietly now as our united miseries were shared and emptied our cans before Cliff turned to me.

"That was good – needed that, thanks," he said, "Now what I need next is to have a pee."

"There's a bucket in the shed," I said, "Use that."

Cliff looked at me with a question on his face.

"When I'm down here I save it then put the contents on my compost heap each evening; apparently it's good for the soil," I said, "I don't mind if you add to it!"

Cliff chuckled as he understood, then stood up and sauntered into the shed, the sound of his zip reaching my ears as he did so.

I sat there mulling over what I had to do when there was a sudden and anguished yell from the shed. Quickly I jumped up and stepped inside, to find Cliff standing there, his penis hanging from his fly, his mouth open.

"Fuckin' great spider!" he gasped, "There – in the bucket!"

I looked and indeed there was a biggish spider there; a common house spider that had either explored the bucket or fallen in. It was unharmed because the bucket was empty at present, but it certainly didn't belong there. Unfazed I picked the bucket up, took it outside and shook the spider out before returning to the shed wherein Cliff still stood.

I plonked the bucket down and waved my hand at it, then looked at Cliff. He was just frozen, his mouth still open, his lengthy penis still hanging; still exposed. I put my hand on his shoulder and shook him and with a sudden shudder he came out of his trance and looked at me.

"Bloody things – they scare me!" he said, "Never liked them much – and then that..."

"All gone now – it's safe to pee!" I said but Cliff was still scared.

"Stay there, stay with me," he said, "Fuckin' hell, that was nasty!"

I suppressed my chuckles as I stood there beside him but Cliff was still all tensed up so I waited quietly for him to let loose. As I did so my eyes almost automatically drifted to his penis and I found myself captivated by it as it lay in his hand. It looked quite long and respectably thick too and he was uncut. Perhaps half of his knob was visible beyond his foreskin and what I could see of his knob seemed to glow a deep purple colour. His penis itself was nicely brown and there was a prominent vein that scribbled its way down the shaft. I felt my own penis move languidly as I observed Cliff's – then discovered that I needed to lick my lips and swallow a mouthful of saliva.

"Come on then – what's keeping you?" I asked just a moment before Cliff began to pee.

A long steady stream of golden piss poured noisily into the bucket and I patted Cliff on the back and turned to leave but he called out to me.

"No, no, don't go, I need you here just in case... and anyway there's something else," he said somewhat mysteriously but obviously still somewhat disturbed, so I just stood and watched until he'd finished.

Finally, the last drips fell and Cliff shook his penis but instead of putting it away he turned towards me, his penis still held in his hand. Things seemed to happen in slow motion now and unable to or unwilling to lose sight of his cock I watched as with a slow movement of his hand

297

up and down his cock he caused his penis to begin to lift and fill out. A few more strokes and it was erect in his hand, now protruding a good six, maybe seven inches or more from his fly. He let go of it and it stood there by itself, his foreskin peeled back, the tip moist, his plum coloured knob looking almost edible and at that moment I felt Cliff's eyes burning into mine.

I lifted my gaze and found I was right but now Cliff was looking far from downcast; instead he had a big grin on his face.

"What d'you reckon then?" he said, "Interested? Fancy having a bit of fun? I've got a feeling you would... and you'd be helping me too."

I knew from the way that my own cock now seemed to be straining in my underpants that my inner mind had revealed its desires; if not to me then to Cliff and I found myself now to be the one unable to move. But Cliff was now more animated and shuffled closer to me until his erection was no more than a foot from me.

"Help me please. I know you want to try it," he said and as he spoke his hand reached out and found mine.

Then somehow I lifted my hand and let it be guided until his shaft filled my palm and as it settled there, Cliff's fingers wrapped mine around his cock in a tight and very arousing embrace.

"Nice?" he asked quietly, and I found my head nodding in reply.

And then his hand was sliding mine up and down his shaft and I could feel his thick penis jerking and straining as we stimulated his flesh together while down in my own trousers my own flesh began straining against the material, feeling very stimulated too.

I'd almost forgotten how good it was to hold a nice cock; to feel the heat inside it, the silky softness of his foreskin and the firmness of his erection as my hand slid over his penis and knob. My fingers probed his shape, exploring his length and thickness, discovering the wetness at the tip and delighting in his size.

"What is it – seven – more?" I asked as his hand left mine, allowing me to slide my hand up and down his cock more steadily.

"Near enough eight," he answered quietly, "Do you like it?"

"Mmmmm," I hummed, "Feels lovely..."

There was relative silence for a while now; punctuated only by our breathing and the occasional gasp from Cliff as I found sensitive places until Cliff broke into my thoughts.

"What about you?" he asked, "Can I play with you too?"

I felt myself nodding again – and then his hands were at my zip; then searching around inside my trousers; then grasping my erection; then pulling it out through the opening.

"Good – you're hard already," said Cliff as his hand extracted my penis from it's enclosure.

The cooler air brushed over my penis deliciously but only until Cliff's fingers enclosed my cock which now surged from the pressure and warmth of his hand.

"Oooooh Cliffffff," I moaned, "Stop it – stop it!"

I didn't mean to say that – the words just fell from me – all I could manage in the heat of the moment, a mindless utterance driven by the erotic nature of the situation. Cliff chuckled, knowing full well that I didn't really want him to stop, then shuffled around until we faced each other, our hands working steadily on each other's penis.

"No, you don't mean that, do you? And you feel nice too," Cliff said as his hand worked on my cock, "That's a lovely handful!"

"Mmmmm," I moaned softly as I eagerly explored his penis, "Yeahhh and so's yours..."

Then I sucked in another quick breath as Cliff's other hand reached into my flies and gathered up my balls which he pulled out of the opening to join my penis. His hand weighed them and rolled them around, squeezed them gently and pulled at them too. Then his fingers

299

slid under my balls and firmly stroked my perineum, coming awfully close to my arsehole. I felt my hips jerk suddenly at his audacious touch before he pulled his hand away.

His actions did little to calm me, not that I particularly wanted to be calmed down – I was so very definitely enjoying this rather unexpected activity, but his touch had both shocked and stirred me. Already my hips were responding and were spasmodically jerking, thrusting my cock into his hand as his fingers slid up and down my length and I could feel my level of arousal quickly rising, could feel pulses of precum being gently created. Already I'd reached a level from which there was no desirable return – all I wanted to do; needed to do; had to do – was to cum, cum and just cum!

There were several days' worth of spunk in me; my balls were overfilled with my sperm and it wasn't going to be all that long before I blew off. I just wanted to let him bring me off but somehow, I held onto my mind and concentrated on his cock instead; concentrated on bringing him to the same level that I'd reached. Urgently my hand worked on his penis, eagerly and quickly sliding his foreskin up and down his hot shaft. I could feel the wetness of his precum with each stroke now, a sticky slipperiness that was adhering to my hand even as the heated aroma of delicious sex reached my nose from our aroused organs.

I felt Cliff shudder and felt his penis thrusting steadily at me and I let my eyes find his. They were half closed in his ecstasy while his mouth was half open, his lips moving, fluttering, quivering – then he must have realised I was watching him, and his eyes opened fully.

"Ollie, I'm getting close man," he moaned, "You're gonna make me blow off in a minute or two."

"Yesss, yesss!" I gasped, urging him on, "Do it – cum for me!"

My hand tightened around his cock and moved faster and at that same moment I realised that Cliff's own hand was holding my cock just as tightly and that I too was very close to release now. But all that did was to make me redouble my efforts, then finding that Cliff's hand was moving in time with mine, so erotically and deliciously so that I found myself suddenly on the brink on an orgasm too.

"Oh fuck – gonna cum as well, I can feel it!" I groaned, "Get ready – it's cumming!"

Suddenly tension increased enormously inside me – suddenly it felt as if I was about to explode but instead of exploding inside, I felt the pressure spurting my spunk from me, squirting it out over Cliff's cock, spraying against his trousers and over my hand.

"Uhhhhh! Uhhhhh!" I grunted as each eruption was ejected, "Fu... fu... fuck, oh fuck!"

"Don't stop Ollie!" gasped Cliff at that moment, just as I remembered to pick up the pace of my own hand around his cock, a hand now dripping wet and slippery with my own cum.

And then Cliff's hand was moving and surrounding mine, holding me tightly. Inside my fist I felt his cock stiffen even more; it seemed to swell in my hand and then Cliff too was pulsing spunk everywhere just as I'd done. His first liquid load splashed up my shirt, then his aim improved, and three more substantial gushers of clean white lava coated my penis and his own hand before his eruptions died away to a meagre trickle. I felt his cum clinging to me and oozing down over my balls, a feeling that sent wicked shivers all through me.

Cliff shuffled closer still until our two cocks could rub together, sharing the cum that liberally coated both of our sex organs. His hands pushed mine away until he was holding both of our knobs, side by side in his palm; knobs that both still oozed spunk, knobs that were covered in veils of white slime and his fingers rolled our cocks together in the sticky, slippery and pungent remnants of our climaxes. For a few moments we just stood there as we recovered, neither eager to move and both enjoying the release that a good orgasm provided until we both seemed to gather our senses and step apart.

"Wow – look at this lot!" Cliff exclaimed, "We've damn well got it everywhere!"

There was indeed spunk all over the place; on our shirts and trousers, on my boots and on the floor; dripping down, soaking in and sticking to our hands and cocks.

"Bloody hell," I answered as I surveyed the outcome of our entertainment, "I think we both needed that!"

We chuckled together as we scoured the shed for cleaning materials and I eventually came up with a couple of old towels which were all I could find. Almost apologetically I proffered a mud-stained towel to him and he used it to clean himself as best he could while I did the same using the other towel. At least we were both wearing old clothes so a few more stains wouldn't be especially noticed (even if the hygiene level wasn't exactly high) and we eventually mopped up most of our emissions. My cock was still somewhat sticky with what was mainly Cliff's cum as I tucked it back into place but somehow, I enjoyed the stickiness; it was a reminder of that exciting moment, as if I'd need reminding!

Then finally we recovered, both of us seemingly rather shy about the event and yet possibly relieved, now that the pressure had been removed.

"God – I didn't really expect that!" said Cliff as he helped himself to another can of beer from the ice box, "But wow – that was good though!"

"Bloody right it was!" I answered, my voice excited if a little unsteady as I too opened a can, "That was so damn good but what on earth made you get hard?"

"There was a look in your eyes, on your face," said Cliff, "You looked interested and kind of turned on while you were standing there – so I just took the chance."

"Mmmmm, glad you did!" I exclaimed happily, "That was fun!"

Cliff chuckled as we stood there and drank, surrounded as we were by the mingled scents of the earth, of fertilizer, old timber, beer and of the more strident scent of sex – it was a very masculine-based theme, unintentional thought it may have been, but it all felt good and there was a real feeling of relaxation between us now. We'd broken a barrier and made a real bond between us too.

Together we took our drinks outside and sat, me in the chair, him on the arm of the chair, silently reminiscing, it seemed. And although we began to talk, we spoke of other matters, anything except sex, almost as if we were both bemused at having let ourselves go. For some while we just sat and relaxed until I glanced at my watch and discovered that the afternoon had passed and that it was now time to deliver my load of vegetables to the greengrocer.

"Oh bugger," I said, "Look at the time – gotta get going – can't be late."

Cliff's hand reached out and held my arm as I turned to move.

"Can we do that again?" he asked, and I found myself nodding eagerly.

"Yeah, definitely!" I replied, "Dunno when though."

"I'm at a loose end tonight actually; well I've got to go out to a meeting in town but while I'm out perhaps I could pop round – I'll have a couple of hours free beforehand," said Cliff, "Are you busy?"

"Err, no, nothing I can think of having to do," I said, then I reached a quick decision, "Yeah – come on round – why not!"

Cliff and I knew where each other lived; we'd found out some months before when we'd first met and now Cliff was merely left with setting a time.

"Be at your place at seven then; I'm sure we'll be able to keep ourselves occupied until it's time for my meeting!" he said with a grin and I gave him the thumbs up as I began loading the car with produce.

Cliff helped me with the last two boxes of vegetables and then left me to shut my shed while he crossed the allotment to his own plot. From there he waved a goodbye to me as I drove away, my heart now beating with more enthusiasm than it had for a while, it seemed.

It seemed a very long wait for seven o'clock to arrive; a time during which I found myself checking everything as if waiting for a lover. I shaved and showered, then I checked my hair, my freshness and the house generally, fussing around like an old mother hen. I expected nothing and yet I checked the bed and the bathroom twice and despite a degree of pretence that Cliff was 'just coming for a social visit' I found my penis to be constantly aroused and turgid and my heart to be beating that much faster than usual.

All I wanted was to feel Cliff touching my cock; loving it, maybe sucking it – definitely playing with it and for me to be able to return the compliment. I felt I was like a teenager, even finding myself watching the road avidly (and yet casually, of course!) until finally I recognised Cliff's car as it turned into our road.

"Oh god," I gasped to myself, nearly hyperventilating, "It's gonna happen!"

And then I was welcoming Cliff into the house and fixing him a drink and bustling around and all a-twitch until Cliff cottoned on to my agitation.

"Hey – calm down Ollie, relax," he said as he settled himself on the sofa, "What are you so excited about? It's only me!"

Cliff's broad smile did indeed calm me – his whole presence seemed to relax me and before long I too was seated and we began to chat, our conversation meandering from topic to topic until we'd found a certain degree of spontaneity by which time we'd also consumed a couple of drinks each. And then one of us, well, it was Cliff actually, mentioned sex. Instantly I felt my heart jump once more and my chest tighten and Cliff too seemed to sit more upright as the underlying reason for our 'meeting' arose.

"I was, errr, thinking back to earlier on..." said Cliff casually, "You didn't mind – you did enjoy it, didn't you?"

I found myself nodding, almost eagerly, somewhat shyly, then gasping a brief reply.

"Yeah, yeahhhh, it was incredibly good," I said, "Yeah, I definitely enjoyed it."

"Thought I'd better check," said Cliff brightly, "'Cos that's what I came round for, isn't it?"

I nodded again, a small movement but I knew that my glowing face would be showing my approval regardless of my limited response – I could feel the heat in my cheeks just as Cliff chuckled quietly.

"Haha, haha!" he chortled, "You're as bad as me really, aren't you? Sort of scared and yet eager too."

"Ye... ye... yeahh, I am a bit I guess," I spluttered, my mind unable to release the right words, "So you are, too?"

"Of course I'm eager and I'm all ready!" replied Cliff, "Look – see – I'm all hard even now and just being here with you has made me feel so bloody horny!"

He stood up and there before my eyes was the prominent bulge of his penis; a solid bar from his apex, up and across his groin. He used his hands to stretch the material over his bulge, an action that clearly outlined his penis in all its glory, even down to the shape of his knob. My hands felt as if they wanted to reach out and stroke that delicious bulge, but my natural reticence held me back – that was, until Cliff made the next move.

His hands moved to his belt – a few quick movements and a hissing of his zip and his trousers slid down his legs. Immediately the extent of his arousal became visible; a generous tent in his boxers and an area of dampness where his tip pressed against the material. He thrust his hips forward in a slow movement that just enhanced the view for me and then his hands were reaching out towards me. I lifted my own hands and allowed them to be drawn to his body where Cliff pressed them against his penis and where my fingers curled to caress his length. His penis felt big and powerful beneath my moving fingers, fingers that also felt the cool dampness of his precum-moistened underwear and I could feel the precum oozing from my own rigid cock within my trousers.

Cliff sucked in a long breath through tight lips.

"Yessss," he hissed, "Feel me, come on, stroke me – put your hands inside!"

The first touch had given me more confidence and now I knew that my mind wouldn't restrict me or let me down.

On the outside of his boxers I moved one hand downwards until I met his bare leg, then I reversed the direction, but now almost eagerly sliding my hand up inside his boxers. His somewhat hairy leg was firm, his muscles tight and hard; then I discovered his wiry pubes and his balls inside his loose scrotum. Briefly I caressed them, feeling their dimensions and weight but my real interest was higher up. I pushed my hand further up his leg opening and reached my target, the solid shaft of his erection, which pulsed and jumped as I touched it.

"Ahhhh!" gasped Cliff, "Yessss! Yessss – that's it – hold me, rub me!"

And now that I'd reached my target, now that I'd found his penis, I was no longer shy, no longer reticent and I let my fingers curl around his penis tightly. It was hot and so firm and so hard despite the softness of his skin. For a little while I just enjoyed the feeling of holding his cock, until Cliff seemed to come alive once more.

His hands pushed mine away, then pushed his boxers quickly down to join his trousers around his ankles. A moment or two later and his t-shirt discarded too and now Cliff was there before me, his chest rising and falling quickly, his hair-strewn abdomen firm and steady, his penis lifting and falling with his breathing. Already his foreskin had peeled back from his knob which shone delectably and which even now had the mandatory small bubble of precum at its tip.

Cliff shuffled closer to me, ran one hand up and down his cock and beckoned me to join him – and in an instant I too was standing there, busy now with both hands as I discarded my own clothes. Suddenly, urgently, I was naked and standing before Cliff, our two rampant cocks just inches apart then with a smile, Cliff's hand united our cocks, holding them together so that I could feel the heat emanating from his penis.

"I want you," said Cliff, his soft voice breaking the silence and as he spoke he sank to his knees, still retaining his hold on my cock though.

I really didn't know what to say so I just remained quiet although my breath shuddered from me as my excitement grew.

'*He's gonna suck me*!' I remember thinking, '*Yes, yes – come on, pleeeeease*!'

And then he was – I felt the warm softness of his lips surround my cock; I felt the pressure as he closed his lips and I felt the thrill welling from me as he began to apply some suction. I watched as if from afar as my hands moved and rested on his head to guide him as he let my cock slide in and out of his mouth.

"Fuuuuck Cliff, that feels so good – so bloody good!" I exclaimed as Cliff worked on me, his head moving back and forwards, my hips following him, "I've wanted you to do this, so much!"

"Mmmmmmm!" was all that Cliff said as he built up a rhythm; a steady movement accentuated by his hand which was now wrapped around my shaft.

And now we were into the meat of the action as Cliff steadily worked on my cock. Both his hand and his lips were sliding steadily up and down my penis, an instrument that seemed to thrill from his actions, seemed to harden and grow with each stroke. I was speechless and breathless as he worked on me, such was the delicious pleasure he was creating. My hips were now jerking my cock into his mouth, an unintentional movement of my body as the delights of being sucked stirred my responses, a movement that I tried unsuccessfully to control. I tried because each movement sent another wave of pleasure to my balls and brought me another moment closer to my release.

"Oooh fuck!" I gasped as Cliff's actions took their toll on me, "Careful Cliff, careful!"

My hands had somehow found his head and were attempting to stop his movements. Briefly Cliff stopped his actions and, allowing my cock to slip from his lips he looked up at me.

"What's the matter Ollie, too nice is it?" he said before sliding my cock back into his mouth.

"Oooh damn right is it!" I exclaimed, "You'll make me cum if you're not careful!"

Cliff pulled away once more, his eyes finding mine.

"I want you to cum – let me finish you off!" he said, "I want you to cum in my mouth – I want to taste you, all of you!"

"Ohhh yeahhhh – oh fuck, yeahhh!" I groaned, my voice trembling with eagerness, "Ahhhh! You'd better not stop doing that then."

Cliff's only response was to squeeze my cock with his hand and then to resume his actions with what seemed like even more enthusiasm, his lips tight around my penis, his tongue teasing my helmet non-stop.

Gigantic spasms kept shaking me and with each spasm I tried to plunge my cock deeper and harder into Cliff's mouth; with each spasm I came closer and closer to losing it and I knew that this wasn't going to last much longer!

In fact, it was on its way even as I thrust – my orgasm felt unstoppable now – a force that would merely eject a spoonful of fluid, but which felt strong enough to move a mountain.

"Watch out Cliff, it's coming... it's coming!" I gasped as I felt everything tighten up inside me, "I'm gonna – I'm gonna... ahhhh! Oh god yeah, yeah – here it cums!!"

With a deep grunt I thrust my cock as far forward as I could. My buttocks clenched tight as my spunk ejected, swelling my cock and firing what felt like vast energetic volumes of cum deep into Cliff's mouth. He coughed briefly and some bubbles of white spunk erupted at the edge of his mouth, then he settled once more, swallowing again then continuing to suck me off until I had no more to give.

"Bloody hell!" I managed to utter, now feeling weak and washed out, "Oh Cliff, that was incredible!"

With a final squeeze of my cock Cliff lifted his head and looked at me. His mouth was shiny and wet and his fingers came up and cleaned his lips of cum before popping the small residue back into his mouth. He smiled broadly now.

"Tasty!" he exclaimed, "Delicious in fact!"

"Was it?" I asked, unable to say anything more intelligent.

"Definitely!" he added as his tongue licked his lips, "I could make a habit of that!"

He laughed now as he stood up and a second or two later he was kissing me, his mouth and breath both redolent of the saltiness of my spunk. We clung together as we kissed until I became aware of Cliff's penis which was thrusting, driving against my stomach. I reached down between us and grasped it, feeling the wetness of his precum in my palm. I wanted him now – I wanted to return the compliment – I wanted him to flood my mouth as well.

"Do you want me to?" I asked and Cliff understood clearly; his hands now urging me downwards until I was kneeling before him.

His gorgeously big cock stood there, pointing towards the ceiling. Its foreskin was furled back, its knob shone and glistened and a small dribble of sticky clear precum was sliding slowly down the underside of his cock; a viscous dribble that clung to his penis. Quickly I leaned forward and licked the little stream up and although the taste was very faint, I nevertheless knew perfectly well that the small dribble was on my tongue. It was a minute taste of the nectar that I wanted so much more of now and Cliff understood my desire and, with his hands on my head, he pulled me towards his groin.

Almost eagerly I opened my mouth and allowed his cock to slide inside, feeling the warmth of his flesh against the roof of my mouth as he pushed inwards. Quickly I tightened my lips around his shaft, a movement that brought a low groan from Cliff and which lifted my senses even higher. I slid my tongue around his helmet, feeling the firm ridge of flesh, then the smoothness of his skin and then tried to poke my tongue into his little hole and as I did so I felt Cliff's fingers tightening on my head as I probed with my tongue. For a moment it felt as if I'd succeeded but it was a trick of the senses that made me imagine that his hole was huge and that my tongue was like a little fingertip.

There came another groan from Cliff, then I detected a small gush of precum that concentrated my senses as I settled to suck him off, determined to outdo his efforts. I was well aware that I'd have to be really good to do that, but I was truly determined now, almost desperately so.

"Oooh fuck Ollie, that's nice!" Cliff said as I worked on him and as he spoke his hips pumped his cock into my mouth more urgently and I had to pull back rather than let his cock fill my throat.

I wasn't skilled at deep-throating – I didn't object to feeling his penis pushing well into my mouth but not into my throat as yet. Perhaps one day soon...

But right now, all I wanted in my throat was his cum, his sperm, that deliciously sticky salty stuff that I knew his balls were full of and which I wanted inside me instead. I locked my lips tight around his penis as my fist began to slide faster up and down his shaft, jacking him off as fast as I could in an eager effort to enjoy his fruitful essence. Already his cock felt bigger and stiffer and possibly hotter too as I twisted my tongue around his knob while up above me I could hear Cliff's breathing getting quicker and more shallow. His breath seemed to be shuddering from him too almost as if he was shivering, but he wasn't shivering from cold, that was certain as he now confirmed.

"Ollie, Ollie – I'm getting close!" he groaned as his hands found my head, "Oh fuck – I won't be long now!"

"Come on then – let me have it!" I answered as I let his cock slip from my mouth for a brief moment, "I want you, here, inside me."

Everything was becoming urgent now – Cliff was going to cum soon and I was suddenly almost desperate to taste his lovely spunk – it was guaranteed to taste delicious!

"Uhhhhh!" gasped Cliff as I renewed my attack on his penis, "Bloody hell – nearly!"

His whole body was shuddering now, quivering with soon-to-be-released urgency – I had to grip his penis firmly or lose it – or let it thrust right down my throat. I sucked hard and let my fist slide quickly up and down his shaft and suddenly Cliff's hand tightened on the back of my head while his other hand on my shoulder began squeezing hard.

"It's coming, here it comes!" he moaned, his voice urgent, "Ready – can't stop now – it's coming! Uhhhhh, oh yessss!"

With a loud grunt and a powerful heave of his hips that drove his penis against the roof of my mouth he opened up. I swear I felt his penis thicken, swell and grow harder just seconds before he gushed hot spunk into me, filling my mouth with his fluid and his cock. I managed to swallow deeply as his product filled my mouth but that only left room for another gush, another thrilling top-up.

I was working his cock hard and fast now, urging it to provide me with it's delicious nectar – I was full of lustful need for the taste.

"Oh Cliff, yeah!" I managed to gasp as I briefly opened my mouth, "More, more!"

And there was more – another blast that felt warm against the roof of my mouth; a blast so sudden that I inadvertently let a trickle slip from my lips.

I wanted to stop and collect it as it cooled against my chin, but my mind was on making the most of my mouthful of warm cum and anyway, at that moment Cliff pumped another warm gush of cum from his cock. It felt thick and sticky and it was wonderful to savour on my tongue; a fresh slightly salty flavour that just made me want more.

Careful not to swallow it all I allowed some of the essence to slide down my throat so I could enjoy him to the full – then immediately wished that I could have some more. And a second or two later my wish was granted as Cliff's penis gushed yet another squirt of cum into my mouth and then another. And now I had to swallow again – although I have to be honest and say that Cliff's penis made one last thrust at that very moment, a movement that contributed to my action.

It was a wonderful sensation to know that my mouth was filled with the sperm of a man; his vital contribution to life. I just knew then that I'd be letting so much more of Cliff's cum flow into my mouth and down my throat if he'd let me, if he'd give it to me.

With a parting kiss I let Cliff's cock slide from my mouth, and I stood up, my face glowing and my chest heaving as if I'd just run a long race, to find Cliff in much the same condition. Dreamily I savoured the remaining sperm in my mouth before swallowing it all – then shook my head as if to clear the congestion from my brain.

"Phew!" I said, "Brilliant!"

"Fuck, that was good!" Cliff exclaimed as he smiled at me, "You were perfect!"

"Weren't so bad yourself," I answered with a big, almost sheepish smile, "Can we do that again some time?"

I knew what the answer would be, but I had to ask, and Cliff's broad smile told me how unnecessary my question had been. His hand came up to my face and I thought he was going to stroke me but instead one finger extended and slid up over my chin before moving away laden with a white blob of cum.

"You missed a bit, just like I did. Share it?" he asked as he held it up and I nodded.

And with his finger held up between us we both moved closer and closer until our noses touched and then our lips met around his cum-laden finger. We both sucked – and then his finger was gone and our lips were together and we were kissing and tasting his cum once again and then pulling one another closer and tighter together. It was wonderful as the two of us let our lips do the talking, as our lips slid wetly over each other, as our tongues extended and explored and it was my turn to be shivering now, not with cold either but with excited emotion because even though I'd only come a few minutes ago I could feel that my cock was hardening once again and was pressing against Cliff's abdomen.

But then Cliff pushed us apart gently.

"Hang on – gotta breathe!" he said, "Wow – didn't really expect that. Love your lips, they're so soft and warm."

"Couldn't stop myself; that was amazing!" I said, sucking in a sudden breath as Cliff's hand surrounded my erection, "Ahhhh, what're you doing?"

"Just feeling you," said Cliff as his hand continued to slowly move on my quickly rising cock, "Been a long time since I had such a nice cock to play with."

"You've done this before?" I asked and Cliff nodded.

"Yeah once – I used to know a guy...but that was ages ago; we got to know one another really well," he said wistfully, "But you're here now – can we sort of get to know one another better, do you think?"

I felt my hips jump suddenly and my stiffened penis thrust through his fist before Cliff took his hand away but already my words were forming.

"Yeah, oh yeah!" I cried, overjoyed at the way things had progressed, "Love to – that'll be incredible!"

"Better make some plans then," said Cliff, already pulling his clothes back on, "But not right now – the time's just flown by – gotta leave you soon, it's an important meeting tonight – to do with the group I work for."

"Oh what – you've got to go already?" I asked plaintively, "I was hoping we could..."

"I'd love to be able to stay Ollie, but not tonight," answered Cliff, "This was like a proper introduction wasn't it and we seemed to get along ok so we simply must get together again... but not right now."

"Oh ok. Suppose so Cliff," I said, fervently wishing that he wasn't having to leave, "Thanks so much for coming over anyway – I really enjoyed that!"

"Mmmmm, so did I," he replied as he finished dressing, "I think we'd definitely better to organise some more meetings; some longer ones I guess?"

"Definitely!" I said as I reluctantly tidied my cock back into my trousers.

My penis was still well-inflated, and my bulge looked quite substantial as I walked Cliff to the door – so much so that Cliff placed his hand over it as he turned in the doorway.

"That's a lovely cock you've got," he murmured, "I'm really look forward to getting to know it better!"

And then he leaned forward and kissed me unexpectedly – and then he was off and walking to his car. I almost needed to chase after him; to implore him to stay with me and my stomach was full of uncontrollable butterflies as I watched him drive away. I turned back indoors, discovering as I did so that my cock seemed to be quite as hard as it had ever been.

"Stop it! Relax," I said to myself as I shut the door, "Anyone would think you're in love!"

What was left of the evening dissipated into a jumble of food and work and coffee and then it was bedtime. Eventually I slumped into my bed, naked and still aroused; my penis still risen to attention, my knob almost glowing with warmth yet trembling with anticipated desire. But tonight I was alone and I lay there with my hand around my warm shaft, wishing that my hand was his; wishing that his cock was there beside me too. But Cliff, despite arousing me, had taken the urgency from my need and instead of wanking as I often did, I found myself now almost cuddling myself as I drifted off to sleep, imagining that it was his arms around me as well.

Inside me there was a mild sense of annoyance that we hadn't been able to enjoy each other for longer but I kept reminding myself that this was merely our first meeting and that we'd both agreed to meet again and finally I accepted the delay. I knew that we'd see each other again down at the allotment anyway and I was well aware that this was the start of something big. The result was that I slept well despite my evening desires and rose eager to get back to join the world; feeling full of physical energy and with a lightness that I could hardly explain, even to myself.

The following morning, after a modest breakfast I was ready once more, ready to face my days' labour and as the warmth of the early summer sun increased so did my activity level and I positively bounced my way to the car as I headed back to my allotment. The morning traffic did nothing to spoil my liveliness nor my general cheerfulness and inside twenty minutes I was driving down the dirt road into the allotments.

There it was a more relaxed world, the traffic was at a distance and the ambience was more of nature herself; the light wind, the warm sun, the humming of busy bees and the twittering of bird blending so easily to form the peaceful atmosphere of the place.

I opened up my shed then turned and surveyed my little domain contentedly, smelling the scent of the earth, of the small array of flowers that I'd cultivated beside my shed and that of growing plants as I did so. It was warm already and so peaceful here in my corner of the allotments. Some of the nearby plots were vacant and few other allotment-holders were here so early in the day – I was almost alone. Quickly I stripped off my t-shirt, then wearing just my shorts and boots I began my chores of weeding, watering and harvesting with plans to get a car-load of goodies to my greengrocer by lunchtime.

The sun almost stung my back as I worked and when I ducked into my polytunnel to avoid it's rays, instead I discovered it's heat. Quickly I opened all the vents, which helped somewhat and then I began gathering my crop including tomatoes, sweet peppers and cucumbers until I had two boxes full which I lugged back to the shed and it was there that Cliff found me.

I only became aware of his presence when, as I was bent over one of the boxes, suddenly a long green cucumber was thrust between my legs. All in one movement I jerked upright, clamped my legs together and twisted my torso around – to come face to face with a broadly grinning Cliff.

"Caught you!" he said cheerfully while pointing between my legs, "Look at you, you horny bastard – you've got a huge hard-on already!"

Half of the cucumber was indeed protruding before me like a huge green erection and I managed to see the funny side of it too and laughed as I unclamped my thighs, dropped the cucumber into my hands then replaced it in the box.

"Bloody one-track mind, haven't you!" I said cheerfully, "Is that all you think about?"

"No – no, of course not, but coming in and seeing you bent over like that...and then seeing the cucumbers," he said with a wicked smile, "And it just got me thinking – well, doing more than thinking actually."

"Uh?" I queried as I frowned; then I caught on.

Cliff's penis was quite clearly visible, its stiff length stretching the leg of his shorts dramatically, almost threatening to tear the material, or so I could imagine.

"Flaming heck, you're not up for it already?" I asked, more a statement than a question and Cliff nodded.

"Course I am – always ready, especially after last night. I think I've been hard ever since," he said, his hand sliding down over his penis as if to accentuate it's size and stiffness, "Aren't you feeling horny?"

As he spoke and as the words sank in, I quickly realised that almost inevitably my penis was interacting with the vibes that Cliff's own arousal was giving off and I felt the growing mass of my cock in my shorts.

"Sure, but not out here," I admonished him, "Come into the shed – there's people around."

Truthfully there weren't many others at the allotments right now and the nearest was probably fifty yards away, but I wasn't eager to give

317

anyone a show! A few steps and we were hidden from sight at which point I clutched my stiffening penis in my hand.

"Ummm where was I – yeah, I guess so," I spluttered, my mind still partially on my vegetable produce, "Not sure really, been busy; hadn't really thought about it until now."

"Perhaps this'll help," said Cliff and a moment or two later his shorts were sliding off and were quickly joined by his underpants then his t-shirt too.

He stood there stripped for action, his lengthy penis jutting from it's small forest, pointing towards the ceiling and towards me. Quickly he bent and undid his shoes then he stepped away from his clothes and in doing so he closed the gap between us until his eager penis was pressed against my hands; hands that instinctively closed around it.

"Ohhhhh yesss," breathed Cliff as I fondled his warm stiff cock, "Come on then, let's do something."

Shaken from my previous state I glanced around, almost furtively, as if to search for lurking perverts in the small shed but finding none and seeing no-one within sight, I leaned past Cliff, pushed the door closed and relaxed. The windows were dirty enough not to allow anyone a good view inside. Quickly I too dropped my shorts and underpants and stood there with my clothes around my ankles.

"What shall we do?" I asked but Cliff already had the answer.

In his hands he once again held one of the cucumbers, lasciviously sliding his hand up and down it's length.

"I was just thinking..." he said, "How much fun it would be if your cock was this big!"

"Hah – as if! Silly idea," I said as my fingers played with Cliff's warm erection, "What the hell would I do with something that big?"

The object in his hand was easily two inches across and some fifteen inches long.

"You could try putting it inside me," he said, "Be a bloody good stretch but I reckon…"

"No way!" I exclaimed, "What, that thing; in your arse?"

Cliff nodded quickly, a twisting smile forming on his lips.

"Where else?" he asked, "Haven't you tried putting things inside you?"

"No – well, no – ummm, of course not, ummm," I lied, "Well, not often."

As I spoke so a thrill shook me from head to toe, a thrill that made my buttocks clench, shiver and pulsate.

There was something especially exciting about that idea because it was an activity that I'd thoroughly enjoyed in times gone past and now memories were flooding back quickly and powerfully. I felt myself shiver with eager anticipation as the thought of fucking filled my fervent mind. In recent years all I'd had inside me was my vibrator and certainly no real-life cock. In many ways I'd tried to avoid that kind of gay intimacy, but I always knew that underneath all else it stirred and turned around inside my mind and that one day it would resurface. Could I really get back into that lifestyle? Dare I?

"Oh well, never mind," said Cliff as he seemed to realise my reticence, "Be alright for us to play though, won't it?"

His words defused my tension and at that I nodded vigorously – that was safe ground, but there were limits.

"Ok but not with that cucumber – you put that thing down!" I retorted, not wishing to have anything so large near my arse and Cliff laughed.

"Get your boots off then – let's get properly naked," Cliff implored, and he stepped away from me to let me remove my own footwear.

I turned on the spot to bend and unlace my boots and as I bent and strained to undo a knotted lace, so a warm hand was laid on my buttock;

a sudden sensation that caused me to almost jump out of my skin, so close to my arse was it.

"Aaaahhh!" I quickly gasped in surprise, "Ohhh, that's nice!"

Somehow his hand was soft and welcoming and needy and a moment or two after exclaiming I felt myself pressing back against him while suddenly realising that my cock was rising, jumping and quivering with excitement.

"Stay there," said Cliff and I complied – partially because I was still working on that shoelace but partially because Cliff's hand was so gentle and enjoyable and so exciting.

As I remained bent at the waist, his fingers slid from my arse downwards to the back of my thigh, then eased between my legs to cup both my nuts. His fingers gently squeezed and rolled them around before releasing them and reaching for my cock, which he grasped from below and manipulated firmly while his wrist pushed my balls apart. There was no way that I even wanted to stand upright at this time and anyway the feeling of Cliff's forearm sliding right between my cheeks was now wildly thrilling as it rubbed past my arsehole, the hairs on his arm deliciously tickling my tender flesh.

I shuddered all over as Cliff's hand released my cock and made the return journey – but this time in a straight line upwards, pausing at my arsehole. I could feel the touch of his fingers – so near to my hole that it made my breathing cease for a few moments.

"That's cute," he said, "What a pretty little hole; it's a perfect star, all puckered and tight – looks lovely!"

I was about to make some cutting comment when I felt his fingers gently pressing against my hole; kind of testing me, like teasing a woman's nipple by playing around her aureole.

I almost jerked upright but Cliff's other hand restrained me firmly and I found myself wanting to remain where I was while his fingers gently moved against me. I felt myself shuddering as his fingertip explored the vicinity of my hole then gasping as his finger seemed to enter my body. My buttocks tightened as he probed but he wasn't pushing hard or deep but just pushing against my body, against my tight but fascinated hole and it felt incredible.

"Fuckin' hell Ollie," Cliff said from above and behind me, "Gotta have some of that!"

For a second or two I was frozen, caught between the two ideas; to let him or to stop him? The trouble was that I wanted this to continue and yet I was scared as well but I managed to remain bent over, my legs trembling and my heart pounding. But something, some part of me, was obviously eager because I managed to step out of my boots and push them and my clothes to one side.

"Go on then, don't stop," I said, my heart in my mouth.

There was a soft "Yeahhhhh!" from Cliff; a cry of excitement and need.

Then I felt Cliff moving a bit and there was an extra warmth pressing against me just a few inches below my hole. It felt smooth and warm as it slid and jerked and just had to be his cock.

"Cliff, oh no, I don't think... No, you mustn't!" I gasped, almost panicking and suddenly frightened again, "Not now; not here – there's people – no, it'll hurt!"

Cliff leaned away, his cock no longer touching me now.

"There's no people and it won't hurt and why not now?" he insisted, his other hand still on my back, holding me bent down, pushing quite hard now, "And anyway, I know you want it."

Oh god – I did and yet I was scared – but scared of what? Scared of being labelled 'gay' or of the pain or of being caught or what? I knew not what I was scared of but I knew that I'd let him! I knew that deep inside I wanted us to do more than just play together.

"You're not going to hurt me, are you?" I asked, guessing then pleaded frantically, "You're gonna need some lubrication or something."

There was no answer from Cliff, but I could hear him rolling his mouth around and then a splat of warm saliva landed atop my crack, quickly followed by the touch of his fingers again.

"Oh fuck!" I panted, "You're gonna do it, aren't you?"

What felt like two fingers were now guiding the saliva to my hole, pressing firmly into my flesh and making me pant and shiver.

"Calm down Ollie, I'll be gentle," said Cliff from above me, "Ok, you ready?"

"Oh fuck!" I repeated, "I dunno – just be bloody careful!"

Cliff chuckled but said nothing; then something that could only be his cock was pressing against me, slipping in the liquid, pushing into my hole.

"Ahhh," I breathed, "Ahhhhh – don't – take it easy!"

"I am, I am," said Cliff firmly, his tone of voice matching the pressure he was applying, it seemed.

There was a strong sensation of stretching now; stretching in a different manner to the easing that my arsehole was more used to of late; different too, to the sensations that I'd engendered as I'd played with myself. But it wasn't revolting me – instead I was now all eager to renew my experience with a cock, so much so that my hand was now wrapped around my own penis which felt as hard as it had ever been.

"Here we go," said Cliff, "Coming in now."

And as he spoke there was a sudden overpowering overload of everything – pain, weirdness, pleasure and sex, along with the feeling of a large object slipping, sliding into my body.

"Owwww!" I gasped as my arsehole suddenly split open; as my sphincter muscles lost the battle; as his rigid penis invaded me, "Oooh fuck!"

"Yeahhhh!" exhaled Cliff, "That's better. You ok? Sorry, I knew it would hurt a bit but it'll get better, a lot better."

"Yeah, yeah, think I'm ok but fuck me, that did hurt for a few moments," I managed to say, my mind whirling from all the wild happenings behind and inside me, "Give me a break for a bit will you – hold still."

I could feel the warmth and solidity of Cliff's body close behind me and somehow it was comforting to know that he was there, and it was a feeling that enabled me to hold still as I became used to his invasion. It felt different to my vibrator despite both being much the same size – much better, definitely sexier and considerably more exciting. I knew immediately that I'd been right to let him invade me – to let myself slip back into my gay side.

Cliff's movements had ceased and I was able to assess and explore the situation now, a situation that left me scared and yet delighted somehow and now I'd calmed down I could feel Cliff's thighs and his rough pubic hairs pressing against my arse – which had to mean that his entire penis was inside me. More importantly the pain was easing now, and I was starting to enjoy the sensation, but it was a shock, nevertheless.

"Wow!" I exclaimed, "You're right in there – in me? You've done it?"

"Bloody right I am," said Cliff heartily, "Just what I needed! Just what you needed too, I reckon."

"Did I say yes?" I asked, "I'm not sure..."

"Of course you did, you were just too scared to relax," said Cliff as his penis moved slowly, gently inside me, "I could tell you needed to get over that hurdle – well, now you have; now you can really be you."

Be me? Who was I? So far as I knew I was nothing more than a single man wrapped in his work and with no particular leaning either way and yet I'd loved it when I'd had sex with Steve and now with Cliff. So what was wrong with expanding my horizons and embracing my complete immersion into gay sex?

'Yes – let it happen,' my mind suddenly conceded, 'He wants you – you want him – go for it!'

Almost immediately Cliff grunted softly, then laughed.

"That's better Ollie!" he said, his voice warm and friendly, "You're with me now!"

My body had adjusted itself in line with my mind it seemed and suddenly I was welcoming Cliff's intrusive penis. A moment or two later and I almost fell forward, just managing to brace myself on the chair and avoid collapsing face down as Cliff thrust quite firmly into me.

"Yeah, oh fuck yeah," said Cliff, "You feel really good now – that's so much better."

I knew I did – I'd unfrozen and come alive and now I wanted Cliff to fuck me, to really screw me! I felt my sphincter squeeze his cock, tightening around his shaft as he moved in and out steadily now; loving the feeling of his study penis sliding inside me, almost urging him on. I began to love the friction as his organ slid against my skin and found that I could even feel the way the rim of his knob bumped up against my sphincter muscles. I began to feel the way his penis pushed against the tissues and cavities inside me, began to feel pleasure and excitement.

I felt waves of sex making my own cock harden once more as Cliff's penis nudged firmly against my prostate, the electrifying thrill sending shivers and muscular spasms through me. Almost as importantly, I'd now also secured a good grip on the chair I was bending over so my stance allowed me to hold my arse steady as Cliff continued to drive his penis into me and equally importantly I'd now regained a grip on my own cock.

"That's so nice now," I moaned happily just as a dribble of precum wetted my knob and my fist, "Ooooh yesss, yesss!"

"You're doing well," grunted Cliff from behind me, "This is bloody lovely mate."

A verbal silence now descended as actions took over with just the sounds of Cliff grunting with effort, the slight creak of floorboards and my breathing evident to me as Cliff's steady onslaught of my arsehole continued.

Eventually I had to ask though...

"Is it good, really good?" I enquired, wondering idly how long Cliff would last, "Are you getting there?"

"Bloody terrific!" he replied, his movements somewhat faster now, "Don't think it'll be too long now, why – do you want me to come?"

I was converted now – eager to complete my reorientation.

"Yeah, most definitely, but when you're ready," I said as my arsehole worked on his cock, "And please do it inside me – don't take it out!"

"Really?" answered Cliff, "You'll let me come in you?"

"Oooh fuck yeah," I said, my voice quivering with emotion, "No sense in you doing half the job, is there?"

Cliff chuckled quietly and although he remained silent now, I knew that it was because he was concentrating on his orgasm. His movements were that much stronger now, really driving his penis deep into me, slamming his thighs and balls against my arse each time and with each stroke he let out a gasp as the effort forced air from his lungs. I kept a tight hold on the chair as he fucked me, realising too that I was responding by moving my arse around, partially for his benefit and partially for mine. Certain positions felt incredible just as others caused his cock to pain me inside and yet that pain was sometimes delicious, the extra bite it caused sending cock-hardening waves through my groin.

This was something I could get used to again; something I could enjoy and appreciate once more but the circle wasn't yet complete. Much as I was enjoying Cliff using my arse, I knew that I wanted to use his as well! But later perhaps and certainly not right at this moment because Cliff seemed to be coming to the boil.

I knew that he was getting close just by the way he sounded and was moving. His strokes were now sharper somehow, his penis driven with more urgency and energy while his cock somehow felt even harder that it had done and all this was compounded by the way his hands on my hips were like talons now, pulling me towards him almost harshly. Cliff was panting too, each gasp rasping from his lips as his actions reached towards his climax.

"Come on – let it go!" I implored him, "Do it – fuck me – come, come!"

"Yeah, yeah, fuckin' am! Ahh, coming, it's coming..." Cliff panted, his thrusts now faster and shallow, "Bit more... yeah... bit more. Oh fuck – here it comes! Uuuughhhh!"

With a grunt that might have been heard for miles Cliff almost uprooted me as his penis drove deeply into my arsehole, held almost still and began flooding me.

"Oh Christ – yessss, yessss!" he breathed as his deep strong thrusts continued, "Oh fuck – oh that's better. There's more – ugghhh – ugghhh! Oh fuck – that's it!"

Four, five, six strong pulsating thrusts had emptied his load of spunk into me, a warm and delicious load of cum that sent thrilling sensations through me; that remained long after his thrusting had ended. Instead of my mind (and my arse) being full of Cliff's energetic penis, now I was filled with the feeling of wetness inside me as well, a feeling of glowing warmth and almost the taste as if his juices had permeated all through me in an instant.

And now Cliff was leaning on me, not heavily but firmly as he recovered, his breaths making his body rise and fall against mine while his penis remained lodged inside me, now just jerking occasionally – quite possibly in response to my own spasms as my arse continued to enjoy his invasion and then Cliff was slapping my back lightly as he pushed himself more upright.

"Wow – that was good," he said, "Bit of a shock to be honest – didn't really expect you to be quite so friendly and welcoming!"

I laughed gently as I realised that I had indeed very much taken part in the action. It hadn't all just been Cliff and his cock – it was my arse that had contributed to the enjoyment that we'd both felt. If I hadn't had been such a willing participant, then Cliff wouldn't have enjoyed himself so much – and nor would I for that matter.

I squeezed my sphincter muscles tight around his penis like a loving hug, but I could feel that his cock no longer had the stiffness that had so thrilled me, and I knew it was time for us to disconnect.

Immediately my mind considered the flood of juices that would need mopping up and I suddenly realised that I still only had those two old mud and cum-crusted towels with which to clean up.

'They'll have to do,' I thought, but Cliff came to the rescue.

"I'm going to pull out now," he said, "Anyway, if I don't it'll fall out soon, I think – and there's a couple of nice clean towels in that bag I brought in."

"Ah brilliant, that's good. Hey – you cheeky sod, you came all prepared for this, didn't you?" I replied as I jerked upright, dislodging Cliff's cock as I did so, "You knew that we'd fuck, didn't you?"

"Not so much knew as hoped," he said as he shuffled across the shed and extracted the towels from his bag, one of which he passed to me.

"Hmmmph!" I grunted as I dried my arse and cleaned up the runnels of spunk that had already travelled down my legs, "What if I'd said no?"

"Then the towels would have just been for you to replace those mucky old things you've got," said Cliff, as he brushed sweat from his chest and armpits and wiped his cock, "But as it is, I'm glad I thought of them. I'll take 'em back home after this and give them a good wash."

"They're not filthy yet!" I replied, "Especially compared to my old ones – they'll do for a bit longer."

"But you haven't come yet, have you?" asked Cliff as he stepped towards me and palmed my still turgid cock, "Perhaps if you could return the compliment…"

"What – come?" I asked as I considered the idea, "Yeah – of course I could!"

"And do you suppose you could do the same as I just did; you know, fuck me instead?" asked Cliff as his fist slid up and down my now risen cock.

"Oooh fuck – not sure I'm ready for that to be honest," I spluttered in reply, but Cliff was already preparing me and anyway, inside me I knew that I was lying.

My words had popped out of me as a natural response; as if to indicate that I wasn't overeager, but the truth was that I really wanted to give Cliff something in return. While the words from my mouth had been reluctant, my mind was very willing; even hoping, to give Cliff just some of the pleasure he'd given me and my cock was most definitely in favour!

"Oh, come on then, I'll do it!" I exclaimed.

Cliff responded with a big smile and then in seconds he'd sunk to his knees before me and engulfed my erection in his mouth, deliciously stirring my juices, my cock and my emotions. I felt my hips jerk as his tongue teased my knob, swirled around the rim of my helmet and fluttering over my foreskin. I heard my breath shuddering as he aroused me and knew that whatever else happened, I'd be having an orgasm before I left the shed. And then Cliff was standing once more but now gathering saliva from his mouth in his own hand before snaking his hand round behind his arse. A few seconds later and he was on his knees; his arms resting on the chair much as I'd done; his arse in the air, his arsehole wet and glistening and inviting.

"Come on Ollie, here I am, take me!" he invited, "Don't waste it."

My mind slipped aside for a few moments as I considered my situation. Not that many days ago the thought of male to male play would have been unusual, my earlier experiences almost forgotten, and it certainly hadn't been on my menu. But then Cliff and I had met and had oral sex, which was a strange enough scenario – and now he'd fucked me! It was going to be the start of a whole new ball game to actually fuck Cliff although it wasn't one, I intended to avoid. I'd be travelling back in time but most certainly not reluctantly because every experience with Cliff was exciting, educational and stimulating. It was also bringing back all my old memories and my exploration was making me discover more and more about myself. I knew I was ready to go further now!

With a big breath I found myself lowering myself to my knees and aiming my penis between Cliff's legs, his hairy arse now less than a foot from my cock. I was almost hyperventilating as the exciting scenario roused me. I so needed to sink my cock into something; I was so eager to climax that I no longer cared where – all I now wanted was fulfilment. I shuffled forward and extended one hand to rest on Cliff's back as I approached him, my erection now guided by my other hand.

"Oh fuck – is it going to be ok?" I breathed but Cliff looked back at me over his shoulder.

"It'll only not be ok if you don't do it!" he said, "Come on – I'm ready – be brave!"

My penis felt excitingly stiff, entirely rampant and ready – all I needed was to get my mind to accept the situation. Then suddenly I found myself imagining the view from Cliff's angle as he'd fucked me and suddenly, I knew I was ready. I'd been concerned when he'd penetrated me and yet it had felt wonderful; even incredible and certainly I'd enjoyed it, so I needed to give some of that pleasure back!

"Yeah!" I said quietly, "Let's get on with it!"

"You what?" asked Cliff as he looked back at me once more.

"I'm ready," I said, now feeling entirely confident, "I'm all ready to fuck you!"

"Yeah Ollie, come on then," said Cliff as he settled back and wiggled his arse at me.

His hole was pulsating, almost blowing kisses at me and glistened with wetness.

"Why's your arse wet?" I asked having forgotten seeing him anoint himself.

"Bit of spit, isn't it," replied Cliff without turning, "Just got myself ready for you. Come on, I'm waiting."

I shook my head in pleasant wonderment but as I did so a wicked thought had entered my mind; a thought that made my erection jerk with excitement.

"Hang on," I said, "Just getting myself ready too."

As I spoke, I reached back and in a moment or two a large cucumber was in my hand – not the biggest in the box but certainly lengthy. I swilled my tongue around my mouth to gather some of my own saliva, then let it dribble onto the vegetable with my other hand spreading the wetness around.

"Ok, here I come," I said, a comment that was answered only by another wiggle of Cliff's rump and a grunt of approval.

I closed in, placed my fingers and thumb astride his hole to stretch the skin and then brought the cucumber up close, then I pushed firmly and having seated the end in his hole I moved my hand to rest on Cliff's back and increased the pressure.

"Ahhhhh!" gasped Cliff, "Fuck Ollie, you feel huge and how come your cock's so cold? Ahhhh shit – no, it's not! What the...?"

He tried to bend more upright, but I pushed him down as I drove the cucumber into his body, then began sliding it in and out steadily.

"Fuckin' hell, you bastard," he groaned, "Oh my God – oh fuck, oh fuck!"

"Just getting my own back!" I chuckled but now I noticed that movement of the cucumber was easier, even though there must have been a good six inches of it inside him.

"You might have let me know you were gonna do that," groaned Cliff, "I've got some lube in my bag, I could have – oh fuck, yesss, yesss! Oh Ollie – yeahhh!"

The thought must have excited him or otherwise turned him on and his arse was now pushing back at my hand – at my big green dildo. I moved my hand from his back and slid it underneath him and sure enough his cock was rigid and dribbling precum steadily. I let it gather in my palm before I began sliding my hand easily up and down his cock, with both of us now revelling in the delightful feeling.

But much as it was wonderful to be holding his penis, my own penis was being ignored and needed attention. The cucumber had done its job – now it would be easier for me to penetrate into his body instead.

"That woke you up, didn't it?" I said jovially, "I'll swap over now – you can have the real thing."

"Yes please, please – ok, been there, done that," moaned Cliff, "I want to feel you inside me, not that thing."

"Don't be rude about my cucumbers!" I said lightly as I slid the vegetable from his hole, "Or I'll put it back!"

"No, no – I want you," cried Cliff, "I want to feel the heat from your cock, I want to feel it moving in me, I want to feel you deep inside me."

"Ohhh yeahhhh, alright," I replied with enthusiasm, "Hang on, you say you've got some lube, have you?"

"In the bag, down the side," he said as he waved his hand and I soon found the little tube.

A few moments later and I'd squeezed some out and anointed both my cock and his hole with the slippery stuff – we were both primed and ready.

After the removal of the big green plug, his arsehole had gaped wide open before me, pulsating pinkly inside before the brown puckered flesh once again contracted into a small dimple. But I knew that his arse was now primed for my cock and that I fully intended to fuck him thoroughly.

I dropped the cucumber onto the floor and shuffled closer to Cliff, bringing my still well-inflated penis into line with his hole. Cliff's head swivelled around; then lifted as my penis approached his body and I heard his breath quivering as he sucked it in.

I slid my cock around in the liquid; dropped another little blob onto the scene of the crime and finally pushed the slippery puddle around to ensure that my cock and his arsehole were thoroughly lubricated – then I leaned closer until we touched.

The tip of my wet and glowing cock now sat in the small depression of his hole, my knob touching his skin, just resting there. I could feel that there was still a nice firm reluctance on the part of his body to allow mine to penetrate but his hole had been stretched and would soon let me in. I wasn't inside his body yet, but the moment was very close now and except for the gentle sounds of our breathing it was quiet as the moment of penetration approached – both of us aware of the pleasure to come, both of us with bated breath as I settled myself into position.

I knew instinctively what to do and yet this was my first time in ages, but my instincts had taken over and were guiding me now; telling me just how to do it and how fast to move things along. There was no rush and even though I was holding back, my cock was still completely rigid.

More than that, I'd begun to ooze some lubrication of my own as the contact between my tip and his arse stirred my juices.

But I couldn't just wait forever...

"Ok Cliff, here it comes. I'm going to push a bit now," I advised him and Cliff grunted his approval.

I shuffled a little bit closer and watched my penis cause his hole to depress, then slowly his sphincter began to ease open and my knob started to disappear within Cliff's body and I realised that I was indeed beginning to fuck his arse.

"Ohhhh, nice!" gasped Cliff deliciously as things started to happen, "Yessss – oooohhhh yessss!"

Slowly and carefully I let my cock slide into him until perhaps a generous inch was embedded now; my knob lodged inside his hole, the rim around it held tightly by his sphincter muscles but as I now increased the pressure suddenly and before I could react, I was in him; my penis was sliding so smoothly into his body. It wasn't until I was at least three quarters embedded that I was able to steady myself.

"Ahhhh!" I breathed as the incredible feeling of having my cock inside another human engulfed me.

"Oh fuck," gasped Cliff happily, "Ollie, that was a brilliant!"

"Sorry, sorry," I answered, "Didn't do it on purpose. Are you ok now?"

"Yeah, no problem, I'm fine – it just felt amazing; it's ages since I had a nice cock inside me," he said, "Don't start banging right away though!"

I laughed; that wasn't my style when it came to sex, I always tried to be a considerate lover.

'Lover?' I heard my mind asking of myself, 'Yeah, suppose I am in a way.'

Unintentionally I must have continued to push and as my mind returned to the present, I cast my eyes down to where my pubes were now squashed against Cliff's arse. My penis was right up inside him! Experimentally I began to move, slowly sliding back and forward, feeling the tightness of his sphincter and the warmth of his insides around my cock. The feelings stiffened my penis again and sent a wave of erotic thoughts through me that seemed to almost force me to respond by thrusting my cock into Cliff more firmly, but he was not only ready but eager to enjoy my efforts.

"Yeahhh, come on then, do it!" he exclaimed, "That's good – that's good."

"Uuuuhhh, uuuuhhh," I grunted as I steadily plowed his arsehole, "Feels good..."

"Feels so much better than that cucumber," said Cliff as his arse muscles caressed my cock, "Warm and loving and so fuckin' good!"

Steadily I screwed him now, our flesh slapping noisily together, our breathing loud, heavy and sonorous. The sounds and smells of sex reverberated inside the shed, filling my ears and nose deliciously, driving me to pump my cock into Cliff's hole with steady energy. Beneath me Cliff was thrusting back at me; grunting and gasping as we fucked, but his sounds were definitely of pleasure rather than pain.

Then, as I thrust hard and fast, I felt my orgasm rising quickly. Nothing so good could last forever and I seemed to have found an angle that stimulated my cock just perfectly and it was bringing me very quickly to the boil. Suddenly my body was alive and excited – instead of the steadiness of fucking, now my penis was leading the way with frantic, driving, pumping thrusts.

"Cliff, Cliff, gonna come soon," I gasped, "You ready?"

My movements were already becoming somewhat ragged as I neared my climax; my penis had taken over and I was going to empty my balls into Cliff's body any minute now.

"Yeah, I'm ready – no – do it on my face instead!" said Cliff between breaths and in an instant, he'd squirmed away from under me and twisted around.

A moment or two later and he was sitting in the chair, his own hand working hard and fast around his erection as he held his mouth open for my penis and my cum. Quickly, he raised his other hand and pointed.

"Here – in here," he said, "Shoot it – come on, I'm ready!"

And so was I. Despite the shock of having his body pulled from around my cock I was still profoundly aroused and almost on the brink of orgasm; all it would take was a few more strokes.

"Ah yesss – here it comes!" I said as I leaned over him and jerked my hand quickly up and down my shaft, "Here it comes!"

With a grunt, a final thrust, a frozen moment and a sudden jerk I let loose from some six inches in front of his face. But even from that close range my aim was far from perfect and my first salvo was both powerful and misguided, blasting cum upwards. Some of my eruption slashed across his forehead; some found his hair, some cleared his head altogether and some ricocheted back at me. The second salvo was far more on target and left only a small splash on his chin and by the third eruption Cliff had his hand and his mouth around my cock to ensure that my aim was better.

Two more spasms jerked my remaining juices from me and then I was just standing there, shivering with emotion while Cliff made the most of my cock and my spunk. His fist was around my quivering penis, holding me steady as his lips and tongue worked on my cock until suddenly, he released his grip on my cock, lifted his head from my groin and slumped back onto the chair. His eyes were shut now but although he was almost supine and still, his other hand was far from idle; it was jerking his own cock quickly until he gasped, thrust his hips upwards and began spurting wildly up and over his own abdomen and chest.

And then he did indeed collapse, his body rising and falling to his deep and heavy breathing while his eyes, although closed, seemed to be crinkled with smiles.

Before my own legs gave out, I too had to sit down and did so on the cushioned arm of the chair beside him while I recovered and gazed down at Cliff's body. His fingers were now idly playing with the white spunk he'd ejected, sliding it over his stomach, anointing his nipples and then lifting blobs of spunk to his mouth. Gently he sucked them clean, then they descended again, collected some more cum and brought it to my lips. Almost subconsciously I allowed his smeared fingers to enter my mouth, enjoying now the texture and scent of his offering before smiling down at Cliff, a warm smile of contentment.

"Wowee!" I said brightly, "That was good, wasn't it?"

Cliff was still busy sucking sperm from his fingers but now he looked up at me, his lips wet and slippery and smiling.

"Bloody hell Ollie, I think you enjoyed that!" he said cheerfully.

"Brilliant!" I replied, "I'd almost forgotten how good that can be…"

He laughed raucously and infectiously.

"Didn't have to think much, did you," he said, "It was all down to that lovely cock of yours."

"And your tight arse," I answered, "And that cucumber!"

"Nah – just forget the cucumber," he answered brightly, "That wasn't so nice – but your cock – that was amazing!"

"It was your nice tight arse that was amazing," I said, "I really enjoyed that."

"But are we going to do that again?" he asked, "Please!"

"Try stopping me!" I said as I used his towel to clean the remnants of my orgasm from my cock, "Not right now though. Gotta get back to work."

"Sure thing – I'll help you," he said, "Soon as we've cleaned ourselves up."

He stood up and winced, then smiled, one hand behind his arse.

"Phew!" he said, "Bit tender there – I'll be all right though."

I laughed at his discomfort. It was he who'd let us into this sexual adventure, so he had to take the consequences. And anyway, my own arse still quivered from the memory of his cock, still felt the liquid of Cliff's sperm as it tried to ooze from me – and still desired more.

"How soon – I mean when – oh fuck, I mean we can do this again, can't we?" I asked as wiped my arse and cock clean, then handed the towel to Cliff.

I began climbing into my clothes, but the only answer received was a hearty laugh from Cliff and a slap on the back.

"Try keeping me away!" he said as we began to move the boxes of vegetables from the shed, "Perhaps we should bring a mattress down here."

"And perhaps I'll keep a cucumber handy too!" I answered as I dumped the last box in the car.

"No way – but some clean towels would be good," replied Cliff, "And I've left the lube in the shed too."

"Hope you've got some more at home," I chuckled as I slammed the car door shut.

"So when can you come round?" said Cliff, his eyes gleaming with happiness and lust.

"Couple of hours eh?" I said as I dropped into the seat and turned the ignition key.

"Yeah!" Cliff roared over the sound of the motor, "See you there!"

I motored slowly from the allotments and paused at the gate. On the dashboard of my car I noticed one of Cliff's business cards and I could hardly believe my eyes.

The card spelled out his address and his name – Cliff Mellors.

"Well fuck me!" I said to myself, "I think I'm gonna have to rewrite that book – they got it all wrong!"

I was Ollie Chatterley while he was Cliff Mellors – the surnames were transposed just as the first names were too. By the book I should have been Oliver Mellors and he should have been Clifford Chatterley and neither of them were gay – but so what! Somehow our affair seemed equally as twisted and wicked as Lady Chatterley and her gamekeeper's affair was... and quite as much fun.

The End

But not for long…

Printed in Great Britain
by Amazon